MURDER BY THE MARFA LIGHTS

An Ariadne French Mystery

by
Denise Weeks

Pandora Press Richardson, TX

Pandora Press

Cover design by Denise G. Weeks
Book design by Denise G. Weeks
Cover art by Jason Cantrell

First Edition, August 2012

deniseweeks.blogspot.com
shalannacollins.blogspot.com
shalanna.livejournal.com

ISBN: 1478185511
ISBN-13: 978-1478185512

Of what significance one's existence is, one is basically unaware. What does a fish know about the water in which he swims all his life?—*Albert Einstein*

The fish trap exists because of the fish. Once you've gotten the fish, you can forget the trap.—*Chuang Tzu*

DEDICATION

To Dennis Havens, who brought Bastey and Hawk to light
and always believed in the Marfa Lights.

ACKNOWLEDGMENTS

I want to thank my parents, Dal Charles Gerneth
and Billye Jo Cantrell Gerneth.
Thanks also to all my teachers, past and present.

I'd like to acknowledge the long mentorship and friendship of the
denizens of the Fido WRITING echo and its ensuing mailing list,
including especially author Dennis M. Havens, who has suffered through
draft after draft of my various books. A big thank you
also goes out to each of my beta readers over the years.

CHAPTER ONE

I was at my sister's house painting her west dining room wall Tahiti Orange when her landline phone shrilled.

"Let the machine pick up." Zoë stepped back to evaluate our progress. She was doing the other three walls Holstein Cream. "It leaves streaks when you paint those W's. I don't care what they did on 'Extreme Home Makeover.' Just go straight up and down, overlapping the edges a bit." She pushed back her dark hair, leaving a skunk-streak of vanilla paint through her bangs.

"That's probably for me." I started backing down the stepladder.

"Who'd be calling you here?"

"I forwarded my desk phone. It's my night to cover supervisor calls on the help desk."

"You and those stupid fish tanks." She glared.

Evading her disintegration ray, I rushed down the hall of her 1920s cottage into the guest room where I could have some privacy to answer the call. "Aqualife Tech Support, The Fishes' Lifeline. This is Ari. How may I help you?"

A tentative-sounding male voice said, "Um. I'm looking for Arialle French?"

Pretty good: he hadn't entirely mangled my first name, the way most people did the first time. My name is Ariadne, pronounced "R. E. Oddney," as if I were an initial-author, like C. S. Lewis or J. K. Rowling.

I didn't recognize the voice. It was a warm, resonant, and infinitely sensual bass that threatened to vibrate my entire body along with my eardrum. I shook off its seductive effects as best I could and assumed a professional tone. "This is Ariadne French. How can I help you?"

"Oh. Sorry, Ariadne." He nailed the pronunciation. "I'm looking at some bad handwriting here. You see, it's handwritten."

"What's handwritten?" My old paranoia danced in the background. If this were a customer who'd spoken to me in the past, I could only hope I hadn't given unclear or misguided advice that had resulted in a tankful of floaters and a house full of howling, broken-hearted children who'd named every one of the fish and had trained several of them to do tricks and come when called. "Do you have a specific fish problem I can help you solve?"

"Er . . . no." He sounded mystified. "I'm calling about a personal matter."

My chest tightened. Surely he wasn't another bill collector. The last thing I wanted was for Zoë to know they were still calling my work number.

Over a year ago, I had signed my nephew Ricky's admission paperwork without a second thought. We had been desperate for him to begin the experimental treatments for his rare cancer. My sister had been incapable of rational thought, and probably couldn't have spelled her name, let alone sign on the promise-to-pay line. I hadn't been worried about money at the time; I had certainly never imagined that so much of the expense would go unpaid.

Before I could get too agitated, the voice set me straight. "I guess I should've introduced myself. My name is Gil Rousseau, Aaron's neighbor and his pastor."

I felt my heart thud against my breastbone. "Aaron Beecroft?"

My one true love. Or so I had thought, up until he'd faded out of contact with me a few months ago.

"Yes. Of course. Sorry if I'm not making myself clear. The purpose of my call is . . . well, I'm afraid I have sad news."

That never meant anything good. In fact, it normally meant only one thing. "No," I said involuntarily.

Gil cleared his throat. "I'm sorry to be the one to have to tell you, but Aaron has passed away."

Aaron? Dead?

Oh, dear God. Please, please, Lord, let it be a prank. Please. "Is this a crank call? Because if you think it's funny. . . ."

"I'm sorry. I wish I were joking. Aaron was found dead in his cabin night before last by his nearest neighbor. She got worried when his lights didn't come on two nights in a row. But his car was still in the driveway, so she used the key they'd exchanged to go check."

"I apologize," I said mindlessly. "I didn't mean to impugn your intentions." *Impugn?* The elevated diction served as a defense mechanism; my subconscious was distancing me from the kick I'd just taken to the heart. "It's just that . . . my God, what can I say? I can't believe it."

"I hope I haven't reached you at a bad time." As though there could be a good time. "Perhaps I shouldn't have called. But I found this number on his caller ID, and I realized that you're probably the same Ariadne." *The same Ariadne as . . . what?* "I thought talking to you in person would be better than sending a registered letter."

Why would he need to send me a registered letter? I was afraid to ask. Instead, what popped out was the thought uppermost in my mind. "So Aaron made it out to Montana?"

"Montana?" He paused. "No, we're in West Texas. Big Bend country."

Aaron had told me he was headed for Big Sky country. Well, close enough. My ears started to hum.

"At any rate. The reason I'm calling is that Aaron named me executor of his will. And you're his sole beneficiary."

Aaron had a will? More to the point, Aaron had anything that was worth writing up a will for? He'd lived out of a duffel bag as long as I'd known him. Except for what he'd charged on my credit cards and put into my name, such as the conversion van and the camping stuff and other odds and ends we thought we'd need for our escape from society. And then a year ago, when I couldn't leave on Aaron's schedule—because my nephew was dying—he had left without me.

"Additionally, I've been unable to contact his next of kin or find anything that could lead me to them. I'm counting on you to help make Aaron's arrangements."

Arrangements. The euphemism brought back Ricky's giant portrait on an easel standing next to his coffin, his wide-eyed freckled face staring optimistically out at me from eternity. My late nephew would've started eighth grade in the fall.

Did the pain ever fade? My tongue clung to the roof of my mouth. With effort, I peeled it loose. "That might be difficult. Because of my job and all."

It was a lame excuse, and it sounded like one.

"Oh. Then I suppose, well, these things can be somewhat taken care of from a distance." He paused. "Do you happen to know who would be his next of kin?"

"His parents. But they're—they haven't been in contact with him for a while. I'm not sure I can help much in finding them. They're full-time snowbirds. I mean, RV'ers. They live in their motorhome and move with the seasons among the RV resort camps. It's a really popular lifestyle." I was babbling.

"Ari? Are you okay?" My sister's words echoed down the hall.

I lowered my voice. "Aaron's an only child. His parents are Myra and Doyle Beecroft. Doyle used to work for the military as a contractor. And there's an Aunt Fannie Belle who lives in Ardmore, Oklahoma, but I don't know her last name. That's about all I know. Aaron and I hadn't been in touch for several months."

I imagined I heard Gil's pencil scratching. "I'll give those leads a shot. But if I don't find anyone, something still needs to be done fairly soon." He made a sound somewhere between a cough and a squeak. "It would be so helpful to me if you could come out in person, at least for a day or two. You could take what you want out of the cabin, and so forth."

His cabin in the woods. <u>Our</u> cabin. The one he was going to build for me, for <u>us</u>. The one I thought I'd lost forever once Aaron stopped calling.

I'd often wondered how he liked true cowboy life after leaving Dallas, where the Cowboys were nothing but a football franchise, not real-life Marlboro Men herding dogies and wearing flannel shirts, ten-gallon hats, and

Wranglers (the only jeans that a working cowboy or rodeo circuit rider will don.) Could I bear to see Aaron's house if he wasn't there waiting for me? When he'd never be there again?

"I'm afraid I couldn't possibly get away."

I thought I heard a click on the line.

"I understand," said Gil. "Perhaps you'd prefer that I use some of the estate's cash to arrange a sale of the furnishings. Of course I'd need your signature to authorize it. Assuming we don't find family, I could have someone box up his personal effects, such as his wallet, glasses, and so forth. Unless you're not interested at all in his, ah, private papers and possessions and such?"

Something twisted in my chest. I still possessed every note Aaron had ever scribbled to me, collected in a white ceramic box he'd given me one Christmas, its top embossed with a serene unicorn. And I kept a bag in the back of the closet containing his various gifts. I'm sentimental, maybe even a little obsessive. Aaron and I had that in common.

Gil continued offering me the shiny apple. But was it poisoned? "I could get some bids on packing and sending the more valuable items. Unless you're saying you'd like to have an estate sale, sell it all, and have me wire you the funds."

Aaron would have hated that. He was particular about his things, especially since he kept so few. And an auction would be the last thing Aaron would want. Strangers handling and bidding on his personal objects, seeing—and judging—him through only the few special things he'd kept. What an intrusion.

I wanted to go out there. See that cabin standing. Imagine him there, living out his days in peace and serenity, maybe longing for me but reluctant to call, thinking I was still angry at him. Feel him sitting there at his dinner table doing his crossword puzzles in ink, like Zoë. I could sit on the edge of the bed where he'd slept. Breathe in his skin's musky smell from the sheets, one last time.

I'm a glutton for punishment.

"One more detail." Gil paused. "You've also been named as his literary executor. He was writing something. A book, as I understand it."

Aaron, writing a book? He'd never read a book since he got out of school, as far as I could remember. Was this the Aaron Beecroft I knew?

Belatedly, it struck me that Gil had said he found my phone number on Aaron's caller ID. But I hadn't called Aaron, hadn't even known where to find him. Gil must've meant my number was programmed into Aaron's phone, or that it was the last number stored in redial. Maybe Aaron had finally called to tell me he was ready for me to come out there. To be with him. And somehow, I'd missed it. Why hadn't he left voice mail? Why hadn't I answered that all-important call?

All of a sudden the bedroom seemed blazing hot. I jerked the paint-spattered bandana from my head, wiped the sweat off my forehead with it, and lifted my hair off the back of my neck. With my free hand, I scrabbled in the drawer of the nightstand for a ponytail holder or rubber band, but came up empty.

"Hello?" Gil said tentatively.

"I'm here." I let out a long breath. "Forget what I said. Of course I'll come. I'll have to make arrangements at work. But this is Friday night, Monday is the Labor Day holiday, and I have two weeks' vacation coming."

"Oh, good." Gil sounded—there was no other word for it— perky. The minister-bearing-condolences morphed into the salesman who'd just closed the deal. "I'm glad you changed your mind. Aaron was adamant, when I witnessed this will for him last year, that you be the one to take care of things. Not that he'd expected to pass so soon, of course. He simply realized that with the amount of money and goods that he'd amassed, it was his responsibility to see that they didn't go to the state."

How could Aaron have a lot of stuff? What kind of work had he found in the middle of the West Texas desert? Had one of his grand schemes actually paid off for a change?

"I've taken the liberty of looking up some of the available flights."

I cringed. But flying would be the quickest way to get there. And my old Ford Escort would never live to make the trip.

"One way, of course. You'll probably want to drive his Navigator home and pull the trailer with whatever goods you want."

A Lincoln Navigator, no less. "That sounds reasonable. Also, I might be bringing someone with me, and that would leave our departure date open-ended." My sister Zoë liked nothing better than going through other people's things.

I thought I heard a faint gargling sound from the kitchen extension.

"Do you need me to wire you the funds? Or I could make the reservations for you, and you can pick up the tickets at the counter at DFW, if that'd be more convenient."

"You're a mind reader." I'd been wondering how I could find a fare that I could afford. It occurred to me that I'd never heard of an executor spending the estate's cash on such nonessentials, but then I had no idea how those things worked.

"I have the flight information on my computer screen"—naturally, because everyone anywhere in the world sits in front of a glowing monitor all day—"for the flights out over the next couple of days. Let me read them off to you."

§ § §

Before I even hung up, Zoë was standing in the doorway. "Who in the hell was that?"

"You were listening in from the kitchen," I accused her, folding my arms. "You heard it all."

"No, I didn't. That damn phone kept cutting out because the MUTE button has a short. Besides, I couldn't believe what I was hearing." She shook her head, looking incredulous. "Some guy you've never met invites you out to his cabin to pick up something or another from an estate? That's bullshit. Who died?"

This was going to blow her mind, as it had mine. "You meant that as a joke, I know. But that was one of Aaron's neighbors out in Big Bend country. He says I've inherited all Aaron's stuff. I'm the only one they can find, and I'm going out there to—you know, make arrangements."

"For Aaron," she repeated dumbly. "Your Aaron?"

"No, somebody else's Aaron." I made the "duh" face. "He's been living in a cabin at the feet of the Davis Mountains."

"You said he went to Montana."

"I thought he had." I shrugged. "He didn't get quite that far." My vision blurred, but I blinked back the tears. If they ever started, I wasn't sure they'd ever stop.

My sister stared. "God, Ari. Some guy called and told you Aaron's dead?" The reality of it began to register on her face. Her tone softened. "What in the hell happened, pardon my French?"

I ignored Zoë's favorite wordplay (because our last name is "French"—it's a family joke). The inside of my nose began to sting, but I wouldn't cry. And words wouldn't form in my mouth.

When I didn't answer, she blathered on, as is her wont. "I mean, Aaron was the health nut of the century. I never saw him eat red meat. He used to ride that overpriced forty-gear bike everywhere and stuck with yoga even after his 'friends'"—she made air quotes with her forefingers—"started razzing him about yoga being girly. He seemed like the perfect specimen." My libido had agreed. "I'm assuming, since you didn't say, that it wasn't a long illness, not as far as they know, anyway. Was it his heart, or an accident, or what?"

"I don't know. I didn't get the details." The reality of Aaron's final vanishing act hadn't sunk in yet. I was still mentally waiting on his "I'll call when I get settled" promise, had been for a year. I'd never given up hope that he'd eventually send for me, even after his cell number started informing me that there was no such subscriber.

"Weren't you paying attention? You should've asked."

"Give me a break. I answered the phone expecting to get a work question about aquarium pH." My throat was tight. "Aaron's left me everything, and I need to go out there right away."

"Wait a minute." Zoë held up her hands and windshield-wipered them back and forth to clear the slate. "How do you know this is legit?"

"Why would the man lie? His name is Gil Rousseau, and he's Aaron's neighbor and friend." I shook off a tiny tendril of doubt.

"He can't be for real. Gil Rousseau? Wasn't that an Impressionist painter?"

I shot her a look. "Give it a rest."

"I will not." Her hands landed on her hips. "Maybe he's some kind of psycho Aaron met once on the road, or in one of those crazy pubs he likes to go to, and they got bombed together, and while Aaron was schwacked he told this guy all about you and even gave him your phone numbers. For all you know, the guy is a perv, waiting out there to take you into the boonies and . . . God knows what."

Leave it to Zoë to think of all sorts of horrid, bizarre things that wouldn't happen. "Spare me the wild imaginings. Besides, Aaron quit drinking." But I bit my lip.

"I'm serious, Airhead. You are definitely not using that ticket, if he actually sends one. That's a typical scheme used by Internet predators, for corn sakes. They lure women to remote love nests, and the women are found months later in pieces in somebody's chest freezer." Her eyes bulged out of her round face. "I can't believe you're so naïve."

"You can come with me," I said in an innocent voice. "For protection. He said he could book a second seat on the flight. All I have to do is call."

"That part, I heard." She tried to wither me with her glare, but I'm fairly resistant to that after thirty-odd years as her baby sister. "Baby" is a misnomer, because I'm only two years younger. "You know I do not travel."

My sister hadn't spent a night away from home since she'd left the hospital. She'd been a virtual recluse all year. A good excuse to get away was exactly what she needed.

Sounding as if I knew what I was getting into might help. "Okay, listen, I'm checking out his story. I'll call out there in the morning when they open to make sure he's real."

"Call where?" She lifted one eyebrow a notch. "What did he claim to be?"

"He's Aaron's minister." I grinned as her chin hit her chest. "The associate pastor at the Church After God's Heart. Aaron's been attending since he got out there. Apparently, he became quite the charity worker and community servant. What, did the speakerphone cut out?" I nearly stuck out my tongue, but restrained myself. "Aaron joined Houses for Humans and built his own log cabin from a kit."

My sister goggled at me. "This is the same Aaron Beecroft who couldn't change a lightbulb without getting a splinter? Who thought Sunday mornings were made for playing online computer games?"

"People change."

"Not that much. Not in barely over a year." She shook her head.

"Either this Gil is a con artist, or he's putting you on. This sounds exactly like Aaron, or rather like one of Aaron's crazy schemes to get you out there. Bringing more money." Turning, she headed for her kitchen. "I need a drink."

Zoë had a point. There had been something in Gil Rousseau's manner that'd implied—even assumed—we were Close Personal Friends. That did seem kind of strange, though I didn't want to examine it too closely because for all I knew, preachers always acted like that. What I wouldn't doubt is that Aaron got religion after watching Ricky's inspirational struggle.

"I'm flying out. Then I can drive back pulling the trailer."

"Aaron still has that trailer you've been paying for?"

"I guess." I'd had to keep up the payments, because otherwise my credit would've sunk even deeper into the slagheap. "The man acts as if Aaron's got money. A lot of it, apparently."

"Will wonders never cease." Zoë held a glass under the ice maker as it ground cubes to a pulp. "I wonder what kind of scam Aaron had going. I'm sure it was a racket." She eyed me. "Have you eaten today?"

I had missed lunch. But I wasn't very hungry.

Being a great cook keeps Zoë a little stocky, not that she cares. Whereas I haven't gotten fat yet, though I dread the onset of scale-creep; it happened to my sister last year when she turned thirty, and even to our super-disciplined mother soon after forty. Thank goodness I still have a couple of good years left, I hope.

She handed me the glass. "Where—how did Aaron get all that money? Furthermore, why didn't he think about paying you back for what y'all charged on your credit cards that you've been struggling to pay?"

I skipped the second question. "I'm sure he did odd jobs. Maybe webpage design." I shrugged. "There's always work in construction."

Momentarily her eyes closed in exaggerated disbelief. "Think, Airhead. That wouldn't bring in the kind of money he'd need to buy land, let alone build on it. Out there, he only had half as much as you two would've had together, and I never believed he could do it on double that. He had no marketable skills of the woodsman stripe, like whittling or pounding nails. Maybe he turned to selling blood. Better yet, his body." She filled her glass with Sun Tea from a huge amber container on the countertop.

I followed suit, resisting the bait. "Not a lot of market for that out there, I wouldn't imagine. But I suppose I'll find out."

She tried another tactic. "You can't take all that time off from work."

"I'll arrange for a temp. The customer service help screens are pretty self-explanatory, and temps can send the tougher questions up to a supervisor. It's only for a week or so."

Zoë's eyelids fell to half-mast. "I still say it's too dangerous. Going out there alone, when Aaron had who-knows-what happen to him. Maybe it was a burglary or home invasion. What if one of your creditors found him?

'Nonconforming lender' can mean Guido from the Mob comes to break your kneecaps."

I couldn't resist a chuckle. That didn't sit well with her.

"Something's fishy." She eyed me disapprovingly with her penetrating hazel gaze. "But you're a grown-up, so I guess you can make your own decisions about your personal safety."

My sister is terribly overprotective of me. It's kind of nice sometimes.

"Where exactly is this cabin? Did you get more details from Peter Pan than just 'second star to the right, then straight on until the gas gauge shrieks'?"

I tried to remember. All I had written down was my flight number and Gil's cell phone. "A little town called Mar-something. Martha?"

"Marfa?" My sister's eyes widened. "Home of the Marfa Mystery Lights? Artists' colony in the haunted desert? Travel destination of woo-woo seekers and True Believers?"

She had to be putting me on. "You're thinking of Sedona, Arizona. Or Roswell, New Mexico."

"You've never heard of the Marfa Ghost Lights? They've turned that Godforsaken desert outpost into an attraction for all the UFO buffs and X-Files fans."

"I don't know what you're talking about."

Zoë shook her head. "You'll find out. Don't count on me coming with you, by the way." She plopped into a dinette chair and made room on the table for a bag of chips by moving her stack of mystery novels, half-completed crossword puzzle books, mail-order catalogs, and general what-have-you to the floor. "I can't afford to go gallivanting. Neither can you."

"Aaron's estate is paying my way."

She sighed. "I suppose this means I'm on my own with this Extreme Home Makeover."

"I can keep painting all night, or until just before my flight leaves."

"When do you leave, again?"

"Tomorrow afternoon."

She rolled her eyes. "You'd better go get packed."

CHAPTER TWO

The flight was what frequent flyers call "uneventful," but that was because I had kept a steady upward pressure on both armrests. I brought along my MP3 player and two books to distract me, yet I ended up gazing out the window at the colorless plains as we floated across the endless Texas landscape.

According to Gil, the closest airport from the east (since there was none at Fort Davis) was Midland-Odessa, George "Dubya" Bush's hometown, oilman territory. I'd never been to far West Texas and had a picture in my mind of cattle among tepees. The area is actually a plateau on the edge of the Chihuahuan Desert that extends down into Mexico, according to the pilot's informative landing announcement.

The runway looked too short for an airliner, but we made it. As I stepped into the terminal, a good-looking guy came forward, holding out his hand for me to shake. I knew it had to be Gil because he was the only one not wearing cowboy boots or carrying a toddler on his shoulders. For some reason, an old line from Alice Cooper (a preacher's kid himself) came to mind: "I'm not evil, I'm just good-lookin'."

Gil's shiny blond hair was in the latest style, not too short, not too long. He wore a tweedy sport coat over dark Dockers and a white button-down shirt, but no tie. His shoes squeaked out their newness as he stepped toward me.

"Ari? I'm Gil Rousseau." His palm was soft, warm, and dry. Momentarily I flashed on Aaron's long-fingered hands, roughened by all that carpentry.

Sweat popped out unbidden on the back of my neck.

"Ariadne French." I had to lip-read, because my ears were roaring from the changes in pressure. Chewing gum and other tricks have never worked for me; I figured from experience that I'd be partly deaf until morning.

"You look just like your picture."

Aaron had shown my photo around?

At least I was wearing one of my favorite outfits, one that didn't make me look fat. Stretchy black tee, charcoal cardigan, herringbone trousers, black boots, pink socks with a pattern of black cats. With my hair in a messy impromptu bun I'd done on the plane when my neck started to sweat, I was trying for "rebellious librarian."

I managed a weak smile. "Let's avoid all the awkwardness. If you'll call me Ari, I'll call you Gilbert."

"Gil, please, and it's a deal. But it's not short for Gilbert—it's Gilgamesh. An affectation stemming from Mother's English major at Vassar."

Ah, he understood unusual names. "Gilgamesh" trumped even "Ariadne" for weirdness.

"You win," was all I said.

He grinned, revealing charmingly imperfect teeth. I appreciated the sparkle in his swimming-pool-blue eyes. Blue as in a chlorinated, kidney-shaped, Windex-clean pool. Fringed with dark lashes and topped by thin blond brows.

Gil retrieved my rolling suitcase from the carousel as I stumbled along behind, clutching my carry-on bag, my tote, and my oversized purse. Zoë was right about my tendency to overpack. "Why did your parents choose that particular name and not Persephone, say, or Minerva? Or, rather, to stay with the Greek version, Athena."

I decided against countering with the usual snide remark about not having burst fully formed from the head of Zeus like the goddess of wisdom and warfare. "I was born on September seventeenth. It's Saint Ariadne's feast day."

"There's a saint?"

"You'd better believe it. Didn't they go over that in preacher school?" I smiled for real to let him know I was teasing him right back.

"Not at Southwestern Baptist Theological Seminary."

"I suppose saints are a Catholic thing." I breathed in the dusty air and looked around at all the nothing. "How far to the hotel?"

"About two hundred miles. It's roughly a three-hour drive."

"Oh, my G—" I caught myself. "My stars. I had no idea. It didn't look that far on the map." Inwardly, I winced at how lame that sounded.

"The concept of an inch equaling a hundred miles is a bit advanced." He was still grinning, letting me know he was joking.

"I'd never have put you out like this. I should've rented a car."

"No need. You've got Aaron's Navigator." He dangled keys next to my ringing ear. "But I wasn't figuring on having you navigate alone. Our places are kind of off the beaten path. When I said I'd meet you, I meant I planned to drive you back." His eyes twinkled unnaturally, like a TV evangelist's.

Like those YouTube videos I'd watched last night of the Marfa Lights in action.

I didn't know what to say, except, "Great."

As I trotted along trying to keep up with this long-legged stranger, I had to wonder again whether Zoë's paranoia had been sensible caution. It was a bit late to admit this to myself, but I'd come out here basically on a wing and a prayer, without even getting an itinerary. I didn't even know Aaron's address; Gil had said it was "outside of town." And I really would've preferred to know in advance that Gil was not a kindly old Andy Griffith minister but a young hottie, the way girls looking at Clark Kent need to be let in on the secret that he's Superman. That resonant James Earl Jones voice fooled me into expecting an elder, not a centerfold.

I hadn't realized how much I'd left up to him. The way Gil had laid things out, it seemed logical. And I had acquiesced, like a sheep. That wasn't like me at all. Where was my head? Of course, I'd been in shock about Aaron. And I still was.

My gut twisted up, but I made it relax. Surely I was safe with a preacher. And I'd verified his identity by phone earlier in the morning. The quavery-voiced church receptionist had confirmed his employment and raved about how much she—and everyone—had loved Aaron. That, I could buy.

Even so, my budding paranoia pointed out how the whole deal could be a setup; anyone could be bought, and I might've been given a false story by a plant pretending to be an elderly church mouse. I took a deep breath and contemplated how crazy-cat-lady that sounded. Besides, screaming and bolting for the Southwest Airlines desk would be bad form.

I forced a bigger smile. "So tell me about where you live."

"We're on the very outskirts of Marfa. Funny name for a Texas town, isn't it? Back in 1883, it was founded as a railroad stop, and some railroad executive's overeducated wife named it after a character in Dostoyevsky's *Brothers Karamazov*."

My sister had known that. She just didn't wanna tell.

In the parking area he headed straight for a forbiddingly large copper-toned SUV. Opening the passenger door, he gestured for me to hop in. "I hope you're not one of those environmentalist gas-mileage commissars that I hear Dallas is full of," he said in a light-hearted tone. "This beast is only a mid-sized, but it's appropriate to the terrain around here, even off-road. Just don't expect eighty miles to the gallon."

Mid-sized. It was a leather-lined behemoth.

"Leave it to Aaron to stay 'green,'" I said, but Gil didn't seem to register my sarcastic tone. Which was probably just as well. The only part of me that was green was my stomach. I felt like the class goat jumping heedlessly into a hot rod with one of the bad boys from school, without even considering why he'd be offering me a ride all of a sudden.

But, I rationalized, that was just my usual caution-to-the-point-of-neurosis kicking in.

The SUV still had that new-car smell. In the dash sat a StreetFinder GPS and a fancy six-CD stereo with XM radio. As I climbed in, I miraculously managed not to bang my head against the door frame, although I narrowly dodged the huge passenger-side visor with its terrifying safety warnings. I can be awkward when I land in unfamiliar situations. It's a lot better now than when I was a teenager. But as Zoë says, "Walking into doorjambs, getting your coat caught in the escalator, and slamming your head in car doors takes a special talent that a hardcore klutz never grows out of."

As Gil started backing out, I got the shoulder harness fastened and my tote settled on my feet without incident. We zipped out of the airport, Gil navigating the mazy streets onto a two-lane highway. Not a Dallas-style expressway, but a road typical of West Texas. Rural Texas. Winding two-lane state highways following the property lines that once divided two family farms. Armadillos belly-up on the side of the road wearing dully surprised expressions. Scorpions.

I stifled a yawn. Gil seemingly misinterpreted my travel-weariness as boredom.

"Scenery's pretty featureless from here until we get into town. Lean the seat back and relax, if you like." He turned on the radio, which was tuned to a classical station. A symphony; I thought it was Beethoven or possibly late Mozart. My sister would recognize it.

I dozed off, dreaming of being pulled along in Zoë's little red Radio Flyer. When I awoke, the car was filled with orange light.

The flat landscape had been magically transformed, illuminated by the Southwestern light of a Texas sunset. I knew the phenomenon was caused by dust blowing in the atmosphere, but while it chokes the lungs it also filters the light and turns it beautiful, all orange and purple. The way God blends colors, they never clash.

Without thinking, I muttered, "It's a hundred and six miles to Marfa; we've got a full tank of gas and a six-pack of Diet Splurge; the sun is goin' to bed for the night; and we're not even wearing sunglasses." Then I remembered I was with a virtual stranger, and felt my cheeks reddening.

"I love that movie," Gil said softly. "Only the original, mind, not the remake."

Relieved that he'd recognized my impromptu *Blues Brothers* pastiche, I stretched my arms over my head. The thought crossed my mind that up in Heaven, Aaron was finally meeting his hero John Belushi in person.

I was sure of it.

For some reason, my eyes started misting up. I rubbed them and searched my tote for a tissue.

"All right?" Gil glanced my way, looking concerned.

"Great." I sat up straight, smoothing down my wrinkled waistband. "Just having a movie moment."

"It's cinematic out here, you bet. This is where they came to film all the movies about the Old West in the 1800s and those simulated moon landings." He winked.

My eyes adjusted as the sunset turned persimmon and we slid into twilight. Silhouetted in the dusk in front of the purpling sky was an animal that wasn't quite a deer, wasn't quite a llama—there was an alpaca ranch just outside Renner, so I'd know—grazing in a fenced pasture as the highway curved to cut between two fancy spreads. "What's that?"

"Antelope." He grinned.

"I've never seen one." I twisted my neck to watch as we passed until the antelope faded from view. "Just like they sing about in 'Home On the Range.'"

"You'll see all kinds of wildlife out here. Hope you're not timid around spiders and snakes." He glanced into the rear view, then put on the signal (even though I couldn't see another car behind us down that vast straight ribbon of road) and changed lanes. "We've got everything that's creepy-crawly. And snakes like to sleep under flat rocks heated by the sun, so you need to keep an eye out if you go exploring. We've got rattlers, of course, but adders are a lot more dangerous because they've got no maracas to announce that they're there and they're nervous."

I shuddered openly. The Golden West, indeed.

As we rolled across the plateau, the horizon flattened out, and I felt that I could literally see for miles. The road was regularly lined with cacti, weird tall columns about as thick as my wrist with a spray of leaves at the top. Some had tall shoots with purple flowers, large spiky-leafed plants that looked like mutated sage. "I never realized cactus would bloom like that."

"The rains came in August, so now things are greening up. Wild Rose Pass farther on up looks like Ireland, jagged rocks with green up top. But you'll see that, if you stay around here long enough to take a few day trips."

Interspersed among the roadside succulents were streamlined silver trailers. One about every mile or so, in fact. In West Texas terms, an absolute plethora. "Are there always so many people camping out?"

"No. That's a way of life up here. Those are mostly restored 1950s Airstreams."

"They're permanently installed?" I'd envisioned people hooking the trailers to their Ford F-150s and pulling them away after a week or so in this isolated desert. That would be about my limit in an Airstream. If that long.

"Right. Lot of people run bed-and-breakfasts in their extra trailers. There's a good-sized following."

The sunset was rapidly fading, leaving in its celestial wake a murky twilight. A full moon popped into view. Or was it the new moon when it appeared during the day? I couldn't recall.

South of Fort Davis, the previously pancake-flat highway suddenly climbed. My ears, still inside-out from the flight, changed their hum from B-flat to E-flat. I worked my jaw around the way my mother always suggested—she swore that would make them pop open—but, as usual, it did nothing but increase the pressure inside my head. I dug in my purse for a stick of sugarless gum.

"Moving into the high desert. We're a mile high here, did you know? Like Denver." Gil's voice was muffled by my internal Civil Defense Sirens. "Dallas is only at an elevation of 625 feet or so above sea level."

"Sea level" made me think of being seasick. Every movement of my head threatened to make me dizzy. I chomped away like a cow working her cud and rubber-plungered my ears with my palms until I felt light-headed. My ears eased a bit, but didn't reopen for business.

The road narrowed and started spiraling up, climbing a version of that mashed-potato mound in *Close Encounters.* Devil's Mountain, if I remembered correctly, and the same devil must've designed this. My head went boink, and I clapped my hands over my ears to hold in my brains.

Gil glanced over. "Change in altitude," he said. "Might take you a while to adjust. Some people stay in bed for a day."

"Oh, joy," I murmured.

§ § §

We pulled up in front of the Thunderbird Motel's neon sign, and it struck me that I'd entered 1956.

From their website, I'd known it was a remodeled reinvention of an old horseshoe-shaped roadside motor court, done by the same boutique hotel group as the famous Hotel San José I loved in Austin, but to see it in person was a trip back in time.

Converted Midcentury Modern cabins that had been turned into a designer inn apparently attracted Dallas society and other high-end tourists, because everything appeared recently spiffed. As requested, I had a downstairs room. I was in the "Ward and June Cleaver" cabin, in sight of the pool. The water glowed eerily green with underwater lights.

Gil beamed, although I hadn't said a word. "I told you you'd like this place."

I breathed in deeply, expecting a lungful of the fresh night air typical of a small town. Then I sneezed. In place of the acrid urban stink of air pollution and bird flu, there was West Texas' pervasive grit. Red dirt and sand blew in on the wind.

You can't have everything.

The room was smallish with an artsy platform bed, fake zebra-skin rug over a painted concrete floor, and a funky chair straight out of the March 1956 Good Housekeeping. I dropped my bags on the duvet cover, which was made out of an earth-toned Mexican blanket. A huge canvas of cubist art hung over the bed. In here, it smelled faintly of that "sanitizer" stuff every school and hotel seems to use. Pine-Sol with an overlayment of Febreze.

The quiet little room had an instant effect. All at once exhaustion overcame me, and I wasn't a bit worried about bedbugs in the crisp linens, even though Channel Eight had recently done a series of exposés on the hidden dangers in even the best hotels. All I could think of was sacking out.

"You love this kind of place. You're going to be so happy here with us." Gil murmured it, sounding as if he hadn't meant to say that aloud. Which made hearing it even more creepy. "Oh, Claudie." He suddenly seemed to rally, and corrected himself. "I'm sorry—I mean, Ariadne. Ari."

What was that all about?

He dropped my bags. Making no move to leave, he stood silently watching me. I could see his face reflected in the large mirror at the other end of the room. His expression was unreadable.

Was he trying to hypnotize me? The thought was unsettling. Of course it was another ridiculous notion. I took measured breaths. He probably didn't even realize he was being weird; he had to be thrashed himself, having made this drive twice in twelve hours.

His voice was still too quiet. "I suppose you'll want to get right to bed."

I turned to answer in the affirmative, but simultaneously realized he hadn't said how he was going to get home. If I was going to keep Aaron's car, how was Gil getting home? He was a minister, so surely he wouldn't expect to stay here. I mean, I hadn't been to church in a while, but "taking care of the flock" couldn't include that, could it? Still, even if he just needed to crash on the—was there a sofa? Maybe they had a rollaway bed. Whichever, it would still be really awkward.

I took a step backward.

The only lights in the room were the ones that auto-magically came on with the wall switch, which meant it was fairly dim. I couldn't read his expression. If Gil was watching me for some kind of signal, he might end up getting one he wouldn't like.

Gil looked at me closely. "You've got a smudge." Putting his hand on my cheek, he tilted my head and with his index finger rubbed the side of my nose. "A speck of something blue."

Blue? From where? Besides, how could he see a color like that in this dimness? It was too personal, too intimate a gesture for me from someone I'd just met. I managed not to flinch.

Ducking away, I covered by reaching over to switch on the table lamp. "Thanks. I'm going to scrub down the moment the door closes behind you. But you're right, after I call my sister to let her know I'm here safe, I'll probably curl up and read myself to sleep."

He winked. That made my heart start pumping for real, but evidently he'd intended it as a gesture of reassurance, because he started sounding sensible again. "The hotel manager is one of our deacons. He knew I was coming. I'll hitch a ride home with him." He glanced at his watch. "It's almost time for the night staff to come on duty, so I'd better scoot. Maybe he'll walk me over to the pancake house for a bite."

I let out a breath I hadn't realized I was holding. "That'll be nice. I mean, you probably need . . . sorry, I'm never this incoherent."

"I know what you mean." Did he? His face certainly wore a knowing expression.

Zoë might've had a point. Except I still couldn't believe this guy was dangerous. He did seem awfully solicitous, considering we'd just met, but I supposed that was the way ministers always operated—shepherds of the flock. Besides, I was too tired to keep up the high level of suspicion and vigilance that this frame of mind required. I'd have to release my control issues and trust the Universe. And the chain on the room door.

Still, I couldn't keep from stammering. "Right, I—I hope we—I mean, tomorrow we can start bright and early. How far from here is the cabin?" While I spoke, I edged towards the window and lifted the corner of the curtain. "Can I see it from here?"

Gil chuckled, getting my Palin reference. "Our little enclave is actually just outside the city limits." He waved one hand. "Real estate here has gone crazy. We're the new Santa Fe."

"The way sixty is the new forty and orange is the new black?" It didn't come out sounding funny, the way I'd intended.

He smiled, as though to himself. "See you in the morning. We'll get right to work."

As I closed the door behind him, breathing easier, I wondered what exactly he had in mind.

§ § §

The synthesized voice on the phone said, "This is your wake-up call."

Long ago, I'd learned to answer the phone and even hold trivial conversations without coming fully awake. Good thing the hotel desk's automated call didn't care whether I made sense.

I managed to position the receiver back on the hook as I swam slowly up out of a troubled sleep. I'd dreamed of Aaron, but couldn't remember the details, only that he was in trouble but just out of reach. He kept looking at me so expectantly, as if I should be able to rescue him.

By the time I was up, dressed, and reasonably coherent, Gil was knocking at the door.

"I hope this isn't awkward. I realized as I was walking up to the door that you might not be up yet." It was nine-thirty, and he knew I had a day job, so he wasn't taking much of a risk. "But Paul—the manager—had to be in early, so I arranged for him to bring me back up here. If you're not ready to go, I'll run over to breakfast and come back for you." He quirked an eyebrow expectantly.

"No, I'm good to roll." I inflated my cheeks in some semblance of a smile, but I could see by the mirror it was a bit pitiful. "I'm a big fan of breakfast myself, so I'll tag along, if you don't mind." I was sure he wouldn't.

"Fantastic." He rocked back on his heels and clasped his hands behind his back while I ran my hairbrush down to my shoulders one last time and slicked on some lipgloss before grabbing my purse. "Not the waffle house, though. They've really slipped. I think you'll enjoy my favorite spot instead."

"Great." Over my shoulder in the mirror, I could see him watching me again. But instinctively I sensed there wasn't anything stalkerish about it. He was going out of his way to be nice, but why should that make me suspicious?

I was getting as paranoid as my sister.

§ § §

The Brown Recluse Coffee Shop was housed in a converted cottage. It was the central morning hangout for Marfa's domino-playing retirees, tourists, and pretty much everyone else.

"They serve only fresh-roasted free-trade coffees," Gil told me as he pushed the door open and held it for me, "because they're environmentalists who try to help the native people of those lands." He winked, as if to apologize for dissing environmentalists yesterday.

I stepped through the door in front of him. Round gingham-skirted tables dotted the western side of the dining room, with orange vinyl booths lining the walls. A used bookstore filled the east bay, probably the parlor of the original house. Behind the reservations table a grand old staircase, roped off, ran up to an unseen second floor. An old Bob Wills tune was playing over the sound system. Zoë always said the Texas Playboys were the Glenn Miller Orchestra of Western swing.

We ordered strawberry pancakes, a rare indulgence for me. Actually, I didn't get a chance to decline, as Gil ordered for both of us. "My usual, and she'll have the same," he said preemptively, winking at the Republican-haired waitress. She returned the wink and stuck her order pad into the pocket of her red apron as she scurried away. I wasn't about to make a scene, especially since he was paying, but soon I'd have to start watching my calories.

The ambiance was relaxing, and I nearly forgot that I wasn't out here for a vacation. Old records—Willie Nelson, Buddy Holly, and other artists who'd been associated with West Texas through the years—dropped one after another in the Wurlitzer. It was like being at Grandma's house, if your grandmother had run an old-timey diner featuring a jukebox stocked with slightly scratched records.

Gil gave me a few sound bites from the nickel tour. "The movie *Giant* was filmed in Marfa. The cast, including James Dean, stayed at the El Paisano Hotel down the street. It was built in 1930, but they re-did it in 2000 and renamed the restaurant after Dean's character, Jett. You've got to check it out while you're here. More recently, the Coen brothers did *No Country for Old Men.* Went way out by the old railyard with the abandoned tracks that run down to Mexico, and got wild-eyed about how they could film in the authentic Old West. Another bunch used an actual steam locomotive in *There*

Will Be Blood."

"If they want the wide open spaces with indoor plumbing and a blinking stoplight, this is the place to come, I guess."

"An amazing number of artists are here, too. What's even stranger, most of them make a handsome living. We've got the Judd and Chinati foundations and a number of galleries. An art museum, complete with wealthy patrons."

I could see the allure of deserting Dallas for such a place. It did seem like an odd choice for an artists' colony, being so far away from coffeehouses that had open-mike nights for poetry readings and all-night billiard halls. But who knew, they might find the pricey booze at the El Cheapo Liquor Store a perfectly satisfactory trade-off for no traffic and gorgeous mountain views.

Gil had an appealing way about him that for lack of a better word I wanted to term "kindly." He seemed to like me, and I was relieved that the weirdness from last night had apparently been in my imagination. As he pointed out various architectural features of the café (there weren't many), he patted my hand. After a few similar sallies, he let his hand rest briefly on top of mine. I felt my body trying to decide whether to respond. The scales tipped towards an affirmative answer.

My frozen heart blinked its teary eyes. Maybe there was a possibility here. Eventually. When I wasn't so emotionally vulnerable and I was better able to tell real attraction from just clinging to whomever's arm was offered.

We chatted about nothing. I soon noticed the way that everyone seemed to be stealing glances at us. If I looked up and smiled, they always got startled and pretended not to have been looking. It seemed that it was unusual to see the attractive young preacher squiring some strange woman around town—who'd have thought it?

What happens in Marfa stays in Marfa, I always say.

"You're a native Texan?" Gil's tone told me he wanted a positive answer. Fortunately, I had one.

"Born in Dallas."

"Some Texans would tell you that Dallas isn't really part of Texas."

"Same way New Mexico isn't really part of the United States."

"Some folks would argue that point, too." He grinned.

I picked up my napkin. Underneath was a daddy long-legs. Much to my dismay, I shrieked. My voice went off before my rational mind knew it was coming. Reflexively, I smashed the spider with my menu. Then I realized I was standing up, trembling.

Gil leapt up as though I were being sucked into a vortex. "What? What's wrong?"

Mortified, I pointed at the underside of the menu with the squashed remains. "Nothing. I mean, a spider—it startled me." Everyone was openly staring by now. The manager hurried over.

My knight in shining armor settled me back into my chair and shooed away the staff. "Just a little spider. Gave her a start. Everything's fine."

"You'll get used to them things around here," said the waitress, clucking her tongue at the pathetic, wimpy city gal. The manager took away the offending menu as the waitress polished the vinyl-coated tablecloth clean, and insisted on giving Gil a voucher for a free meal next time. "You'll learn. At least you're not one of those crazy tree-huggers who won't even swat a fly," he said happily as he walked away.

"I'm thinking of converting," I said, to be contrary.

"To nonviolence? Way to stand out in the West." Gil let me know he was joshing.

"At least I could still do it, because the last time I checked, the USA didn't have an official state religion."

He shook his head, smiling wanly. "Yes, we do. There is indeed an American religion. Unofficial, of course, but a state religion. It's the worship of the Almighty dollar."

"Point taken." I smiled weakly, gauging the table's height as I contemplated crawling underneath. Because people were still looking my way. The only reason I kept my seat was that I couldn't risk plopping down on top of a full-fledged spider colony.

Gil was on a roll like sprinkles on a doughnut. "Separation of church and state doesn't mean what people think it means. It only prohibits the establishment of a national church, such as when Henry the Eighth established the Church of England after the Pope wouldn't grant him a divorce from Catherine. It's not intended to keep prayer out of school, or take the Ten Commandments out of a courthouse, or erase God off of the coin of the realm. It means you can't be required to worship at a certain place or in a certain way, but they didn't intend to make it a social crime to admit in public to being a church member."

I cleared my throat. "Worry not. As long as there are exams, there will be prayer in school."

He grinned. "Heard that one already. And it's the God's truth."

Gil held my gaze just a shade too long, just long enough to make me feel uncomfortable. He probably intended that as a sign of sincerity. Preachers learned to look people straight in the eye, seeing into the windows-on-the-soul, and the like. Still, it was a tad disconcerting.

Especially when he kept doing it all the time.

After a leisurely stack of "hotcakes" (as the waitress called them) and the best coffee ever, we were back on the dusty trail.

§ § §

The approach to Aaron's cabin took us to the crest of another ear-popping hill—although it could only be called a hill in comparison to the rest of the rugged, rocky terrain. It was at best only a local high point off the main road. The ground looked like it was mostly volcanic rock and sand, the occasional tuft of prairie grass popping out a tendril here and there. On the way, we passed Gil's own house, a large adobe-style like the ones in all those generic Southwestern paintings. His sloping yard was studded with thick-trunked yucca plants, several of which were in bloom. On the nearest flat spot was an Airstream behind an outcropping of rock, but Gil explained it was someone's summer home and currently unoccupied.

Up a bit farther were two more Airstreams that looked like they had settled in for a long stay. If the trailers were layers one and two, the log cabin was the cake-topper. It was perched on top of the arroyo amid a stand of junipers, the only trees I'd seen for miles. The cabin gave the impression it had sprung up among the native plants under the clear turquoise sky, free from the pollution and ozone I'd left behind in the DFW Metroplex.

A flagstone path climbed up and wound around the side of the house to the front porch. Aaron had a small log-walled courtyard, inside of which was a gravel garden. It reminded me of one of those executive gift things, that mini "Zen meditation garden" with white pebbles that you combed across a plate. But surrounded by the white gravel were plants: cactus and succulents and even a couple of bushes with ragged flower buds. I recognized one of them as a dwarf pomegranate; Zoë had tried to grow one of those, but never could get it to thrive.

In the far corner of the courtyard stood a pipe shaped like a shepherd's hook, with a spigot that had a large flat round paver directly underneath. For watering plants?

Gil saw me looking. "An outdoor shower. To wash off the grit so you don't track it into your adobe abode and scuff up the wood floors. We have dust storms just like Abilene, or worse."

Aaron's front door was an ornate cast-iron gate backed by a glass door. A plain linen curtain hid the cabin's contents. I was suddenly afraid the spell of serenity would be broken, that we might encounter red burnout velvet drapes, black imitation leather sofas, and the other trappings of the waiting room of a Mexican bordello. Aaron'd had typical bachelor taste. I almost had a panic attack as Gil worked at the deadbolts and swung the door wide.

But I was pleasantly surprised. It was very Ralph Lauren faux-country Frenchish. The place was filled with flea-market finds, but that had been a hot trend for a while. One wall featured a huge flat TV and all the equipment for a home theater. The open den/kitchen combo had floor-to-ceiling windows looking down the side of the mountain into the valley. Still, that wasn't what made me gasp.

Every wall, it seemed, had a built-in aquarium. Forty gallons and up, not just the ten-gallon dime-store specials. The size that dental offices often keep in waiting rooms to calm down jittery patients. Glowing like radioactive rectangles at eye level and swarming with life. Schools of opaline gouramis, several angelfish as big as my palm, a large shoal of neon tetras. To my right, a long speckled catfish hung from his suction-cup mouth on a tank's glass wall.

Gil looked at my reaction and laughed. "Ever seen anything like it?"

What was Aaron doing with all these fish? He hadn't seemed that interested back in the day when we had fish and he'd left all the tank care to me. Worse, I knew I couldn't transport the live contents all the way back home, at least not easily. I gravitated toward the far wall for a closer look.

The tanks were mostly Aqualife equipment. I wondered whether Aaron had called our number, hoping to get me on the help line. But I'd have known his voice anytime across eternity. So either he must've let others help him, or he'd picked up enough savvy from living with me. I gave away all but one of our tanks after he left, because I had to move out of our upscale leased house into the low-rent Casa el Dumpo apartments and start living cheaply.

Lining the long half-wall of the main room—built into the wall, I saw as I got closer—were what appeared to be the saltwater tanks. A large silver-blue discus swam around, watching us suspiciously from behind jagged decorative rocks. The other exotics shot back into the jungle of water plants when I drew near.

The cabin's interior doors were rustic, having been nailed together from salvaged vintage barn-floor planks, as Gil the wannabe realtor pointed out. There was a built-in breakfast booth of oak, plus custom cabinetry in the kitchen; it must've taken time and skill. Assuming Aaron had started with a raw piece of wood and spent time sanding, finishing, re-finishing, re-sanding, and so forth until he'd produced a work of art, I was impressed. He must've spent a lot of time learning his craft.

"How did he ever. . . ." I trailed off, running my hand along the finished edges of the poured-concrete kitchen countertops. "I mean, working alone."

Gil shook his head. "Everyone pitched in, in return for Aaron's work in the community. We had nail guns and all the equipment that we use in Houses for Humans."

That was the Aaron I knew, coming into a community unknown and using his quiet charm to form a network of people who owed him favors and then calling all the favors in at once. He probably sprang for pizza and beer—or, considering his sudden conversion to righteousness (or at least to being churched), cola and diet soda.

We hadn't been inside a whole minute when there was a pounding at the door. Before I could even turn around, the front door slammed open. A nasal Fran Drescher voice, sans Queens accent, emerged from a panting, life-sized brunette Barbie doll.

"Who's been driving that car? Y'all still here? Where are you?" she called out in a worried tone. She seemed out of breath. Probably from running up the side of the hill under the burden of those huge boobs. Spying me, she added, "WHO are you?"

Gil stepped out of my shadow. "Orleans, I'm glad you're here. There's somebody I want you to meet."

"Gil! I was upset when I saw the SUV gone, because . . . oh." She looked at me again, and this time I registered. "You must be that girl Gil said was coming out here." But she didn't hold out her hand.

In small towns like this, as I knew from having lived in insular Renner most of my life, when a stranger's car appears in the neighbor's driveway, the townsfolk notice and come running to see who it is. Of course, this wasn't a stranger's car—but to see a dead man's car disappear and reappear was probably even more intriguing.

"So what's going on?" She taloned Gil with one claw and put her other fist on her hip. Somehow she also managed to cross her legs at the knee, while still standing up, which I thought was pretty slick. She looked like an animated kite.

I introduced myself. Gil circled around me and gripped Orleans's upper arms from the back. "Let's step outside and let Ari have a moment, shall we?" His tone of voice was not unlike my dad's when he wanted to Have A Word With one of his daughters, or more likely with my misbehaving mother when she was threatening to throw one of her public hissy fits.

He guided her out onto the porch. The door was pulled to behind them, but I could hear the murmurs of a hurried, hushed conversation.

I wandered over to Aaron's computer desk, set into an alcove between the kitchen and media room. A mini "away room," I figured, in modern real estate jargon.

The desktop was cluttered with several handheld games and a few vaguely calculator-looking gadgets. He had a laptop and a desktop system with a large LCD monitor. I didn't feel I should power up any of the equipment, though that would be interesting to do later. I sank down into the desk chair, feeling tired already. It was at Aaron's height, meaning that my feet didn't touch the ground. I have a long torso and short legs, the exact opposite of him. But because I'm so long-waisted, when I sat, I had a perfect view of the desktop and the wall.

Behind the desk, mounted on the paneling, was Aaron's huge corkboard, covered with Post-Its and clippings and even some of our old familiar Dilbert cartoons in yellowing newsprint. He'd always had a corkboard that he called his mindmap, even back when we'd worked together as entry-level Associate Software Engineers at InVerse.

My heart melted. Up until now, I hadn't seen anything that made this personal; it could've been a showcase house on any real estate TV program. But now I knew it was Aaron's, and I was in his inner sanctum. A heavy sigh escaped me as I surveyed the board.

Among the Dilberts and yellowed "Far Side" panels was a large postcard showing an armadillo in front of an outhouse with the caption, "Indoor Plumbing?" I didn't get it, and it didn't seem to fit the theme. Untacking it, I took the card down. My fingertips felt indentations on the back. Writing.

I turned it over and found myself reading a letter to me.

Aaron's handwriting resolved after a blurry moment into text on the back of the card. "Ari, babe! Hello, lost love. Or whatever we are to one another. (Here he'd drawn a smiley face.) I know we didn't part on the best of terms. But I need you to come out here. Something's wack and I know you'll be able to figure out what it is. I need your help right away. Call me when you get this." He gave a landline number and a cell number. "Love and shuckies, A." His usual signoff.

Something squeezed my innards. Gil still hadn't said what happened to Aaron. Had he?

I didn't want to be a suspicious paranoid like my sister. But sometimes they really are out to get you.

"Wish You Were Here" would've been enough to bring me running. Aaron knew that. So for him to write that to me—sounding fairly adamant that I come right away—it had to be something serious.

And yet he hadn't been able to bring himself to mail the card. Maybe if he had. . . ?

Behind me I heard Gil's heavy footsteps and a decisive closing of the door. Before thinking too deeply about what I was doing and why I didn't want to take the chance that Gil might see me with it, I shoved the card into my purse.

Too quickly, he was behind me. "What interesting things have you found?"

Had he seen my sudden motion? My hands started trembling and I knew I would stammer out something incriminating. I had to think fast.

I covered by pointing at the ring of Post-Its around the monitor screen, listing groups of numbers. "Oh, I was just trying to figure out what the heck these are." I snatched a note and held it under his nose. "Do you have any idea?"

His expression softened into his happy-face. "Those are GPS coordinates. Probably various unpublished geocaches that he's waypointed. A group of us from church go out geocaching together all the time. It's a blast. I'll show you how they work." He reached over and picked up one of the vaguely techie calculator-looking things on the desk. "This is a handheld GPS unit. You put the coordinates in, and it shows you where to find the geocache." He started tapping in numbers off the note. "See? This shows the old quarry to the west of us. If you select 'find route,' it'll lead you right to the cache, or as close as it can get, according to how many satellites it hears. Aaron's got this one marked as a find that he added to."

I looked up, putting on my best "admiring the big strong smart man" expression. "Back up. I have no idea what you're talking about."

"Oops. Geocaching is a new sport for people—mostly techies and hikers—who like the outdoors and a challenge. There are a lot of groups devoted to it online." I must've still looked as bewildered as I felt, because he paused to think. "It's like a worldwide scavenger hunt. You get the locations of caches off the Internet."

"Caches?"

"Somebody hides a box of trinkets and a logbook in some public place, not buried, but in a hard-to-find or not noticeable area. That's a geocache. The container is hidden behind a rock or next to a tree, for example, and typically gets covered with dead branches or bark. It's usually waterproof and sturdy. Like Tupperware, or for a smaller one, an old 35mm film container."

"Sounds simply thrilling." I softened the sarcasm with a grin.

He burst out chuckling. "Hard to explain the appeal, but it's the new nerd craze. You use your GPS unit and put in the coordinates that you get off the Internet and go find the cache, if you can. Then you can take out a trinket and put another back in its place. Usually there's a rubber stamp in there that you can use to stamp your own personal logbook that you keep. Or you can stamp their logbook with your personal chop if you want to do more than sign. Then you'll go online and put your name down as having found the cache. People brag about being the first or second to sign the logbook. Then you can set up your own cache in a state park or some public area and have people go find it in return. I have to admit, it's kind of neat, despite all the geekiness."

"I can't picture you doing that." Though I could picture Aaron doing it, if he got to wear hiking boots and use a computer thingie to find stuff outside.

"You'll have to experience it first-hand. It's a great excuse for a hike or a nature trail walk." He beamed. They must teach that sparkly expression at seminary. "Come on, let's take a look around. Then I'll have you run me home, and you can come back up here and settle in. You can go get your stuff from the hotel anytime. You don't want to stay there, do you? When you can stay here for free. Satellite dish TV, broadband cable modem, food in the fridge, running water and all."

"I suppose." I wanted to be sure I could feel comfortable here at night before I committed to staying, but I didn't want to tell him that. I was still kind of wary that he might offer to sack out on the couch. Though I had to admit I might not remain entirely opposed to the idea, once I knew him better. I might even be, I grudgingly admitted, somewhat attracted to him.

Both attracted and repelled. That didn't make any sense, even by the laws of magnetism.

He walked me around as if I were a buyer with potential. The cabin was really nice. Two bedrooms, the master connected to a large bathroom that looked straight out of Architectural Digest. The interior-walled media room, an exercise room that could be a sunroom except for the folding treadmill and stationary bike. Closets containing mostly boots, jeans, flannel shirts, knit tees. Nothing I didn't expect to see. I fingered the towels in the half-bath behind the kitchen. They felt like Egyptian cotton, top-quality.

All at once I was exhausted. "I'm afraid I'm sort of, as Grandpa used to say, 'tuckered out.'" That was funnier if you knew that my mother's maiden name was Tucker, but anyhow I managed a smile. "I'd better go ahead and take you back home. I'm sure you have better things to do than spend the day baby-sitting me."

"Not at all." For a moment I thought he was going to hug me, but he squeezed my shoulder at the last minute instead. "But yeah, you probably want to regroup. Let's roll."

At the doorway, I stopped and faced him. "Gil, I've been wondering. What happened to Aaron? I mean, he was so healthy. Had he been ill?"

Gil shook his head. "He died of a heart attack alone in the cabin. We'd just been out working on a Houses for Humans project the weekend before, and he'd seemed fine. There's no explanation. Just one of those awful things that we'll never understand in this life."

Okay, so that was the official line? In one-third of cases, the first symptom of heart trouble is a fatal infarction, I had read one day in the JAMA (in the hospital while I was waiting for my nephew Ricky to finish with a treatment), so perhaps some people would believe that. But not me. Not Aaron, who was so conscientious about what he put into his mouth ("This is what you're rebuilding the cells of your body with every day, Ariadne"). He worked out regularly and rode his bike everywhere. Nope, I didn't buy it. Unless somebody came up with some evidence of high triglycerides.

I shook my head before I could stop myself. "I just can't accept that."

"You still loved Aaron." He paused. "May I ask—why? Most people would have nothing left but righteous anger after what had happened between you."

"I'm not most people." Gil of course had no way of knowing that both my sister and I were oddballs who walked their own paths, unusual during a time when homogeneity is valued and conformity is the watchword of the day. "I can be upset by and angry at your actions and still not stop loving you and wanting you to give me an explanation, even if it's just a placebo so that I can keep loving you. If I love someone, that's forever. I've always been that way." I clamped my lips firmly shut before I could break into a verse of "Suite: Judy Blue Eyes" by Crosby, Stills, and Nash.

He nodded. "You feel astrally linked to certain people. They remain a part of you even after they're no longer physically present. This is a somewhat deeper belief system than is promulgated in our pop culture today. Everyone sees things as transient now. You would have to go back to the ancient Greeks and start reading to find people who believe as you do, and follow it through Western Civ I to understand how the culture has changed."

"Gil, please. I don't care if I understand. Besides, it's getting so deep in here it's ruining my boots." I almost smiled. The next thing he'd probably say is that I was obviously "married to Aaron in my heart," or some such platitude. That thought made me mad again. "And don't psychoanalyze me. You don't know me, and so please let's not go into all that Goddamn bullshit about how my love for people should stop because of this or that logical reason, dammit."

Fortunately, the profanity didn't offend him. "It's all right. Anger is perfectly normal at this stage of grieving. As is your refusal to believe that Aaron could be called home so arbitrarily. Calling it 'denial' may be a little simplistic, but there's something in the human soul that searches for comfort at times like this. It's almost as if a heart attack is too easy an answer to the larger questions, maybe even trivial."

The larger questions? I searched his gaze, looking for something I didn't find. Those twin swimming pools he used for eyes didn't show a ripple. "The last word I'd use right now would be 'trivial.'"

Gil adopted a mournful look, one suitable for a misbehaving puppy or a man skittering on thin ice. "What I mean is, we all prefer to think the death of a loved one is connected to—special circumstances; that's all I meant."

What was behind that lack of actual semantic content? Okay, Zoë had it right: something was definitely fishy around here.

Ha, ha. My brain, when rattled, sent up an aquarium pun. Well, worse things have bubbled up from that huge undergravel filter.

I couldn't help wondering: in Texas, wasn't there an inquest whenever there's any kind of suspicious or questionable death? Was there a report somewhere? Couldn't I get a look at it? Should someone call someone?

Probably.

But now I was sure that I needed to know what the medical examiner's report actually said.

I might've taken Aaron's postcard at face value as an excuse to get me here if he hadn't died, but maybe . . . maybe he'd been afraid for his life. And perhaps he was right to be suspicious.

I knew I had better watch my step.

CHAPTER THREE

It wasn't far back down the hill to Gil's lair. I remembered passing it on the way in. He didn't live right adjacent to the church, but he pointed out the building, a huge adobe cathedral only a couple of blocks away. His house, though, seemed nearly as big as we pulled around in the circular drive (I'd surrendered the keys to him, pleading fatigue, but really I wasn't sure how to handle such a land yacht and preferred to try it out with no witnesses.) How did an associate pastor outside a metroplex make enough money to afford something like this? Perhaps he'd inherited a bundle.

"Like to step inside for a minute?" He twinkled his eyes at me again, and I couldn't help comparing him to a Macy's Santa. "I love showing off my place. Designed it myself, with a little help from the architect."

Taking up so much of his time was making me feel guilty, but. . . . What the hell. I could use a respite from assimilating all that Aaron had done and accumulated in one short year away from me. It didn't seem as if he could've been away that long.

Gil's adobe hacienda was U-shaped, the stucco walls of its courtyard enclosing the open top with a wrought-iron gate. The court covered a larger area than Aaron's. Opening onto it were arched windows from every room and a line of French doors from the west wing. But the major attraction was a set of massive double front doors with twelve carvings on each, arranged three across by four down. When I examined the carvings more closely, I realized they were the symbols for the signs of the Zodiac.

"I especially love this clay tile roof." He gestured upward. "That makes a mighty nice sound when it rains. Like living under a vibraphone."

"I can well imagine."

In the front hall, a shocking orange wall re-oriented me as my eyes adjusted. Gil grinned as he saw me gaping at the huge framed piece of abstract art on the wall—a Mondrian-style array of rectangles, but all in muted Southwestern terra-cottas and celadons—with a skylight acting as its museum-like downlight. "Local artist," he said. "Has showings all the time, if you're interested."

Mexican tile in the entry rose on the right-hand side into a tile staircase that curved upward to the left to create a small indoor balcony that reminded me of the outdoor balconies seen in stage productions of "Don Quixote." Perhaps that came to my mind because in the corner stood that clichèd 1970s icon, a fake suit of plate mail.

The rest of the interior walls were either bare logs or quiet shades of green. Pea-green in one room, a greenish greyed taupe in the next. Straight ahead was an open-plan kitchen/living room whose back wall was glass doors through which I spied a large atrium containing an in-ground pool.

He must've noticed me goggling. "I know what you're thinking. The church must be pretty flush, or else when it comes to their staff, fairly excessive and indulgent. How many people of modest income in Dallas have a heated pool indoors? But that's how we do it out here, because dust storms are pretty commonplace, and the filter on an outdoor pool gets clogged up. The dust devils are also the reason I can't wear my contacts." He reached into his pocket and slipped on prescription glasses. The metal frames with lozenge-shaped lenses circling each eye made him look so much more intelligent. Professional.

I still hadn't eaten lunch; suddenly my stomach rumbled loudly. Gil grinned. "Come on back into the kitchen and we'll see if I can't scare up something right quick."

I perched on an ironwork barstool at the kitchen island with the sun streaming in behind me while Gil scrabbled around in the refrigerator and cupboards. He brought out a plate of veggie crackers surrounded by cheese cubes and slices of an unfamiliar squishy fruit. "Ten bucks says you've never had this." He poked at one of the pieces of fruit.

"No bet."

"That's from a native cactus called a strawberry pitaya. Mine bears all summer, or whenever it feels like it."

I reached out for a piece. It was a small pink fruit all slushy inside with tons of tiny seeds like a strawberry kiwi. Feeling brave, I popped one into my mouth. It was fabulous. Like a cross between a strawberry and a banana.

Bells rang out, sounding the Winchester chimes. I looked up expectantly, wondering whether Gil had a church-modified microwave, but then realized it was the doorbell. Since the front door was standing ajar, the visitor barged on in. Noisily, judging by the sounds on the tile. Cowboy boots, I predicted.

"Hey, Gilster, I brought back your—oh, I see you have company." Into the kitchen strode a square thirtyish man in worn jeans, boots, rock concert tee, and gimme cap with a blond ponytail poking out the back. He was carrying a large metal toolbox. When he saw me, he stopped short and stared, as if he were seeing something he definitely shouldn't be seeing. "Claudie?"

My mouth fell open the way it does when I'm at a loss for words, which isn't often.

Then he did a double-take and said, "Oh, sorry. I thought you were someone else. You resemble a former church member." He grinned, displaying phosphorescent-white teeth, and held out his free hand to me.

"Nice to meet you. Whoever you are." He glanced at Gil meaningfully.

Gil's delayed response was too jolly. "Buck! How goes it, bud? Buck Travis, this is Ari French." To me he said, "Buck is a musician and handyman. He volunteers at Marfa's independent radio station, KMAR-FM."

"Ponyboy is my handle on the air. *Ponyboy's Roundup*. People sort of came to call me that over the years." He tossed his hair in a gesture I recognized as subconsciously flirtatious. "After the character in that sixties novel."

"*The Outsiders*." I smiled, recognizing the reference and appreciating why the appellation had been applied to him. "What's your playlist?"

"Classics."

No surprise, considering it was public radio. "My sister is a classical music fiend. Are you a Mozartean, or do you prefer Beethoven?"

He laughed. "Classic rock-and-roll. My playlist comes from me, not from my bosses or the advertisers, so what you hear is the truly great stuff, some of it obscure. You can hear me Monday through Thursday from eleven AM to one PM, immediately following the Super Roper Redneck Revue. We stream live audio at marfaindyradio dot org."

"I'll check it out." I noted the URL on a scrap of paper I found in my purse. "It's refreshing to meet a real broadcaster. Most of the DJs I know have gotten stuck in syndicated corporate radio." The changeover from independents to syndicated "Jack" and cookie-cutter "Clear Channel"-owned companies, controlled by conglomerates, had affected almost every Dallas-Fort Worth station.

He nodded. "I prefer a place that doesn't know 'Jack.'"

I caught his reference and smiled. "You and me both."

Turning back to Gil, he swung the toolbox back and elbowed him. "Well, I won't keep you two." He winked.

From the expression on Buck's face, I knew he thought I was either a new convert from the church or a potential convert to Gil—as if he were trying to seduce me. Why did that vibe come up so frequently?

"Did you know Aaron?" I asked before anyone could confirm or deny.

Gil signaled something to Buck with his eyes. It was the kind of private gesture my sister and I often used to communicate. However, I didn't have Buck's decoder ring. "Ari's the woman I was telling you about who came out to claim Aaron's cabin."

"Seems I recall you telling me about that." Ponyboy brightened. "Maybe we'll see you tomorrow night down at the festival. *Numinous Hatred*—that's my band—we're playing three sets on the Bluebonnet stage."

I looked at Gil, widening my eyes to let him know I'd enjoy going. That had always worked on Aaron.

"Happy to hear you got a gig. Maybe we'll catch you there." Gil wasn't committing.

"Hope so." Ponyboy winked at me again. "Nice to have met you. Gil, I'll catch you at Sunday school." He touched the brim of his hat in a mock-salute and was gone in a puff of cowboy dust.

That was my cue. "I'd better run, too." I slid off the stool.

"So soon?" He looked at my plate. "You've hardly nibbled. Can't I take you out to lunch?"

I shook my head. "You've been way too kind already. I should let you get back to your church duties. Anyway, I need to just crash, stretch out, and rest. Get my things from the hotel, clean up a little. You know."

Gil chuckled in a way that suggested he was indulging me. "All right. I need to drop in at the church office. They like to see me now and then. But I'll catch you later."

§ § §

Back at Aaron's cabin, I closed the door and leaned against it, feeling overwhelmed. The SUV had been a smooth alligator to handle, but now that I was here, I felt like leaving again. I hadn't decided whether to sleep in the cabin tonight—or, truly, whether I could. Everywhere I looked, the specter of Aaron floated between me and the fabric of reality.

How much of his memory-jogging Presence could I take? I had my limits. What I needed was a good cry. Yet now that I was alone, the tears wouldn't come.

Slumped against the door, I sighed. The fish stared curiously at me from their fluorescent crucibles.

"Lucky old fish, just floating around paradise all day," I paraphrased from an old pop song. "It's always daytime in there, isn't it?" The lights never went off in the tanks. The bubbles rose soothingly across the artificial scenery of the back glass. Everything was right with their world.

I took a shower and changed into my other jeans, the ones with five percent Spandex, and a beige tunic-length sleeveless cotton tape-yarn sweater. I thought I could get away one more day without washing my hair, if I kept it braided.

I was searching Aaron's cabinets for the fixings for a quick meal—he had dry beans and rice, bottles of salsa, a freezer full of various pre-chopped peppers and onions, and a crock pot on the countertop, but that would take too long; I needed something quick—when I heard shells crunching outside.

It was the sound of tires on the driveway.

I opened the front door as a black-and-white car pulled up and parked. A sheriff's badge and department logo was painted on the door. A uniformed man got out, flashing me his ID as he approached up the steps.

"Ms. French? Detective Max Varga. I need to ask you a few questions."

I could say the same to you.

I managed to smile. "I'll help if I can. But I may not have any answers.

I just got in town, and I haven't seen Aaron since he moved out here from Dallas."

Officer Varga was not-entirely-ungorgeous in a sandpapered, Russell Crowe-esque way. His forest of stubble told me he either hadn't shaved this morning or had a one o'clock shadow from too much testosterone. Or perhaps he was deliberately growing a beard. He was a compact, muscular type about my height and had a sprinkling of freckles on his pecan-colored complexion, fawny eyelashes in the same camel-taupe as his hair, and sunglasses pushed up into his hair so that the front was spiked straight back. He smelled of wintergreen Life Savers.

"Nevertheless. You probably know more than you think." He looked at me as if I should start the conversation. I figured it was probably a technique they learn at the Police Academy to make idiots like me spill their guts.

"Well, come on in," I said, just like my mother would. I stepped back and held the front door wide for him, because it seemed pretty silly to stand out here where the neighbors could gawk. Not that there were many neighbors, but people probably glanced out of the windows of those Airstreams now and then.

He blinked, standing outside in the sun without bringing those sunglasses down. Maybe, like my sister, he used them as a hairband.

"Wouldn't this be more comfy inside?" Now I was begging the cops to invade my space. I really was turning into Mother.

Stepping inside purposefully, as if in a Raymond Chandler story, he glanced around. Then he swiveled a three-sixty to take in the full effect. "Whoa! This guy a fish scientist of some kind?"

"No, just a hobbyist. They're fascinating, aren't they? Each aquarium is an encapsulated biosystem—a beaker, if you will."

He gazed at me somewhat suspiciously. Uh-oh, I had openly intellectualized. To counteract the bad impression I'd possibly made, I flashed my ten-dollar smile, flipped my hair forward in that girly I-like-you maneuver, and gestured for him to enter the great room. I pulled out the wicker chair for him and sat in a matching one. "It's interesting that you already knew my name, Officer, let alone that I was here. Though I suppose that's how it works in a small town." Settling my chin on my fist, I tilted my head coquettishly. "What made you decide to come by?"

"Got a call." Following my lead, he sat.

A call from that Barbie-doll woman Orleans, no doubt. She'd found out that I inherited and she was peeved. My best approach would probably be to act the slightly flirty ditz with a Jessica Simpson touch.

I simpered at him. "Oh, that's nice. But I wasn't aware that there was any police problem with Aaron's estate, or whatever. Surely it's not against the law for a stranger to come to town."

"Depends on the stranger, of course." He glanced down at his steno pad. "Pretty standard, just checking things out. Under Texas law, anyone who dies outside of a medical facility becomes a case that has to be followed up and closed."

"I did not know that." I fluttered my lashes.

"Yep. We're busy tryin' to track down the appropriate relatives and so forth, just your basic everyday routine."

That told me that Gil was either flim-flamming me about being the one who had to find the next of kin, or else he was doing a search on his own to find Aaron's family for other reasons. I smiled encouragingly. "So has the investigation turned up anything about what happened to Aaron?"

"Why don't you let me ask the questions." His tone wasn't menacing, just matter-of-fact. I folded my hands in my lap like a good schoolgirl and waited.

The first thing he wanted to know was how my full name was pronounced and spelled. As he copied it down, making sure to get it right, he tried to put me at ease by talking about his own name. "I'm originally from Ecuador. I go by Max around here because people won't say 'esTEBben' instead of 'ESTY-bohn,' and they make it sound the way that Mexicans would say it." I got the feeling that he was telling me something, or maybe he thought I was a bigot.

"You'd hate to hear some of the ways they've twisted R. E. Oddney." I grinned.

"I can relate." He consulted his spiral. After getting my full name, rank, serial number (which I was sure I'd had filed off), and home address, he tapped his pen on the steno pad's metal coil. "What was your relationship to Aaron Beecroft?"

"Well . . . it's complicated."

"You were lovers?"

He didn't mince words. "Yes. We were going to get married . . . at least that's what I assumed." I tried to toss off a Phyllis Diller-esque cackle, but it came out as a bark.

"He came out here to build the house . . . and you stayed behind. In the Dallas area."

"To work, yes, and save some money." I sighed, and decided to meet his gaze, just in case that made the truth more believable. "Actually, my nephew Ricky was critically ill and dying when Aaron left. He needed to go ahead with our plans—everything was all set—but I couldn't leave. After a few weeks I still hadn't heard from him, but I didn't have time to worry. I wasn't fully functional, anyway, because my nephew's health failed so quickly and dramatically. I kept expecting Aaron's call. But I was helping my sister cope. She's—she was—a single mom and our parents—well, it's complicated."

"They're living?"

Suppressing all the smart remarks I used at home to answer that, I simply told the truth. "Yes. But we don't have a lot of contact. I was the only one helping Zoë and Ricky." I sighed. "I had been laid off from my job as a programmer a few weeks before, and so Aaron went ahead and quit his, as part of our plan to move. My layoff prompted him to start the process a little earlier than I'd had in mind." A lot earlier, actually.

"You worked together?"

"At the same company, yes." I gave him contact info for InVerse, because he seemed to want it, although I couldn't imagine how that'd help. "We were both burned out and wanted a fresh start. But then Ricky got sick. When we found out what was wrong, I got him into an experimental treatment plan."

My face must've told the rest of the story. The officer nodded, looking down to study his shoes. After a moment he said, "What they never tell you is that it costs the same whether the patient survives or not."

So he got it. Maybe he'd been through the same kind of experience. I feel a special kinship with others who've lived through it, either with loved ones or by themselves. But I never ask for details; if they want you to know, they'll tell you.

I took a deep breath. "Anyway. With what was going on, I couldn't possibly leave with Aaron, and we both knew it."

He inclined his head, cueing me to go on.

"So he was ready to go, and I told him to go ahead. He wasn't handling the hospital-medical experience well." Neither was I, and Zoë even less. "We'd given up our lease by then, and there wasn't any way I was going to move in with my sister or my parents. I lived up most of my savings just getting re-settled in a temporary apartment"—the one I was still stuck in—"and I had to take another job, which I did. I found one that was less demanding. On purpose."

"You were already overwhelmed. It's sometimes pretty difficult. Some people can suffer from PTSD." Post-traumatic stress disorder.

"I don't know that it was quite so extreme, but yes, I needed calm and structure to cope. Gradually over the weeks when I didn't hear from Aaron, I became concerned. I mean, there were a few postcards, but nothing with a return address. He had told me Montana, but obviously he didn't get that far. I realized I had no idea where he'd landed. Whenever I tried his cell phone it said the customer was out of range, and so I just. . . ." I shrugged. "What was I supposed to do, hire a private detective with funds I didn't have? You see, around that time I had to start making the payments on the trailer and camping equipment and so forth that Aaron had taken along, as I discovered that he wasn't making them when the collection calls began. Aaron also continued to charge on some of my accounts."

"Why didn't you challenge the charges?"

"I did question them at first. They traced back to Aaron's signature—I mean, he signed my name." I had to be circumspect; I didn't want the police claiming that I had any reason to do Aaron harm—even if many people would say I did—and pointing to possible PTSD as a cause. "But it was him, not a stranger."

"And you didn't prosecute?"

"There was no point. Unless I wanted to take him to court, which would just end up making the lawyers rich, and I figured he probably didn't have any money for me to get. It wasn't all identity theft; I had willingly co-signed for some of the stuff that he stopped paying on." No one ever understood this, not even Zoë. "I'd have had to press criminal charges. And that would've ruined his life, and I had no guarantees anyway. I kept thinking—" I broke off. "Up until just now, I still had in the back of my mind that I'd eventually be coming out here to be with him." Another heavy sigh escaped me. "It's complicated, Lieutenant."

He glanced around the room. "Man seems to have come into some funds since then."

"Yes, well, we're talking a little over a year ago. He obviously did well for himself after—after he left." I realized I was wringing out the hem of my sweater, and hurriedly dropped it. "I'd rather not dwell on that. It doesn't matter any more, anyway. What I'm interested in is what happened to Aaron once he got here. From the way this is being handled, I think I can assume it wasn't his heart."

He studied me with his appraising brown eyes. I was starting to feel like a diamond, or at least a cheap zircon. "No, it doesn't appear to have been. But you could probably contact the coroner's office for a copy of the report. There was an informal inquest."

"Was there any. . . ." I couldn't say the word "autopsy," especially because etymology implied it should mean "surgery on oneself," and "postmortem" was equally cold. "You know, any procedures done to find what actually happened to him."

"That's what I'm here for." He looked down, then back up. "Did you benefit in any way from his death?"

"I'm the heir." I managed not to let my face twist into a frown. "Apparently, I get it all. The will hasn't been read yet, and the estate is in probate. For details, you'll have to ask the executor, Gil Rousseau."

"Hmm." He made some notes. "We'll be needing to talk to you again."

"I'll be in town for a while. You know, for the funeral and so forth. Until things are taken care of, up to two weeks." I licked my dry lips. "What kind of detective are you?"

He looked confused.

"I mean, which department?"

"Homicide, ma'am."

So they shared my suspicions. No, it was more than that. This had to mean they had some kind of evidence to go on.

In fact . . . I had probably just been identified as a person of interest, if not a major suspect. Yet.

I ushered him out and watched the dust rise along the approach road as the shell-gravel crunched under his tires. I hoped I hadn't just met a good-looking young hotshot who was more interested in circling me and evaluating his chances for convicting me than in why Aaron was murdered. If he was. Oh, God . . . what if he really was?

Finally I turned back to the front door and started inside.

"Miss! Oh, miss?" A quavery female voice hailed me. Louder, the voice called, "Hey there, new neighbor!" I turned.

A sixtyish lady was hurrying up the steps, spry as a teenager and seemingly not worried about tripping. She gripped a pan of brownies. "My name's Cora Parker. My husband and I are—we were—Aaron's closest neighbors, as the coyote stalks."

Uh-oh, I was too casually dressed to meet the neighbors in this small a town. I pulled out my ponytail holder and shook my hair loose around my shoulders, letting the layers work the way they were supposed to. "Ariadne French. I'm Aaron's"—what was I?—"um, friend."

"I know, dear. Gil told us we'd be seeing someone show up here." Her magpie glance took everything about me in at once. "I thought I just saw the police leaving. Is there a problem?"

"No, no. They just wanted to talk to me about Aaron's death. Because it was untimely. They're just doing paperwork. Just routine, nothing."

Her eyes said she knew I was hiding something, but she didn't press.

"Won't you come in?" My transformation was complete; I had turned into my mother the socialite.

Fortunately, my instincts were good, because that was the proper M. O. for dealing with ladies of Cora's generation.

"Land sakes, police and their paperwork." She brushed past to set the pan of brownies on the kitchen countertop; then she whipped off her apron and folded it into a square, which she tucked under her arm. "Why, you don't need that kind of hassle your first day here."

"It's all right. I want to help them, if I can." I smoothed down my sweater, although that still didn't turn it into a cotton piqué blouse with a Peter Pan collar.

The woman's bright, birdlike eyes searched my face. Then she nodded. "Let's get your mind off of all that. C'mon with me. You can meet my husband and see our spread."

Spread! Yummy. But my visions of marmalade and cream cheese were dispelled as I realized it was a Texanism. She meant their property.

CHAPTER FOUR

Suddenly I was ravenous. I sneaked my fingers under the plastic wrap and dug out a double brownie, then hurried to catch up with Cora. A woman with a mission.

Cupping my treat between my palms, I gingerly followed her down the bricked steps leading through what I had to consider Aaron's back yard, past his fire pit and "cowboy hot tub," which I hadn't noticed before, because I hadn't looked at the back yard closely. The tub was a large plumbed copper trough that I supposed swirled hot water for spa-diving.

Cora's yard was mostly gravel, but not quite as Spartan as the others around. A few zinnias and sunflowers sprouted in her rocky garden among the cacti.

A tall older man stood in their barren field of a front yard, tossing a lasso. I hesitated, feeling that becoming a substitute for his practice on a calf would be a poor introduction. Then I realized he was aiming the loop at a metal statue, which I recognized from high school rodeo as a roping dummy. He spied us and twirled the rope in our direction *à la* Roy Rogers. "C'mon down," he called, sounding just like the announcer on "The Price is Right."

Holding the tip of his tongue between his obviously-capped front teeth, he swung the lariat. The noose slipped deftly over the practice steer's neck, and he snapped the rope taut. "Yee-ha, little dogie," he crowed. "See that? That one's for the record books."

"Buzz, stop that foolishness." Cora wiped her hands on her balled-up apron, even though she hadn't touched anything and I couldn't imagine what she might think had gotten on them. "This here's Arrietty French, the girl come to get Aaron's things. She don't need to see you playin' at that and think you're a tired old coot."

He grinned, winding and looping the rope around his shoulder and elbow the way real cowboys do. "I was tired, and now I'm tired again, so I suppose you could say I'm re-tired." He held out his hand. "Francis James Parker, but call me Buzz, little lady."

He was old enough that the "little lady" didn't seem sexist or affected. "Ariadne French. Everyone calls me Ari."

"Airy it is, then." His face took on a triumphant little-boy expression. "I tore up my shoulder the first time I swung this rope around. Now look at me. Well, you saw." He pointed at the dummy. "A man's got to do something for fun, and I'm too old to chase girls."

"You'd get your fanny whupped if you tried," put in Cora.

Buzz reminded me of Tommy Lee Jones or Clint Black without the hat. I suspected he was putting on an exaggerated country-boy act for my benefit, and appreciated the effort.

"Where you from, hon?"

"Renner. Just north of Dallas."

"The big city." Buzz grinned, and I wished he had a watermelon seed to spit for effect. "You probably thought you were comin' out to a cattle ranch, didn't you? Lot of tourists start scratchin' their heads when they see this landscape. Way out here, we've got lotsa dirt between light bulbs."

"I noticed."

"This is really a plateau on the High Chihuahuan Desert. Extends on down into Mexico," he drawled laconically. "Everyone's gotta xeriscape—that's where you make do with very little water. There's the rainy season for two months, and then there's the rest of the time. Water saving is the word of the day—your garden ain't lawn, ain't flowers, but succulents and cacti and a whole lotta gravel."

"So I see." I scuffed the toe of my sneaker across his "lawn" and dug a shallow line. "But it's pretty in its own way."

He continued playing the role, apparently a frustrated actor enjoying his audience. "Out here, y'know, well, I mean it's like there ain't no Wal-Mart. Drugstore—Steen's—is twenty-six miles as the crow flies. Over at the airfield—it's just for private planes, y'see—you'll often find people flyin' in using light planes from El Paso and Midland, headin' to the Whole Foods market or somesuch gourmet place out there. The Santa Fe or the Katy is likely to rumble by just about anytime pulling a hundred freight cars, at all hours, so be prepared to sit if your road crosses their tracks."

"Well, I love the sound of the train and train whistles, especially at night." I smiled.

"Then you're in like Flynn. Out here there's small farm-to-market roads take you up the hill, no interstate. You'll see." He looked at Cora a moment, then evidently decided she would be complicit in his offer. "Later on we can go cruising in Nellybell"—he indicated his Pat Buttram-worthy old rusted red pickup sitting on a concrete pad near the detached garage—"and show off the sights."

"The sheriff was just over to Ari's house." Cora lifted an eyebrow.

I felt my color rising. "Actually, just a police officer."

"What for? Any trouble over there? He's got a security system. I'll have to show you how to work it."

"I'd appreciate it—I didn't notice a keypad. But it's nothing like that. He just wanted to check in with me about, you know, what happened to Aaron." I decided this could be a useful lead-in. "What do y'all know about what happened? It was such a shock."

"Wasn't it, though?" He shook his head.

"That slut—I mean, that awful woman, Orleans Hall, found him." Cora clucked again. This contradicted Gil, who had said "the closest neighbor," if I remembered correctly, and no one was positioned closer than these two. "She was always showing up, hangin' around him, never got the message that she wasn't any more to him than a booty call."

My expression must've betrayed my surprise—I wouldn't have expected her to know the term, let alone use it—and she cackled. "I'm old, but I'm no fool, honey. It's a damn shame you didn't come out here with him. He didn't like bein' alone, and that's the only reason he ever took up with her."

"Oh." Really, what else could I say? My heart leaped at the chance to believe.

"That girl would try to fool God by showing a dime to the collection plate but tossing in a nickel and think she was getting away with it. She uses up friends fast as an old junker burns 10W40." Cora sighed and ran her gaze up and down me appraisingly. I wondered what my dollar estimate was. "He often talked about his missed opportunities."

Really.

"Aaron should've known better. But men seldom do while they're young." She sighed.

Buzz glanced her way. "Enough, hon. Anyhow, Aaron was a fine young specimen. Volunteered in the community, contributed to the church. It's a damn shame."

"Did you hear what killed him?" I've always been good at fishing.

She narrowed her eyes. "I thought they said it was a heart attack. Though it's hard to believe it with a young kid like that, great shape, nice bod—"

"Watch it," Buzz murmured, readying the lasso again.

She frowned at him. "Let's us women go inside and talk."

"No need, just don't want you talking about the boy like that. Gil did say he had a weak heart. Though I thought that claim sounded pretty unlikely myself. Never saw him eat unhealthy food, watched him go jogging and work out, and so forth. Didn't see any evidence of a health problem."

"What did the sheriff—I mean, the police—actually say?"

He stuck out his lower lip in thought. "I never thought about them getting involved. Been some gossip about it over at the Brown Recluse."

"How would I find out who might know more?"

"I don't know, little lady, but you do bring up a good point. Why don't you ask Gil about that."

"I will." Gil was the last person I wanted to talk to about that. I'd sooner call the Cheap Detective, Max. I supposed that was what I'd have to do to find out where to go for the report, even though Gil didn't seem to want me to have it. "So what are the sights I shouldn't miss?"

"My wife's collection of cacti, for one. I know that's why she really brung you down here. Go take a look." He readied his rope, then aimed it at us, wearing a puckish expression. Cora hurried away, and I was on her heels.

Around back, she had dozens of species of cacti. "This is ocotillo; you've probably seen yucca, rainbow cactus over here, and here's a variety of prickly pear. There's another, with fruit. But you don't want to touch that." The huge thorns that protected the squishy green rounds were daunting. "There's something you haven't seen: a strawberry pitaya."

"Oh! Gil fed me some of that earlier."

Her eyes brightened. "Did he, now. Hmm, I don't know where he keeps his plant." Her brows bounced. "Any-way-how, this is my hobby, this and needlework. And reading. When you go into town, you'll see where we trade in our used books at the coffee shop, the Recluse. We go there all the time. Pretty much everyone in town does."

"We had breakfast there this morning. It was really nice."

Buzz shuffled around the corner *sans* rope. "Man likes some iced tea now and then."

"Get it yourself." Cora stuck her tongue out as he brushed past, possibly headed for the kitchen.

"Are there any other sights nearby I shouldn't miss?"

"If you like art, they've got galleries. Sellers a-plenty," Buzz called over his shoulder. "Probably find a travel guidebook over at the Recluse that'll give you ideas. Otherwise, mostly I'd recommend our justly famous bouncing supernatural lightballs. They're a must-see." He winked.

My stomach growled. I'd sent down that double brownie, but it wasn't satiated. In fact, I was a little sick to my stomach, likely from eating so much sugar on top of so much nothing.

Cora eyed me. "We're about to have lunch. You're welcome to sit down with us."

"No, no." I waved away the suggestion, feeling that it would be less than neighborly to take her up on such an offer at our first meeting. "I'll be fine. I need to get busy."

She shot a look at her husband. "Let's walk you on back down to the cabin, then. I'll show you where Aaron's dwarf pomegranate bush is; I ought to explain the special care."

Although I wasn't even sure I'd be staying, they already seemed to be assuming I would be their new neighbor. And that we'd get along fine, and that we'd have a lot of fun, in fact. That made me feel wanted again, just a little. I couldn't help warming to them even more.

Buzz trailed us as Cora picked her way expertly down the slope. "You really don't wanna miss the lights. Might not want to go alone. Gil be taking you?"

I smiled. "He hasn't mentioned it. Really, I don't mean to monopolize so much of his time."

Buzz pursed his lips. "Believe you me, if he didn't want to spend time showin' you around, he wouldn't be fooling with you." Before I could react to the obscure suggestion I heard him making, he pointed at the courtyard wall. "Instead of yammering about the lights, I ought to be giving you a visual. Here, I'll show you what they're like, kind of." He waved at the front door. "Go inside and flip that first switch to your right. Then come out here and see. I think we can see 'em even in the sun."

Sure enough, Aaron had his own Marfa lights. Set on top of each corner of the courtyard wall were chunks of slag glass that he had cemented somehow over a normal carriage lantern. When they were switched on at night, I could imagine the effect, an eerie glow. "That's cool."

"Always is," said a tenor voice.

I thought I recognized that voice. I turned around, and here came Gilgamesh again. Clutching his Bible.

"Ahoy." He smiled.

I couldn't help it: I was starting to really like the guy, despite the holier-than-thou trappings. And his way of popping up out of nowhere. And even the occasional unwelcome overture.

He'd been doing some research.

"'Ariadne' is Greek for 'holy'—'most holy,' from Cretan Greek, *ari* 'most' and *adnos* 'holy.' That's out of my Greek dictionaries. You were right: there is also a Saint Ariadne. She's the patron saint of slaves and others who are in bondage."

Zoë had often wondered aloud how our parents had known my future when they named me. I used to slog her off, but now I felt it was creepily appropriate.

"Slaves? Really? Are you sure not of fools?" I challenged him to cover my unease.

"I'm only going by what I've read. Saint Ariadne was a Christian slave in the household of a Phrygian prince in what is now Turkey. When pagan rites were performed in honor of the prince's birthday, she refused to take part and was flogged, so she ran away. Fleeing from the authorities, she was cornered against a chasm in a stone ridge. The rock opened miraculously before her and closed behind her, providing her with an escape that proved to be her tomb."

"How convenient," I murmured. I thought I heard Cora snort.

"So she's one of them martyrs," said Buzz with a chuckle.

"I know the feeling," I said.

Gil looked amused. "Reason I stopped by is, I was headed over to the Finaglers' home, but they aren't back yet. I haven't been able to locate any next of kin for Aaron, though I have several calls in and I do expect some news later, I hope. But time marches on." He blinked. "I wondered if you might be interested in helping to arrange his service. Order of worship—like, the music, any readings, that sort of thing."

I suppressed an involuntary shudder. "Absolutely not." If I went into one of those fake-lilac-scented marble-walled crypt places, I'd have a flashback to seeing my nephew laid out pale and still, my sister like a zombie, and my normally über-stoic mother hysterical on the floor. With Daddy actually crying real tears looking down into the box at where they said Ricky was, although Ricky wasn't really there, just a wax figure in a polished carton, a mannequin with its arms crossed and holding a lily. I didn't know how I was going to handle avoiding any such "viewings" in the future and forever in perpetuity, world without end, amen, but I certainly couldn't look at Aaron like that. Or anyone, for that matter, not this soon.

I forced a smile that even I could feel was wan. "I don't think I'm up to that today. Do I need to sign anything?" Surely I wouldn't have to commit one way or another. After all, Gil was the executor. Strange how "execute" seemed to be at the root of that.

"No, no, just thought I'd offer."

"I trust you. Anything reasonable, whatever you think. Just no angel-voiced soloists singing 'Morning Has Broken,' please."

"I'll second that emotion. Torturous, is what that is." Cora cleared her throat. *This guy doesn't live far enough away*, was the vibe from her.

But her old man didn't pick up on it. Clearly Buzz didn't care who he talked to, as long as he got to extemporize; he was a good old friendly Will Rogers type. Jovial. The loose-lipped ship-sinker kinda guy. "We were just tellin' Ari here about the mystery lights. We were thinkin' of takin' her out there tonight to show her."

Cora looked at her husband as if she'd like to scalp him. Sometimes he could be a bit too loquacious, I could see.

"Excellent idea! It's usually about six o'clock when people start to gather out there."

"We always like to go see if we can tempt 'em out again." Buzz winked. "You know, they don't always show themselves to doubters. But I always see 'em."

I was confused. "The tourists?"

"The lights." He grinned.

Gil checked his watch. "Okay, well, sounds good. I've got to land a couple more places and then try Finagle, if I can catch him. See you then!" Gil waved, and for some reason I glanced down at his Bible hand. Up against the dark leather cover like that, his hand didn't look as tanned, but what really stood out was the light stripe on his fourth finger. Left hand. Where a ring could've been up until recently.

Like where a wedding band usually fits.

Some people wore their class rings on that hand, I suppose. Or had some other reason for such an appearance. A skin condition, vitiligo, an old scar from a jungle gym injury. I didn't know. This wasn't the time to ask about it, anyway.

Cora's gaze met mine; she rolled her eyes, and I couldn't help giggling. Buzz glanced over questioningly and I nodded and smiled. I made my tone congenial. "Sounds like a plan to me."

§ § §

I was about to faint from hunger, but I couldn't exactly ask Cora where the closest burger or taco joint was. It would be like asking if she had any food in the house: she'd feel she had to insist on my dining with them, and I didn't want to wear out my welcome on day one. I'd learned early, from my mother, about the burden of obligatory invitations offered only "to be neighborly."

In Aaron's kitchen, I managed to scrounge up two Ho-Hos and a bag of stale Nacho Cheese Doritos. These served as sustenance while I worked on lunch. I set up the crock pot with an impromptu rice-beans-and-veggies concoction (by dumping in various cans that weren't dented and didn't look too rusty) and found a twelve-pack of diet cola in the fridge. For later, I set Aaron's Sun Tea jug out on the porch in a sunbeam that bathed four bags of green tea.

I still felt a little nauseated, but that was because I had eaten nothing but junk and fried food. After I checked to make sure the crock pot was heating up, I made a few calls and was promised a callback by some clerk who would tell me how to get a report about Aaron, if possible.

I couldn't waste time sitting here worried and jittery. I'd have to learn to drive that monster sooner or later.

Aaron's Navigator started at a touch. The StreetFinder fired up and bossed me, something about locating the satellites. And I had been right about the different handling. The barge was like a spruced-up tank after my many clunkers.

After punching a few buttons, I finally got the radio turned on. It was tuned to a country station, which made me laugh, but then I realized that was going to be just about the only kind of broadcast radio around here. Patsy Cline and Jim Reeves' "I Fall to Pieces" came on, and that made me think of Aaron, so I tuned around until I found an oldies station that wasn't too hissy. I didn't know how to find Ponyboy's station, KMAR, except online. I could see that there was a tuner for satellite radio, but I didn't have time to fool with it. When Aaron bought a luxury vehicle, he went first class.

I bounced into town and retrieved my belongings from the hotel, settling up my bill and returning the DVD I'd borrowed to watch in the room on the free player. I let the StreetFinder lead me through town—which took all of ten minutes—and discovered a Tex-Mex hole-in-the-wall that had a drive-through. I drove away with a Stuffed Veggie Sopaipilla (not a dessert item—that was what intrigued me), a Frito Bandito Burrito, and a sack of chips with salsa and guacamole. Enough to add ten pounds to my butt in one day.

When I walked back into Aaron's house, the scent of him hit my limbic system and knocked me into the past. I stopped just inside the doorway to catch my breath.

I must've smelled his essence earlier, beneath the conscious level, but this time, I was alone with it. Without Aaron. The full import of everything that had happened struck me hard, and my knees buckled. I landed on one of the twin recliners in front of the media center.

The coffee table made a good TV tray. I set the food on it numbly and flicked the TV into life. Aaron had probably eaten dinner here more often than not. Between the remote and one of those wooden tic-tac-toe games played with marbles was a cell phone.

Aaron's fancy video-equipped cell phone.

Before I realized what I was going to do, I had the cold plastic pressed up against my cheek. Tears ran out of my eyes without permission and streaked down my face. This was most likely one of the last items he'd held in his hand.

This wasn't fair. I couldn't believe Aaron was gone, out of my reach, never to return. And why hadn't he tried to bring me here sooner? He'd cared enough to leave all this to me; he should've mailed that postcard.

I flipped the phone open and saw that, as I'd expected, it was dead. The pathetic fallacy. I went over to the desk and found the charger and plugged it in. The tea probably wasn't ready, so I retrieved a couple of diet colas from the fridge and trudged back to my recliner with a much-reduced appetite. I did manage to choke down most of the sopaipilla.

I'd have to start worrying about financial stuff pretty soon. Like maybe the mortgage here, and the car payment, and even his cell phone plan. Maybe I could afford to keep his phone, if I managed this inheritance intelligently.

Inheritance. What a double-edged dagger that word was as it plunged into my heart, reminding me why I was getting all this.

I played with the remainder of my food and stared at the re-runs on the cable channels until a knock on the door around five forty-five brought me the smiling visage of Our Man Gil. The sun lit from behind the top layers of his hair, and he looked entirely ringed with light. Like some kind of Heavenly messenger.

I shook off that crazy imagining and stepped back to let him inside. "Isn't it too early to leave?"

He shrugged. "I figured I'd treat you and the Parkers to a quick dinner first." I supposed I could just order dessert and enjoy their company. "It won't start getting dark until after eight. But by then you'll be ready for the main attraction. You'll finally see what brings the tourists and curiosity-seekers to these parts."

§ § §

We rode out there in Nellybell, which was an adventure in itself. The truck didn't have a whole passenger seat because a metal organizer and tool box that Buzz explained he'd needed all the time in his air-conditioning business still lived there. Wedged between Cora and Gil in the back, wishing my butt hadn't spread quite so much sitting at my desk job, I bounced along as Buzz navigated the bumpy highway.

We'd eaten at a homestyle barbecue joint outside of town, which took a while because everyone else went back for seconds (I managed to beg off and have only the blackberry cobbler, which wasn't as good as Zoë's), and now it was getting dark. The mountains were silhouetted in the orange glow of the sunset.

About nine miles east of town out on Highway 90, we took the exit marked with a sign reading MARFA MYSTERY LIGHTS VIEWING AREA (NIGHTTIME ONLY). The sign's background was purple, which I thought was unlike most Highway Department signage. Buzz parked next to a concrete pad dotted with picnic tables and trash receptacles. "There's the viewing station."

A brick patio area looking like the outdoor café seating for a chain restaurant? This was the site of magic?

We parked in the area provided, and instead of getting an eerie feeling of anticipation, I suddenly felt like some UFO nut who was going to Area Six-and-a-Half to spot Greys. I wondered what in the heck I had been thinking to come here with these crazy eccentrics, and burst out laughing. Gil looked at me, and I said, "Nothing. Just . . . I've never been to something like this before."

"Neither has anybody," said Buzz. "Less'n they've gone up to Alaska or Canada to watch for the Aurora Borealis. But this is a lot more reliable than that. As long as you have faith." He winked at me, and I wasn't sure just how he meant that remark.

There were several couples already leaning on the railing, with a few families straggling in behind. One woman was ready for anything, settled into a fancy camper's chair with her cooler of longneck brews. At least we wouldn't be alone in our folly.

The Texas Highway Department and the Chamber of Commerce had provided a wooden stand holding convenient little brochures about the viewing. I couldn't believe the state government took such a woo-woo thing seriously. But it also speeded up my pulse. Was this for real?

I plucked a brochure out of the stand. Just enough daylight remained for me to read the small print.

Sightings of Marfa's mystery lights were first recorded in 1883, but the Native

Americans knew them long before that: Apache legend tells of an Apache chief lost in what we would call the astral plane and searching for his tribe, and the lights serve as his beacons. These lights were reported since before electricity or vehicles ever reached the Big Bend area. Theories about headlights or ranch landscape lighting also wouldn't explain why some observers hear a high-pitched "tuning fork" noise in only one ear while watching.

The Ghost Lights of Marfa still shine as brightly as ever, and are still as mysterious—despite many scientific studies—as they were when they were first seen by early settlers who drove their herds into the Marfa area in 1883, including Robert Ellison. Driving his cattle west from Alpine, he saw strange lights in the distance on the second night out, while camped just outside Paisano Pass. Fearing that they were Apache signal fires, he searched the countryside by horseback, but could never catch up with them, and eventually realized that the lights were not man-made. Other early settlers assured him that they too had seen the lights and had never been able to identify them.

Numerous photographs and video footage have captured these lights in action. Marfa Lights are generally considered harmless. They are even rumored to have helped a lost man during a blizzard by providing warmth and guiding him home.

It was getting too dim to read. I folded the brochure into the pocket of my jeans.

"It's good that we came on out today. Because this weekend, it's going to be crazy." Gil gestured at the crowd. "It'll be the Marfa Lights Festival in town, starting tomorrow morning. Remember, Bucko mentioned it? They have it downtown at the old Presidio County courthouse. Food and crafts, live music, line dancing. Do it every Labor Day weekend." He smiled. "Around eleven Saturday morning, there's a Macy's-style parade through town with floats, the Marfa High band, fire and police trucks, horseback riding and rope tricks, and all that. People wear costumes related to the lights." I couldn't imagine. "That afternoon and all evening they'll have the music festival, with special guests like Willie Nelson or Asleep at the Wheel. Not them this year. I've forgotten who it is, but it'll be good."

"Wow," I offered, noticing a couple more people settling in along the railing, some with binoculars. One couple lined up their young children on the railing and told them to hang on tight. Obviously, tourists took this viewing seriously.

"Of course, being from Dallas, you've probably seen it all." Cora smiled her secret Mona Lisa smile. I wondered what sort of wicked thoughts lay behind that little-old-lady mask.

"No, I'm still a country girl at heart." There was definitely more to Cora than I'd seen at first glance, but then nobody ever questioned a little old lady and her sincerity, so as long as she didn't get vague or absent-minded Cora had it made. "I love to take Sunday drives and nature hikes."

"To visit abandoned farmhouses?" Gil startled me from behind. "Looking up into the night sky hoping for a visitation—like now?"

"Hush," said Cora, moving around to put Buzz between us.

"I saw a UFO once." Gil spoke softly into my ear. "Out in the Nevada desert." His hot breath on my earlobe gave me shivers. But I couldn't move away. "I suppose it wasn't a UFO, though, but probably a top secret vehicle test by the Air Force. I watched the news the next morning. Several crew members of United flights, including some pilots, saw a disc at the same level as their plane. Dark gray and well-defined against the clouds, it was like a rotating Frisbee, they claimed, but spinning so slowly that some couldn't be sure it even moved. It had no apparent lights on it, but there was a glow all around. It hovered above the airport for at least three minutes, then shot up out of sight, leaving a strange tunnel through the clouds. Like somebody punched a hole in the sky."

"Quit trying to spook her, Gil," said Buzz quietly at my other elbow. Tension drained from my body at the sound of a rational voice.

"Jimmy Carter saw a UFO." My voice sounded a little choked. I cleared my throat. "And Dennis Kucinich, along with various other Presidential hopefuls."

My only answer was Gil's measured breathing near my ear.

The crowd was quiet, waiting patiently, as if we stood on hallowed ground waiting for some long-expected vision. In the absence of big-city lights, the stars looked like pushpins holding up the velvet sky. I started to relax again.

Until I felt somebody's arm slip around my shoulders. Sure enough, it belonged to Gil. That tightened me right up. As I turned my head, he hugged my shoulders as if we were there together on a date. He looked at me closely. "Feeling nervous yet?"

"I'm not afraid of the paranormal." I shook off his arm as politely as I could and moved between Cora and Buzz.

But Gil came up behind me again. This time, both hands landed on my shoulders, squeezing. He actually ran his hands up under my sleeves and rubbed my bare skin. I managed not to jump or recoil. His palms were dry and cool. Mine were so sweaty they were slipping off the handrail.

Before I had time to say anything, Cora piped up to Gil, a mischievous gleam in her watery-but-sharp gray-blue peepers. "So, Gil, speaking of viewings, did you get Aaron's set up? We'd like to schedule that in so we can be sure to make it." Her eyebrows headed towards her forehead's furrows, reminding me of that curious cartoon gopher. "Every Wednesday night we go to the library to see the movie, you know, whatever that artsy-fartsy indie film council sends out. And we have a standing date for bridge on Tuesdays and some Thursdays. The sooner I know what to cancel, the happier I'll be."

"Oh . . . um." Gil released my shoulders and stepped away, seemingly realizing how inappropriate he was being, especially in front of his parishioners. "As it turns out, I did manage to complete most of the arrangements regarding music, order of worship, and so forth." Gil shifted from foot to foot. "But we haven't set any schedule yet."

"Whyever not? We wouldn't want to miss family night. We're about his closest neighbors." I couldn't have sworn to it, but I was sure Cora threw me a wink.

"Well, actually." Gil cleared his throat. "His body hasn't been released yet. Some kind of snag at the coroner's office. Has something to do with not having been able to get in touch with a next-of-kin. But as I mentioned earlier, I'm working on that. Expect to be hearing back fairly soon."

I thought of what the policeman had said about them doing the contact. "Aren't the cops getting in touch?"

Gil looked startled. "Well, I'm helping. I didn't want his folks to hear it from the authorities if I could reach them first."

That made sense.

But it disturbed me that he'd been out to that parlor to make all those arrangements when Aaron wasn't even there. All right, as far as I was concerned, Aaron wasn't there; Aaron had moved on to wherever it is that we go, Heaven to me, the Summerlands to others, a vague Afterlife as wisps of the Overmind to someone else. Whatever. It's just that he wasn't still in that clay form, so it wasn't important. But the vision of his body lying in a cold drawer somewhere gave me chills and a sense of the void lurking beneath it all. I really hadn't needed to know this, let alone think about it in the desert dark.

It struck me that there could be more of a reason for the authorities to be holding his body. After all, couldn't they release it to the funeral home and have Gil act as the custodian, because he was executor and personal representative or whatever the hell they called it? I was pretty sure that was often done. Unless there were suspicious circumstances.

I really needed to make a few calls.

"There's nothing out there," said a quavery voice. "Let's go, Earl. We can still catch the late movie on cable." A rustle in the murk behind us told me Earl and his girl were already giving up.

Buzz grabbed my wrist and pointed. "There! I think I see some activity. Look there, just to the right of the red light on the radio tower."

There was a distant red light atop a tower. That, I could see.

"You can be sure that any light to the right of that, a light that'll flicker or appear and disappear, is a Marfa ghost light."

I didn't see anything. "What am I looking for?" I didn't realize I was going to whisper until I started to speak, but the crowd was down to a low murmur, so it seemed appropriate.

"Depends. People see large and small, all colors—mostly orange, yellow, white, occasionally green—I've seen 'em divide and recombine as another shade. They'll be dim or bright as a flash, might move up and down slowly or bounce."

"Do you see any yet?"

Gil chuckled. "Not quite dark enough. Will be in a bit."

As I positioned myself at the railing between Cora and Buzz, Buzz pointed. "You need to scan the southwestern horizon, looking toward Chinati Peak." His finger traced the approximate area. "Just keep looking. Let your eyes adjust to the sky. And have faith."

Gil cut in so that he was between me and Cora, but he kept his hands to himself. Still, I imagined I could feel his breath on the side of my cheek. After a moment he murmured, "Look for the ones that sparkle. Anything that keeps a constant shape, like an oval, is probably a reflected car headlight off Highway 67. The real ones change shape rapidly."

I felt a chill run up my collarbone as his jacket sleeve brushed the side of my upper arm. "Do you feel a little—spooked?"

"Not really." Gil leaned forward to rest his elbows on the railing. "I grew up in southern Nevada. I don't find ghost lights even a little odd, because we lived around similar phenomena, including good old Area 51. That whole mountainous rim surrounding Lake Mead is alive with mildly unnatural events. There's strange stuff in the night desert, stretching out all the way east to the Grand Canyon. I've seen things as I drove through the night between Las Vegas and Phoenix, back when I was going to seminary and working odd jobs at night, that would've made great 'X-Files' or 'Twilight Zone' episodes."

Hadn't he said he went to seminary in Fort Worth? Vegas seemed an unlikely vacation spot for a student of the ministry. Or had I misunderstood?

"For instance. . . ." He ran his finger across the back of my hand in a manner that, if any other guy had done it, I would've called suggestive. "Out there in Alien Greys territory, where the government used to do all that above-ground nuke testing, I've seen a lot of unexplainable weirdness. They've got angry ghost lights. Cars melt and their occupants disappear or are found wandering beside the highway in the morning in shock, or turn into babbling idiots who have to be put away for a long rest. Some people think those lights are a government laser weapon project that went awry."

"Conspiracy theories," I managed, moving my hand out of his reach. "Your car never melted, I take it?"

"No. But out here the lights are friendly. The Apache and other Native tribesmen saw the lights long before any European immigrant. Legend says that God—they call Him Great Spirit—made these mountains by throwing out all the jumbled rocks left over after Creation. The Devil then sneaked in and added beasties that bite, sting, and prick. When a lost soul departed by being bitten or stung, they say, he or she became one of the ghost lights wandering the desolate landscape until the end of the world, when they'll finally be re-gathered into humanity. Other Native stories explain the lights as the phosphorescent souls of braves who were betrayed by treachery and killed in battle, and who won't leave for the next world until they feel they've gotten justice."

Okay, now he was seriously creeping me out. Maybe that was his intention. "They teach you this stuff in seminary?"

"Comparative religion." He made another move towards my hand. "You've got to keep an open mind. God doesn't explain everything to man, after all."

I shifted toward Buzz, but he was occupied getting his hearing aid turned off. Apparently he'd experienced some loud buzzing and popping on past visits, and he didn't want to get zapped again.

"Nothin's happening," whined a teenager who was perched on the railing. "Come on, let's go." His girlfriend hopped down and scurried off after him. It seemed as if the rest of us were on a platform of fools.

Staring out into the blackness, all I saw were the same old stars, only much brighter than they seemed in Dallas. There wasn't any ambient light in the parking lot or on the pad (other than the red glow-spots at our feet), so it was getting well and truly dark out. But I didn't know if I was seeing tiny flashes, "seeing stars," or what. My ophthalmologist had confirmed that I had floaters in both eyes. Maybe that was all I was seeing. What were the dust motes floating in the night sky? Magic, or my floaters sparkling?

"I'm not sure what I'm seeing. How can I be sure?"

Buzz rumbled in my ear. "You'll know one when you see one. There's no mistaking it."

I squinted into the darkness.

The crowd gradually fell quiet. Slowly I became aware of a faraway orange glow, without really knowing at which instant I started perceiving the light. It was an irregular sphere of living orange, like the stuff inside a Lava Lamp, about the size of a cantaloupe. At first I wasn't sure it was really there, but it got more substantial all of a sudden and I knew. It didn't crackle as ball lightning can, nor did it waver and flare like swamp gas or some mirage. It was impossible to tell whether the light originated from ten yards or ten miles away.

"See?" Gil whispered, but I couldn't answer.

The sphere turned a duskier reddish-orange and shrank. It rotated like a globe, flickered momentarily, then disappeared. The crowd let out a collective exhalation, as though we'd been holding our breath.

The light popped back, even brighter.

This time, no one dared gasp.

Two more lights popped up on either side of it, reminding me of the June Taylor Dancers. The satellites could have been up to a foot in diameter, but I knew my sense of perspective was skewed by not knowing how far away they were. They seemed too close for comfort.

A dull hum began in my ears, but it wasn't entirely aural. I felt it pushing at me, sensed it with my fingertips. Trying to see with only my eyes here would be like trying to put "Night on Bald Mountain" into words. Floating in the darkness, we seemed to be tipping backwards on the Tilt-A-Whirl while my stomach clawed upwards like a cat climbing the draperies.

The orbs of light danced up and down. It could've lasted ten minutes or half an hour. I was mesmerized. Two balls of light collided, then merged the way cells do in science-class simulation animations. The remaining two backed away from us and then froze in the night sky, holding steady.

In my right ear, a high-pitched vibrating *whee* began. It really was like somebody hitting a tuning fork. My hands involuntarily flew up to cover my ears, but it didn't make any difference. My pulse beat out a really bad jazz riff, fast, arrythmic, and uncoordinated.

Suddenly a white ball popped on overhead, as if to signal the end of the evening's antics. The larger orange orb divided into two, making it a trio again. As the noise faded, so did the glow in the sky. The last remaining ball winked at me one last time, then receded into the infinite horizon, like a special effect from Pixar.

My heartbeat returned to a regular rhythm. I could breathe again.

Gil squeezed my shoulder. "You're cold."

Was I?

The lights were apparently finished with us. Most people stayed on, hoping to see another show, but Cora poked Buzz in the ribs and he announced that it was past his bedtime.

From a roadside vendor in a truck, I bought a T-shirt proclaiming that I had seen the Marfa Ghost Lights. Zoë would be so jealous.

§ § §

They dropped me off at the door. I turned down all offers to "c'mon in and set a spell" at anyone else's house for a nightcap, or as Buzz phrased it, "a shot of nerve tonic: Jack Daniel's is what made the South the South." But Gil insisted on walking me to the door. Buzz shot Cora a meaningful look that he must've thought I didn't catch.

I turned at the door. "Sorry to be a party pooper. I need to wash my hair and get this war paint off my face." It was true enough; the airborne sand meant I felt dirty again, even though I'd had a shower in the afternoon. I also needed to reboot my psyche and soothe my jangled nerves.

He ran one finger down my cheek, pulling a strand of hair off my lip that I hadn't realized was glued to it. "You were really affected back there, weren't you?"

"No, I. . . ." Why was I tongue-tied? Maybe I had been a little spooked.

"You don't have to be embarrassed. A lot of people have a spiritual experience out there. It can be quite affecting." He smoothed back my hair. I seemed to be frozen in place, unable to slap his hand away—and not really wanting to. "I felt really connected tonight. It was as if—" He broke off, examined my face closely, then continued. "This may sound crazy, but I felt as if Aaron were there watching us, and he . . . approved. Of us."

I didn't know what to say. There wasn't any "us." Someday, if I got to know Gil better, we might become friends. But right now, schmoozing me on Aaron's turf? Maybe even hitting on me? That was too much. I turned and fumbled with the lock.

"I know you're still in love with him. Were, anyway."

I took a deep breath. "It's true that I wasn't really through with him. I'd been expecting him to call eventually. I know he got busy."

"Not that busy. He should've called you. I believe he wanted to, and I never understood what could have been holding him back. Ari, I think he really loves you. Loved you."

Hearing Gil make the correction knocked away my last underpinnings; I dropped the key and slumped against the doorjamb. Gil caught me and circled me with his arms. After a moment of resistance, I relaxed into the embrace. It felt good to have some support, to have physical contact with someone who cared—and who had cared about Aaron. I hadn't cried for Aaron yet, and the tears came streaming out.

"It's okay." He repeated it over and over, rocking me back and forth. After a minute or two, my discomfort level rose alarmingly. His concentration was a little suffocating, or maybe his PheroMonica after-shave was really strong. But I wasn't sure how to extricate myself without being abrupt. And now that my thoughts were calming down, I wondered why Gil should be so intent on making me, er, soothing me. I got the feeling that he'd planned all of this in order to get me to the emotional edge. Well, now I felt emptied out, and I wasn't ready to let him fill me up again with all kinds of crazy, conflicting emotions.

Could he be infatuated with me? I hadn't given him any reason to be. Had I?

No. Besides, I was flattering myself. Being crazy, imagining things.

Still, it certainly appeared that he was trying to become more than just an acquaintance.

"It's too soon," I managed to gasp. Realizing how that had sounded, I hurried to fill the silence with words. "I mean, I can't let myself fall apart yet. I need to be alone to think." I pulled away, somewhat roughly. That left me a little unsteady on my feet, but I stabilized myself by grasping the doorjamb. "I'm sorry. Can I just—I need to go."

"Whenever you're ready, I'm here." Gil looked at me soulfully. Whether he meant "ready to talk" or "ready to console you" or "ready to be your new man," I couldn't have said.

And I could not deal with it. Escaping as politely as I could manage by blathering various platitudes and promises to see him first thing in the morning, I got the cabin door closed behind me. It was such a relief to be alone in the blue glow of the bubbling aquariums.

Maybe I'm a bit more of a recluse than I thought.

§ § §

Speaking of recluses, I didn't see a problem with using Aaron's smartphone to call my sister. His cell phone, because that way there wouldn't be long-distance charges. It only took me a minute to figure out the oPhone; on some level I'm still a programmer, and it was kind of fun fiddling with the device.

Zoë let me know immediately that she was very displeased with me for maintaining radio silence instead of touching base regularly. She was still worried about my host's intentions.

"I meant to call. It's just that, well, Gil has been really great. Things have been happening. I saw the Marfa Lights." I told her about it, exaggerating as needed in an attempt to engage her travel bug. She'd always been a bit of a UFO buff.

But it didn't work this time. "You still could've called."

"You could've called me."

"How?"

She had a point. I'd left her to fret all day and all evening with no contact information. "You're right. I just wasn't thinking."

"Do you ever?"

I read off Aaron's house phone and his cell phone number to her. "Now you can call."

"Trust that I will. Anyway, your apartment's fine and so is your damn fish." The only one I had left, a lonesome red Betta that she was feeding for me. "When will you be home?"

"Soon. I haven't even started doing any of the legal stuff yet."

"Why the hell not?"

Because Gil hadn't mentioned it, and I didn't know quite how to bring it up. "Sufficient unto the day is the evil thereof," I quoted from Scripture, mostly because she hated it when I did. "That's on the agenda for tomorrow."

"Make sure it is. I'm not really comfortable with your staying out there among people you don't know much about."

"I'm all grown up."

"I know you are. That's what worries me." She sighed. "I get the decided feeling that Gil is a con man who lucked into Aaron's death and is out to bilk somebody. Namely you."

I knew my sister was paranoid, but this really took me aback. "What makes you say that?"

"This is all too convenient. Besides, the way you describe him and how he's acting towards you. . . . He's just too nice."

"Come on."

"I mean it, Airhead. Now, don't ask me to put my finger on exactly what bugs me. This is my intuition talking. All those fancy clothes you tell me he has on when it's summertime in the desert. It's the kind of thing Willy Loman might do out of desperation to make that sale, or Jack Lemmon in *Glengarry Glen Ross*."

"Minus all those dirty words, of course," I said as dryly as I could manage without getting my tongue stuck to the roof of my mouth again. "He's a minister, remember. He dresses up every time he leaves the house. Preachers don't have casual Friday."

"Maybe." She sounded doubtful. "Maybe it's just the way you describe him. It's just that, from the way you talk, it's kind of as if he's auditioning for a part."

"Well, don't worry. I won't be throwing him on the casting couch."

"Take this seriously, Ari. I think you're being too trusting. Stay away from that man as much as you can—and from the Marfa Lights, for that matter. Just watch yourself."

"I always watch myself," I said, trying to lighten the mood with a homage to Groucho Marx. "It's other people I have trouble watching."

"No, you don't. You're awfully good at that, I'll grant you." I heard clicks on the line. "I've got another call coming in, though I'm sure it's just a nuisance. Call me tomorrow. Or before. Anytime, if there's any problem."

"There won't be. Please stop worrying." I left her to her mystery call, hoping it wasn't yet another siding salesman and feeling pity towards the salesman if it was.

I had definitely not been encouraging any attraction Gil might feel for me, and I would know if he had some kind of scam up his sleeve. Wouldn't I?

Gil's quick-on-the-trigger upturn of lips sometimes seemed fakey, and he had made a few overtures that I'd had to fend off fairly firmly. But that didn't mean he was fit to plug into the next film version of *Psycho*. I was glad I hadn't mentioned to my sister any of those little flirtatious—okay, heck, full-on seductive—moves Gil had seemed to be pulling on me. With luck, that would all be forgotten in the morning.

I was such a Cleopatra.

Impulsively, before I closed the phone, I clicked on "Photos" to look at what Aaron had seen fit to record.

He'd taken a picture of that pomegranate bush in the courtyard, in full bloom. An orange Texas sunset with streaky clouds. A spider, a really big hairy one—eew. I clicked quickly to the next. Murky, with tiny colored dots on a black background—maybe the Marfa lights? And then one that stopped me.

It was a close-up of that woman I'd met—Orleans Hall, the nasty one—flashing her boobs.

My face burned and I felt my blood pressure ratcheting up several notches. Orleans had her head thrown back, laughing like those idiots on the *Girls Gone Wild* videos.

Viciously I snapped the phone shut and tossed it on the desk.

CHAPTER FIVE

So, the fish. Didn't I need to feed them?

I still couldn't get over the aquaria in every room, on stands and built into the walls, even in the bathroom. The effect was magical. He'd been theatrical in setting up a cool theme for each tank. Schools of neon tetras against a back wall of bubbles, one tank of guppies hiding among plants, plus the exotic stuff. One tank appeared empty, but I was sure there was something lurking in the foliage. Possibly the plants themselves were some kind of exotic prize. I didn't know. I didn't feel like looking anything up.

The access closets were cleverly designed to allow you to reach the tanks from the back or side for cleaning, feeding, or netting.

The saucer-sized discus in one of the salt tanks swam around looking at me suspiciously, but the others disappeared behind the rocks when I loomed near. Why didn't they go to the top and expect food? They should've associated people with fish flakes. Then I saw the autofeeder carousel. The one on the salt tank was nearly empty, so I found the flakes (the expensive brand) in the access closet and refilled it. They still eyed me with suspicion, but once I backed far enough away they all flared their fins and hurried to the top to eat.

§ § §

I prepared for a restless night in Aaron's bed. The sheets looked fairly clean, though I'd had to talk myself out of stripping the bed—which I'd never have considered doing, had I not seen that stupid photo. As I dozed off I thought about how I was getting to sleep where he last slept . . . how I was breathing in his scent, however faint . . . and how I didn't care how dysfunctional of me that might be.

I came awake in the night to find three cantaloupe-sized balls of orange light flickering at the foot of my bed. I felt no fear, but what the government calls shock-and-awe electrified me, every hair on my body standing at attention. Then I felt a comforting touch—Ricky's presence.

I knew I was awake, because I glanced at Aaron's alarm clock, a fancy job that projected the time in red digits on the ceiling. Three-fifteen AM, the dark tea-time of the soul and the traditional time of miracles: an hour ripe for visitations. I raised up on my elbows, waiting for a sign, but somehow even propped up I dozed back off.

Then I heard Aaron's voice. "Watch out," he called to me from far away. My eyes snapped open, and at first I couldn't see anything because they weren't focused. But the full moon shafted through the sheer curtains at the window, and I saw Aaron standing at the foot of the bed. Maybe the Marfa lights had led him. He frowned at me. "Be careful, Ari. He isn't what he seems."

I tried to speak, but I was sleep-grogged and my muscles flapped, inert. My elbows were frozen and deadened where I'd been leaning on them while I slept.

The sound of Aaron's voice went straight to my heart and vibrated inside my very center. "I'm watching over you. Don't worry. But take care."

On the far wall, I saw the shadow of wings. Obviously, Aaron had become an angel. He smiled, and my heart soared. Joy radiated from every part of the Aaron-angel. But then he faded away, receding just as the lights had. Before I could react, the glow faded from the room, and I could move again.

I couldn't believe he was gone. Mostly, I wished I could go with him.

What do they call a vacuum of sound? I was in a cone of silence. Not even the sound of a desert cricket.

I blinked. Then I started to rationalize.

Isn't that what people do? Use their rational thought processes, apply logic to the unfathomable. I reasoned that I must've been dreaming. Between waking and sleep, in a hypnagogic state. That had to be it; I'd just woken up from a particularly vivid dream about waking up. It'd been the effect of those Tex-Mex peppers, or maybe bad berries in the cobbler.

Reasoning wasn't working. Although I hadn't been afraid at first—I'd felt completely at peace—now adrenaline squirted into my bloodstream. Stupid endocrine system. My heart thudded against my ribs, and I felt a panic attack coming on.

I snatched up the pillow and comforter and dragged them into the living room, switching on every light as I passed. I flicked the television and radio on and fell into a troubled sleep on the sofa.

§ § §

Howdy, Texas blasted out its morning theme, "San Antonio Rose," and I stirred. The sun was bright in my eyes and the muscle in my right calf was jumping.

I about fell off the sofa, cracking my shin on the coffee table. The twitch prefigured a bodacious leg cramp, I was sure, from sleeping all balled up on the sofa, tense, trying even in my sleep to remember not to roll off. I stood up and sure enough, the muscle went *throb, throb, clench.* But I pulled on the dent in the middle of my upper lip (that's a trick my grandmother taught me—the anatomical term for the area is "philtrum," but try explaining that to anybody and watch their eyes glaze over) and the cramp slowly ebbed away. I rubbed both calves and found them freezing cold. The air-conditioning vent pointed right at the leather seating group, and it had come on full blast sometime in the night.

Morning charley-horses (as Zoë calls them) always start me out in a semi-foul mood. Digging out the detective's card ("Esteban 'Max' Varga," as printed), I put in a call to the Sheriff's office to find out about the report on Aaron. I hated to end up calling him after all, but he was the shortcut to finding out who to contact. Apparently he was already out catching varmints and shooting up the countryside at seven in the morning. I left a message on his voicemail.

I showered and threw on my jeans and the Marfa Lights tee, then ran a comb through my wet hair and French-braided it. By the time I'd found my shoes, I heard tires crunching on the shells outside.

As I always did at home, I pulled open the front curtain to let in the morning light. It turned out to be a good thing that I don't wear bathrobes, that I get dressed in street clothes the moment I get up—that's because of my mother lounging around in those damn nightgowns all day when she was drinking or depressed, and I had hated it, and the stink of Pall Malls and martinis on her, well, thinking about it still nauseates me. But anyway, here came Sparky the Happy Squirrel scampering up the drive. Didn't he ever sleep? Go to his office to counsel and console church members? Do the grocery shopping?

He bounced in wearing a "Good Morning, Class" face. Even his hair, slicked back in the classic Baptist-preacher style, was perky. A voice worthy of Bucky the Friendly Beaver said, "Morning, Ari! Hope you got some rest. Wasn't that quite a show last night? Really something." At least he wasn't carrying his briefcase or Bible. That meant I wouldn't have to turn down his offer of exciting Amway products at a discount if only I'd become a distributor.

"Come on in." I smiled, relieved that he meant to forget last night's little scene at the door. "I don't have coffee made or anything."

"You're not the Daily Grind. I just stopped by on my way in to the church office. I think you're going to like what I've got to tell you." He wiggled his fingers. "Good news. I've gotten in touch with Aaron's parents and they'll be here tomorrow. They expect to stay here, if you don't mind."

Oh, my God.

Myra and Doyle Beecroft had always regarded me as the not-quite-measuring-up temporary girlfriend, good enough until somebody better came along. We'd met a few times, but never made more than the required pleasantries, let alone stayed under the same roof. My heart fell out of my chest onto my toes.

Gil was so oblivious. "They have their own RV, and they can park it just outside. Isn't that perfect?"

Perfect. "That's fine. Great. I look forward to seeing them."

In a way, I supposed I would. I reeled my heart back in and got it settled inside my ribcage. This was Aaron's family, and they were part of him. I could handle this.

"I've got us set up for Monday afternoon." I must've looked confused, because Gil pointed at me as if to clarify things. "At the lawyer's office for the reading of the will, I mean."

"Is this like on TV, where there's a provision that you won't get what's bequeathed to you unless you attend the reading?" I was half joking.

"Don't believe anything you see on TV." He rolled his eyes. "You'll each get a copy of the will then, and we'll get this probate ball rolling. There are several issues that I think can be dealt with right away, with temporary orders, if necessary. For one thing, we need to get you access to the estate's cash for dealing with the details."

"That's easy enough. We'll simply wire it to my numbered Swiss bank account." I didn't even have a dotted Swiss bank account, but he couldn't know that—not for sure.

Gil flashed a limited version of his smile. "This attorney's really sharp. His name is Woodrow Hawk, and he's right here in downtown Marfa. And he'll get things moving immediately, assuming Aaron's parents feel up to it, all right?" He marched into Aaron's kitchen.

"If you're about to fry up a dozen eggs, don't bother. There's not a single one left in the nest. Let's go over to that coffee shop-bookstore place again." My crockpot experiment would keep in the fridge; that kind of dish is better after it sets a spell, as Texans say.

"I've got a better idea. You haven't forgotten the parade, have you?" He checked his watch. It was a fancy gold-and-silver job. "We need to get to the park fairly soon to get a decent spot, though as long as we get there before ten, it'll be all right. I need to stop by my office for a bit and take care of some things, but that won't take long." He pulled down a large woven picnic basket from the top of the fridge. "I'll hop over to Jodie's Catering where we get all our church food done to get this filled up. You're gonna love her chicken salad. Then we're off to the party." He paused. "You're not a vegetarian or a vegan, are you?"

"No, chicken salad sounds fine." As long as it wasn't full of paprika and hot sauce, Tex-Mex style. But if he liked that stuff, I could cope. I didn't have a huge appetite, anyway.

He reached into the picnic basket and pulled a plaid blanket partway out, as if confirming it was picnic-ready. "And then on Sunday after church, if you're up for it, we can go geocaching."

I took a deep breath. It was time to tell him that I felt I had taken over his life. But it was a delicate situation. How could I phrase this? Why was Gil being so nice to me? Spending so much time on me? And, not to put too fine a point on it, seemingly getting the Jones on for me?

We'd clicked, and I felt the chemistry between us as well. But I'm not that good-looking. I mean, I don't have any obvious defects, but I'm fairly average. Still, even Daddy, who saw genius in everything I attempted as a kid, no matter how bad I was at it, never urged me to enter a beauty contest. I simply couldn't accept that this great-looking guy could have any interest in me beyond keeping me happy so he could wrap up Aaron's estate. Yet Gil seemed to expect that I'd become his new neighbor. I still hadn't decided about that. Being instant best friends felt weird, though. Gil knew so little about me, and I knew next to nothing about him.

He looked up. "Sunday's okay, right?"

I decided not to question Fate. The gift horse didn't need any teeth, so long as I could ride it and feel the wind in my hair.

"On Sunday? I don't want to monopolize you."

"No worries."

Didn't preachers have to spend most of the day Sunday at church? I wasn't sure. My parents had been involved in a fundamentalist group when Zoë and I were young teens—which explained why they felt the need to toss her out and nearly ruin her life when she got pregnant with Ricky at sixteen—and they'd spent almost all day Sundays in church, either in ecstatic worship, study groups, or planning meetings. But I knew that not all churches were like that. Gil probably expected me to attend morning services, come to think of it; I'd have to find some excuse to beg off. Or maybe I ought to go, just to see Gil in action. But in fact he hadn't yet asked me.

I made a sally, mostly for appearance's sake. "You've got so much to do to get your sermon ready, and so forth."

"Don't worry about that." He stuffed the blanket back into the basket, along with four sets of plasticware and the Melamine plates that'd fallen out with it. "Just relax. I'm taking care of things."

Aaron's landline phone rang.

For a moment I panicked, because I wouldn't know what to say to any of Aaron's friends who might not yet know what'd happened. Then I glanced at the Caller ID box. The display said it was the Sheriff's office.

Thinking fast for a change, I decided I'd rather not let Gil hear everything I wanted to ask the authorities, so I just shook my head. "Not for me."

Then the answering machine piped up in Aaron's voice.

My heart leapt into my throat as tears blurred my vision. It was a shock to have his voice booming into my ears. The resulting attack of stupidity explained why I didn't stop the machine's "monitor" mode, and Gil heard the Lieutenant say, "Ari French, this is Detective Max Varga returning your call." He gave a return phone number.

Oops. "I guess it was for me after all," I said, feeling my cheeks burn. I explained about Lieutenant Varga having paid me a visit.

Gil looked none too happy. "The police came here to hassle you about

Aaron's death? I know they've got to investigate, but there's no basis for suspicion at all. Why would you encourage him by calling?"

Whoops, he'd been paying attention. "Nothing important, just a couple of concerns I had. I'll call him later."

He looked visibly annoyed. "You don't need to burden yourself with that. You weren't here and didn't see anything, so what's the use of going into all that with them?"

"They came to me. I figured I needed to cooperate."

Gil's mouth twisted. "Well, you should've told him you wouldn't talk to him without a lawyer. You need to know your rights, and one of them is you have the right to have a lawyer present. It's dangerous if they get some crazy idea in their minds because you're an outsider." He slammed the top of the basket with both palms.

I didn't like this side of the pacific preacherman.

He expelled a breath. "How about next time you just say, 'I choose to remain silent, and I want my attorney?' Then call me."

Gil appeared to know an awful lot about the proper procedure on a suspect's part. I had to assume that was probably because of experiences with parishioners, or whatever Protestants call them.

I took a mollifying tone. "I didn't realize. I wasn't thinking of it as being threatening."

He seemed a bit distracted. "Well . . . all right. I suppose you couldn't help them coming to you. But don't volunteer anything. And try not to upset yourself with all that foolishness." He still looked irritated.

Why the hell did he care if I upset myself? It was my body to destroy as I liked. Had he been most anyone else, I'd have called him on that.

Yet even though he was being all weird right now, I still wanted to hang out with him . . . go on a date with him, even. I can be an idiot like that sometimes. He was cute, and Aaron was gone—and had left a hole in my heart. What can I say? In a sort of pathetic way, I had to admit I needed Gil.

So I made nice, and after some small talk he was whistling "Yellow Rose of Texas" and bounding out the door like an eager Pomeranian on the bunny trail. "See you around eleven—that's about an hour."

I decided I'd better straighten up the front room in case Aaron's parents showed up early. They probably had the key, or maybe they knew about Aaron always hiding a key at the top right-hand corner of the back door frame; I made a mental note to check to see if he was still doing that before I went to bed again believing the doors were secured. I folded the comforter and started fluffing the sofa pillows.

Coming up with a handful of change behind the middle pillow, I dug deeper, finding three wrapped cherry cough drops and a few dried-up fries. I pulled the bottom pillows off to finish the job, wondering where Aaron would keep a handvac, and something glinted underneath.

Blue. A star sapphire. Set in 14K gold.

Aaron's class ring from Stanford.

I dug it out. He was always losing that because it was just a shade too big, and the plastic ring-sizer that he used to make it a quarter-size smaller constantly slipped off. But he'd always found it again.

I clasped it against my chest for a moment. I gave it a quick kiss, then slipped it securely into my jeans' coin pocket. As, I suppose, a good-luck token. I wanted it near me. It had never strayed far from him.

Then I remembered. I had brought along a neckchain of white gold that Aaron had given me one Christmas. It was in a velvet pouch stuffed down into the toe of one of my black ballet flats that were still in my suitcase.

Sure enough, there it was, a 30-inch white gold Omega rolled chain. I hadn't known why I was packing it at the time.

After hesitating a moment, I threaded the ring through, then fastened the chain around my neck. The ring landed between my breasts, accenting the bosom area, which wasn't ideal. I dropped the pendant down inside of my bra so nobody'd see it and question me.

If wearing Aaron's ring like this made me feel better, it wasn't anybody else's business.

§ § §

I needed coffee. Not that cheap supermarket stuff Aaron kept, though. What I craved was a real cup of coffee. Like the one I'd had yesterday at the Brown Recluse.

It couldn't hurt my attitude to get out a bit, either. I needed to exercise my legs and my freedom. Gil's playing the perfect host and chaperone was becoming a wee bit stifling.

On Aaron's desk I found his mobile GPS. I slipped it into my purse, figuring I'd check out how it worked in a free moment. I didn't want to appear completely ignorant if we did go out geocaching. There were a couple of other gadgets that I couldn't identify but hoped to find time to inspect, as well, so I dropped them into my tote. The excuse I used on myself was that I might get stuck waiting in line or in the lawyer's anteroom, and if I had the tote with me, I could fool with these gadgets then.

I grabbed a handful of interesting-looking CDs—some of them Texas music, it looked like, of course the usual Wagner (Aaron loved Wagner almost as much as Schicklgruber had), and a few of our old favorites—to listen to in the car. Willie Nelson singing "StarDust" had been one of our shared guilty pleasures.

This time I didn't even have to use the StreetFinder to navigate to the Recluse. I was reaching for the front door handle when it banged open and Orleans Hall nearly knocked me over.

She stopped short. An expression of rage clobbered her angular features. "What are you doing still in town?"

"Um. . . ." My brain was overwhelmed by the question. I hadn't had any caffeine yet, after all. "I'm settling up Aaron's affairs."

"Affairs! That's a hoot." She crossed her arms. Her tone was confrontational and nasty. "But maybe that's appropriate, since you were nothing to him except an affair. Really not even that, more like a quickie fling. You don't love Aaron. He didn't love you. So what are you doing inheriting?"

Words tried to form in my mouth. All I got was a jumble of letters.

She jerked her thumb towards her amazing (and photographically shown to be authentic) chest. "I was his woman. I'm the one he should've remembered." She looked wistful for a moment. "He had the greatest feet. Never stinky, no toe jam. Beautiful toenails." Then her features hardened up again. "Scuttlebutt around town says he owed you. But I don't buy that. If he really stole your money, then why didn't you sue?"

I sighed. "It's complicated." She wouldn't get why I hadn't wanted to ruin his life, even though he was now messing with mine from beyond. "The credit card companies don't want to hear your life story; they just want their money. And it costs more to bring legal action than it's usually worth."

"Bullshit." She tilted her head. "Why don't you hate him?" After a pregnant pause, she gave a little nod. "If he'd done that to me—not that I believe he did it to YOU, either, you little liar. But if somebody did that to me, they'd be sorry. I'd hate them. I wouldn't be able to wait for Hell to populate with his sorry ass."

That was the same as saying she wouldn't hesitate to kill someone who crossed her. I've never been able to put myself into the shoes of someone who thinks like that. Although I'm no angel and I do have wicked thoughts, they never run in that direction.

Zoë says it's because I have low self-esteem. All my life, whenever someone I love has done something awful to me, my first reaction has always been, "What did I do to make you do this? How can I fix it? Why did I deserve this and how might I become worthy?"

I loved Aaron. I wanted the best for him. I didn't stop loving him just because he stopped loving me, if he had. I still loved him, and probably always would. That's forever. (My mental jukebox once again cued up "Suite: Judy Blue Eyes" along with REO Speedwagon's "Keep On Loving You.")

But all of this was none of her business and she didn't really care, anyhow—hers were challenge questions, rhetorical at best. Even if she got a coredump of my psyche, she wouldn't understand it.

I shrugged. "It'd be easy for me to become bitter and lash out in hate. But I saw my sister fall into that trap for a while, and she's only now climbing out. Mother has wallowed in that pit for years, and I've seen the effects. So I always try to remember that when a state of permanent anger and bitterness holds allure, I should resist. It would be easy to swallow those little red pills of resentment sold on every corner. But despite their candy coating, the aftertaste is foul."

She looked blank. "I don't take pills." Metaphor was lost on her. "But you can bet, if somebody screws me, I'll get back at them if it's the last thing I do."

"And it often is."

"Damn right." She hadn't taken that exactly the way I'd meant it, but at least she was starting to synch up again. "That's what I mean. It's like . . . you're all flippant and cynical. You aren't even sad. Your so-called grief is as fake as that whipped cream in a can."

All right, I knew that I wasn't displaying a lot of emotion, either in public or in private. But that was because I didn't want to lose control; I couldn't open the sluice gates for fear of the flood never ending. Once again, though, my defense mechanisms weren't her concern.

Leaning forward, she poked me in the chest with her right index finger. "There are too many holes in your story. You're a fraud, and I'm going to fix you."

My mouth was a sandbox, and I took an involuntary step back. "Listen, I'm sorry that you got hurt. But I'm hurting now, too. Can't we just live and let live?"

She tossed her crinkly bleached hair. "I'll bet you're one of those cult freakos like those people in the Airstreams. You're all in this together. Well, I'm not going to let you get away with it."

What cult freakos? If there was a Church of Freak in town, I hadn't been made aware of it. Of course I couldn't come up with a snappy comeback. I never can, until ten minutes after the opportunity passes.

I slipped around her through the open door into the restaurant, which was suffused with a solemn quiet. I couldn't imagine why. Who had turned off the jukebox?

Everyone was too obviously trying not to look at me. I wasn't certain whether it would be more gossip-worthy for me to just turn and leave, or to proceed up to the counter as though I took it in stride whenever I got attacked by jealous harridans. I had pretty much decided on option two when Ponyboy—Buck, the radio DJ and musician I'd met at Gil's—emerged from the bookstore bay.

"You." Orleans glowered at him. "I might have known the two of you were in it together. Believe me, this isn't the end."

She stalked out the door, leaving a wake of confusion in my mind.

He guffawed. "You should see your face. She meant nothing to Aaron except a booty call, for what that's worth to you."

I looked at him. "What did she mean, cult?"

His hair swayed as he rolled his head around in dismissal. "Nothing. It's not a cult. Just that a few people who live down the hill from you have a small independent home church arrangement—faith healing, snake handling, like that. You know." I didn't, not really. "They tried to heal Aaron when he wrenched his back, and he said it helped him. Went right back to work on that Houses for Homeless thing the next morning."

"Wow." What else could I say? "She seemed to be imagining some big . . . hoax going on."

He took my arm and guided me towards the short-order counter with the round barstools. "She's just cranky. People have the right to worship or not, as they wish. She doesn't need to impose her standards on everyone else. Besides, her bar is set pretty low."

The restaurant slowly returned to its normal buzz. The sound system clicked on. Willie Nelson's "Crazy," sung by Patsy Cline. I smiled at the implied commentary.

"I would never have suspected she had any standards."

Ponyboy laughed again. "She works at the Marfa Bodyworks Spa. She took the job as a pedicurist and foot massage-acupressure-reflexology aromatherapist because she's a foot fetishist. They fired her from the shoe store—you don't wanna hear why." He winked.

"I'm sure I don't." Maybe Aaron had borrowed money from Orleans, and when he wouldn't pay it back, that could have made her inclined to kill him.

Or maybe she just got too carried away with one of her foot massages, and strangled him . . . by the ankle.

"And she's creepy besides. She has no room to complain about the Church of Salvation and their snakes. I don't care for snakes myself, but you don't live in a glass house and throw stones." He shook his head, his hair undulating sexily across his shoulders. "That girl keeps tarantulas as pets."

"So you know her pretty well?"

"No. I mean, no better than everybody in town does."

"Everyone here knows everyone else?"

"Pretty much, yeah." He grinned that lopsided grin.

"Okay, well, then." I've always been a city girl, so I really can't imagine, but I know this is true in smaller towns than Renner.

It was my turn to order. He stepped back while I negotiated with the barista for something that was more like coffee than dessert. You'd have thought that out here, they'd have old-fashioned java that melted the silver spoon when you tried to stir it, but the clerk was a teen who didn't seem to understand that I really did want full caffeine and none of that syrup. I picked up two pecan Snickerdoodle cookies while she fussed with getting my to-go lid on the hot container.

Buck was chuckling when I turned back around. "You're not into the usual 'half-caff mint mocha soy latte with three left-handed squirts of sugar-free vanilla syrup and two of caramel mocha' monstrosity, like everyone else in Dallas?"

"I'm a native Texan, not a Yankee import. My mama didn't raise an espresso-latte hound. I'm the daughter of a hardcore Folger's man and a 'Good to the Last Drop' Maxwell House fiend." Taking a sip, I managed not to choke. The brew would've scalded a bear.

"I like fiendishness in a woman." He winked.

Now, maybe he was just being neighborly. Some guys have a flirtatious manner about them, and it doesn't necessarily mean anything. But I wondered exactly what impression Ponyboy had gotten from Gil, or from me when he saw me at Gil's, and for some reason, I suddenly felt as if everyone in town thought of me as Aaron's dumb, "easy" chickie. It was disconcerting.

Worse, I had to admit that I found this guy even sexier than Gil. He was just the type that I'd always wanted to go out with when I was in high school, yet that I wasn't cool enough to attract. And he was giving off exploratory boom-chicka-boom vibes. Okay, maybe I was imagining that, but I didn't need complications. The guy was a friend of Gil's. *Whatever that meant.*

"I won't keep you," I said, edging towards the door. "Thanks for rescuing me back there."

He nodded. "So, like, I'm sure we'll run into each other again."

"Have a good day." I turned to go before I could do something clumsy, such as spill this boiling oil all over him or myself. The carry-out cups should've carried warning labels.

He called after me as I opened the door, barely managing not to bash myself in the forehead with it. "C'mon down to the Marfa Lights Music Festival. Early as you can get there is best. I'm playing at noon on the center stage."

I glanced back. He was smiling as though he meant it.

He saluted. "I'll be looking for you."

§ § §

I didn't want to miss the festival, and I figured everyone in town would be there, but I was on a guilt trip about imposing on Gil and didn't want to presume. When he arrived, bearing a basket of food and a cooler full of soft drinks, I tried once again to cut him loose. "Please don't feel responsible for me. I hate to take up all your free time, as I seem to be doing."

"Oh, no, it's fine. I was supposed to be out planting shrubs at an upland habitat restoration site this morning as a volunteer, but I've called and they've got plenty of people. I'd much rather see the parade." He pulled a megawatt smile out of his cheeks. "I'm entitled to have some fun, too, you know. God created everything on Earth for us to enjoy, even secular stuff, so rest assured I don't always have to be arranging ski trips for the youth group or planning a revival."

"Good to know I'm not a burden."

"You?" He chuckled. "No way you could be a burden, even if I had to carry you around."

Maybe he really WAS into me. Liked me "that way."

This was very confusing. I had been trained from birth not to be attracted to preachers or motorcycle gang members. And I usually didn't flirt with everything that moved. The air out here seemed to be conducive to a certain kind of . . . freedom, I'd have to call it. Or maybe I was just cracking up.

Still, while here I should stay open to new experiences. And I hadn't been to a parade for years.

§ § §

The parade was all Gil had led me to imagine, and then some. People were in costume, all right. Many of them had come as Marfa lights. That meant they wore fluorescent or glow-in-the-dark trash bags on their bodies and had glow-sticks or flashlights mounted on their foreheads, which were smeared with bright orange face paint. The "light brigade" jumped around doing gymnastics between the marching band and the baton twirlers, and circled both of the floats, which seemed to have a similar theme.

We stood on the edge of the grassy park grounds watching and applauding with the crowd. After the last of the parade passed us, we picked our way through the knots of people to find a good picnic spot. Gil spread out the blanket and pulled out an amazing array of food.

I tossed my hair back over my shoulders. "If I keep eating like this, I'll outgrow my clothes."

"That wouldn't be all bad," he said mysteriously. "I mean, I think a lot of women are too bony and anorexic. You're supposed to have curves."

"But I don't want to look like a beach ball with legs." Still, I took a sandwich and some of the potato salad.

"You could never look like that." He gazed at me soulfully.

It was a little disconcerting.

"You haven't seen my female relatives. Except for my mother and my sister, they generally run plus-sized. And my sister's no twig."

"You don't need to worry so much." He didn't look away.

I'd been aware for a while that Gil had a habit of holding eye contact just a nanosecond too long. Most likely, he didn't even realize he was doing it, and might mean it as a way to show how sincere he was; I was probably the only person who'd ever interpret it as creepy.

But I averted my gaze. "Tell me something, Gil, if you know. Where did Aaron get the money to build, let alone do all the rest of this? I mean, I know he had some savings." He'd left with everything I'd saved. "But not nearly enough for that whole house and all that's inside. Where was he working?"

Gil shrugged. "He did some consulting, something in software." He turned to gaze into the distance. "He said he'd come up with something that was going to be really profitable, and he was trying to start his own company.

Form a corporation with himself at the helm, and then sell the thing he'd invented."

"An invention?" The chicken salad wasn't bad. The grapes might be a little off. Mayonnaise leaked out of the sandwich, and I wiped my fingers on a napkin. "Was it a program?"

"I think so. You know, computer stuff."

I didn't intend to let on that I knew anything about software. Programming was never my passion, although I'd majored in computer science because I knew I could make a living for myself and thus wouldn't suffer the way my sister had as a "dropout." I had gone directly into software quality assurance when I got out of college and started at InVerse, where I met Aaron. I was the QA representative assigned to his code modules, and thus I was destined to dog his every design step, attend every meeting he held, sign off on all his walkthroughs, and the like. We spent a lot of time together, and we clicked. Okay, I fell for him, really hard, and the kicker was that we still worked well together, a sort of synergy. But I wasn't the coder he was, not by a long shot. Still, I thought I could probably figure out the general drift of his code, if I could find some of it.

Assuming he'd stayed in the habit of using comments that were more meaningful than "increment X" or "process data." I'd seen an awful lot of that over the years.

So I turned on the feminine wiles. "Computer stuff?" I tilted my head like a show dog. That usually prompted people to explain further.

Gil waved his hands. "Something about keys."

"Keys? For pianos, for houses—for what kind of lock?" I tossed my hair flirtatiously, even though I knew it wasn't nice to toy with him.

Gil didn't seem to know details. "I did a little computer stuff once myself, in that part-time night job I had in Phoenix when I was going to seminary. Glorified data entry. We had to type in keys to validate the locked software every now and then. Maybe he was working on an automated patch for that. Lot of people don't like having to keep track of validation keys, and so it might sell pretty well."

Sounded like shareware to me. And where did Gil go to seminary again? I thought he'd originally implied that he was at Southwestern Baptist Theological Seminary in Fort Worth . . . but I'd just remembered that when we were watching the Marfa Lights, he'd referred to driving between Phoenix and Vegas. So had he gone to seminary in one of those two spots instead?

As I was formulating a tactful question, I heard a "Yoo-hoo!" from the east.

"Cora at three o'clock," Gil said in an Air Force flyer imitation.

"Hey! Over here," I shouted. Cora saw me and waved back.

Gil looked a bit miffed. Well, he could keep his soulful gazes in check for a couple of hours.

Cora and Buzz seemed to know everyone. Buzz was "working the room," glad-handing everyone who passed, as she stood inspecting the board that told what events were happening where. Giving a final nod, Cora turned away from it, grabbed Buzz's hand, and threaded their way through the crowd over to us.

"Is that a sandwich?" Buzz winked at me. At least I knew he was harmless.

"Sure is. Here, have one. They're really great." I started filling the other two plates for them.

"Oh, my. I couldn't eat another bite." Cora rubbed her nonexistent belly. "We were just over at the food vendor carts and I had a pickle and a pretzel."

Behind her back, Buzz made a "Yuck" face, and I laughed.

She slapped at his arm without even looking back. "I'm too old to be pregnant. I just like sour and salty together."

"Then you'll love the potato salad." I bit my tongue as I realized how that sounded. "I mean, it's pretty tart."

"Too much vinegar," Buzz pronounced after a bite. "But still tolerable good."

Cora set her plate down after a couple of bites. "I need to visit the little girls' room. Come with me." She shot me a meaningful look.

"Women," said Buzz, rolling his eyes. "Can't go to the toilet alone."

"We can. We just don't have to." Cora struggled to her feet, and I followed.

"I know this may be none of my business, dear," she said as we picked our way carefully through the standing and lounging crowd, across the rocky grass—how they got grass to grow in that park was a poser—and headed toward the restroom facility, a WPA-built brick structure that looked pretty roomy. "But I noticed the other night Gil was putting his arm around your shoulders, and kept picking up a piece of your hair and putting it back off your forehead, and such. And today he's sitting pretty close to you."

"You noticed," I said lamely.

"Well, it would be pretty tough to miss. And it's impossible to ignore those longing stares. My stars, the way he looks at you ought to be rated NC-17."

I felt my cheeks heating up as we entered the ladies' room, a stinky place that was perhaps not the best choice for extended hanging-out. "Yes, I know, but I've got to work with him until this estate is settled up, and." I shrugged. "I like him. I don't want to lead him on, but. . . ." It was difficult, because I had experience with how impossible it was to handle certain people; my mother doesn't understand boundaries, either. "You know."

"It's just easier to make nice." Her tart tone surprised me.

"No, I didn't mean like that." I was a little taken aback. "I meant, I'm flattered. And I think it's just a little crush, anyway. He hasn't done anything untoward." My hackles rose. Perhaps I'd been a little suspicious of his intentions myself, but she was not only questioning my judgment but practically implying I "made nice" with everybody. Maybe that was what Aaron had let them assume. I couldn't help being a bit stiff in my response. "I appreciate your concern, but I think I can handle myself."

Cora raised one invisi-brow (probably groomed to oblivion in the Pencil-Line Eyebrows era.) "I'm sure you can, dear. But really, now. He may be taking things more seriously than you are."

She was from another generation. She didn't understand.

"I know you're not inviting his attentions. But I thought I should tell you something." She met my eyes in the mirror.

"Okay, tell me." I braced myself. He was an ex-con? He was gay? He had some kind of social disease I could catch by sharing Bibles?

"He's recently divorced. Only became final about two months ago."

I had seen the wedding-band stripe earlier. "In Dallas, that's not recent at all." I smiled into the mirror, catching a fleck of something on one of my front teeth. I scrubbed it away and applied fresh peach lipgloss.

"Well, if you don't want to hear." Cora sounded like my grandmother used to when she was about to go all pouty and clam up. "I was just telling you for your own good."

I sought her gaze in the mirror again, trying to look chastened. "No, please, go on. I need to know whatever you can tell me about the situation."

Her eyes brightened. "There was a town scandal over Gil's wife and Aaron. People said they were having an affair. Went on right under Gil's nose. Everybody in town knew, of course. Aaron never admitted to anything, but Gil's wife left, and he said she needed space, so we never challenged him. I understand she went to New York. Where her parents live, I think. Anyway, they got the divorce."

"REAL-ly." I sounded like Rosie O'Donnell, but whatever. The idea of Aaron sleeping with other women had occurred to me, obviously, but the reality of it was hitting me hard.

"Really." She nodded, as if this verified everything she'd believed about the downfall of modern civilization. "I can't say for sure, but I imagine that affair was for real, and it was just easier to break up than work it out. Poor woman, she never meant a thing to Aaron, but men are like that. They can just use a woman and then toss her aside, like a used Kleenex. You can't hold it against Aaron, because that's how men are taught, that they're entitled and it's okay to take advantage whenever women throw themselves at them. Besides, I don't think Claudia is cooking on all burners; she's always been addled. The Women's Auxiliary brought in a consultant and we all got our colors done and Claudia insisted she was a Spring when she's obviously a Summer; she looks like a dead leaf in lime green."

"So do I. But I wear it sometimes."

"Well, you shouldn't." She eyed me. "That's only one example. Claudia's sort of a flake. She played the odd duck the whole time she was in the church. You couldn't take her seriously. Aaron really didn't take that Orleans seriously, either. For him, she was a convenient lay, or whatever they say nowadays when they mean a shack date." She waved it away with one hand. "Men, they've always been the same. Through the ages, this kind of mess went on. It's just that now everybody does it out in the open."

"Yeah," I said as noncommittally as possible.

"Nobody cares a shred about decency any more, I swan." My grandmother used to use that expression. "Well, I just thought you should know."

"Thanks for telling me."

We both took care of business and washed our hands as quickly as possible. A gaggle of preteen girls came crashing in the door, taunting one of their number about some boy who was clearly "out to jump her bones." Their decibel level was approximately the same as that of the amplified guitars outside, if you were standing a few feet from the stage. They crowded us away from the mirror.

Cora gripped her tote and led the way out of the bathroom and back into the crowd. "Unless we have a plan, those men will lounge on the grass eating for the rest of the day. Where to next?"

It was getting close to noon. I pointed. "How about the center stage?"

Cosmic forces were at work, because we walked right up to a band whose bass guitarist was my friend Ponyboy. His hair was down loose, wavy, and lush just past his shoulders. So it hadn't been one of those gimme caps with the hair attached, like director Kevin Smith wears now because his wife made him get a business haircut.

On the stage, he was wailing away on the guitar. It was the kind of country-rock song that my sister calls "Crock," but that I like—it's like the Eagles, or more like the songs Mike Nesmith did when he was in The Monkees. Texas roadhouse. About a train whistle and how as it dies away it takes part of your heart with it. It wasn't awful, and it might've even sounded promising if I could've understood all the words. Amplification can distort voices.

Cora covered her ears. "I'm going back to the picnic area to see if they're over there," she shouted into my ear. I waved and pantomimed that I'd meet back up with them here. I hadn't been worried, because Gil knew I was carrying Aaron's cell phone, so we could get reconnected.

Even thinking of the devil can invoke things; I heard warbling from my purse. I wasn't used to Aaron's ringtones yet, and it was awfully loud out here, but I caught it because it was dissonant and in the wrong key to be part of the music.

It was my sister. "Where have you been? I've called three times. What the hell is that noise? Turn that stereo down. I swear, you are going to put yourself deaf."

While Zoë raved, I found a quieter spot near the edge of the treeline. "I'm at an outdoor concert. A festival. Gil brought me here. Along with the neighbors," I added quickly.

"You aren't getting involved with him, are you?" Her tone was fully suspicious. "Airhead, I know you're smarter than that."

"I'm not." Not smarter or not involved—it was her pick.

"Be sure you don't. It's tough, I know. You're vulnerable right now. But be strong."

"Nothing's going on." I shouldn't have joked with her about his intensity earlier. Maybe I should straighten him out about my intentions not to get involved . . . but then that would blow any chance I had of getting to know him better later, if I wanted to. On some level, I was still intrigued by Gil.

"You don't want to marry a preacher. You're not the type to play preacher's wife and host all those church members all the time and show up every time the church doors open and never get a new dress without the congregation taking note and pointing out how extravagant you are. Or how shabbily you dress and what terrible taste you have. You'd never go on a vacation without people murmuring about where the money came from and saying it could've gone to charity and so forth. It's just not worth the hassle."

I remembered the church that had temporarily owned my parents, and although I knew most churches were nothing like that, I granted that Zoë might have a point. "Well, people do it," I said, because I'm a rebellious little sister who hates to be told what she shouldn't do.

"Not you, Airhead."

I suspected she was right, but I couldn't possibly admit that. "We're not even going steady, OK? He's just being a good host. I'm sorry I didn't call. I got busy."

"Yeah, I'll bet." She snorted.

It was time to smooth her feathers. "Not with romance, duh. I found out some interesting things about the circumstances of Aaron's death." I filled her in briefly on what I'd discovered so far.

"You're not playing Nancy Drew, are you? Just do what you have to and get out of there." She paused. "Are you sure that detective hasn't gotten the wrong idea—such as, just maybe, he can pin this on you?"

"Pin what? He hasn't really said for sure it was murder."

"He's from homicide, you said." Her tone indicated clearly that I would never be worthy to bring the potato salad to the Mensa picnic.

"But he knows I wasn't even here at the time." Didn't he? "He mentioned that I could get a report from the inquest."

"Why don't you do that, for grins."

"Now you want me to sleuth. Shouldn't you be a bit more encouraging and ask some leading questions?" I said, matching her sarcastic tone.

"If I think of one, I'll lead you to it."

"Did you make sure you turned both the deadbolts in my door and left the lamp timer on so it looks like I'm home as usual?" The neighborhood around the Casa el Dumpo apartments could be pretty rough.

"Yeah, yeah." She dismissed that change of subject. "Listen, use your connection with that guy. The guitarist. Ask him about Gil and about the other people. You know how to work it; use some of your crystal blue persuasion on him."

"That song is not about drugs or magic," I told her. "Tommy James said in his book it's about his conversion to Christianity."

"Whatever. Your version is the old eyelash-fluttering technique; I'll bet you've already been doing it. Flatter him by telling him you know the bass guitar may seem simple to learn but takes a lifetime to master—and that he's well on his way. Talk about Clapton and Hendrix. You're good at bullshitting." I rolled my eyes, even though she couldn't see me. "Take that little spark you felt between you and fan the flame a little. Maybe he'll inadvertently tell you something you need to know."

Even though I'd done a bit of the girly stuff on every man I'd met so far—I thought of it as being friendly, Texas style—I balked at actually admitting to it, let alone scheming about it. "I hate the kind of women who manipulate people."

"Well, grow up. Those are the women who find things out and live to fight another day."

"You're conflating two proverbs."

"Wait until you see what else I conflate if you don't hurry this thing up. Take care of business and then get out of there."

"I'll call you in the morning, after Gil and I get each other's names tattooed on our butts and when I know what's on the schedule. Okay?"

I hung up with the nagging feeling that there was something else I should've told her . . . or asked her.

§ § §

As the set ended, I went up to the edge of the stage and caught Ponyboy's eye. He didn't look surprised. In fact, his expression held the hint of a smirk.

The smug bastard had counted on me, as if I were a teen fangirl. The idea made me want to bolt, but I rammed down the rebellion and smiled. After the last nair-nair twang faded, he leaned his guitar against the amp and headed my way.

As he came offstage, I fell into step with him. "I loved that last song. You're really good."

He preened. "We think so." He veered towards one of the nearby lemonade stands.

"Why don't y'all get on 'American Idol'? Or some show like that where they work with bands."

He grimaced theatrically. "Please. No wonder the arts are going into the crapper, with those people manufacturing acts like they were toasters." Shaking his head, he patted down his shirt pockets as if looking for smokes, then seemingly remembered he'd quit. "We don't want that kind of sellout lifestyle. Want to do it our way. Once you get a recording contract or TV gig, The Man owns you."

I nodded extra-vapidly. "Yeah, I see what you mean."

"No-talent divas and TV stars are the saints of today—and their reliquaries are sold on eBay."

Once again he seemed a lot more erudite than the average cowboy bass player, but of course I had no idea of the road that'd brought him here. He might be a Rhodes scholar: look at Kris Kristofferson. This guy could be similar. The idea intrigued me.

After he'd gotten his lemonade, I stepped up to order one, feeling parched all of a sudden. Probably because of what I was about to wend my way around to asking. They sold me a small diet version, and I turned back to him. "I wanted to thank you again for rescuing me from that little scene in the coffee shop. That was weird, wasn't it? I guess she and Aaron were fairly close."

"They had an arrangement." He looked away; I was losing him. Oops. Guys hated to be reminded of ugly scenes that women had made. I'd need to steer the conversation using another tactic.

"Oh, well, she doesn't know me. Anybody can get the wrong idea," I said breezily. "She's probably pretty fond of Gil."

He eyed me speculatively. He had to be wondering whether Gil and I had something going. What did I look like, the lonely little petunia in the onion patch? What with all the suspicion, I felt less guilty about leveraging out some information.

"You know, I wonder whether you could help me out with something." I tried to look less like a gossip and more like a Concerned Party. "I heard that Gil is recently divorced. How involved is he with his ex? Like, I mean." I waved my hands vaguely, as I imagined That Kind of Woman might. "Still involved?"

"Let's go somewhere more private." We headed back to the area behind the stage, where the next band was beginning to set up. "Keep an eye out for Gil and the rest of your crowd, will you? I'm going to level with you, because you look like a decent sort."

I glanced around, as if I were accustomed to making sure the coast was clear.

"Aaron had an affair with Gil's wife last year."

So Cora wasn't the only one who knew. And that meant it was probably true. I took a hurried sip to cover my dismay and almost choked. "Too tart," I gasped out. He patted me on the back until I indicated I was all right, that he should go on.

"Everybody knew, but just didn't say anything because they all respected Gil so much and he just seemed not to want to know, as if it would all blow over soon, or as if it were just another cross he had to bear." He shook his head. "You know, the martyr syndrome. But it was going on under his nose, and he had to be ignoring an awful lot of clues. That's how some people cope. The affair ended when those two realized they had nothing in common."

That was too deep an analysis to be a lucky guess. Had Buck been Close Personal Friends with either Claudia or Aaron?

"There was a lot of speculation and recrimination and all that, but nothing was ever said in public except the marriage was ending amicably."

I managed to speak without coughing. "That's how I heard it. And the wife got confused and ran away, supposedly off to her parents in New York."

He shook his head. "That's what they told people. She isn't really in the Apple, but just down the road to the west, in Alpine. She's playing the artist—doing ceramics of some kind. Has a little studio and the whole bit. Anyway, Gil apparently reconciled with Aaron and didn't hold it against him because he said Claudie was confused already and that it had been her fault. That it was for the best." Tying his bootlace, not looking directly at me, he let me absorb the news without checking out my expression. I appreciated that, because I was freaked out by that concept.

It gave Gil a motive for killing Aaron, though.

"Where is her studio exactly?" I still sounded strangled.

"I imagine I could dig up her address, if not more. But I've got another set." He gestured at the stage. "Catch you later?"

"I'm sure of it."

CHAPTER SIX

Now I was convinced that Aaron's death was no heart attack and not an accident. But where the hell did I start looking for the truth? It seemed overwhelming to try, let alone prove anything.

Cora walked up behind me, trailed by the guys. "There you are. Why didn't you answer your phone?"

"I didn't hear it ring." Checking, I saw that they'd tried me twice. "Aaron must not have assigned you a custom ringtone. The default ring for this phone sounds like one fingernail dragged across a harp, and I can't hear it even when it's quiet." I gestured towards the stage, where Ponyboy and his crew were tuning up again. "Do you want to settle in and risk hearing more of their stuff, or shall we go see what there is to see?"

§ § §

We circled the grounds, and I enjoyed the rest of the festival. Gil had toned his mooning down somewhat, but still acted interested. I couldn't help it—I had to admit that my body was responding, and that I was still interested in him, intrigued in spite of the recent revelations.

I never said that I always listened to my better judgment.

The fest continued late into the evening, giving me time to sunburn (that SPF on the bottle isn't always trustworthy) and get covered with mosquito bites. Who knew mosquitoes could breed where there was so little visible water? By the end of the day, I was ready to get back to the cozy, welcoming cabin.

Had Aaron really been tight with Gil, and maybe Buck, and all these Western individualists? They didn't seem like his type. He'd always been a techie type, kind of snobby about people who didn't know their way around a ham radio or computer, but here he'd been living in the sticks and apparently loving it. Of course, I had little to go on other than the evidence of the cabin itself and what these people told me about him. Could there be some kind of scam going on, the way my sister suspected there was? I mean, Aaron didn't seem to fit with this crowd. Maybe they had something on him. Something that got him killed?

Gil might've discovered Aaron's algorithm and how good it was; I couldn't see Aaron being naïve enough to talk about it with him, but the slightest slip of the tongue could pique Gil's interest. Maybe a representative of one of those companies did Aaron in to get the stuff without paying.

Speculating like this would drive anyone crazy. I shoved the picnic basket into the cargo area of the SUV, wishing I hadn't eaten any of Gil's too-tart, fattening potato salad. And hoping I didn't have terminal onion breath. Even though I was tired enough to be irritable, I had to play nice until I dropped him off and got back to the blessedly quiet house, humming with nothing louder than aerator pumps and tank bubble wands.

I think our family is descended from turtles: we like to be able to withdraw and regroup at the end of a trying day.

§ § §

Despite the late night, on Sunday morning I was already up, scrubbed, and lounging in front of the Cartoon Network when Aaron's house phone rang at eleven-thirty. Church services must've run long.

Gil was on his way over. "I just got a call from Aaron's mom on their cell phone, and they are right now turning off the highway. ETA five or six minutes."

I leaped off the sofa and into my good jeans. I decided on a blue button-down Oxford shirt and combed my hair, putting it into the Alice in Wonderland half-ponytail style. That looked too infantile, so I brushed it out again. I ended up with barrettes holding back the waves from yesterday's French braids, finishing just as Gil beat on the door and shouted, "They're here!"

Only by force of will did I avoid a flashback to *The Goonies*.

A huge maroon-and-white RV (painted in Texas Aggie colors) groaned its way up the road and pulled into the drive. The door opened, and out fell a plump dark-haired woman who ran over to Gil. Mystery Woman greeted Gil by throwing her arms around his neck and sobbing. "Thank you for being so good to my brother."

Those dark circles under her eyes had to indicate a fairly bad hangover. Aaron didn't have a sister.

I'd never seen her before. She looked about twice Aaron's age, but was still too young to be his mother, Myra, unless she'd been reverse-aged by aliens. Then Myra emerged, looking the same as always: chubby, determined, sunglasses nestled in her dark bouffant, dimpled thighs quivering below her khaki shorts. As usual, she gave no sign of noticing me.

The engine noise from the motorhome finally died away and a man's voice boomed out. "No hookups, no problem. We're self-sufficient."

Doyle, Aaron's six-foot, three-hundred-pound couch potato of a father, climbed out, looking like a horse who'd been ridden hard and put away wet. The years hadn't been kind to him: his face, neck, and arms were wrinkled like an index card that'd been folded over and over, then forgotten and left in the washer for three wash cycles. He glanced my way, but gave no sign of recognition.

It was enough to get me noticed, though.

"Who is SHE?" yelled the younger woman, pointing at me over Gil's shoulder.

Gil glanced back at me. It was the first time I'd seen him look unsure of himself. "Um, yes, Marisol Rose, this is Ari French. Ari, you wouldn't have met Marisol; she only recently rejoined the family."

Before I could ask what the hell that meant, Gil gestured with his eyes for me to be patient and ask him later.

"Why is she still here?" Marisol's face crumpled into a pout. "You found us. We're here. She can go now."

Gil smoothed back his hair with the hand that wasn't restraining her. "Um, I'm afraid I don't quite follow you."

Myra approached me, tottering on wedge heels. "Hello, Ariadne. We appreciate your coming out to baby-sit the house until they could get in touch with us. It was really thoughtful of you." She waved one hand dismissively. "But now I'm sure you have other things to do, so feel free."

Wait a minute. . . .

Gil held out his hand for her to shake, but she didn't seem to realize. "Mrs. Beecroft, I'm so glad to meet you at last. Aaron spoke of you often." I thought ministers weren't supposed to lie. "But let me correct your impression right quick. Ari isn't just baby-sitting. She's mentioned in Aaron's will as far as his final arrangements."

"Well, she can take whatever little keepsake he willed to her right now and get on out, because we're here now." Myra stuck her nose into the air and sniffed. "What is that smell? It smells like DIRT out here."

Gil cleared his throat. "Things aren't quite that simple, as you'll discover when we get over to the legal office. Ari actually is the major inheritor in the bequests."

Aaron's mother laughed. "You can't be serious. If you're talking about some fake will she has come up with, well, you can forget that. We've got a lawyer in Dallas; all I have to do is dial his cell. He'll take care of any little problems pretty quick."

"I wouldn't call this a little problem." Gil looked mildly panicked.

"Of course not. I mean, of course it isn't a problem." Marisol Rose looked as if she'd like to pop loose a few thorns. "We have the lawyer and we're going to break that will and we're going to get all my brother's stuff, so she might as well leave now."

I gave up waiting for the honeymoon to be over and started trying to figure out how to finalize the divorce.

"Now hold on a second." Gil's diplomacy was failing him. "In fact, I'm Aaron's personal representative and am legally bound to carry out his wishes. Which do include Ariadne."

"You haven't been letting her STAY here, have you?" Marisol's eyes narrowed into nickel slits. "That can get you in big trouble, buster. An executor or whatever you are is supposed to handle the property carefully. If she has been in here and has broken or disturbed anything, you're in for it."

"I haven't stayed here." The lie popped out of me. It had a recoil; I took a few steps back. "I've been, um, inside with Gil a couple of times. I'm staying with the neighbors next door. Actually, tonight I'm moving to a motel in town."

Marisol looked me up and down. "Of course you'd say that. But we'll find out the truth."

Mama Bear looked at Gil, but her laser eyes failed to set him on fire. Not for lack of trying. "I am not happy with these arrangements at all. I wish you had told me what you were doing."

So did I. Why hadn't Gil worked all this out in advance? Why hadn't the possibility—probability—of their throwing hissy fits when they found out I was inheriting struck me before? They were Aaron's rightful heirs, I supposed. I wasn't any blood relation, and we'd never been legally tied to one another. And he had left me behind and moved on.

Sure, he had put me in his will—I guessed; I had only Gil's word to go on there, as I still hadn't seen a copy—but that could've been whim. He wouldn't have expected to die anytime soon. He might've been angry at his family and written the will that way in hopes of stirring up trouble. Which he'd accomplished. When it came right down to brass knuckles, though, I had felt all along that I didn't have any morally valid claim on all this stuff. And I didn't need it, or this.

"Look," I began.

Doyle cut me off. "Our lawyer is a high-powered expert. He's challenged plenty of fraudulent wills in probate court. You might as well give it up now."

Gil rallied. "I can assure you that I personally witnessed the will. She wasn't involved."

"I'll bet. You just didn't know about it. We've never approved of her influence on Aaron." Doyle glared in my direction. He'd become even more rough-edged than I recalled. He must've gotten filed down pretty drastically by life over the past few years.

Myra sniffed. "Our lawyer also handles estate contests involving mental incompetence. Why would my son leave his estate to this slut when he has a perfectly good family?"

Why, indeed.

"Can we remain civil here?" Gil rallied, but wasn't quite up to the role of white knight.

"Noooo." Marisol's voice whined out of her nose and into the stratosphere. "This is ridiculous. Whatever she's down for, surely we're next in line. I mean, if she had died before he had, then wouldn't we have gotten everything?"

That sounded ominous.

Gil tried to take a stand. "You'll hear it all this afternoon at the reading. I wish you wouldn't make any assumptions until the will is actually read. Then we can talk, all right?"

"There isn't any room for talk. You have nothing to say about it."

"Actually, as his personal representative," Gil began, but was shouted down. Marisol and Myra headed for the front door.

Marisol shot a verbal volley over her shoulder. "Some people have no reason to be here."

It was all I could do to keep from yelling, "You got that right, 'sister.'" He'd never mentioned any sister, and I found this claim pretty fishy. But I also felt in my heart that she had a point about the inheritance. And I couldn't help wondering why this aspect of things hadn't crossed my mind before, and why my own (authentic) sister hadn't brought it up. Zoë'd been stunned, like me, I supposed. I'd been overwhelmed by Gil and his confidence, probably, and my curiosity about coming out here to see overrode all reason. Well, now I had seen. And I'd seen enough.

Still, right now these people were pissing me off. I stepped into the Furies' path. "This place was built with my money, at least in part. I do have some claim on it."

"Excuse me?" Myra pinned me to the spot with her glare.

"Might I point out that some of my equity went into the building materials? Aaron took advantage of me by 'borrowing' my credit cards while I was too busy coping with a crisis to pay close attention. But what he bought was for our future here, so when I first found out, I waited for an explanation to come from him by phone or mail. It never did. I think this is his way of settling that debt."

Marisol whirled on me. "So that's what you did? Told him he'd better give you all his stuff because of some imaginary"—her forefingers made "air quotes"—"*debt*?"

"I never asked for this," I said, half to myself. "He didn't consult me. All I'd like is—" What? The car, maybe. I felt entitled to whatever might still be in my name, or charged to my credit. I could just quit paying on all those bills. It didn't matter—my credit was already ruined. I wasn't going to keep paying so they could have things; it was Aaron I'd cared about. Screw them.

No wonder he'd never had much to do with his family.

"What proof do you have that he owed you a dime? Let alone that he wanted to"—air quotes again-"'share the wealth'?"

"Horse manure," shouted Doyle. "He never had any intention of sharing things with her. This little gal is just a round-heeled opportunist," he said into Gil's face, wagging a finger in my direction. "You can't be taking her seriously."

"I'm afraid I have to follow the directives in Aaron's will. And as his representative, I do have a say in these matters."

They all rushed Gil, who'd clearly been unprepared for a confrontation. He held them back by shoving out his arms referee-style, but I could see he'd be overcome pretty easily if they decided they wanted to take him. If only I had studied one of the martial arts other than "Lie On Sofa"; every one of these jerks outweighed me. It didn't look as if they'd come to blows, but one never knew.

"Want me to call the police?" I asked Gil, although I wasn't sure whose side the law would rule on.

"No! We can reason together," he said.

"Reason away, as long as she goes now," Myra said.

Did I really want to duke it out with these trashballs over a few material things? Was anything here worth fighting over?

If I walked away, Zoë might call it wimping out. Or it might be respecting boundaries and allowing others their rights.

I had to admit that these people, odious as they were, had the more obvious claim. Until the provisions of the will were implemented after it was probated, they as the relatives were the ones with the legal right to tell me I was trespassing. The police had presumably processed the scene of the death long before I arrived, so detective Max wouldn't be likely to respond well to the suggestion that these people might destroy evidence and further clues to a possible crime, as I had in effect done the same thing by staying there. That approach led to a dead end, if not over the cliff.

The family felt I should leave the premises immediately. Was this a problem for me?

I decided it wasn't. Gil should've told them the details about me and hashed all of this out. He was going to have a hassle if they brought a charge of fraud. If he had taken care of business properly on the phone, this wouldn't be happening.

"I'm out of here," I said, though no one was listening.

As they continued to rave about responsibilities and lawyers, I started edging past Gil to get back into the house for my purse, tote, and duffel. I'd grab only the basics—including the keys to the Navigator. I might have to stay in town to deal with the legal paperwork. But I didn't have to stand here and watch this circus.

Gil stood in front of the Terrible Trio with his arms straight out from his shoulders, looking like some kind of faith healer whose current had suddenly stopped flowing as they noticed me making a move. "What's she doing?" cried Marisol. "She's getting in!"

I barely beat them inside to grab my duffel and tote. On impulse, I snatched Aaron's laptop, case and all. Damned if I'd let them magpie-skim all the stuff that looked salable. They'd probably hide expensive trinkets in that RV and tell the estate it didn't exist. Besides, if I really had the title of "literary executor" as Gil had originally claimed, I needed to find whatever Aaron might've written, and that would be on his laptop; he'd always had it with him. I swept a few more gadgets off the desk into my tote, for good measure.

There wasn't time to get my clothes and toiletries or my suitcase, but they probably wouldn't disturb those. They'd better not. I'd get Gil to retrieve them later. It shouldn't be that tough to figure out which clothes belonged to me, as Aaron never wore women's denim skirts when we went together. Of course, people change.

By this time they'd backed Gil into the house and the two women were coming right for me. I had my tote and duffel under my left arm with the laptop and snagged my purse as I headed for the back door.

"See y'all in court," I couldn't resist shouting cheerily. Let them worry about me being there to fight them and possibly prevail—although I hadn't decided whether to try.

Outside, I headed down the hill for Cora's house. Before I could figure out what I was going to say, I was knocking.

Cora was still in her Sunday best. Decked out in floral linen and pearls, she surveyed me in my not-quite-casual-Friday get-up. "You look all out of breath, dear. Won't you come in?"

"I think I will, for a minute." I jumped inside and slammed the door behind me, then lifted the corner of the curtain to look back toward Aaron's. They didn't seem to be following me, which was good. "I just came by to tell you that Aaron's parents have arrived, and I won't be going back into that house."

I summarized the situation, even though Cora didn't deserve to have that dumped on her. She just kept nodding, looking a bit disconcerted. "I didn't even get my clothes, I was so angry."

"I can see that, dear. Why don't you have a glass of iced tea and cool off?" She led me away from the door and towards her kitchen. "Isn't it a shame they can't deal with this. With his final wishes, I mean."

"Well, I sort of see their side of it. I would negotiate. But they're very upset right now, and there wasn't any point in talking to them while they're half crazy. They do seem to feel it's their way or the highway."

"That's too bad. Perhaps if they do end up with everything, they'll find it doesn't mean what they think it will. I've never seen anyone enjoy an inheritance the way they thought they were going to."

"Yeah." I'd seen that happen, too. With my grandmother's estate, among other things. The prolonged fighting had alienated the brothers and sisters permanently, and all over a few bits of crockery and furniture. "I hate for them to sweep in here like this, because it shatters the fantasy I'd built around why he chose me. Let's face it, he wasn't exactly at his most ethical, using my money to finance his dream project. I believed he was sincere when he told me it would be for both of us. I kept expecting him to send for me, even after all this time. That was pretty stupid of me, wasn't it?"

My brain seemed to be doing a core dump. Cora didn't need to hear my life story. However, it insisted on pouring out as she loaded two glasses with ice.

"What can I say? I loved the guy. All the while I was doing my best to make ends meet and catching a full measure of crap from my sister, who just knew he was taking advantage." I leaned back to vibrate the edge of the curtain. Still no signs of movement from the cabin. "When I got Gil's call, I convinced myself that this showed I was really his true love all along. But maybe it was just done on a whim one night after he'd been drinking. He wasn't used to booze any more, and it had started to have bad effects on him before he quit. Who knows? Of course he couldn't have possibly anticipated that he'd leave the world suddenly." Could he? "Sorry. I'm blathering."

"It's all right, dear." She filled the glasses from the Sun Tea dispenser on her countertop. "You're safe telling me. I always find it flattering when people confide in me."

That wasn't what I'd meant to do. Why did I always spill my guts when I got nervous?

I edged back towards the door. "I'm sorry to put you to any trouble. I suppose I'd better get out of here, because I don't want them coming after you."

She glanced sharply at the curtain. "They wouldn't dare."

I looked at the tea. I was parched. "Could I get that to go? I don't want to carry off one of your good glasses."

She had a set of orange plastic travel cups secreted away. I transferred my tea into one of them, snapping on the top gratefully. "They can have the furniture and so forth. I believe the car is mine—I mean, I'm taking it for the moment. Gil gave me permission, and I have no other means of escape." Cora nodded again, though I could see she had a few doubts about my legal right of access to the SUV. "Could you—I mean, later on, whenever Gil can get that bunch out of the place for a while, could you retrieve my clothes and things and keep them for me?"

She patted my shoulder. "Call me when you've settled down and you're ready for me to bring your things." I knew the phone would remember her cell number in "Incoming Calls" from when she'd tried to call me at the festival, but she handed me a yellow sticky note with their house phone. "If you lose this, we're in the book." She examined my face again. "You sure you don't want to stay with us?"

"I think I need my own base, but thanks." I knew how quickly houseguests started to reek, especially people you didn't know that well.

Those jerks probably had no idea how to take care of the fish. With luck, they wouldn't mess with the tanks. The autofeeders were full, and everything was set up. Worst case, there wouldn't be anything left alive for me to worry about.

I pulled back Cora's kitchen curtain and watched out the window a few moments until I verified that Aaron's family was still not pouring forth in pursuit of me. They were probably busy taking inventory, and weren't likely to come streaming out. The Navigator wasn't blocked in by the RV, either. It was on the other side of the circular drive.

"Good luck, dear," Cora whispered as I scurried away.

I got the engine started without worrying about whether they heard. They were probably squabbling among themselves as to who would get the towels.

"That went well," echoed through my head in Zoë's voice as I sped away.

I was making a three-point turn onto the highway when Aaron's phone warbled out "Wayfaring Stranger." I hit the speakerphone unit on the visor, and Gil's voice boomed out.

"I had no idea they'd be so hostile," he said.

"It doesn't matter. They're right. I just want the SUV, nothing more." I had fixated on the car. Well, why not? Look what they were driving. "I wish you'd explained things to them a little better before they arrived. Although it might not have mattered. They're incredibly combative."

"They acted perfectly cooperative on the phone."

That would be in line with what Aaron had always said about them—manipulative, cunning, the sort to play along with smiles until they found ways to get what they wanted, no matter what.

"You're entitled to the bulk of the estate. Aaron specified that his will be read in public, and so he must've anticipated this. It's common that the family in these cases will fight any other beneficiaries and even one another."

"I don't need all that stuff. How can I justify taking it away from them? It's a lot more important to them than it is to me."

"Ariadne. . . ." Gil sounded defeated. "I've stuck my neck out on your behalf in several ways. In fact, we need to talk about what we've already committed to—like covering your airfare and your driving the car."

"Do you want the car back now?" My throat started to burn.

"No, no. But what I'm saying is—if you're not going to fight to be the ultimate beneficiary, there might be problems. If there's a challenge, nobody should be allowed to drive the car for a while. Of course there hasn't been any formal challenge of anything at this point. We should try to reduce the chances, if we can." He cleared his throat. "You'd need to return it. Not this very minute, I mean, but soon."

So I'd have to rent a car. And the airfare that I'd charged to my Visa would be another burden. Why, again, had I come out here? Poor impulse control. "Look, I need to get away for a while. Mind if I call you back later?"

"You're not leaving town."

"No, I'm not letting them chase me away. I understand I have legal obligations. I'll be at the lawyer's office for the pow-wow. Please find out whether there's some kind of paper I can sign to release the other stuff to them or start negotiations. Whatever. Right now, I have some other things I want to do."

"Okay. There's an elders-deacons meeting at four that I want to sit in on, and then evening worship, so I'll be out of pocket for a while. I'll catch you later."

Only if I don't see you coming.

§ § §

The pounding between my temples had slowed by the time I got into town, which took all of ten minutes. But I didn't know where I was going. I couldn't fly home until after the will was read. I couldn't go home to Aaron's because that wasn't my home. Hotels weren't home.

At first, I'd thought I could feel mildly contented here. Maybe that was because Gil had been so welcoming. I'd started out so excited about seeing the place Aaron had chosen for . . . well, not for us. For himself. But anyway, now all those semi-comfy feelings were floating into the clouds like a sack of Scrooge McDuck's money.

I pulled over in front of the Presidio County Courthouse, an 1886 stone-and-brick landmark in the center of Marfa's town square. For lack of any other way to work off my excess energy, I got out of the car and walked inside. I might as well sightsee a bit so I could tell Zoë I'd Seen the Sights.

There was a notice posted on the front steps informing citizens they could sign a petition in favor of adopting a new city slogan: "We've been leaving the lights on for you for 120 years."

I couldn't even smile.

Eighty-six steps up inside the courthouse tower brought me to the overlook room, where I had a 360-degree view of the town and surrounding countryside. The vista should've been breathtaking. All it did was bring on a touch of agoraphobia. I needed something to damp down my impending anxiety attack, not feed it. Deep breaths helped a little.

But I didn't belong here. I felt as if I had squeezed my eyes closed and set the library's globe spinning, then stabbed my finger at it to stop it wherever fate chose, and then said, "That's where I'm going to live when I grow up." Or maybe I'd used that globe that they used to have in the lobby of the New York Daily News building, the one that was in "Superman." Was it still there? Could I hitch a ride on it? Had I already?

With calm came second thoughts about not fighting Aaron's awful family. I hated to let them win. A quick cost-benefit analysis was in order, though. There could be drawbacks to winning this fight beyond the time wasted and what it might cost.

For one thing, I couldn't afford to inherit this stuff.

I'd heard that people who went on game shows often ended up selling the prizes they'd won when it came time to settle up with the IRS. There would be taxes to pay on the estate. And then payments on everything that wasn't free and clear. Aaron undoubtedly had a mortgage and a car payment and other liens, and the utilities would come due soon. This cellphone would need to be paid. Maybe I could at least hang on to that. And a few more luxuries, if I managed the inheritance well.

Inheritance. What a double-edged dagger that was as it plunged into my heart to remind me why I was getting all this. To gain the material wealth, you had to lose an awful lot.

Bailing out, on the other hand, would be one way of sparing myself. I can't abide tugs-of-war and family in-fighting. It's because of all the fighting in my family, the way my parents are—the way my mother is—and because of everything that happened when Zoë got pregnant unexpectedly (and unwedded-ly) with Ricky in the first place fourteen years ago. It's too hard to deal with.

Still, these people were not my family. Thank God. And I had no baggage with them. They were definitely all problem children who didn't deserve a thing. Maybe I was playing the little fool.

Why should I be all accommodating and let Aaron's family—who obviously despised me—have the last word and the lion's share of the inheritance? Aaron'd had no compunctions about using my money and my credit rating for his own benefit, and taking my credit score for a ride like Chill Wills riding the bomb down in *Dr. Strangelove.* He counted on my remaining blissfully unaware that my money had helped get him a powerful SUV and a fairly spectacular house. If I hadn't survived him, who would Aaron have left everything to? Not them, I'd guess.

Furthermore, who the hell was this Marisol chick? Aaron had no sister. At least, he'd never mentioned one. Could she have been adopted out and only recently found? Might he really not have known about her? She looked nothing like any of them. Who was she, really? And why was she wasting Earth's precious oxygen?

I must've zoned out for a minute, because it was shocking when my eyes focused and my head snapped to attention. It took me a moment to realize what I was looking at: it was a blue sedan that looked just like Gil's headed down the road that led out of town. I watched as it curved around and continued out of sight. Of course, there could be other cars around that looked like Gil's. And he wouldn't leave that bunch alone in Aaron's cabin, would he? Maybe he had something to discuss with a parishioner. Or wanted to ask another legal eagle about this situation he'd gotten us into.

Gil's car could've been stolen. By Marisol. So she could go find someone else to berate. Maybe she'd run out of acid and needed a refill.

I left the courthouse before anyone could try to offer me tourist help or an area map. Being Ms. Nice Girl wasn't going to get me where I needed to be.

§ § §

Since I was stuck in town for a while, I figured I might as well do a bit of investigating.

First order of business was a bite to eat. After getting a fruit smoothie and an oatmeal raisin cookie at the lunch counter, I dug out Aaron's cell phone and dialed that musician's number. He answered on the first ring. That told me that his caller ID probably knew Aaron, so maybe they'd talked often? Hmm.

"It's Ari French. Did you ever dig up Gil's ex-wife's address and phone number?"

"Oh, yeah, you wanted to find Claudia. Sure, I can get you that now." After some keyboarding noises, he read it off to me. Then he proceeded to give me driving directions.

I drive by landmarks. However, Buck's way of explaining was typical Guy-Style. "Head south on 91 and then take 82 east; get off on Travis and keep going east until you hit FM 1478, and it'll be on the northwest corner." I do a lot better with the typical distaff version of directions: "Go down to the first Taco Bell past the gas station across from the feed store, turn left and look for where they tore down the old dime store, you know, where the Jones place used to be, and go a little farther until the first spot you can turn right. Keep going until you see a big stone church with a purple truck out back. We'll be upstairs."

But I simply thanked him and told him I hoped to catch their show tonight. Then I keyed the address into the StreetFinder, kissed my fingers and patted its top for luck as if it were some techno-Ganesha, and set off following its instructions to Alpine and into Claudia's domain.

§ § §

Gil's ex-wife didn't have a garden, but she (or somebody) had invented a weatherproof version of pretend ocotillo cacti. They'd used barbed wire-wrapped rebar as stalks and wired polished red rocks together as the flowers. The faux ocotillos lined her front walkway.

When I saw her, I did a double-take. It was like looking at one of those age-progressed police portraits of children. Only this was me, ten years from now. Assuming I wore well.

Me, but blonder and a little slimmer.

That kind of explained why Gil looked at me the way he did. And why he had seemed to "know" me and like me right off. He'd probably seen a photo of me that Aaron had around the house, though I hadn't seen one on display anywhere (which had been disappointing). And he'd instantly felt pair-bonding because of the resemblance. That made his behavior towards me seem a little less disturbing and a little more pathetic.

It's weird to face your doppelgänger. People say that most of us have a double somewhere. I was meeting mine.

Claudia didn't look fazed. She whipped off her red bandana and wiped at the dried clay that covered her palms. "I see you found me. Word travels fast around here, so I knew you might be headed this way. Come on in."

Pony had called ahead? Nice touch.

She led me back to her all-white kitchen. "I know you're wondering about me—about Gil and me, and about Aaron and me, I mean." Claudia obviously didn't believe in beating around the cactus. "Yes, Aaron and I had a fling. But it wasn't cheap and tawdry, the way it must sound." She sighed. "Gil and I were long overdue for our breakup. I made some mistakes, but so had he. It's complicated."

"Of course." I sat on a barstool as she puttered between the sink and stove, apparently making coffee. "I appreciate your straightforwardness. Especially since it's none of my business."

"Well, it's understandable that you might . . . want to know a little bit about the situation." She tossed her hair. There was an ess of clay at each of her temples where she'd forgotten and pushed flyaways back with her fingers. "I realize it's tough for you. You must feel pretty strange walking in here and finding out that things weren't quite as you probably thought they were."

"I hadn't been in contact with Aaron for some time, so I had no idea what to expect."

"Oh." She seemed surprised. "The way he talked, I thought he was in fairly frequent contact with you."

"I only wish."

Regarding me curiously, she went on. "That's surprising to hear. At any rate, he'd been working on an algorithm that he thought would prove quite profitable. He said he had clients wanting to integrate his new security system into their network, which would help keep their network secret—'hidden in plain sight,' as he put it." She tucked a wayward strand of hair behind her ear. "I thought he was looking forward to being successful—from the way he talked, independently wealthy—so he could send for you."

Tears welled in my eyes. "He could've sent for me when he was flat broke. He knew that." I willed the tears to back up. "Maybe he would've had me come. But unfortunately, something happened." I held her gaze, as if making a challenge. "Do you think Aaron's death was an accident?"

Her eyes widened. Looking nonplussed, she lowered her tiny butt onto a stool. "What do you mean? Aaron had a heart attack."

"No, he didn't." I wasn't sure how much I should tell her, and since I didn't have a "Murder, She Wrote" script to follow, I couldn't imagine the damage I might be doing to the case if she turned out to be the culprit—although I seriously doubted that already. Suspecting her was difficult because I had always wanted a twin. "The authorities suspect he was at least helped along, if not deliberately killed."

Claudia sucked in a breath, as though my news had knocked the wind out of her. "I can't believe it."

I decided to push the slider up another notch. "The police are looking at several people. Gil, for instance. And more seriously, at Orleans Hall."

"If something bad happened to Aaron. . . ." She shook her hair out, as though she could shake off any discomfort as easily. "They couldn't have had anything to do with it, I'm sure. I don't like to cast aspersions on people." As if she'd convinced herself, she nodded. "I'm sure the police are doing everything they need to in order to find out."

I let her drop the subject. "So how do you like it out here?"

"I love my studio." She met my gaze again, but at a slant. "I'm working as a potter-slash-ceramic artist and waiting tables in the evenings, and I'm much happier than I was as a stay-at-home." She shook her hair back. "I couldn't stand it, being a minister's wife. I never realized what it entailed. Your time is never your own. Most of the time they're called on at the last minute to do all this marrying and burying and counseling of church members. I always had to be Miss Perfect, and if I ever came to church looking less polished than Cindy Crawford, there'd be talk that I was ill or drinking. I just couldn't take another day."

"So it wasn't true that Aaron broke up your marriage."

"No, no. He was there, he was available. A fling. What he did for me was show me that there could still be love and freedom, that I was still young, that there was time for me to make a change. He showed me I needed to do that. And the only way to do it was make the break. It was time." She looked off into the distance. "Aaron was a great guy, Ari. Talked about you often."

Oh, God. I didn't want to know that.

"He had his problems, and he and Gil didn't always agree. I'd had the feeling lately that there was a barrier between them, and that it wasn't all because of me and our little . . . indiscretion." She sighed. "Gil and I still talk. We're friends, after a fashion. You know, once you've been with somebody, part of you always stays connected to them."

I knew.

"Of course there's more to the story. These things are always complicated. I would still be with Gil today if I hadn't found out that he'd lied to me. Discovered it in a most uncomfortable fashion." Her faraway gaze told me she was remembering, and her jaw tightened, so I knew that she wasn't going to reveal all her secrets. "That was the last straw. He'd been covering up something that he should've told me, and I just—anyway, it was a symptom of how he wasn't the person I thought he was. Rather, the person I wanted him to be, who I tried to make him into, and that never works. Like in that Boston song, 'A Man I'll Never Be,' where the woman sees the guy in an idealized fashion, and he realizes he can never live up to that, though he thinks somewhere inside he has it in him to be the man she thinks he is."

Claudia wasn't quite as impassive about this as she wanted me to think.

Maybe Claudia was responsible for the spider. The one I'd seen in the cell phone photo. Perhaps the death she'd intended for Gil—who'd used her, in some sense, and then cheated on her—had landed on Aaron instead, by accident and not by design. This place was far enough out in the country that there were probably lots of spiders around, and she looked as if she knew the terrain and was comfortable in it.

I could've sworn she wiped a tear out of the corner of her eye as she shook her head. "Listen to me. I'm philosophizing, rambling. Forgive me. You don't want to hear all this."

"It's okay. I like to wax philosophical myself."

She smiled, tilting her head, her long hair falling to one side like a sheaf of golden wheat. I could see why Gil was still in love with her. And her resemblance to me was really only superficial. Claudia was a great beauty, or had been a few years back.

"Do you miss your life in town?"

"Not very much. I think Gil feels a little lost." She looked wistful. "But anyway, he's fine with this. He needs to move on, and I think he's ready to do that." She glanced at me, and again I felt as if I were being sized up. As a potential date, as a life partner for Gil, as what? "Take it slow. You don't know what you're getting into. It's not just the associate minister who has all those duties at the church. It's his woman, too. And you may find you're not the type of person who can help shepherd. You have no life of your own. It takes a certain personality to survive and thrive. Just—think carefully before you commit to anything."

"I'd need to be committed if I were even thinking that." I smiled. "I mean, we've barely met. I hope you're kidding."

"No, I'm serious." She looked wistful. "We're probably not destined to be friends, but I wish you well, and I think for your own good that you should learn everything that comes with the job before you commit yourself to it."

"Don't worry. I don't even have an application in for that job."

She smiled and patted my arm, inadvertently smearing it with a dab of clay.

Her studio was an artist's dream, evocative and airy yet set up to sell. Her potter's wheel was behind a glass wall so that customers could watch while she spun vessels out of clay, and there was a little silver bell to ring when you wanted to be waited on at the wraparound counter. The work was that of a skilled artisan. I couldn't believe she'd only started playing at this recently.

I bought a large pot that she had on sale, one that had a flaw in the glaze, but which looked as if it were lighted from within. It was orange-red and reminded me of a Mason jar holding a firefly.

Or perhaps a Marfa light.

CHAPTER SEVEN

The Lieutenant was parked out in front of my hotel on the main drag. Didn't cops go to church? Apparently not, at least not if they were on duty. He was at the corner leaning against his patrol car when I parked on the street.

Without bothering with trivial time-wasters such as "Hello," he approached me, letting me know from his demeanor that he would be talking business. "I couldn't get you on the house phone."

"Yeah, well, I'm not staying there now." I stepped out of the SUV. "I need to give you the cell phone number."

He nodded. "Driving this Navigator with permission?"

My heart sped up. "I'm not sure. I didn't ask. Gil Rousseau originally told me that everything was to be mine, so I started driving it. Is there a problem?"

"Aaron's mother called and tried to report this car stolen, but Gil came on the line and explained that it was actually under his authority and that he'd explicitly given you the keys and granted free use of the car. Still, if I were you, I'd get something in writing from the estate. As I understand it, they're going to dispute, and they seem determined to find problems."

He took down the number of Aaron's cell phone. "Lucky thing I ran into you. Wouldn't want you to get pulled over by somebody just driving a patrol car who didn't know the situation."

"They're already trying to have me arrested?"

"Not too unusual in these kinds of cases. But they called again a few minutes ago and practically ordered me to bring you in on suspicion of murder. I tried to explain to them about setting up a case, but they didn't want to hear that."

My mouth went dry, but I played brave and nonchalant the way the suspects do on "Law and Order." "They're used to having their own way, I think."

"Something like that."

I held out my wrists, playing brave, although I was pudding inside. "So are you going to take me downtown?"

"We're already downtown. The station's just around the corner." He jerked his head toward the end of the block. "But no, there's no official reason at all for that. No one's said that foul play was definitely involved, except for the insistence of the parents and one other citizen." I thought I knew which citizen he meant. "We're still investigating. I would ask that you not leave town for a while."

"I won't be leaving until after the disposal of the estate, or within two weeks when my vacation ends, whichever comes first." Gil had told me the probate would be a one-afternoon deal, that he had all his ducks in a row. He just hadn't realized one of us quackers would be swooped down on by a hawk.

The officer nodded again. I couldn't read his eyes behind those tinted aviator glasses. "Want to take a stroll?" He started down the street towards the minuscule tourist area. I fell into step, wondering whether he was trying to help me or planning to screen me for clues. "So they've got a preliminary report on Beecroft. Originally thought it was natural causes or an overdose, but looks more like an allergic reaction that got out of control, wasn't treated. Seems they suspect there was some kind of toxin that overburdened his system."

For some reason, I thought immediately of that strawberry pitaya Gil had offered me. It had a strong flavor that could mask a bitter elixir. Could that have been easily poisoned? Gil was one of the few people in town with one of the plants, he'd said.

"Apparently he had some alcohol in him and took a trank as well, so it's a dangerous mix."

Tranquilizers and booze? "Aaron hates pills. He never drinks. I mean, drank." I winced. "Not any more. I'm sure of that."

"Maybe not when he was around you." He shrugged. "Interesting thing, though. There's a spider bite on him. The coroner wouldn't have noticed, but it was in an . . . unusual area." He wiggled his fingers as if to imply that I should guess where he meant. "She stumbled on it. It had gone unnoticed by the forensic team during their cursory examination, because it's so high on the inside of his thigh. But it was sufficiently nasty-looking that she excised some of the damaged flesh and put it through chemical analysis. Expected to find the venom of a local spider: there are several that we see all the time. But the lab hasn't been able to get a match with any known spider from around here. Said the sample was loaded with something, though. They've sent it off to some big-city lab they use, but the results will take a while."

A spider bite. Somehow I had known they'd find one. "Venom that they're having trouble identifying. Isn't that"—I searched for a word other than "suspicious"—"fairly odd?"

Again, he shrugged. "The area around Marfa is prime spider country. Tarantulas, brown recluses, black widows, all the old favorites. But the vast majority of spiders don't threaten us, and many can't even penetrate human skin. Venomous spiders that can kill a human are rare—there are only two native to the USA—and their venom is well-known. It was the allergic reaction that probably killed him; he couldn't take it, what with that weak heart. Guy with a heart condition like that, well, a normally nonfatal toxin could overburden his system."

The only problem with that reasoning was that Aaron didn't have a heart condition. I said so.

Max Varga frowned. He flipped a few pages back in his notebook. "Common knowledge around town is that the guy had a weak heart, a valve weakened by childhood rheumatic fever."

"I never knew that." And I didn't believe it.

What I did believe was that Orleans, Aaron's apparent "go-to" booty call, was the girl most likely to have had access to him while he was asleep and vulnerable. And as far as I was concerned, she was also the Girl Most Likely To. If he'd tried to dump her, she might've taken action. Plopping down a hungry Mexican tarantula of the more toxic variety could work without looking like a deliberate killing.

"Does a spider just attack for no reason? Wouldn't it be possible for someone to plant a spider on purpose where you'd startle it and get bitten?"

"Anything's possible." He regarded me, looking amused. "Why would you think of that?"

"There are a couple of people around here who are spider fanciers, that's all. Friends of his. It just seems unusual."

I didn't want to make specific accusations yet.

The detective flicked imaginary dust off his sleeve. "Seems like just an unlucky accident. Lot of spiders around here. Guy was a geocacher. Means he hiked around where there could be snakes, scorpions, other nasties. I see a lot of tourists who get hurt marching around like that in the desert. Common thing."

This seemed to imply that they would close the case for murder pretty soon, unless something came up on the big city toxicology re-screen. Or even if it did.

I bit my lip. My gut said this was murder. But which of Aaron's new cohorts did it, and why? And how would I ever prove anything?

I turned to the detective and stuck out my hand as if to shake. "Well, I appreciate all your help. I'd better get back." To what, I didn't specify.

He looked uncomfortable. "Before you go, I need to take care of a couple of questions."

Columbo must be his hero.

"We still haven't ruled out foul play. This report is only one of the factors that keeps me interested." He spread his hands, unable to speak without gesticulating. "What I'm asking you is just for my report, though, pretty much routine."

"Okay. What did you want to ask me?"

"Well. The parents told me that you should be the major suspect, as you're inheriting. That obviously you'd been in contact with Aaron and had bent him to your will, and/or hypnotized him or brainwashed him."

This was getting serious.

"I've never even been to a single CIA training course."

He blinked. "I'm just telling you what they said. Basically, that he was coerced and made to will everything to you, and then you killed him." He flipped pages in his notebook. "We need to know where you were on Wednesday night."

"In Dallas. Working the phones at my desk until six. I work for Aqualife, the aquarium manufacturer, in their call center. I clock in and out on a time clock, so I can verify my hours. My boss came by late in the afternoon, and she'll probably remember our conversation because I arranged to forward the phones over the weekend." Oops. Now he'd claim I could've forwarded them to my cell phone, because he wouldn't believe I couldn't afford even a "go" phone without a contract. "Then I went home."

He frowned. "Alone?"

"I suppose I was." Had I been with Zoë? "I went to the grocery store one night. I can't really remember."

"Well, see if you can. Do some research, talk to people. Find somebody who can verify your presence with them on Wednesday night between six and midnight."

That was tougher. The days had blurred together since Gil had called on Thursday and I'd left on Friday. Home seemed like a faraway dream, and the weirdness of Marfa a vivid reality. But I vaguely remembered having had a blind date—a "bland" date—on a weeknight. Had it been only this past week? It already seemed a lifetime ago.

Now I hazily, dimly recalled that—if I remembered correctly—I'd gone to Happy Hour to meet this guy Eddie because a mutual friend had set us up. Our mini-date hadn't gone that well: he had left after a couple of drinks, and then I'd belted out a couple of standards at the Karaoke bar for the heck of it before I went home. Could that have been Wednesday? I thought so.

"Wait. Last Wednesday night, I did have a date of sorts. I don't know if he'd even remember me; I think I was more impressed with him than he was with me. But anyway I could call him and see. Or maybe the people at the bar would remember me, because 'New York, New York' requires a solid range of two octaves, and my voice cracked."

He didn't follow suit by cracking any smiles. "Can you check? I really need to confirm where you were."

I envisioned the wheels turning in his head. I could've had a date, then flown here, driven out to the house, offed Aaron, and then reversed the process. But I'd have left quite a paper trail if I'd flown. I couldn't have made the drive all in one evening, and others could confirm that I was at work by nine on Thursday. He couldn't possibly be taking me seriously as a suspect.

Eddie might remember. "I'll get in touch with a few people right away. I appreciate that you didn't drag me into an interrogation room."

He smiled. "No need for that. You're being very cooperative. We're copacetic."

"Copacetic" was an old Air Force term my dad used to use. I hated it. But it meant things were all right. For the moment.

We parted in front of the El Paisano. I needed a place to stay, and if it was good enough for the cast and crew of *Giant*, I could handle it.

§ § §

One step inside the lobby, I walked right into Orleans' trap. She leaped out of a chair, dropping her dilapidated fashion magazine, to crow. "Ha! So Aaron's family threw you out."

She'd heard already?

"I told that silly Gil to forget about you and send you scuttling right back home, but he insists you'll be coming to the funeral." I'd forgotten about that little detail again; it was easier to block it out. "Marisol Rose is picking out the music, and I told them that just for you, they should finish up with Loretta Lynn's 'Women's Prison.'"

Oh, God, I had heard that song accidentally one night on the radio and at first had mistaken it for one of those Irish story songs of heartbreak and wrong, like "Long Black Veil." We were riding in the car, and when Loretta went into that hymn at the end, the same one some idiot had arranged to have sung live at Ricky's memorial service, Zoë had smacked the radio dial so hard I thought she might've broken her little finger, but it ended up with only a stone bruise.

"I have no idea why Gil has glommed on to you like he has." She regarded me as if I were a fish head on rice. Of course, my resemblance to Claudia now made his unusual affinity for me so much clearer.

I tried to step around her, but it ended up as a Don't-Walk Waltz.

Her hands went to her hips. "He's never been too rational when it comes to women. But don't expect anything in return for the booty calls. All dogs are gray when the milk is free."

She had her folksy proverbs mashed up. But I was, for once, struck speechless (I was already dumb), so she went on *sans* challenge.

"If I were you, I'd get the hell outta Dodge. Finish up whatever legal stuff you have to do to release the estate to his family by mail." Who said I was definitely going to release the estate without a fight—and where had she learned about that? "If you don't, this town is going to have to get together and set you straight."

"I am straight. Aren't you?" I walked away, half hating to turn my back on her. But I didn't feel a blade plunging in, and she didn't pursue me further.

I had my answer to Aaron's murder. Orleans did it. A lizard scuttled down my backbone as I peeked into the wall mirror for a glimpse over my shoulder to gauge her reaction, but she'd already disappeared.

Orleans "did" Aaron, in the common parlance. She got him drunk, and he wasn't acclimated to the stuff any more. Then she slipped him a Mickey and dropped her pet spider on him. Somehow urged it to bite. Watched until she was sure he was dead, and then took Spidey home for a celebratory six-pack. The final irony was that she was evidently helping plan his funeral.

Funeral? I could've smacked my forehead. What had I been thinking? From the beginning, I'd known there'd be a service . . . and of course I had to go. Gil—and Aaron—expected it, for sure. But I hadn't thought about it clearly, filtering my visualization of this trip through a hazy screen of Vaseline like one of those 1960s fashion photo shoots.

My little black dress was way too daring; it was a cocktail dress that worked well in the big city, but what had I been thinking? Small towns aren't Dallas. I hadn't packed a single thing that'd be appropriate to wear to a small-town Texas funeral.

Once I got registered and hauled my lack-of-luggage to room 116, I made a few calls back home. The first order of business, even more important than finding a black dress, was to find someone who remembered seeing me in Dallas late Wednesday night.

I phoned around, leaving messages for several people. I got my boss's voicemail, of course. That Eddie guy I'd been out with didn't answer. He probably thought I was going to declare I couldn't live without him, and was avoiding me via Caller ID. There was no point in asking Zoë to testify, as I hadn't been with her, and I didn't want her to lie for me.

It would be interesting to know who Aaron had last been in contact with. Why hadn't I thought of this before? I paged back on Aaron's cell phone to see who he'd called and who had last called him. Good thing it held the last twenty entries. At 10:30 PM on Wednesday evening, I found an incoming call from "Tinkerbell." Tinkerbell?

The number was local. I rang it, but got no answer, not even voice mail.

The last outgoing call he'd made—and this was interesting—had been to good old Gilgamesh at eight PM. The content of that conversation would be interesting. I wished I could replay it as easily as I could go through this call history. I'd have to figure out how to get Gil to tell me about the call without tipping him off that I suspected him of being involved. That I was fishing for—whatever I'm fishing for.

Then I checked in with Cora. "I am <u>such</u> an idiot. I need to ask you another favor," I told her. "I knew perfectly well why I was coming out here. But I got here without a single outfit formal enough to go to—to attend the—um—"

"Aaron's services?" She clucked. "Now, that's only natural. You had your mind on other things, I'm sure. I'd be glad to lend you anything I own. Come on down and let's see what'll fit."

Of course nothing did. Cora was flat as a board and was shaped like a skinny chicken leg. I am curvy on the edge of zaftig and about a foot taller. The closest mall was miles away. Hell, the closest WalMart was in Alpine near Sul Ross University.

"I don't even want to go to his—the funeral." The word crumbled to dust on my tongue. "I shouldn't be imposing on you. This is so stupid."

"Never mind, dear. We're not licked yet. Come on." She traded her fuzzy houseshoes for slip-on Skechers and took me down the hill, weaving among the pack of Airstreams. They were rotund affairs that looked a lot less stable close up than they had from the road, but hidden among them—the campfire at the center of a circle —stood a classic double-wide.

She knocked three times (just like in the song) in rhythm. "Vernette! It's Cora. I need a favor."

The door opened. "You just caught me. I was about to start getting ready for our six o'clock service." Vernette was a raven-haired pale Black Irish lass with freckles, tall and curvy.

"I guessed right," Cora told me smugly. "Looks like she's about your size." To Vernette she added, "This gal needs a dress suitable to wear to Aaron's funeral."

Behind her, a tall, gaunt man—so pale that at first I thought he might be an albino—perched on a rickety futon in his undershirt, arms raised, praying in tongues unknown to me. There was a woman sitting on a folding chair in front of him, and another woman had her hands placed on the first woman's head. "Rictu veem alarata," the man announced in a stentorial tone, as though speaking to a teeming auditorium. His voice carried: he was an orator like those trained by the old-time dramatics and debate teachers.

"My husband, our lead pastor. Hold on, he's in the middle of a special healing." Vernette lowered her voice as we stood watching the action in the living area for a moment. He continued speaking, but I didn't recognize the words. Maybe they were in that unknown tongue the Bible mentions.

"Perseus Ottinger, Preacher Man," Cora's voice said into my ear, so quietly that I wondered if I'd imagined it.

Vernette motioned to us, and we tiptoed past the duo as if an unwarranted noise would break the spell.

Halfway down the length of the trailer, I stopped. This was not a church charity closet I was about to raid. It was Vernette's personal clothes closet. Suddenly I felt absolutely like Oliver Twist, making the fool's pathetic plea of "Please, sir, can I have some more?"

Cora smacked into me from behind. "What's the matter?"

"Maybe I shouldn't presume to borrow. In fact, this was a terrible idea. I have no right to impose on you. Forgive me for coming." And I started to back up, but Cora's toes were in the way.

Vernette grabbed my arms. "Nonsense, child. You have a need, and we are here to fill it. God has put us here to help others who are in need."

At the very end of the hall was an array of what looked like hamster cages and terrariums. Gently she guided me away and into a side alcove, where there was a cubbyhole of a closet. Pressing on a wall-mounted TapLight, she illuminated it and studied the contents. After a moment she pulled out two suitably dark dresses. "I think one of these will be perfect on you."

The first was too severe and a little tight around the ankles. The other was a knee-length charcoal frock of rayon/spandex knit that wasn't cheapie or too clingy, with a demure square neckline and jet beads dotted around on the shoulders like dandruff. Actually, the beads lent a soberly sparkling effect and would put lights in my hair. Long sleeves so no one could claim I was Jezebel. It only came down just below my knees, but I could get opaque black tights at the hotel's little drugstore (assuming they carried tall sizes) and wear my black flat patent Mary Janes.

This could work.

But then if I accepted the loan, that took away my best excuse for skipping out.

I met Vernette's approving eyes in the mirror.

"Are you sure? I mean, I really appreciate your offering me this, but. . ." I gazed into the wavery mirror with all its cracks and crazes. I looked just like Mama in her college graduation photo. That didn't thrill me. However, I'd pass for a decent churchgoing lady, and that was what I needed to do.

Vernette patted me on the back. "The Lord gives us means so's we can help others. The first commandment is love the Lord with all thy heart and all thy soul and all thy mind and all thy strength, but the second is love thy neighbor as thyself, isn't it, hon? Jesus commanded, 'Feed My sheep.' That's what I'm here to do."

As we left, I let horrible guilt wash over me for ever making snide, hipster remarks about "religious fanatics" and "church weirdoes." I was ashamed for prejudging such a large segment of society. And I hated Orleans even more for being so judgmental and nasty about these nice people, who were after all only doing what they believed they were meant to do.

Even if I still privately thought snake handling and poison-guzzling qualified as exceptionally offbeat theology. "Testing God," my mother would call it. Still, they had the right to believe as their hearts led them. Who was I to judge?

Aaron's phone rang. The ringtone was "Wayfaring Stranger."

Gil sounded as if everything was peachy and we'd never had any uproar. "I wanted to touch base with you. We've set the meeting at Hawk's office for tomorrow at ten AM. We couldn't coordinate it for any earlier, because of the holiday." Monday would still be Labor Day, regardless of my personal crisis. "He's coming in special just for us, as the family has asked us to expedite."

"No problem. I wouldn't want to inconvenience anyone." My tone betrayed my irritation with him.

"Ariadne . . . I'm sorry. I really regret the way they're behaving. But there's more to this situation than just a family spat. We need to get the will read and start the process of probate."

"I don't care about inheriting, so long as I get all my stuff back out of the house. I'd like to keep this SUV, if possible. If it's paid off, I mean." I didn't know what would happen if I "inherited" one that was still owed on, although it could be that the estate had money to settle with.

Cora peeled off discreetly with a "I'll see you later" and headed for her house as I padded towards the car, gripping the phone in a stranglehold and pretending it was Gil's neck.

"But—you're entitled." Gil made a noise of exasperation. What was his game? What did he care if I accepted or refused the estate? What was it to him that I didn't know about? My paranoia struck deep.

"As my daddy would say: 'What's it to you, sir?'" Almost instantly I regretted taking a nasty tone with him. I softened a bit. "Tell me something, Gil, just so I won't fall out with shock when I get to the reading. Who would have inherited if I hadn't been around?"

He hemmed and hawed. Finally he came out with the stunner that by now I almost expected. "If you had predeceased him, Aaron's estate would have been liquidated with profits going to the church building fund. We're hoping to put up a new Sunday School building and buy several lots behind the church for future expansion. It's what he thought would be best."

Oh, really. "Nothing at all for his family?"

"A few personal things. There are some individual items named as it is, mostly small trinkets. And his parents get any stocks, bonds, IRA/ROTH accounts, or savings accounts. But the bulk of the estate is willed to you. I think you have a case if you decide to fight."

"It's not in me to fight them. I don't know if I will." A sigh escaped. "Gil, I know this sounds crazy, and God knows I need the money." I winced, but I didn't care any more if he thought I was one of those wicked city women who cursed and took the Lord's name trivially. "But it's not worth it to me. I mean, I don't need that stuff, and they're his blood relatives. I hate fights, and this promises to be drawn-out and painful. Still, I haven't decided for sure." Before he could respond, I added, "I don't want to talk about this any more. At least not right now. Let me think."

"I have to get over to the church for the deacons' meeting and then for the evening service, but we'll be out around sevenish. How about dinner?"

"I have plans." Of course I didn't ,but I didn't feel like seeing him just yet.

He was quiet a moment. "Okay. Well, I'll talk to you later."

After I hung up, I felt guilty about hurting Gil's feelings. At least he'd sounded hurt. He couldn't be that emotionally invested in me already, could he?

And another thing. It had been eating at me all day. Why weren't people saying that they missed Aaron, talking about what a great guy he was, and hugging me with the requisite crying and sniffling? I supposed there'd been a touch of that from Orleans, but everyone else seemed too blasé. Hard-hearted. Philosophical to the point of coldness. Even worse than in that Robert Frost poem about how the ones who aren't dead naturally return to their regular lives.

Maybe Aaron wasn't dead at all. What if this were some elaborate scam? The convoluted setup for an elaborate scheme to rip me off. The only flaw in that reasoning was that no one had yet taken me hostage nor asked me to write a check in order to get the African prince's money out of TimbukThree. Plus, Officer Varga seemed fairly well convinced; typically, they made sure someone was dead before they opened a homicide investigation, didn't they? Still, in my current state of mind I couldn't help feeling majorly suspicious of everyone and everything, especially Gil.

These were crazy thoughts. I was just tired. It'd been a while since I ate, too. I'd be better once I had a hot shower and some more of that Tex-Mex food.

§ § §

Back at the hotel I landed on the bed like a wrung-out rag that'd been used on sixty camels. What I dreaded most was calling to tell Zoë where I was staying. Maybe I wouldn't tell her.

No, I had to. What if she had an emergency and found out by calling everyone in town trying to find me?

I wouldn't put that past her.

But first I took a shower, postponing the run for Mexican food. That potato salad had put my stomach in knots, or maybe the events of the day had. My stomach also advised that I stop procrastinating and call Zoë. With a large helping of put-upon and a good deal of trepidation, I dialed.

My sister was sitting at home watching a telethon and fretting. I could hear Steve Lawrence belting out a ballad in the background.

"Just checking in for the evening." I told Zoë about the spider that had bitten Aaron and how it fit in with some of my suspicions, thinking that would entertain her—as cynical as she was, and as much as she liked to mock my crazy theories—but instead, she fell apart.

Her voice actually trembled. "Leave that to the police. Get your butt back here."

"I can't. There's a lot of family in-fighting, though, and the reading of the will is tomorrow. After that, I'll probably be headed out fairly soon." Assuming that was okay with Max Varga.

"If not, I'll fly out and drag you home by the scruff of your neck. Maybe I should come out there and see what's really going on."

She'd never act on that threat, would she? I didn't need that. "Suit yourself," I said, tempting all the Fates, "but I couldn't leave immediately, anyway. I need to prove I was in Dallas and not out here last Wednesday night."

"What?"

I explained about the little detail of needing an alibi. Oddly enough, the explanation didn't soothe her at all.

"Oh, boy. I can see it now. This jerk you met that night won't remember you, or he'll be kind of vague about the exact times, and they'll point out that he could be lying for you, and you'll say how could he have known he should, and they'll say you called him and told him to cover for you in just this instance, and you'll say that's ridiculous for him to stick his neck out, as y'all hardly know each other." She took a much-needed breath. "And they'll say, 'We can't just take your word for it, lady.'"

I could see how I might have a problem. "Let's not borrow trouble. Maybe I'll hear from Eddie tonight." Easing the laptop out of its case, I discovered a couple of paperbacks that tumbled out with it. Good, some bedtime reading. "I'll be just fine."

"I'm flying out tomorrow." What? The Fates had heard. I should've asked for a pony. "You can pick me up at the airport; I'll call with my flight information as soon as I get it."

"But—" I took a deep breath. "There's really no problem."

"I'll be the judge of that."

I tried to scare her away. "If you're here, you'll have to come to Aaron's—service."

"Hell, no, Airhead. I couldn't do that. You won't ever catch me dead at another one of those, and I mean that literally. When the time comes, just put me in a trash bag and leave me at the curb. What I meant was, I'm coming out there to make sure you don't get railroaded on a murder charge."

"That's not going to happen. It's not like that."

"But it can get like that pretty quick. I can see it's hopeless to reason with you. I'm coming."

My sister has seen too many mystery movies and TV programs.

"Hold off, okay? We go to the lawyer tomorrow. I'll know more then. I'll call you immediately if anything happens that makes me uncomfortable." I took several deep breaths, but it didn't ease the pounding behind my eyes. "Just stay put, and if I need you, I'll call. You don't need to suffer just because I made a blunder."

She wasn't happy, but I knew she was relieved at not having to travel because she hung up very softly.

I didn't even have a nightgown or a change of clothes with me in this room, not counting Vernette's dress. There was that "I Saw the Marfa Lights" tee in the car, but I'd save it for the lawyer's office in the morning, along with these jeans. I didn't want to spend money on James Dean pajamas even if they had them in the gift shop, but I would pick up some pantyhose before the service.

I cracked the laptop and started snooping through Aaron's files.

CHAPTER EIGHT

Aaron told everyone he was writing a book.

But it was really software documentation. For his algorithm.

The text of a promotional brochure I found on his hard drive told the story.

"CRAPPR v.7 is one of the most important pieces of cryptographic software ever written, employing algorithms and techniques never before seen. It provides user-side simplicity for secure E-mail, communications secrecy, user authentication, and data-integrity verification. CRAPPR is a tool for anonymous, secure, and encrypted file sharing and message transfer within a limited pool of private nodes. Users communicate and collaborate in full security, sharing ideas through the chat interface and data through the download system which is hidden under the normal Internet channels."

It sounded good so far.

"Most similar tools boast of RSA encryption"—I knew this was the industry standard encryption algorithm—*"but CRAPPR goes it one better with our proprietary Calty-Patterson modified patched algorithm. It's the most secure P2P—peer-to-peer—connection protocol currently in the development stage. Features include our unique non-RSA public-key cryptosystem that eliminates security risks from symmetric ciphers, the provision of secret public-key facilities to allow high-security scenarios, and encrypted digital signatures to eliminate security risks from cryptographic hash functions (most of which have recently-discovered security issues).*

"Once the project is implemented, users will communicate with only their trusted nodes through the DarkNet"—whatever that was—*"which runs under the surface of the everyday Internet (partial mesh), operating independent of your physical network topology. To be clear, this is not a separate physical network but an application and protocol layer riding on existing networks. Link-level encryption secures links, and public keys are used for authentication. The automatic key distribution security model is primitive at the moment, but is under modification and will be complete when the finished system is delivered."*

Whatever that meant. Apparently, it was weasel-talk explaining that he wasn't qui-i-ite finished converting the model in his mind to a pile of code. The document went on for several pages in this vein, but I could see he still had some editing and fleshing out to do.

I knew a bit about cryptography and in particular about public key encryption because he had insisted that I learn in case I ever needed to use secure communications, but I didn't know anything about constructing the algorithms, except vague hand-waving over buzzwords about multiplying

what's here?" and then a set of what I now understood to be geocaching coordinates.

My heart pinged. If only he'd contacted me some other way—say, by calling Zoë. He knew her phone number and it was still the same, even though my landline and e-mail address had changed when I'd had to move out of our luxurious duplex and into the Casa el Dumpo apartments. Of course he also knew she didn't like him, but hey. She'd have passed along his message to call back or given him my new e-mail address.

Wouldn't she?

I let out a breath as a raspberry and scribbled down the coordinates on a scrap of paper that I stuck into my wallet. Then I copied them with my cursor and went to the GiggleWorld website to look up the location. It was probably the middle of a nearby waterfall or some other cool place he had planned to tempt me with so I'd be eager to come out here. . . .

My room's door opened as if on its own, and I nearly jumped out of my skin.

"Yoo-hoo." Gil walked in, and I recognized him in time to suppress my shriek.

Maybe there was some kind of warning pheromone that he gave off; underneath my spinal-cord startle reflex, I had somehow sensed it was going to be him.

It was always him. Bopping in with a wide grin, as if I were always supposed to be happy to see him. He was like some evil doppelgänger of Elmer Gantry.

I slammed the laptop. Before I could engage my higher editing functions, my mouth let loose with, "Who the hell let you in?"

He looked pretty taken aback. Hurt. Apparently, preachers were kind of like doctors and celebrities in that people never objected to them strolling in whenever, and hotel clerks and nurses' stations pretty much let them have free access. "Clyde, the desk clerk, is a good friend of mine and sings in choir in our church, so he didn't think it would be a problem for me to come on up." An electronic room key waggled in his fingers. His tone conveyed how deeply wounded he was at my outrage.

"I don't much appreciate good old Clyde's attitude." I shoved the laptop under the pillow that I had been using as a lap desk. "I don't like people barging in unannounced. You startled me. I knew I hadn't ordered room service or extra towels."

"I didn't realize I might scare you." He sounded contrite.

But he did scare me, I admitted to myself. Damn this town: everything here conspired to stretch my nerves to the snapping point.

"Most everyone in Marfa still leaves their doors unlocked. Nobody thinks anything of people walking in on them during the day—at least, people they know, especially their good friends." And we <u>were</u> such good friends.

"Just about everybody knows each other here. Of course, you're bound to be more cautious up there in the big city."

I hated his Simple Country Preacher act. "I thought you were still in church."

"We just let out a few minutes ago." His lower lip popped out in a pout. If he'd had a hat, he'd have been kneading the brim and looking down in shame. "I guess I was way out of line, and I apologize. I didn't think. You might've been undressed. But anyhow, you're decent, so we're all right now, aren't we?"

I buried the laptop further—on the off chance he might recognize it, although I knew that was fairly paranoid of me—by pulling the chenille bedspread up as though I were making the bed around my knees. "If you mean I'm dressed, I suppose I am. I've got nothing else to change into except a T-shirt. But seriously, don't do that to me. Never sneak up on people. It makes them crazy."

"I understand. I won't do it again." He looked chastened. "So, anyway, I came to check on you, and tell you that we're scheduled at the lawyer's office at eight in the morning now. We ran the time up early so as not to waste our whole day. Hope that's all right."

I still wasn't ready to make Pax, Truce, King's X. He wasn't going to wriggle off the hook that easily. "You should've called me so I'd know you were on your way over. At least ring me from the front desk. Why didn't you?" I had the feeling he'd been hoping to catch me at something.

"Ari, I just wasn't thinking. I'm pretty stressed coping with those crazy hillbillies. Aaron was nothing like them."

I clucked my tongue in mock-sympathy.

"I know you said you have plans tonight, but they must have been cancelled, because here you are." He smiled, as if letting me know he was on to me there. "I thought I'd come over and offer to take you to dinner as kind of an apology for the way a lot of people have behaved. You didn't really have to get out of the house just because they said so, you know. I'm still in control of the estate as the executor until probate is complete, which will take a while."

"That's all right." I let out a deep breath. "I told you, I'm not tied to the idea of getting all that stuff. In fact, it makes me tired to think of wrangling over it. That's sure not what Aaron wanted." Briefly I wondered, again, why Aaron would stick me with this hassle; he must've known how they'd react. Maybe he thought material goods would make up for what he'd done to hurt me, or he believed that it was the noble thing to do, but really. This was just reopening half-healed wounds.

"So can I at least buy you dinner?" Gil blinked. In this light, he looked like a young Paul Newman. Sort of.

I relented and shooed him out so I could make myself more

presentable. Or at least get reasonably ready for a public viewing.

God! What a choice of words my subconscious had sent up. I wasn't dead yet.

And I definitely wasn't looking forward to having to see Aaron laid out . . . waxy . . . still. . . an effigy. My mouth went dry and I choked on nothing. I knew Aaron no longer inhabited the husk of his physical body, but I was going to have an extremely tough time when That Time came. Especially since the last funeral I'd attended had been my nephew's, and if all of that came rushing back at me, I'd be flying down Main Street like a bat released from an unheated belfry. I could only pray that I'd have the strength to cope.

I zipped the laptop into its case and slipped it back under the pillow. Spreading the covers up over it, I trusted that the "Do Not Disturb" sign would keep the maids from barging in to change the bedclothes.

Like a storm trooper (and feeling almost as determined and pissed), I marched out of the room and almost ran over Gil. He was waiting in the hall, leaning against the wall under a sconce like John Wayne waiting for Maureen O'Hara outside the saloon.

"You're going to love this little hole-in-the-wall." He offered his arm, and we headed out.

I had to wonder. What was Gil's real reason for "checking up on me" like this? I figured maybe he just wanted to be sure I wasn't having dinner with someone else. Though why should he care . . . uh-oh.

Despite the yawning social chasm Gil seemed to sense between Dallas and Marfa, courtship was pretty similar in either place. I couldn't afford to be sending mixed signals. I thought I'd made it clear that I didn't intend to get involved with anyone now. Especially not someone way out here, someone associated with Aaron, someone I couldn't necessarily trust, and whom I could fit into my twisted little puzzle of the possible plot against Aaron. I just wasn't ready to deal with complications. I wasn't that much of a fool. Was I?

Gil gave me that patented weatherbeaten, crinkly-eyed Country Singer look along with his easy smile. *Oh, God.*

§ § §

As we passed the entrance to *Jett's Club*, the James Dean tribute bistro that served as the hotel's main restaurant and bar, I spied Ponyboy headed across the room and hailed him. "So much for running into each other," I said, with that perverse kind of pleasure in being with one guy and flirting with another.

"Actually, I've been kind of tailing you." He grinned to let us know he was kidding. "But I'm glad I caught you. I wonder, since you enjoyed the festival so much, if maybe you'd like to see a real West Texas event. There's a preliminary chili cookoff in Alpine tomorrow afternoon, because of the holiday weekend." He patted his hair, which was another of those flirtatious gestures, according to my studies of body language. "It's not an open event where you'll get all kinds of swill and slop, by the way. You might say this is a Terlingua primary, a rehearsal for the Big Bambu of Texas chili awards. Maybe you'd like to go." He addressed the sort-of-invitation to me.

"I've never been to a chili cookoff, believe it or not."

I imagined I could hear Gil's teeth gritting. "Buck, my boy, that's really nice of you, but she's exhausted. After her journey out here, the festival all day, and these late nights, she needs a day off."

"No, I'm fine," I said.

Gil gripped my upper arm the way my mother used to do in warning, when she didn't want me-the-dumb-child to blurt out one of her secrets. "Well, it's too bad that you really won't be able to make it out there. We'll be busy with the legal stuff tomorrow."

"Surely not all day?" I smiled peaceably. "I mean, the lawyer meeting is at dark-thirty. Let's say it runs from eight to nine, or ten at the latest. Then I have the rest of the day free." I addressed myself to Buck. "So this is a pretty advanced show, among blue-ribboners only?"

Pony grinned, showing his mildly gapped front teeth. That was technically termed a midline diastema, and lots of sexy Englishmen seemed to have it. "They're people who're competing to go to Terlingua for the Texas championship at Tolbert Park in a couple of months. These early rounds narrow the field, and the best entrants garner points. They cook up the exact same prize-winning stuff as they will for the big contest." He squinted one eye in the way guys do when they know they've got you, but just need to reel you in slowly.

"I've always wanted to go to a chili cookoff."

He quirked one wild-haired eyebrow. "Turns out I'd be available to escort you."

"Oh, would you really?" I fluttered my lashes.

"Why not? I'm goin' anyway. Musicians don't turn down free food."

Gil's mouth dropped open. But as I had not been officially invited anywhere as Gil's date tomorrow afternoon, I felt free to take him up on it. "Sure, I'd love to. I want to experience the local flavor, excuse the pun."

"I guarantee you won't be disappointed."

"I know I won't." I was indeed putting on the flirt for Gil's benefit. I didn't know quite why I wanted to yank his chain, but maybe it was because he was just so ever-present and took for granted that my time was all his. And I figured Ponyboy was making the offer partly to irritate Gil, as well. "Come get me when you're ready. I'll probably be back around eleven, at the latest. Is that too early?"

"They start cookin' around seven in the morning, so they'll be able to offer samples startin' around lunchtime. I'll stop by here to pick you up on my way out. Probably noonish. Got a cell number?"

I wrote it on the back of a hotel postcard. He glanced at it and I thought I saw him do a brief double-take. Too late, I realized I had put down Aaron's number and hadn't explained how I came to have the phone.

"Okay, tomorrow, then." He re-tightened the red bandana encircling his head and tossed his hair in a sort of goodbye gesture. A well-known flirtatious gesture, to students of body language. "See you."

I said to Gil, "Close your mouth; there are flies out here. Now, where's this gourmet bistro?"

§ § §

It looked more like a dive to me. The *Mystery Lights Bistro* proved to be a true gem in Marfa's downtown lineup, complete with one of those old-timey large front windows in which was displayed "a genuine meteorite that hit out in the desert in the 1960s" and several handmade pull-toys sitting on top of an antique table. Above the front door hung a rustic "welcome" spelled out in horseshoes. We passed under the lucky sign, but none of the luck spilled out on my head.

"Two?" asked the perky waitress.

Glancing behind me to see whether there were invisible hordes of pookas following us, I nodded.

There were about eight tables. But only two were uninhabited. The patrons ranged from a young couple with a high-chair toddler (currently distributing chunks of banana evenly around the floor) to a foursome of gray-haired seniors. Each table featured flickering votives, fresh flowers, and antique-looking carved wooden chairs. (With no cushions, my tailbone pointed out, but I could manage.)

Gil beamed at the waitress. "I've brought a foreigner here to Marfa's number one culinary delight." I hadn't gotten a good smile out of him yet.

She purred and whipped from behind her back a linen-lined basket loaded with cranberry cornbread and puffy yeast rolls. I knew if I ate more than one of each, I couldn't eat dinner, but it didn't slow me down. Especially when she set down the honey butter.

I ordered the field greens salad, which turned out to be the results of somebody mowing the weeds in the back forty, tossed with lumps of goat cheese, pecans, and watermelon balls. But it was pretty good once I drizzled the Southwestern avocado-ranch dressing on top.

In front of Gil the waitress set a huge slice of pork tenderloin glazed with some kind of sour cherry sauce that I could smell all the way on my side of the table. He offered me a few bites, but I felt as if I were eating off my dad's plate.

No sense not having fun when you can, so I kept the conversation light and even told a couple of my sister's special clean jokes, reserved for just such an occasion as dining with an offended preacher. Gil sulked for a while (though nobody who hadn't seen his usual Merry Sunshine demeanor would even have noticed it), reminding me of a spurned teenager, but eventually he warmed up again and seemed to forget (or at least forgive) my planned outing with his competition.

He leaned back expansively, patting his midsection gently as if checking to see whether the food was really in there. "You know, Ari, I hope you do decide to stay here in Marfa. I mean, to move here and make Aaron's cabin your new home. There's so many things to see and people to do." His grin told me that hadn't been a slip of the tongue, but purposeful wordplay.

Gil put the B back into subtle. By not being subtle at all.

He rested his chin on his linked fingers and gifted me with another of those lingering glances. "You'd be a good neighbor, just like Aaron." His eyelids eased down to half-mast, the classic "bedroom eyes" position.

It was time to play hardball. "Speaking of Aaron. I was looking at the call history on his cell phone, and I discovered that you were the last person he talked to the night he died."

Gil's eyelids shot back up. "I was?"

"You were." At least that had been the last outgoing call. I assumed it had connected. "What did you say to him?"

His fingers twitched as though grasping at nonexistent straws. "I have no idea, Ari." He let out an uncertain chuckle. "Aaron and I used to chat about whatever came to mind."

"But you do remember talking to him."

He allowed as to how he might've talked to Aaron that night, but claimed he didn't even remember doing it, let alone recall the conversation. "We spoke fairly often."

"About?"

His hands flew out to illustrate. "Church activities. People. Whatever was going on. You know."

"And this conversation faded out of your mind, even though he died later that evening?"

"Ari . . . I didn't know when I talked to him that he was about to leave us." He pushed back his hair, that stray forelock that looked, right now, like Aaron's. "I had my mind on other things. Life's not like the movies, where people remember every little detail and recreate entire conversations for their 'memoirs.'"

Funny. I could do that with particular scenes from my life, especially from my childhood, and with certain conversations Aaron and I had held. Vivid snatches of scenes, complete with sound bites, scents, the works. I had always imagined Aaron was at his best when we were together, but how could I know whether I had helped make him the best version of himself that he could be? I couldn't help wondering whether Aaron did find his best life out here, after all.

I was aware that it was unusual, in modern times, for me not to hate

Aaron or resent him for all of his apparent transgressions against me. But, for whatever reason, I only ached over his mistakes. Possibly it was my low self-esteem, the feeling that whatever people do to me, they're justified in doing, or something like that, which is typical of children of alcoholics and survivors of verbal and physical abuse, I am told. Or perhaps when I say I love someone, that's forever and unconditional—it doesn't stop just because we both change. It's eternal. Still, "He turned on me" and "He turned me on" aren't normally isomorphic.

At the end, had Aaron thought of me? Had he received the "Two-Minute Warning" that George Carlin used to talk about, where time was suspended and dilated long enough so he could repent and make peace before the curtain fell between the two worlds? I hoped so. In my heart I knew he was at peace in that better place where I've always believed we end up, even if he was a typically imperfect person. That was just part of being human.

Turned out I wasn't emotionally empty, as I'd thought, because I started crying.

"Aw," Gil said. "It's starting to become real, isn't it? That Aaron's moved on."

He had already moved on when he'd left me behind, but now I had lost him for sure. It was a blessing that the restaurant used cloth napkins, as my nose suddenly needed to be honked.

Gil slid his chair over next to mine, and somehow all at once I was crying on his shoulder. He started patting my back, but in no time his hand was moving in circles that became too much like caresses. "You're so soft," he murmured. "So sweet. We're such a good fit together."

Startled, I pulled away. I wiped my face on the backs of my hands and stammered out, "Oh—I—I'm sorry I—I fell apart like, um, like that. Let's not ruin the evening by saying something stupid."

Undaunted, he started humming that very song, as sung by Frank and Nancy Sinatra. It took me entirely too long to recognize the duet from Zoë's vast collection of "licorice pizzas," otherwise known as "cool wax" or vinyl records. She'd started collecting them at all the thrift stores before anyone realized they should be marked up as usable nostalgia.

"Gil, please." Drying my face on the crumpled napkin (heedless of the nose-blowing), I shook my head. "I'm overwhelmed enough just trying to deal with the problems at hand. I can't deal with this, too. Not right now."

"Sure. All right. I don't want to pressure you or rush you, Ariadne." He reached for my hand, squeezed it, and then released it. That would've been effective on the old me. I'd have fallen "look, sine, and hinker," as the old song goes, for such a demonstration of Sensitivity and Simpatico. I used to be a real sucker for the Alan Alda types. But I'd learned the hard way that surface gloss often served as a useful top layer to hide a much more cunning personality.

Maybe I was being unfair. Gil might really be Mr. Sensitive. But at any rate, I wasn't going to encourage his romantic fantasies any more. "I'm serious. I don't need you putting your expectations or your trip"—I sounded like a hippie, but it was descriptive—"on me."

Gil smiled, but this time it was a gentle smile. More personal and immediate than his preacher-smile, and for once I didn't feel that I was watching his performance at the podium or being talked to by a salesman-slash-tour guide.

He switched on the bass. "You're right. You've been through a lot these past few days. Let's talk about nothing," he said in his basso profundo. They don't call that a "trick baritone" for nothing. "Zip, zilch, nada. *De rien.* Null. The empty set. The set that does not contain itself. And in nothing, is not everything therein contained?"

I could listen to that voice forever. It was something like Aaron's, something like my dad's. A little like that of one of my stage heroes, James Earl Jones. A vibration with molasses in it. Addictive. I considered covering my ears so I couldn't fall under its spell.

"What rhetoric. No wonder you became a preacher." I almost managed a smile myself.

§ § §

After dinner, we walked very slowly down the block. I'd have gone faster, but it was a pleasant temperature out, so I paced him. "Got to let a meal like that sit," he commented as we approached the hotel. "Or, as my kinfolks in East Texas would say, 'set a spell.'"

I was pretty sure he expected me to invite him back to my room. Frankly, I needed comfort and reassurance after all this stress, a release of tension and a reaffirmation that I was going to be fine, and that could often be found in a willing partner's arms, even if you're not deeply in love. So I was tempted.

But encounters like that always complicate matters, and I always end up regretting such impulses. And we had business to transact, so there'd be no walking away and not having to deal with the aftermath. Even though I can be pretty ignorant, I'm not stupid, so I knew better than to make that kind of hormonally-driven mistake.

Usually.

Stopping just inside the lobby, I turned to him. "That was really nice. I enjoyed everything. But now, please respect my privacy and give me space. I'll see you tomorrow morning at the reading."

I wasn't sure how he'd take that. But he didn't press. "I'll call you when I start off in the morning. Do you want me to pick you up?"

"That won't be necessary."

He gave me directions, and it sounded easy enough to find from where I was. "Take care of yourself, Ari. See you tomorrow." He waved bye-

bye and departed.

I entered my chamber and was struck with glumness. Closing the door, I felt that I had narrowly escaped something. Even though I also felt I might've missed out on something good . . . yet it wasn't the place or the time.

I flicked the television into life so I wouldn't be so alone.

§ § §

The meeting at the lawyer's office was even more dismal than I'd expected.

Woodrow Hawk was a kindly, fortyish Native American with silver streaks running through his straight jet-black hair, the ends of which sat on his shoulders. He was good-looking; even his big nose, it occurred to me, added a certain gravitas to his bearing. On the back of one hand he sported a tattoo, maybe some sort of tribal marking, but I couldn't quite make it out.

"We're here today to restate the final wishes of Aaron Leland Beecroft. Now, this isn't anything official. That 'reading of the will' scene you get in B-movies isn't real."

I guessed I had seen too many B movies.

"Texas law states that the executor has five days to mail out a copy of the will to everyone who's in it, and that's generally how it's done. We don't hold a reading unless it's requested in the document itself by the decedent. However, here we do have it stated that Aaron wished for it to be read to his heirs and beneficiaries. So we're complying, and what we're doing here today is part of an attempt for us all to try to get together and cooperate."

Did Texas law require that all interested parties meet face-to-face for a group reading, when requested? Sounded like it. So I had to survive an hour or so in the company of these very strange strangers. And it was getting hot in the little office, despite the cool breeze blowing out of the air vents. I fanned myself and noted that Aaron's mother was doing the same. His dad looked pretty ruddy, but I couldn't tell whether he was sweating or crying.

Mostly I couldn't believe how stupid I'd been over the past week. Coming out here like a young fool for the adventure of picking up my inheritance, indeed. Why hadn't Gil just FedExed me a copy of the will in the first place? Why had I come so eagerly without checking things out?

I cleared my throat. "Excuse me. I have a couple of questions. When the heirs want to dispute the will, probate can't go forward, according to my informal research." What the World Wide Web believed wasn't always strictly accurate, but I'd consulted it last night after I got back from that awkward dinner. "I'd like to say right up front that I don't need everything Aaron had. I'm interested in the car, if possible, and a couple of keepsakes, and then I'm willing to discuss a different distribution." I had in mind one of the many worthy causes, but felt it was tactically sound to let the "enemy" think I was considering their claim. Donations from an estate went pre-tax, whereas if I inherited, I'd first have to pay capital gains taxes off the top. "Can I request that change through an affidavit or whatnot?"

The lawyer looked amused. He straightened a pile of papers on his desk. "Legally, no such *post hoc* negotiation can take place, though I'm sure it happens. More likely it works when the various parties are basically on good terms. On one side, the law says that the intention of the testator must be carried out to the letter. In the eyes of the law, the decedent is a living presence during the probate process. If he wrote in his will that Aunt Flora gets the '63 Chevy, cousin Jimmy the lawnmower, and good buddy Sam the collection of 'Hooters' magazines, that is how things are going to be distributed, no matter how much Jimmy whines about wanting to read all those thought-provoking articles that he dang well remembers his cuz' promised someday would be his."

Hawk had the Simple Country Lawyer schtick down pat. I nodded in confusion.

He chuckled. "Does such an argument get Jimmy anywhere? Not really. He's welcome to present his case to Sam informally, but Sam is under absolutely no obligation to hand over the magazines, leaving Jimmy with a lawnmower for which he'd have no use, since he lives in his pickup truck. It's like any offer to swap: the prospective swappee has every right to say no. And though Aunt Flora could make better use of the lawnmower than the '63 Chevy because she is a far tidier person than Jim or Sam, and already has an '05 Hyundai Sonata, it's out of the court's hands. She'll be the quickest to realize this and will drive that Chevy to the levee as soon as it's legally hers, and sell it for whatever she can get."

"But—all right, assume that I fight this dispute and win. I won't be able to stay here in Marfa more than a couple of weeks, so I need to do this long-distance. I might not have title to the car for a while, but it's my understanding that the executor can allow me use of it, because he controls the estate until the end of probate. And he can pay me back for any expenses I've incurred. Do I understand correctly?"

"I don't know where that 'understanding' came from, Ms. French, but it's off base. Any such arrangement would violate the ethics of the executor, who is for all practical purposes an officer of the court." He shot Gil a stern look. "Until probate is settled, remember, all that property still belongs, in the eyes of the law, to the decedent. Even letting someone use a car, for example, is technically unlawful. Nothing can legally happen until probate closes and the distribution of assets takes place."

Aaron's clan glared at me as if he'd just said I'd cheated at tic-tac-toe and had to take my circle out of the square.

"I'm sorry. I was just trying to—I mean, I only have two weeks to spend here, and I realize that probate might take months."

"The length of probate is affected by many things. Probate judges are sharp people who have usually seen it all. A bunch of hysterical family members might send a chill of apprehension through most of us. But the judge would take the histrionics in stride. Very little could happen that judges haven't seen before." He met my gaze. "By the way. Only family members are heirs; others are beneficiaries of the estate."

"I object," Marisol cried, as if we were in an episode of "Matlock." "To your characterization of us as hysterical and doing historic—histriolic—" She spluttered to a halt.

"Point taken," Hawk said mildly. "Poor choice of words. All I'm trying to say is that judges follow the precedent of the law as set by similar cases decided in the past, and it's all pretty standard. They're not easily swayed by emotional displays. They can't allow themselves to be."

Marisol glared, then looked away, muttering.

The Hawk surveyed the group face by face like the Lion King gazing down upon his people—or a bird of prey surveying the scene to decide which prospects might be the best choice for dinner later. "I am not unsympathetic to the family dispute here." His gaze settled on Matriarch Myra. "I'll work with the other lawyer that you folks mentioned you've retained. But basically, I think you'd be better off to just accept the wishes as stated in the will."

Myra looked as if she wanted to spit. "That's a fraudulent piece of trash."

Hawk shifted in his chair. "Charges of fraud are fairly uncommon. But there needs to be a basis in fact." He leaned forward. "Have you any evidence against this document? Solid, written proof that you could present in court? Rumor and hearsay doesn't count as evidence."

Marisol firecrackered again. "Evidence! Isn't it obvious?" She pointed a claw at me. "She's just a gold-digger who got him to change it, or changed it herself, then killed my brother."

My heart teleported up next to my tonsils and proceeded to pound out a Cherokee rain dance. I gulped air and tried not to show any outward reaction.

Mr. Hawk eyed Marisol. "Careful there, ma'am. Those are pretty serious charges."

Gil reached over and squeezed my hand, but I ripped it free and settled it across my chest, holding it down with the other one. Gil's face told me he got the message.

Hawk frowned. "Throwing around unsubstantiated charges of coercion, not to mention murder, could cost you dearly. I'd advise you to think before you speak." It was his turn to glare at Marisol. "As I said before, the court makes its decisions based on—here we go with this again—provable fact. This document has a provenance known to me. In other words, it was signed and witnessed in front of me, and thus I have reason to believe it should be considered valid."

"Why won't anybody listen to me? Why doesn't some policeman

investigate her?" Marisol was pointing at me again, and undeniably would have burst into those unpronounceable histrionics had Doyle not spoken up.

"Pipe down, girl." Not "daughter," not "Mari." The old man's voice sounded dusty and hollow; it cracked, like a vessel not used for years that had just been filled with hot water. "You'll have your chance to talk about all that. This ain't it."

"I'll remind you only once more," the lawyer intoned, "that any charges you make which turn out to be slanderous and unfounded could cause you financial pain far beyond any benefit you might see from this estate." Hawk waited for her to settle down. After her pointer finger had wilted and curled back into her fist, he continued. "These types of situations typically boil down to a choice between two 'genuine' documents, one bearing a later date than the other. Unless coercion is a provable factor, the will with the latest date always stands. What I'm about to read is a fairly recent document that was filed with this office." He blinked at Myra, whose hat was trembling, feathers and all. "Do you have any competing document?"

"No. But . . . but. . . ." Myra tried to form a coherent sentence, but apparently bluescreened.

"I witnessed this will myself." Gil had found his voice. "Aaron was of sound mind. We hadn't been drinking."

"I should hope not," Marisol managed.

"Aaron really wasn't one to imbibe. Although it isn't expressly forbidden by our faith. It's not encouraged, but." Gil shrugged. "All I'm saying is that neither of us had any alcoholic beverages that night."

"Aaron quit drinking a couple of years ago. Not for any moral reason, but because he said it made people act stupid and wasn't constructive. I mean, he hated to be out of control." Why did I feel a need to get that on record? As with so much that was happening, I wasn't sure what was wise or why I bothered.

"So he didn't see the entertainment value in throwing up. Was that the only area of his life you didn't have time to corrupt?" Marisol shot back.

Hawk stomped on her bow-and-arrows. "I cautioned you not to be contrary. This is your final warning." He looked pointedly at his watch, a beautiful silver face on a beaded turquoise band. "I have another client who'll be arriving pretty soon on an emergency basis, and this is normally a day off, so I suggest we get down to business." He handed around copies and began to read aloud.

The will contained what Gil had told me it did, with a few bequests to each family member—except Marisol.

When she didn't hear her name called, she started frantically paging through the document. "What the hell are you trying to pull?"

Hawk paused. "Excuse me?"

"Don't start something," warned Doyle.

"Where's my inheritance?" Tears formed at the corners of Marisol's beady little eyes.

"I have no control over what's in the document." He raised one hand. "And if there are any more interruptions, I'll have to reschedule, as we're running short on time."

That temporarily silenced the group's foot-shuffling.

After going over the rest of the terms briefly, he stood. "If you have any questions, I need you to hold them and submit them in writing. Right now, I've got to bring this to a close."

With him on his feet, the rest of us couldn't exactly keep sitting there. I got up and found my knees weak. I felt Gil's gaze boring into my back. I turned to head for the door, and our eyes met.

I headed him off at the pass. "I'm going off to taste chili at noon. Until then, I need to be alone for a while."

He nodded, once. The easy smile was gone.

§ § §

Cyberspace soothes me as music the savage breast and booze the savage imbecile. I needed to surf the Web and get happy—not to mention find out some things.

I stomped out into the parking lot fully intending to dig my things out of the SUV, throw the keys into Marisol's cake-trap, and go back to the hotel to surf until Ponyboy showed up. But I couldn't get around town—or even back to the hotel—easily without the SUV, and I didn't feel like hitching rides. Why should I just hand everything over meekly? The cop didn't seem inclined to accuse me of Grand Theft Auto. The lawyer had scolded us, but he didn't seem like the type to call the police on me, or whatever. Surely it wouldn't hurt to keep the car a few more hours, even if it wasn't quite kosher.

Starting the car firmed up my resolve. I tooled out of there as everyone else emerged into the sun, blinking. The important thing was to get away from these people. I'd worry about all the legalities later.

I was somewhere between out of sorts and seriously angry at Gil. Plus, on the terror scale, I'd rank about an Airwick 7. Nerve-wracked and doing everything possible not to think about it. Apparently, Gil had already helped me breach the court's trust (technically), and I could be in trouble for taking the car. If they suspected I'd taken any other things of Aaron's, they'd probably send a posse after me. I could only hope it would be headed up by Willie Nelson and Kinky Friedman.

So I might've "borrowed" a few of my old boyfriend's things for a while. Get over it. And they had no claim on the class ring, really. Did they? I mean, I'd tried it on before now and then. And they definitely didn't buy it for him or pay one cent towards his self-financed education. It wasn't diamond-encrusted or set with shiny opals (only a synthetic blue star sapphire), so I wasn't worried about its value, other than the sentimental.

I needed the laptop so I could investigate, and I couldn't very well take it back if I couldn't even go into the house without navigating Marisol's bulldog fangs, could I? Gil and I needed to work something out. Much as I didn't want to see him, at least for a while, I'd have to call him later tonight. I had to get rid of this car and settle whatever was between us so we could conclude our business. And I still had the entire memorial to get through.

Apparently, I wasn't going to get paid back for the hotel. The last thing I wanted to do was call my sister Zoë and have her wire me funds, but I might have to resort to that. *Shit.*

Hawk had made it clear that I had a perfect legal right to inherit. The law was on my side. Still, I was trying to do what I felt was fair. Doing the right thing. That should get me karma points.

So why couldn't I shake the nagging feeling that this was SO not going to go my way?

§ § §

I had a new theory.

Aaron invented something that made people want to take it away from him because it could be hugely profitable. This could easily have led to his murder.

As long as I had known him, Aaron had been smart and ambitious. His ambitions were focused around his teenhood dream of starting a computer game company. I didn't see how he could do that and still keep out of the grasp of that corporate world he hated so, but I was willing to believe he'd figured out a way to manipulate the suits to his benefit, instead of the reverse. Now he had an algorithm that could be very profitable, and it was likely that he could start any company he wanted with the proceeds. So let's say he was in negotiations to license his Magic Formula (I didn't really understand the nature of the beast, despite the e-mail I had read) when one of the corporate types or another hacker who knew what he'd come up with did him in. Where was the Magic Formula now? Had it died with Aaron?

This was making me crazy. I parked at the hotel, went back up to the room to change, realized I had nothing to change into, and took a quick shower instead. A person could get kind of sweaty and sandy just walking around West Texas, what with that red dirt blowing in the wind.

Pulling on the same old sandy clothes and shoes (shaking them out hadn't helped much), I headed for the street to walk off my anxiety. I always get my best ideas when I'm mobile.

I wasn't hungry, though I had missed breakfast. And last night's salad hadn't stuck to my ribs (even though my ribs weren't yet sticking out). How much chili I'd get to sample this afternoon—or if I could stomach any of it—I didn't know, but I was hoping for something light.

One nice thing I'd noticed about this small town was that no one judged me on my wrinkled, slept-in, filthy clothes. At least they didn't make it obvious if they were, the way they would have in upscale Dallas. Everyone acted like anybody might as well come into the Brown Recluse café and bookshop looking like ten miles of bad road. I felt more like "found on road dead," but I smiled and they served me an egg-ham-and-cheese burrito that would've knocked off any socks I happened to be wearing. The smell alone made me drool.

The place was really kitschy, but felt like home. For a time, I could forget why I was here and just enjoy Marfa's unique appeal.

§ § §

Aaron's cell phone sang out.

"Just thought I would let you know I'm bringing the family back into town," said Gil's voice. "No, we won't be coming by your office this time. We're going to see some of the sights. No need to worry. We'll be home again in about two hours if you need to call us. I hope you can finish that research by tomorrow. Well, keep us posted."

"What?" Then I twigged. Gil was pretending to be talking to someone else—a bit of misdirection for the jerks' benefit. He was signaling me that it would be OK to come get my clothes.

He sailed into the finish line. "Good luck finding those documents. I'm sure you'll have it all taken care of by our next meeting. Take care, now." He hung up without waiting for a reply.

I intended to take care. Good care. Of myself.

Another meeting with the Bickersons, huh. What were they up to now? I finished my coffee and left a generous tip.

In another minute, Cora rang the phone. "The coast is clear. Gil loaded those crumbs into his church's van and he's ferrying them someplace. He winked at me and that's how I knew he's going to be gone a while."

"Thanks. He called. I'll be right over."

"I'll have to go in with you; I have a key he left with us. They've probably got it locked up tight."

They'd more than likely grabbed that hidden key, and any others I didn't know about. "I appreciate it. I would feel strange about going in by myself."

CHAPTER NINE

As soon as we got inside the cabin, I was nearly bowled over by the terrible vibes. The entire place seemed to have changed character. For one thing, it reeked. Aaron's vaguely patchouli personal scent had been replaced by tobacco, okra, and drugstore perfume. I held my nose.

"They don't keep a neat house, do they?" Cora tsked as she ran her gaze over the scattered suitcases and outerwear.

"I hope they haven't harmed the fish." I checked the tanks. Everything was OK, though the discus swam over and stared at me reproachfully.

Could Aaron have invented a radical new encryption system using nanotechnology? Those fish didn't look bioengineered—although that discus looked as if it would like to tell me something, but it just didn't have the required vocal equipment. It spoke, but nothing came out but bubbles, *blub-blub.*

I could definitely relate to how frustrated it must feel.

Making the rounds, I checked the details of each tank—temperature as given by the cling-on thermometers, pH as shown on similar sensors, and the status of the bubble wands, as well as various other vital signs; everything looked copacetic. Strange that there wasn't a lionfish, though. Aaron used to love lionfish in salt water tanks while I hated them, but he always kept at least one. They're lethally poisonous, which was my problem with them, but he claimed they were "fun to watch." Could the Beverly Hillbillies or Flasher Girl have killed one? Taken it out to examine it and let it suffocate? Flushed it?

That empty tank bothered me. "Cora, do you remember what used to be in this? Did he have a hamster? A lizard?" There wasn't a water bottle, so that couldn't be it. And fish didn't live over cedar shavings.

She grimaced. "That thing? Oh, he had a spider in there. It was that woman's idea, I'm sure." Orleans again. "One of hers, no doubt."

"There wasn't anything in here when I arrived."

"No, I reckon she took it out at some point after . . . you know. The church was over here that night as soon as the ambulance left. Philomena called everyone, as is her wont, and we all milled around as if there was something we could do. But since there wasn't any family to minister to and console, we left. She could've taken the thing anytime, and good riddance." Cora shuddered.

Orleans could've used it on Aaron and then gotten rid of it. She could've merely dropped Mr. Arachnid into the sand outside, and her murder weapon would've disappeared, guilt-free, into its own private Tanelorn.

I kind of wanted a recent photo of Aaron for myself, but I didn't see any; none were on the corkboard, which was odd because he'd always liked to tack up his latest shots. Come to think of it, I hadn't yet seen any photos of me in Aaron's house, although Gil had greeted me at the airport by claiming he knew me from my picture. And I knew that Aaron, shutterbug that he was, had several favorite photos of me that he used to display. Did Gil have the photos? Had he taken them for himself before I got here?

That would be more than a little creepy.

In the bedroom, I retrieved my clothes and other detritus. Aaron had a couple of broken-in denim shirts that were right next to where I'd hung my stuff. Could I help it if they sort of fell off the hangers and into my suitcase along with my stuff? A plaid flannel shirt that I'd bought him also found its way into my luggage. They'd come in handy if I stayed here much longer, as the desert can chill down at night.

A woman's scream pierced the air. Cora must've left the front door open. I rushed into the main room to find her frozen near the window. "That wasn't you?" I panted with relief.

She jerked the front curtain aside. A woman was standing in the door of the Airstream down the hill, screaming and flailing her arms.

"Come on," I said without thinking about anything other than needing to help. We ran down the hill and inside the gaping door, past the woman who banged into me as she pelted for the next closest trailer, yelling, "Gathering, immediately! Gathering!"

Inside, the healerman had his hands on someone and was literally shouting.

"Lord, please don't take this blameless innocent," he intoned, this time in language I could understand. "Your servant is so desperately needed here. But if this be Thy will, please help us, Lord, and Thy will and not ours be done," he added in a semi-whisper, apparently out of a sense of obligation.

The woman under his vibrating hands lay prone on their built-in sofa and looked floppy. Her mouth gaped open and her eyes weren't focused.

It was the woman who'd so kindly lent me the dress. His wife.

Cora shouldered me out of the way.

"Vernette!" Cora shouted at her. "Vernette, can you hear me?" She shook the woman's limp foot. Unresponsive.

Someone else shoved me aside from the back. Several people streamed up and surrounded the woman. Soon a circle of the devout stood around the woman, praying and begging God to raise her.

I couldn't take this. It brought back every time that Ricky had a code called in those final days and we'd basically done the same, in our more restrained Episcopalian way. They were asking God to raise her up, the way He did Lazarus, because they knew He could still use her on earth.

But I didn't have a warm fuzzy feeling. Cora backed out of the group at last, after what seemed an eternity of calling on eternity. Taking my arm, she led me outside. "Call 911, dear. They don't have a phone."

I reached into my pocket and dialed.

We heard the church begging, their prayers and beseechments cutting through the faraway sound of the sirens. I knew that prayers are always answered, though the answer is often "wait" and sometimes "yes."

Sometimes God says no.

Through my tears, I noted that from this door, I had a perfect view of anyone coming or going out of Aaron's house, front or back.

§ § §

When the ambulance arrived, the EMTs ran inside and started pounding away, doing their best. Cora looked at me and shook her head. "Come on, dear. We don't need to be in the way."

Buzz met us in their front yard. "What's the ruckus about? I could hear that wailing and gnashing all the way back in my workshop, over the sound of the router."

Cora explained briefly, brushing away a tear as we entered her warm kitchen. "They were in there laying on hands and praying, fully expecting for God to raise her." She'd been baking; pies lined the counter, scenting the air with nutmeg and cinnamon.

"Did the damn—excuse me, blessed fool handle a snake?" Buzz asked.

"Does it matter?" Cora traced the edge of the dinette table with her fingertip. "It's such a shame. That's a real blow to the church, as well."

"They should know better, though. Mark chapter 16, verse 18, doesn't ask you to do that." Buzz shook his head sadly. "Tempt thou not the Lord thy God."

"Please." Cora sank into a dinette chair and stared out the window.

I turned to the ever-practical Buzz. "Was Aaron sympathetic to the group? I mean, they lived so close. Did he know them?"

"He was neighborly." Buzz seemed noncommittal. "I think he'd had a few talks with them, and went over there to see if they could do something about his back once. Don't know if it did any good. They couldn't talk him out of dating crazy women."

That got Cora's attention. She glared at her husband a moment before her sharp birdlike gaze settled on me. "I've been meaning to mention, dear, that you might rethink some of your strategies. Perhaps it's a bit much to be going around town with both Buck Travis and Gil. People might see that as 'dating.'" I could hear the scare quotes around "dating" in her tone.

Did everybody in this town know everything about everyone else? I'd have to be careful not to trip. And it must be a horrendous problem for surreptitious nose-pickers.

I smiled easily (which wasn't easy). "I'm not dating anyone. I have business to finish up with Gil, and Buck was just being neighborly, offering to show me what a chili cookoff is like. We're just spending the afternoon, not the evening."

Cora tsk-tsked, but went on to discuss with Buzz the challenges of handling this latest death as a good neighbor. It seemed to involve hours of baking and casserole-making, exactly as it would've with my mother.

Probably I appeared to them to be picking out a replacement man, seemingly doing comparison shopping between Gil and Ponyboy. And all the while I was actually trying to play one man against the other so I could gain the advantage and learn more. I didn't mind if my field-playing got around town as long as they all retained the impression that I was naïve and trusting. Because I knew better than to start trusting them . . . didn't I?

§ § §

When I got back to the hotel, it wasn't quite twelve. But as I walked into the lobby and was hit by the freezing-cold, fake-lavender-scented air conditioning, Ponyboy dropped his newspaper on a side table and leaped up from the loveseat. He frowned and looked at his watch.

"It's just now noon," I said, knowing I sounded defensive. His *you're-tardy* act put me off a bit, but I was so shaken by the morning's tragedy that I fairly glommed on to his arm. Getting away for a while was going to be such a relief. People having fun, doing happy, normal activities in the sunny fields of midday. No more death, no thoughts of funerals.

He smiled, that Willie Nelson grin again. "Okay, I was just hoping you'd get back sooner. You said eleven."

"I was unavoidably delayed." Not wanting the hotel desk clerk to get an earful—or anyone else who might be lurking around—I pulled him outside. "I think you'll want to hear this."

He had a pickup, a black Dodge Ram complete with Yosemite Sam mud flaps, but it was painted with psychedelic ripples of color to let people know he was a nonconforming free spirit. I wouldn't have been surprised to be climbing into a love-in Volkswagen van from the Seventies, used for hauling the band.

As we drove, I told him what had happened. Tears streamed out of my eyes as I described their attempts to raise the woman. He just kept shaking his head, clucking his tongue, and glancing over at me, with the occasional interjection of, "Man, oh man," or "Jeesh-a-loo." Finally he said, "I guess Orleans was there, too, wasn't she?"

That came out of left field. "No. She wasn't."

"Really?" He tilted his head as if thinking. "I'd have expected you to see her. She's been hanging around there lately. She said the preacher's wife—that same woman—had been trying to evangelize her."

He hadn't mentioned this before. In fact, he'd given me quite the opposite impression. "And she was interested?"

"Don't know. Seen her over there quite a few times lately, though." He seemed contemplative. "If I didn't know better, I'd have thought she was casing the joint." He glanced over at me briefly. "You know, scoping it out. As if to steal something. Only they don't have anything worth stealing. Nothing you could sell, such as computers or MIDI equipment like I've got."

For some reason, he wanted me to believe Orleans was not merely a slut, but a criminal. I decided to reserve judgment on that and picked up on what he'd last mentioned. "You're a computer music type?"

"I have sequencers and synths, yeah. Don't use them when we play festivals, but in the studio I do. Like to fool around with them. Used to do quite a bit of programming myself."

"Oh?" I'd found I could elicit more information from people by being a minimalist than by asking a bunch of pointed questions. Nature hates a vacuum, including any silence in a closed car.

"Yeah. Like a lot of people, I used to work in computers. I burned out."

"Just like me."

He grinned. "I heard about that."

From Aaron? I closed my eyes briefly. But I wasn't going to fill in the blanks for this guy. "Better than fading away. I got laid off just in time. So what made you get out of the rat race and follow your bliss as a musician?"

"In my case, it was a good kick in the butt—involuntary."

"You got laid off?"

"Not exactly." He sounded a little sheepish. "Used to work for The Man in the form of a government contractor with ties to a government agency. Worked in Special Projects for years until I suddenly lost my ticket—my clearance—over some minor infraction."

I lifted one eyebrow.

"Possession of a plastic bag of weed. It happens."

"Yes, it does." It might, but I thought it was pretty irresponsible. Workers with clearances were generally hyper-aware of anything that might endanger that ticket.

"Anyway, turned out it was the best thing that could've happened, as I had my head so far up my butt with all that codemaking and codecracking that I'd forgotten what's real. Code doesn't last. Music does. Have you ever heard of an upgrade that made Hank Williams obsolete?"

"Never will." I smiled. "How about Bob Wills? Hoyt Axton?"

"Well, maybe Hoyt." He grinned back.

"How can you say that? Don't you know he wrote 'Bony Fingers'?"

He laughed. It was unclear whether he had actually ever heard the song, even in the context of a ghost story, but I didn't care.

"His big hit was the one about the bullfrog, Jeremiah—you know, 'Joy to the World.'"

"Big hit for Three Dog Night, you mean."

"That's the version I like."

I had found a kindred soul, soothed by old music. Classic rock. The music of my life—my childhood, anyway. Perhaps we were more alike than I'd realized.

But I'd have to stay on my guard. What other "special projects" did Buck know about?

CHAPTER TEN

The cookoff grounds weren't quite what I had expected.

A wide, weedy field—somebody's back forty, probably—full of milling people in shorts and T-shirts. Tents and booths in a line as far as you could see. And the smell. It was like being inside a bottle of chili powder. Over our heads, banners announced that this event was sanctioned by the premier chili-loving body in Texas, the Chili Appreciation Society International. The general atmosphere reminded me of when I was a teenager and Zoë dragged me down to Willie Nelson's ranch (before he went bankrupt) for the annual family picnic and music festival down near Luckenbach.

"Feast your eyes on the world's most talented chiliheads," Ponyboy said, grandly gesturing. Under each tent were stoves with boiling kettles; stirring the pots were all sizes and shapes of people wearing aprons of chili pepper-printed fabric. And aprons with slogans: "Kick it Up A Notch." "Chili: the national food of Texas." "Fire in the Belly." My favorite was one that several chefs sported, with a picture of a pinto bean with a red circle around it and a line through the circle.

Ponyboy pointed at that one. "Putting beans in chili is a hanging offense here."

"I kind of love beans," I admitted. "Black bean chili."

"Well, it's not chili then. It's bean stew."

I nodded.

"You're not a strict vegetarian, by chance?"

"No. I tried that for a while. But I couldn't keep my weight under control. Otherwise, I'd still be vegging it."

I was inclined to wander, but he wanted to visit every booth that was ready to offer samples, methodically, in order.

Every booth had a theme. Many contestants were dressed to fit the theme.

We started at "Chiliheads with Dreads." The booth's occupants were costumed as chili peppers with green stems on their heads and red dreads hanging down past their shoulders (thanks to their knitted caps), which I thought was fairly creative. They loaded palm-sized cups with samples and handed me one, along with a plastic spork. "Ours is the classic Texas red, but the best version," said the middle-aged cook.

The chili was lumpy but sweet. I guessed a secret ingredient aloud.

"Molasses?"

The contestant simply smiled enigmatically. "I've spent years adjusting the seasonings—not in this particular pot, mind you, but over time I guess I've cooked up hundreds of quarts of chili."

"What's in it?" I examined it more closely. It clung to the spork and didn't run off in threads like thinner canned brands.

"The perfect blend of beef, spices, and sauce to grab the judges by the tastebuds."

I took another bite and diagnosed finely chopped meat; diced vegetables including onions, carrots, tomatoes, and peppers; tomato paste; garlic; chili powder; and cumin. Maybe cinnamon?

"You'll find all kinds of stuff in the pots here, though—usually based on beef or pork, either ground, pulled, or cubed. Sometimes sausage. Occasionally ground turkey or chicken. Some people put wild game—armadillo." He winked. "But we're traditionalists. All 100% Texas-raised, born-and-bred Angus beef."

"I'm relieved to hear this one didn't contain wild game." I shuddered exaggeratedly. "What kind of chile peppers do you use?"

"A blend. There are more than 150 varieties, including chipotle, poblano, jalapeño, and habañero. The heat comes from capsaicin. We use a combination of fresh and dried. Fresh peppers generally taste sharp and clean, while the dried ones lend a rich, roasted-vegetable flavor. We grind our own." He held up a rusty old coffee grinder. "They're all different. Chipotle is really smoky, while Habanero has a sweet citrus undertone."

"If you live through the burning sensation and can still taste anything after that."

The cook smiled. Ponyboy started edging towards the next booth. "Well, thank you," I told the cook. Without thinking, I reached for my purse.

Holding up both palms, the contestant looked morally affronted. "We're pleased to serve up our concoction free of charge to everyone stopping by."

As we headed for the next booth, I asked Ponyboy, "How can they afford to give the stuff away?"

"This is a contest for money, kiddo. Some people have sponsors." He indicated the signs promoting one brand of chili powder or another. "You can win a special award from one of the companies if your recipe ranks high and it uses their stuff. But most people keep their recipes under deep cover."

"Chilly Chili" featured different salsas because the main attraction wasn't ready yet. A frenzied-looking young man, tall and skinny as a pencil, was hunched over the kettle, tossing in spices and glancing around to make sure no competitors could see. I figured that was at least in part an act he was putting on for the crowd. While I was watching that little show, Pony sneaked a fully loaded tortilla chip into my mouth, and my lips accidentally closed around his finger. That was way too personal and not what I would've intended, but a spinal cord reflex is a spinal cord reflex.

To cover, I swallowed the stuff too quickly, which kicked off an amazing bout of hiccups. He signaled the attendants at the booth, and a teenaged girl with her face greasepainted orange—she was apparently dressed as a cheerful tamale—tried to hand me a beer.

Feeling sheepish, I held up my palms. "Can't do it. Not even Oklahoma near-beer. Do you have a non-alcoholic version?"

"Oh, the Dubya special?" She reached for a Buckler's, the stuff the forty-third Prez drinks because he can't handle real booze, either. "That better?"

"Makes me feel more secure," I said, ducking my head and swilling a few mouthfuls to cool off the heat.

The next booth proclaimed, "Hotter'n Hell." The huge black iron cookpot they were using would be more accurately termed a cauldron, and it looked witchy. Double, double, toil, and sausage.

They passed me a sample cup, but the fiery scent knocked me over. Seeing my reluctance to dig in, Buck laughed. He threw the contents of his cup into his mouth all at once. "Man Spontaneously Combusts at Chili Cookoff after Eating Bowl of Hell Fire Chili," he quipped, without even coughing.

"Where angels fear to tread." I managed a weak grin and waved the sample away.

He reached into the pocket of his leather jacket and handed me a roll of Sugar Free Tums.

Before we moved on, Ponyboy bought a small bottle of Frank's red hot sauce to take home. He stuck it in his pocket while I marveled at the ability of mere glass to contain such a solvent.

He cut his gaze at me. "I hope you're not allergic to anything, because the secret ingredients can be pretty arcane."

"I hope you're teasing." I knew some cooks were pouring in beer, some adding wine, usually red wine. But the alcohol, supposedly, would mostly cook out, so I wasn't worried about losing control of the situation if I had a taste or two. "I can guess some potential secret ingredients: Dijon mustard. Cinnamon. Peanut butter. Chocolate." I shook my head. "But if there were anything in this stuff that I was allergic to, I'd already be swelling up like a blueberry."

"Nice image." He winked. "That's what happened to your girlfriend Orleans once. One of her spiders nipped her, she claimed, and within the hour her hand was turning blue and swelling. It didn't look blue to me, honestly, and I told her I thought it was partly in her imagination, but she ran off to the hospital in Alpine anyway. Turned out she'd gotten a thorn from some cactus lodged under her fingernail when she'd been out scouting for spiders, and she was having an allergic reaction to that or somesuch."

"I'd have erred on the side of caution myself." I studied him for a moment. "How did she get so interested in arachnids?"

He didn't stop to figure out the word from context, which hinted to me that I was right to suspect he wasn't just a simple country musician who'd never been out of Palo Pinto county. "Oh, she started out after she'd visited some church out in the country where they handle spiders and snakes as part of the way they show their faith. Even though Scripture says, 'Tempt not the Lord thy God.'" He paused, so I nodded. "Anyway, she got fascinated with spiders and creepy-crawly things." I felt something slithering up my arm, and jumped away. He laughed, showing me that it had been his hand, crawling up my arm like the itsy-bitsy finger "spider" that you use to amuse (or scare) a child. "I take it they're not your favorite hobby."

"I'll stick to fish and cats, thanks. So she keeps those things in cages?"

"Yeah. Has quite a few of them. I don't like to think about how she feeds the things. Word on the street is that when she invites a new boyfriend over, some of 'em get downright terrified and bolt."

"I can well imagine."

A look that I recognized as predatory entered his gaze. "Oh, are you afraid? Because a fear of spiders can indicate a certain type of gender identification confusion. More precisely, a fear of bisexuality. You probably already know that, because of Aaron."

What was he telling me? That Aaron had been, had become, or always was . . . what? It didn't matter, and I didn't want to know. I pasted on a weak smile. "Aaron wasn't afraid of spiders. Neither am I."

He winked. "Right. Big Doctor Freud claimed everybody was bisexual. He also said that spiders can represent your evil, masculine, and angry mother." Shades of Aaron's bitch-mother on wheels. Grasping my arm as if it were his to claim, he elaborated. "Female spiders are more powerful than their mates, and they kill by sucking their mates dry." That was certainly evocative of Myra Beecroft. His eyelashes fluttered coquettishly as he squeezed my hand.

This had to stop. "Like vampires." Pulling my hand free, I said, "I just don't wanna be bitten." I winced inwardly at my unintended double entendre. I needed to change the topic, and fast.

How had that hideous Orleans managed to latch on to Aaron, even as a booty call? He was fairly squeamish himself and hated being tied down, in any sense. Or had he changed? More to the point, had I ever known his true self the way I believed I did?

At the next booth, "King Kamehameha's Hawaiian Concoction" boasted ingredients such as pineapple, coconut, and exotic herbs "that shall remain nameless," said the King with a wink. He was tall and fat, in full battle array, complete with loincloth, crown, and grass-skirted attendants. I didn't dare contradict.

When we walked away with our samples, Ponyboy pulled out the little bottle and used his Frank's RedHot sauce very liberally over it. "I can't stand it. The very idea of piña colada chili!" He made a face and tossed the container after a bite.

I thought it tasted pretty good.

But Three Old Hags' chili was my favorite, not too sweet yet not tongue-burning. There was a kick to it, probably a good dose of cinnamon. The contestants were nice little old ladies who reminded me of my grandmother and aunts, offering their samples atop squares of cornbread. At first bite it seemed tame, but in a moment it proved itself spicier than the Hawaiian cocktail.

As we walked away, my mouth started burning.

"That could be theirs, or the people's before. Sometimes there's a delayed effect." Ponyboy handed me his cornbread, which I stuffed into my gullet to damp the sensation. That worked pretty well.

As the afternoon wore on, we circulated, testing "Cheney's Shotgun Blast," "Hillbilly Fare Chili," and "Hot Rod Top Gun Meld." I feared I'd need to sneak off somewhere to belch. He took my hand, not so possessively this time. It seemed natural as we strolled along, so I just relaxed and enjoyed the attention, trying not to worry about whether it sent the wrong message. I was tired of having to overthink every human reaction and wonder how my every move might look to others; that was too much like my mother's approach to life.

"I heard about the brouhaha over at the cabin," he said conversationally. "Did you get anything of Aaron's before they ran you out?"

"They didn't exactly run me out." His phrasing rankled me a little, and I shook my hand free. "I chose not to cause a bigger scene. And partly because of their awful behavior, I didn't bother to tell them that in my tote, I happened to be carrying Aaron's laptop and GPS unit and a few personal things. Aaron left his things to me, anyway. That bunch is just out for loot, so I don't feel guilty. I'm not sure what I'll fight to keep, if anything."

Now why had all that come out of my mouth when I'd had no earthly reason to blab it to him? I examined the label on my empty beer bottle. There had to be more alcohol in it than the Nutrition Facts admitted to, because if I wasn't a little drunk, I should've been too cagey to answer that at all, let alone truthfully.

The bottle wasn't Buckler's, after all, but the similarly named Burper. I panicked briefly before tossing it into the next trash bin we passed. That was an alcoholic brew. No wonder it had tasted as if they'd milked a diabetic guinea pig. And when I drink, my judgment deserts me. "I think I need something to eat."

He glanced over, grinning. "Don't you know how to enjoy a slight buzz?"

So he'd known all along. Maybe that woman hadn't just grabbed the bottle next to the correct one; maybe he'd sent her a high sign.

Maybe it was time for my paranoia to kick back in.

In the center of the circle of tents were groups of children hanging over portable fences to pat clever little goats at the petting zoo and getting their faces painted with erasable flowers. "Want to try bingo?" He indicated a spot where people were shouting out letters and numbers. "All it takes to get a card is, you donate a fiver to the cause."

I shook my head. "I never win anything and I'm a sore loser."

"All right. Onward." We passed a small stage where a bluegrass trio was setting up to play. I wouldn't have been surprised to see baton twirlers in front of them, tossing the fire batons in an impromptu contest.

At last the booth we'd had to skip earlier started waving people over for a sample. I was full and shook my head as he hurried to get a fistful of the stuff. Finally I followed, mostly so I wouldn't get lost in the crowd.

"Worth waiting for," Ponyboy said. "I tried this last year and it should've won." He tested the contents of his plastic container with one finger and licked in an entirely too erotic motion. "You won't want an entire sample of this one. But I'll give you a taste." He dipped a blue corn chip and thumbed it onto my tongue before I even registered that his hand was approaching my mouth. Embarrassed at the sudden intimacy of the gesture, I turned my head and realized that the fastest socially acceptable way to get rid of the stuff would be to crunch down. The blue corn was nothing special as far as I could tell, but the chili seemed pretty bland.

And then I breathed in. A billion mousetraps simultaneously snapped along the inside of my cheeks, my sinuses erupting in an incredible, painful rush. I felt my eyes bugging out, although that could have been my imagination.

"Magnificent," he murmured through a mouthful. "Have your endorphins kicked in yet?" He appeared mildly stoned. "It's the rush of the capsicum. It gives you a sort of high."

My eyes were watering, but I managed not to whimper. Instead, I grabbed a bottle of spring water out of a galvanized tub of ice that stood nearby and ripped the lid off without even twisting it.

He grabbed my hand before I could splash any water on my swelling tongue. "That's like hosing down a grease fire. Definitely not what you douse it with." Reaching behind the counter at the same booth, he retrieved a pat of butter. "Stick this on your tongue. This, or sour cream, is what the judges use."

"Works on Mexican food." What I actually heard myself articulate was more like, "Wowk um Methkin foob." My tongue slowly started to come to, tingling as the butter molecules coated it. It still felt like a swollen extrusion of dried toothpaste.

"Five-alarm fire?" He sounded a little more sympathetic. "Sorry about that. I figured you'd be somewhat acclimated, you being a native Texan and all."

I nodded, even though I felt like slugging him. My tongue and throat still burned. Sucking in air like a frustrated ex-smoker without a stogie, I managed a raw whisper. "Do you think I could have another? Pat of butter, I mean?"

"I'll go you one better." He bought me a container of plain yogurt from the same vendor, out of a mini-fridge which they apparently kept filled with stuff for emergencies. As all the men (evil, going to Hell, and not soon enough to suit me) looked on and chuckled, I shoveled it in, even though the plain unadorned stuff is fairly bitter, and held it on my tongue and against my scorched palate.

Once I could talk again, I scowled at him. "How do you stand it?"

"Takes a little getting used to, but it's worth it. As soon as the fire is out and I can feel my tongue again, I dive back in. You gotta get on the horse in order to ride."

That was obscure yet suggestive. I sucked down yogurt and kept quiet, but I was through testing chili for the day. Ponyboy was evidently eager to be able to say he'd tried every last one.

Around four the Exalted Grand Chili Judges swept the baton twirlers off the dinky stage to announce the winners. The crowd pressed forward, and we were swept along with it. I got pressed up against Ponyboy, but he was a gentleman and didn't squeeze any of my parts. He got points for that.

The judge had long frizzy blonde hair and a raspy voice like Bette Davis. "We ranked each recipe based on taste, texture, consistency, spice blend, aroma, and color. The winning entries each had a unique attribute that set them apart."

"And enough heat to melt the polar ice caps," I added.

"Civilization's doing a great job of that already," he said into my ear. It tickled.

First place went to HellFire Chili; second to the bastards who'd tried to strip the top five layers of flesh from my throat; and third to my favorites, the Three Old Hags. Ponyboy clapped and hooted in support as the little old ladies scurried forward to get their five-hundred-dollar prize.

"Pretty good for an afternoon of cooking." My palms stung from applauding. "So now they're all finalists who'll get to compete at Terlingua?"

He shook his head. "They don't have the keys to the Jeep quite yet. They've gotta compete in a few more rounds, in other cook-offs all over Texas, and gather up enough points before they can enter. There's a few more weeks until November, so they'll probably all three make it."

What a thrill to spend every weekend tooling around the countryside cooking for strangers. But that was their passion.

As the crowd settled down, the music resumed at a quieter pace with a balladeer who reprised a number of old Western hits from the early 1950s. I popped my last two Tums as we wandered away. "What time is it getting to be?" Zoë was right about my needing to wear a watch. I have several really nice ones, but they make my wrists feel heavy and I'm always afraid I'll scratch the crystal.

"Oh, 'bout beer-thirty." Smiling, he led me south of the stage. "What, you're not tuckered out already?"

I knew where this could be heading. He'd let me know that he was available and that he was attracted. I had tried not to send mixed signals and hoped I hadn't been somewhat of a tease, but I've always believed that a date doesn't mean I owe anyone a make-out session. And right now, I had to do what was right for me.

Affecting an Aunt Fannie Belle drawl like the one he was currently putting on, I said, "I'm afraid I'm plumb worn out, as they say in Luckenbach." I rubbed my stomach.

"Ex-cellent," he said, watching my gesture with approval. "But can you pat your head at the same time?"

"No." I smiled back. "Seriously, I'm tired and I'm too full. My stomach feels like the inside of a corroded school bus exhaust pipe, and I have a metallic taste under my tongue where no taste should be." I hiccuped again, without even having to force it. "All the traveling is catching up with me. I really think I need to go back to the hotel and rest awhile." I seriously felt I should throw up, but I didn't want to damage my esophagus by running that stuff through it again.

He spread his hands and shrugged. "Up to you. I suppose I've seen everything there is to see."

Ponyboy had seen all he was going to get of me, anyway. Even though he was exactly the kind of Bad Boy that I'm always irresistibly drawn to.

Just like his namesake in *The Outsiders*.

§ § §

As he escorted me into the hotel lobby, I got the distinct ESP signal that he was about to assume he could continue right on into my room. I might've caved, but it was mid-afternoon, my stomach was distended, and I was dirty enough already. I needed to change clothes (into what, would be the question) and take yet another shower.

"I need to get out of these clothes and lie down a while." Belatedly I realized how that must've sounded, and turned to him. I met his expression of hopefulness with a firm lip-press. "Alone, I mean. There are a few phone calls I need to make, take care of some business."

My mild hints earlier combined with this firm statement finally switched the seventy-five-watter on over his head. "Yeah, I have some stuff to do, too." This guy's smile seemed genuine, unlike Gil's quick-on-the-trigger upturn of lips. "I'll stop by tomorrow morning. Be in the area."

Did I want to spend another day with him? Too dangerous.

"Let me call you first. I don't know what I'll be doing."

He shrugged. At least he didn't say, "Your loss."

§ § §

As soon as he was out of sight, I had an anxiety attack. I needed to settle down, but even after a cool shower, I was too jittery to sit still. The television irritated me, and the room smelled like that fake lavender disinfectant, which was making me nauseated.

I booted the laptop, but I still couldn't find anything that looked like Aaron's source code. The e-mail messages he'd sent were either cryptic (speaking of that DarkNet and his cool-kids-only algorithm) or depressing. I found a few poems he'd apparently written, but although they were tender and apparently sincere, they were kind of lame. Still, to hear his "voice" that way was bittersweet. The silly poems made me cry.

Slamming the computer closed, I started pacing around the room. I couldn't dwell on what had happened to Aaron and where his source code could be hidden. It was making me a few cashews short of completely nuts.

Remembering the excuse I'd given Ponyboy, I thought of calling my sister. I had a couple of questions I wanted to run past her, anyway. She answered on the first ring.

"Were you expecting me?"

"Call it ESP." She rustled some papers. "Listen, I'm looking here at a map, and I'm wondering. Why didn't you fly into El Paso? That's a larger airport, and it would've been closer."

"No, it wouldn't have. We're 159 miles southwest of Midland/Odessa, but 162 miles southeast of El Paso. So going to El Paso, I'd have overshot and would be backtracking to the east. This was smarter." It occurred to me that Gil might've wanted to have that long drive so we could "get acquainted."

"I guess." She didn't sound convinced. I hoped she wasn't doing any route-plotting for herself. "I've been doing a little research on all of this, and while the church office says Gil the Bamboozler is who he says he is—if that's really his name—I'm not happy with the way this is going."

"You called the church?" That jolted me out of my jitters into a panic. "I can't believe you. I'm a grown-up. I can handle things. That makes it look as if I'm checking up on him."

"I didn't give them my real name. Besides, you are, aren't you?" She grumbled something inaudible. "I can tell you're in no mood for civilized conversation. Shall we go back to our respective activities?"

"Wait—I have a computing question. What's a DarkNet?"

She didn't answer immediately. "What's the context?"

"It's referred to in some of Aaron's e-mails about what he's been working on. Apparently, it's a secret network that rides underneath the Internet. He writes that the one he's going to design and implement will be universally accessible, in theory, and therefore aboveboard; however, no one without the key can read the messages or receive attached files."

"If you know what it is, why are you asking me?"

My sister could be so literal. "I meant, what do you know about them? Have you ever heard of one?"

"Only in passing. I don't understand it, either. The Internet is about free expression and sharing with everybody. What would you use that for?"

"It would be great for intelligence services. You know about numbers stations—encoded messages to operatives sent on shortwave radio channels? Well, this would be more secure and less mistake-prone."

"Uh huh." She sounded as if she'd had no idea what I meant. "Wait a sec. I'm web-searching." After a moment, she read from her screen. "A darknet is a private virtual network that allows users to use public channels to connect only to people they trust. It's a closed group designed for file sharing using the public Internet network and piggybacking on it, but that is inaccessible to Internet users and isn't passing general traffic."

I could have searched for that myself. But I listened.

"In simplistic terms: a darknet will be able to receive data from the Internet, but its nodes will have IP addresses which don't appear in the network lists and which would not answer pings or other inquiries. They can take information from the larger net like Data Motels: data checks in, but nobody can check it back out except the private user with proper authorization and keys." She hmm-mmed. "The beauty of it is, these are file-trading networks that can't be tracked by all the Internet policing agencies and companies. Nice for pirating movies and software and music files."

"According to Aaron's e-mails, it's way more than that."

"Why else would anyone want it?"

"Well, governments and businesses and anyone who has secrets to share with a limited group. Such as, let's say, maybe spies—corporate spies and other kinds of operatives." I told her about the Special Projects folder that was empty or encrypted so that I couldn't find any files in it, even with a downloaded disk zap program.

"Hmm." Zoë sounded thoughtful. "That might be Aaron's ticket, all right. You've heard about what the special interest groups are up to? How they've been trying to figure out how to make people pay for the 'net and track everything you do? They want to require digital signatures, a national Internet driver's license, and so forth. All of that stuff that leads to control of information that should be free. And, of course, next they'll require that you give them your encryption keys, which will let them listen in on anyone's secrets."

"I thought Congress wasn't going to allow that."

She laughed. "Governments, including ours, are not to be trusted. They plan to clamp down on the 'net by instituting a digital Mark of the Beast, a personal crypto-certificate that everyone's going to have to have. It tags every online transaction, letting authorities track exactly who did what, where, and when."

"People will never go for that."

"They will, because the certificate system is going to be portrayed as a cure for spam, fraud, and other Internet annoyances. Instead, it'll be a handy-dandy Big Brother surveillance tool. And so what Aaron is—was—designing would be a way to ride under the existing network and avoid being monitored by Big Brother. Let's call the intelligence community Little Brother, and say he could steal a slice of the pie right out from under the other's watchful glare. It could be really profitable to license this to them, I suppose. Maybe Aaron really was on to something." Her voice lowered. "Do you have the source code, or just the executable?"

"Neither. I'm still trying to find a copy of anything. He'd never be without a backup, so even if I can't get to it on this laptop, there'll be a copy somewhere. At least the source code for the encryption algorithm that was going to hand them all these neat abilities." I peeked out the window; it was still daylight, barely. "If I can figure out where that software is, then maybe I'll know what happened to him and why."

"Stay away from it. I wouldn't want it. That's like saying you want some of this toxin that causes a fatal plague and you're not going to drop it or spill it . . . but you always do. You're clumsy. It's like the acid that eats through all known substances—what are you going to keep it in? No." I heard her moving around the kitchen. "If he was into the Mob or the CIA or whatnot for a few dollars, they might not take kindly to you having that algorithm. Or maybe they're using you to find the code, now that the opposition has killed Aaron. It could be a trap."

She always imagined these wild *Enemy of the State* scenarios. I heard her settling back down at the computer to click a few keys.

"You can't handle this, Airhead. I'm coming out there."

"No!" I couldn't deal with both her and Gil. One at a time was bad enough. "I'll stop looking into it," I lied. "All I want now is to get this over with. This hasn't been the greatest vacation so far. Just let me get Aaron's business wrapped up. I'll have minimal contact with anyone until I can get out of here."

"You'd better." My sister was sounding more and more like our mother. "Be careful, Ari."

§ § §

The desert cooled down as the sun lowered on the horizon. There was no suggestion of a breeze on the sidewalks of this town, though. Even outdoors, I felt claustrophobic.

A walk around the block usually restored my nerves, but something had made me hinky. A circle of the quiet block hadn't worked off my remaining craziness the way it should have. It wasn't just the concern I'd heard in my sister's voice. I had a weird feeling of foreboding, even though there was no particular reason for it.

In the twilight I could smell chili cooking on the breeze (or maybe that scent was stuck in my nose). The main drag was empty, and the quarter moon was already popping into view. I was standing under a streetlight brooding like a rejected hooker when a dark-green car pulled up to the curb next to me.

In a *Taxi Driver* flashback moment, my heart kicked into gear and started to race. Then the driver's electric window quietly lowered, and instead of a menacing De Niro clone, the face of hotshot lawyer Woodrow Hawk peered out.

CHAPTER ELEVEN

"Glad to see you've quit driving that SUV," Hawk said. "But isn't a little dangerous to hang out on street corners after dark?"

I didn't want to admit to still having the car. "Perhaps not as dangerous as talking to strangers who drive up."

"Nonsense. Hop in," Hawk said. "There's somebody I want you to meet."

Briefly I ran through the possibilities for disaster of being kidnapped in plain sight by a lawyer on Main Street and dismissed them as paranoid fears that my sister Zoë had drummed into my head. And had just tried to reinforce. I felt rebellious. "Okay."

Maybe I was a little too easy, but I was also curious. I was still a bundle of live wires, because my glands had poured out the adrenaline usually reserved for encountering a dangerous stranger. As my heart slowed, I circled around the wide front of the low-slung old land yacht—perhaps more like a sleek old WWII battleship—and let myself in the passenger side.

The car could've rolled straight off a showroom floor and into a time machine to be deposited into the twenty-first century. Although it was apparent that someone smoked in the car regularly, the aged leather upholstery was immaculate, and the powerful engine hummed politely. If it hadn't been for its style and its considerable size, I would have thought it was a reproduction, a new collector's car. An indulgence that a successful lawyer could afford.

"This is a cream-puff Oldsmobile Toronado," Hawk said. "1969. Pretty advanced for its day. Front-wheel drive, dual carbs, a big V-8 that'll still leave just about anything else in the dust. Built on the same frame as the Cadillac El Dorado, but a shade lighter and with a bigger power plant. Great lines, too, I've always thought. It's hard to believe it's pushing forty. Actually, it's a little over the crest of that hill, now that I think about it." He smiled with a warmth that seemed genuine. "Of course, it's hard to accept that I am, as well."

"I'm impressed." I returned the smile. "To what do I owe the honor of riding in this classic?"

He adjusted the rear view mirror and checked it before pulling out onto the deserted road. "As I said. There's someone I want you to meet."

"Oh?" I was a minimalist again.

"'Saint Walter Bastanchury. Lives on the outskirts of town, pretty quietly compared to the wild days when he played brass in Vegas show bands. You'd probably recognize his old stage name if you were a collector of classic vinyl." Zoë would. "Or maybe not. I'll leave it up to him as to whether he wants to tell you who he used to be. He likes to keep a low profile, and what's more personal than the name a man chooses to be known by?"

"I couldn't agree more." I supposed he was a saint in nickname only. Lots of musicians get dubbed that.

Hawk twisted the old-fashioned knob of the car's radio; some kind of monotonic chant hissed into life. After trying to make out the words for a moment, I realized I didn't know the language. The rhythmic murmur was strangely soothing.

"It's Navajo. A prayer to the Earth," Hawk said. "I wish more people would heed it. I'll bet you don't understand the words, but the general drift is pretty easy to figure out. Anyway, now one more person is listening to the prayer, and we believe that strengthens the plea."

"Ah. It works that way in my faith, too." At least I thought it did, or if it didn't, it should. "You're Navajo?" I knew that wasn't a tribe native to West Texas.

"Apache. The languages are similar. Related. Like German and Dutch, or Spanish and Italian."

I remembered the Navajo Code Talkers who helped the Allies in World War II, and nodded. "Both in danger of extinction."

"We try to pass the culture along as best we can. The kids today, you know. Aren't interested in anything from last week, let alone last year."

Thunder rumbled in the distance. Either that, or the angels were bowling among the arroyos. I squinted out the windshield at the cloudless sky.

He inclined his head. "Storms'll come up right quick with little warning around here." It wasn't even cloudy, but I knew that could change, and quickly, in this part of Texas. The common wisdom was, "If you don't like the weather, wait a minute."

After a brief silence, Hawk glanced over at me. "Decided what you're going to do about your situation with the inheritance yet?"

"No. I'm stymied."

"Don't know why the man didn't specifically exclude them if he didn't want to burden you with them. Then again, I suppose he wanted to leave them those specific effects, and that was the only way to do it. Except that Marisol—she's not mentioned at all."

"I wonder why." I hoped he heard the sarcasm.

Hawk choked out a faint smoker's cough. "Almost any lawyer will tell you that the smart way to cut someone out of a will is simply not to mention his or her name anywhere in the document. The old saw about leaving your disfavored son a dollar doesn't work well; the mere mention of the kid creates a dilemma about possible typos or misstatements, and it causes a situation in which counterclaims can be made. If she'd been named for a penny, she'd have been legitimized and could grab a chunk of the estate—if she got a good lawyer and had a sympathetic judge."

"I didn't say how—I asked why." When he didn't answer, I asked the other question that was on my mind. "Is this saint we're going to see also a judge?"

"Walter?" He laughed. "No. Far from it. Though I do trust his judgment in a lot of things."

"What does he do?"

"He's retired, in a sense. That doesn't mean he's shut down his brain, though. He knows Marfa better than any man alive—or any woman, either."

I decided to kid him a little. "Is he an expert on the Marfa lights?"

"Believes in them fervently," he allowed with a shrug. "That's his privilege. Doesn't matter to me if someone believes they're aliens, angels, or just jackrabbits with flashlights—that doesn't bother me. He respects my beliefs, so I respect his. I'd better warn you, neither of us is what you'd be likely to figure for a mainstream Christian."

"No need to warn me. I not only sat through my diversity training, but actually understood it. Not only am I into tolerance, but also I've always been curious about other paths. My faith is strong enough that I have no fear of meeting believers in something else." I've always believed that it's all the same God, but I kept that part to myself, as I always do. "I'm part Choctaw myself. One thirty-second, according to my mother." Even if she couldn't be trusted in other respects, I believed her there. "Actually, she gets it confused and says she's one-thirtieth."

He grinned. "That's a neat trick. Maybe she has an extra chromosome hidden in the back pocket of her genes?"

I couldn't help but wince. "Puns are the lowest form of humor."

"Still, you can't help but wonder whether that branch of the family tree forked at all." Pulling a Natural Spirit cigarette from his jacket pocket, he pushed in the Toronado's lighter. He didn't ask if I minded, and I had the feeling I shouldn't speak up.

In the distance, I could see a haze over rocky peaks.

§ § §

Walter's place was a double-wide on a gravel path about two miles off the highway.

Distantly, I thought could see the faintest hint of the Marfa lights—or was that a reflection of the oncoming headlights on the highway?

"Not dark enough yet," Hawk said, a half-smile playing on his lips. "But Walt's place is an ideal viewing station. Better than what the state has set up. You'll see. It's really something." He turned his attention to the rear view mirror.

Lightning flashed in the distance over the Davis Mountains as we navigated the gravel road toward Walter Bastanchury's white mobile home. Yet I never heard any thunder, although I was sitting there counting. Supposedly, the number of seconds between the lightning and the thunder is the number of miles away the strike was, because sound travels more slowly than light. At least that was what I'd always heard.

We were outside Marfa, nearly to Alpine, before I broke the awkward silence that'd settled over us. "Sure is quiet out here."

"Strike you as a little eerie?"

"That's as good a word as any."

Hawk chuckled. There was a dry, cough-like rasping quality to his laugh. He probably had COPD from all that smoking.

As if reading my mind, he said, "I know you're no fan of tobacco. And you're going to be exposed to plenty of it at Bastey's place. Tell you what. I'll buy you a big steak dinner to make up for it."

"You don't have to do that." What was it with men out here, always angling for a date . . . or was I flattering myself again? "I'm more of a Tex-Mex fan, actually."

"There are a lot of great places you'd never find without somebody local to help you out."

"I'm okay." I shifted a little uncomfortably. Surely he wouldn't take me out into the desert, have his way with me, and dump me? No, but then it was kind of dumb to go on this adventure, so I had only myself to blame if something untoward did happen.

Pulling my skirt down over my knee, I checked Aaron's cell phone. A single bar.

We passed the vintner. The sign read, "Luz de Estrella Winery." *Starlight Winery.*

Hawk jerked his head toward the place. "We're nearly there. He's their closest neighbor."

"Must be nice. We can actually grow that kind of grape in Texas?"

"Oh, yeah. In fact, Texas vines saved the French ones a few years back when they got mold in their fields or something—ask Walter; he can tell you all about it. This is what's left of the old Blue Mountain label, including their chief winemaker. Came here from the Hill Country to this more picturesque location, I guess because they wanted mountains instead of hills, and every Friday—weather permitting—they host viewing parties for the Marfa Lights. They've got Cabernet Sauvignon, Shiraz, sauvignon blanc, Viognier, and Gewerztaminer, all made mostly from Texas-grown grapes." I was more interested in hearing about the Lights than about the Juice, but I nodded. "Last thing I bought was a bottle of their 2005 Chenin Blanc, made from grapes grown in the Guadalupe Mountains. Thoroughly enjoyed it. You should pick up a couple of bottles for yourself next time you're out here during the day."

As if I'd ever be out here again.

At last we pulled alongside a white metal mobile home with green shutters and a small concrete stoop.

The flashes of lightning seemed noticeably nearer. I stepped out into the sullen, humid heat left behind by the storm. Our footsteps crunched down unnaturally loud on the same gravel that'd been virtually inaudible inside the Toronado. I scurried along behind Hawk as he used the advantage of his long legs to climb to the front door in a few steps.

He knocked, a simple four or five raps. No secret codes, no fanfare. I heard a grumble of thunder and felt a qualm, an electric alarm inside my chest. Strange, because I usually enjoy storms and find the rumbling soothing—if I'm safely inside. That wasn't why my systems were all on alert, though. Should I really have come all the way out here with a virtual stranger? Not so virtual, I thought; I wasn't safely in cyberspace, but out in the cold cruel physical world.

At first sight, Walter Bastanchury was anything but scary. Around five-nine, with the spare build of a lifelong ectomorph, he was on the far side of seventy. His skin was as wrinkled as a bloodhound's, with similarly outlined jowls, and somehow I knew he was another lifetime smoker. His close-cropped white beard more or less matched his hair, both of which had a faint yellowish tint from nicotine.

"Birdman. Come on in." He had taken long enough to answer the door that I'd gotten even more rattled. My feet seemed glued to the bottom step. "Little lady, c'mon up; I don't bite, or hardly ever, and even then not very hard." He guffawed. "What's your poison?"

Hawk stepped inside. "The usual. Ari French, meet Walter P. Bastanchury. The P is for Pidgeon, or maybe Pervert." To Walter he said, "She's the woman I told you about on the phone."

"I'm not senile yet, Hawk. I remember the conversations we had days ago, let alone hours ago." He twinkled at me. "What'll you have to wet your whistle?"

"Bless you if you have iced tea."

He pulled a huge jug off the kitchen counter. "Sat in the sun all day today brewing. Green tea blend. Good for what ails you."

Both men chose stronger libations, Hawk requesting a pricey single-malt Scotch, Walter pouring himself a wide snifter of something labeled *Rémy Martin XO*.

He gestured towards the back of the trailer. "You'll excuse me for a moment. You don't mind if I smoke?"

"Ah, a true Southern gentleman who actually asks." I couldn't resist. "Haven't you heard smoking's totally out of style? They say it's not good for you."

"Then how come I'm in the best of health at seventy-eight?" He winked and trundled into another room.

I looked questioningly at Hawk. "Why doesn't he just carry his cigarettes in his shirt pocket like you? Or roll them in his sleeve like Fonzie?"

Hawk smiled. "He rolls 'em, all right. You'll see."

The thunder got louder and more insistent. The storm was moving our way. I wondered how safe it was inside a metal trailer during a real Texas boom-crash-flasher.

Walter's living room was orderly and neat, not something I'd have expected from an elderly man living alone. I could tell he didn't have an interior decorator, visiting girlfriend, or even a daughter—at least not one who was trying—because the place reminded me of a dark 1970s-era paneled man cave, the classic "bachelor's study" look. The walls were covered with walnut-stained cabinetry, and all the furniture was old-boys-club dark leather. He didn't lack the upscale electronics: a sleek flat-screen monitor sat on a mahogany desk against the far wall, and over the radiator (if that was what it was) hung a large-screen HDTV.

Hawk noticed me studying things. "He's a solitary old cuss. Has a wolf, too."

I raised my eyebrows. "One of those huge dogs, like a Spitz or a Husky?"

"No, a wolf. A gray timber wolf. It's chained up outside, unless Walter has turned him loose to forage for dinner. He believes, as do I, that we show the land more respect by sticking to its indigenous fauna than by bringing in such monstrosities as Staffordshire Terriers."

Despite his affected diction, which had to be a put-on (or a side effect of the liquor), I wasn't sure whether he was kidding. "Does the wolf come in the house?"

"If Walter gets unwanted company, which sometimes happens, his watch-wolf is up for whatever task he's ordered to carry out." He shrugged. "The wolf is his totem animal. His pet is kind of an avatar for that, when he does his Circle meetings."

I didn't think I wanted to know more, so I merely nodded.

"My totem is pretty obvious." He quirked one eyebrow at me. "A regal bird wheeling in the sky. Guess which."

"The hawk, of course."

He inclined his head to acknowledge that I was correct. "When I commune, Totem Animal comes. He accompanies me on spiritual quests and journeys. I know a lot of things that way, stuff that white men either never cared to know or have forgotten in their greed and rush toward the grave under the impression that wealth will bring happiness. Great Spirit tells me in my heart that the land is being ruined—just as they said in that alarmist film about global warming, we are creating a different planet." He shook his head sadly, and I was reminded of that crying Indian on the old TV litterbug public service message, played by Iron Eyes Cody—who turned out to be a Sicilian actor from Brooklyn. But it was a great commercial.

This was getting weirder.

I wondered whether I should spout something philosophical or just fall back on the trusty old wit of, "Gonna be a gullywasher, ain't it?" But nothing philosophical came to me, and I hated to quote a cliché, so I sat in silence while he apparently mused on what he'd said.

He reached into his pocket and withdrew another Native American "Spirit" brand cigarette. "Sorry if smoke bothers you, but it's going to get a lot worse when Bastey gets back."

I felt my nose wrinkling. I hated to appear a prig or an ultra-straight, but I'd never been a fan of pot. I'd always been inclined to fan it away whenever the smoke at rock concerts curled up into our row where we stood waving our Bic lighters. Hawk was right—the stuff reeked, the stink clung to your hair and clothes (especially denim), and the better the grade, the worse it smelled.

If they were going to claim that Aaron was killed because of a drug deal gone wrong, then it was a smokescreen (I winced inwardly at the pun). I would have to dig deeper to see what everyone was hiding.

Walter ambled back in wearing a childlike, secretive smile. He'd been gone quite a while; maybe his stash was hidden outside. Deep in the blue clay several miles beneath the trailer. I pictured a bricked well going down into the earth's marrow where he could send down a bucket containing a pet toucan trained to retrieve—or, more logically, a set of tongs—and pluck out a handful of cannabis. Reaching for his cognac, he quaffed half of it in one open-throated swallow.

I must've been staring, because he stared back with a loopy grin. "Some people might call me an alcoholic." He seemed to be waiting for me to make some kind of comment.

I took the high road. "If you're asking me, I'm in no position to judge. We all have our temptations. Our addictions." One of mine had been Aaron Beecroft. "Do you consider yourself an alcoholic?"

Walter Bastanchury laughed in a way that reminded me of the 1950s actor Gabby Hayes, one of my dad's childhood favorites. "No, my dear, I don't. I'm not even sure that alcoholics really exist, though I've got more than a few acquaintances who'd fit the generally-established view." He blew out a long cloud of breath. "It's easy to become habituated to alcohol. Pot, too, of course. In my case, my reasons . . . my need to smoke weed is far stronger than any craving I've ever felt for a drink."

"Speaking of condemnation, although we weren't. What would you think of peyote?" Hawk met my gaze levelly. "I'm not a recreational user; it's part of the ritual of my Apache religion. It allows sacred communing. Do you think that's acceptable?"

At last I suspected I knew what they were up to with this cozy tête-a-tête. "Bastey" had expressed a desire for a little proof beyond just Hawk's word that I was cool, or trustworthy, or worthy—or whatever—and that it was safe to tell me whatever it was they needed me to know, so they were running me through an improvised questionnaire. A hippie exam, but an exam.

I've always been really good at tests.

Because I wanted to look sincere—because I was, and I wanted it to come across, not just because I was learning from Gil how to fake sincerity—I cocked my head. "Well, here's the way I see it. I've never heard of much peyote use outside Native American religious ceremonies, at least after the 1960s went up in smoke and everyone stopped reading Carlos Castañeda. Is it okay?" I shrugged. "If it's your religious practice, then it just is. I don't see it as the kind of menace that crack cocaine is, or methamphetamine. Now, if you're asking if I'd ever be interested in trying it, I wouldn't."

His eyes glittered. "Contrary to what the Drug Czar would have you believe, it hasn't turned me into a savage. Yet."

"No, of course not. But it's just not my style. For one thing, I'm too much of a control freak. For another, I've heard that it can bring on vomiting. That alone would keep me from experimenting with it. I hate throwing up."

Walter shot me an amused look. "I know a fellow who vomits if he eats, or even smells, liver."

I grimaced. "I don't eat liver, either."

They laughed. A cannonade of thunder punctuated the sound.

Walter pulled a joint from the palm of his left hand and flicked his Bic lighter to get it going. "You don't know what you're missing."

"Oh, I've got a vague idea." I'd probably get a contact high from sitting in here. I supposed that was the price for their information. Well, it had better be a show-stopper. "Aaron, back in the day, before he joined Gil's church and converted or committed or whatever, wasn't above the occasional toke. I never thought toking and drinking improved him, frankly."

Maybe I wasn't giving Gil enough credit. After all, it seemed that Aaron had become a true straight arrow out here.

Walter lowered himself into his recliner. "Tell me about the Aaron you remember."

Ah, now we were getting somewhere.

What could I say that wouldn't reveal too much of the wrong thing, such as my depth of feeling and its intensity? "He was ambitious. He was one of the best coders I've ever seen; he said that when he thought of a function he wanted to program, lines of code would scroll by on the screen in his mind's eye, and all he had to do was type them in. He also loved debugging."

"Computer stuff of all kinds." Bastey raised his eyebrows.

"Aaron had this gift for math. That's part of what attracted me to him in the first place." I started to sigh, but realized it would give me too much of an involuntary toke, so I turned it into a cough. "I met him right out of college when we both worked at InVerse, a software startup that caught the wave that year."

"He was a standout?"

Aaron was an amazingly fast coder and an enthusiastic game-player who had an office full of math puzzles and those Mensa-sponsored intellectual board games. Hand him Rubik's cube all messed up, and he could whack it into shape in ten twists without even looking. He'd invented an algorithm for MasterMind and kept the game sitting on his desk so he could challenge visitors to a round, or to a game of Go, because he said it was far more interesting than chess. If pressed, though, he had an Alice-in-Wonderland carved wood painted chess set that he'd play you on, and an acrylic three-level chess board he'd picked up years ago at a Trekkie con.

But he wasn't a standout in a gaggle of nerds, not really. Surrounded by geeks at work, I started thinking maybe it wasn't that unusual to be able to integrate by parts in your head. I didn't discover just how unusual that ability was until I became YAB (yet another burnout) and got laid off, and suddenly I'd had to interact with the mundane, non-math-nerd world. It was like Harry Potter getting thrown out of Hogwarts and getting stuck back in the Muggle world.

I shook my head to clear the images. "He was special. Not only was he a computer whiz—a nerd—but he also wanted to be his own boss. He hated working for The Man."

"Were you two compatible?"

I was madly in love. He was the love of my life. The biggest mistake I ever made was not leaving Dallas with him that day, although I couldn't have made any other choice and still lived with myself, because of Ricky. I'll never get over Aaron.

I pretended to consider the question, gazing up and to the right because I'd learned in some corporate team-building class that this was supposed to be the body language for truth-telling. Maybe a little of Gil's sincerity-building was rubbing off. "I thought we were well matched. Until he left, and then stopped contacting me, and finally ran up a bunch of bills on my credit cards. Then I had to do some rethinking." I smiled sadly. "But as you can see, all it took was one phone call from a total stranger to bring me running out here to a place I'd never heard of because something happened to Aaron."

Hawk sipped at his Scotch. "Good."

Another explosion of thunder followed, hard on the heels of a stroboscopic lightning flash. The first patters of rain bounced off the roof. Walter drew deeply from his hand-rolled joint. It must have been Maui Wowie, or whatever the equivalent is nowadays: the odor was nauseating.

I glanced in Hawk's direction. Jokingly, he held up his palm like a cartoon cigar-store Indian statue. "How."

I held up mine. "When?"

He grinned. Then he turned to Walter and smiled beatifically. "So what do you say, Basty? Is this gal to be trusted, or not?"

Walter regarded me. "You've known pain. I can read it in your eyes. And not just Aaron's death, either. Your eyes look ten years older than the rest of you. What are you? Twenty-five?"

"More or less. Actually, a lot more." I managed a ghost of a smile. All my training in body language couldn't keep my lower lip from tensing up in silent acknowledgement of my thirtyness. "But I'm an old soul."

"This'd be easier if you were sixty. But we work with what we're given."

I perched on the edge of an ottoman. "That sounds vaguely religious."

Walter grinned. His teeth were stained and dingy. "Conventional religion plays no part in my life. If it did, I'd have to find a new line of work."

"I thought you were a musician."

"'Were' is the operative word there, missy. That was years ago. Though I did make out pretty good in Vegas for a long time, playing tenor sax."

"Sax is a woodwind, not brass," I murmured in Hawk's general direction. He didn't seem to hear. "Why'd you give that up?" Immediately I regretted asking; it was pretty obvious that he wouldn't have the wind for that wood now.

"I didn't. It gave me up." "Basty" shook his head ruefully. "The day came, as it always does, when my time doing that was over. And I got into something very—different. A pursuit that allowed me to live well, back here where I grew up. However, that's been a while. It was a very different Marfa back then."

Hoping to head off any long, drawn-out reminiscences, interesting as those might be to me in some other context, I held up my palms in surrender. "If you're trying to give me a rationalization for your smoking pot, it's not necessary. I'm not going to judge you. As I told you, Aaron occasionally smoked pot before he came here."

"Aaron bought his pot from me." Walter put my gaze into lockdown with his eyes, which were a washed-out, greyed blue. "And that leads into what I need to tell you, not because it's any of your business, but because it might just help the rest of the story make more sense. But like I told you, you ain't gonna like it much."

Nor was I sure I wanted to hear it. But here I was.

As it moved our way, the thunder seemed to add an octave to its lower register. It reminded me of the booms on Zoë's old Boston Pops record of Tschaikovsky's *1812 Overture*.

Walter reduced the level of cognac in his snifter by almost half in one draught, then palmed another joint out of his sleeve and lit up. "Storm's movin' across to the east."

"Whatever it is you think I won't like, it's all right. If I need to know." I squared my shoulders and resisted the urge to cover my mouth with any old rag I could find to filter the stink. "Whatever you've got to tell me, I can take it."

"You're a witness, Hawk. You heard her." He pointed at the lawyer, then back at me. "But first—to soften the blow, you might say—I need to make a confession about how I live now, how I pay my way. I do believe you're not gonna tell anybody, not that preacher man Gil, not your pal Max Garza." That detective. "And even if I'm wrong, I won't be staying around here long enough for anyone to catch me at anything."

That got Hawk's attention. His eyes opened wider, the brows rising a good inch.

I waited for Walter to continue. He was staring down into the cognac as he swirled it in the glass. Either he was mulling over what he'd just said, or he hoped the liquid would offer up an answer like some impromptu Magic Eight-Ball. Suddenly he looked up. "Hold on a minute. I caught that look, Hawk. You maybe misunderstood me. I'm not saying I'm dying, or anything like that. What I'm doing is planning a move. Very soon."

Hawk's eyes narrowed, his gaze becoming penetrating. "You? Leaving Marfa? I can't see you living any farther away than Valentine."

Walter snorted, sending smoke billowing out, even from, it seemed, his ears. "Goddamn Marfa. It's gotten too yuppiefied for my tastes. That silly-assed imitation Prada store out on the highway; these ripoff restaurants all capitalizing on the fact that James Dean stayed here when they made that movie back in 1955. There's women here who'll bend your ear for an hour, telling you they was in high school back then, and how James Dean kissed them on the cheek. Helluva trivial high point for anybody's life." He shook his head. "We're getting all the Dallas types who ruined Santa Fe, Nancy-boys with more money than sense, and now that Santa Fe's a tourist trap, they've come here to pull the same crap on this area. That's why I want to leave Marfa, Hawk . . . and Miss French, was it?"

He paused again for another good toke. Then he looked straight at Hawk and held the joint aloft. Hawk shook his head, but did get out of his chair to bring back the Scotch bottle and pour a triple shot into his glass. Walter shrugged and sucked enthusiastically on his crooked, twisted-looking doobie.

"So, anyway," he finally said, having gone through that same suck-it-in, hold-it-there, expel-it-noisily routine that I'd seen done by furtive weed smokers under the bleachers in high school. "I'm pulling up stakes. Moving somewhere closer to nature. More rural, you'd probably call it. Kenton, Oklahoma. Wide spot on a road hardly anyone ever travels. Five miles from the Colorado border, out in Cimarron County, the farthest west in the Oklahoma panhandle. It's the only town in Oklahoma that's on Mountain time. You wanna disappear off the face of the earth, that's the place to do it. Freakin' yuppies'd rather puke on their Pucci loafers than stop long enough for a cup of coffee. Won't ruin the place through so-called gentrification." He spat out that last word.

Hawk nodded. "Marfa has the lights and the mystique that comes with them, not to mention fifty-plus years of James Dean legend-making. It was like a pigeon waiting to be plucked. I'm surprised this didn't happen sooner."

"What s'prises me is Marfa hasn't flat-ass blown away by now." Walter's joint had gone out; he puffed away at it to get it going again. It came alive as he pinched it and took a hit. "Damn fine shit. You can take my word for it." He looked at me speculatively. "Now, wait a minute. I know what you're thinking. I don't sell weed for a living. Oh, if you wanted to buy a lid, I could probably accommodate you. But I'm not in the drug game."

He rose to refill his snifter. I heard the downpour running off the roof outside and splashing on the gravel. It was a lot louder under a metal roof. The storm only made me more eager to actually have the man get to the point. It was maddening trying to wait while he went through his hippie routine.

I stood. "Could we get to whatever it was you wanted me to know about Aaron?"

CHAPTER TWELVE

Walter Bastanchury cast a glance at Hawk, who gave an almost imperceptible nod. "Okay. If I can't trust you now, I guess I never will be able to." His chest heaved as he sighed, miraculously without coughing. "I smuggle people. Illegal immigrants. In an old hippie van. I drive to a rendezvous spot and pick them up—and I make sure they have a manila envelope containing the right amount of cash. Well, most of the time I insist on payment." He stared into the distance. "I take these guys to another location—it varies—and hand them off to someone who takes them to the Midwest. It pays well, when it pays—and that's most of the time. It allows me my luxuries, and most of all it allows me to buy top-grade weed, which I really don't believe I can live without any more. And you want to hear the kicker?" He displayed his teeth again. "I can't stand friggin' Mexicans."

What did this have to do with Aaron? I was starting to feel played, as if they were just having fun stringing me along, and more than a little exasperated. "That doesn't surprise me," I said. "Aren't they a cross between the native peoples and the Spaniards? The Apaches' ancestral enemies. For bringing smallpox to America." I tilted my head again. "But helping people across isn't always a bad thing." I didn't want to get into my personal feelings and the legality of it all, but if this is what it took to lead him into his revelations, I could play them right back. "How many generations ago has it been since our forebears floated over in the stinking hold of a Spanish tramp steamer?"

He chuckled. "Okay, you've passed your test, missy. Now, I'm gonna give you one more chance to turn tail and let sleeping dogs lie, and if you insist I go on, don't blame me if you get disillusioned."

"I don't have that many illusions left," I said before I could change my mind.

He finished the cognac in one last gulp. "I know this town pretty well. Better'n most. I knew your boyfr—but wait: tell me, was you and Aaron ever married?"

"No."

Hawk was slumping deeper into his chair, whether to make himself more comfortable or because he was fixing to pass out, I couldn't tell. I wondered what my chances were of getting back to Marfa in one piece.

"Well, maybe that makes this easier. Though you never know," Walter said. "You've prob'ly been asking yourself about who this sister of Aaron's is, that one you didn't know he had. Ain't it odd, don't you think, that he never mentioned her? Assuming you'd met the family and all."

"I met them a couple of times." I took a couple of deep breaths, steeling myself. "Aaron said his family wasn't close. That he was adopted. But he later confessed that'd been a lie; still, he'd fantasized all during childhood that his real parents would come rescue him from those idiots who were raising him. But no one ever came to save him, and he concluded there'd been a mix-up at the hospital that would never be corrected, and by that time he'd resigned himself to being a misfit. He never got along with them, because, well. They were basically dolts. And they still are." I glanced towards Hawk, who had sunk into the chair like a hen settling on her nest. "As I found out for sure earlier today. At any rate, I don't believe that's his sister. I have no idea why they'd be parading her around if she isn't, though. Is that what you wanted to tell me?" I braced myself with a slug of iced tea. Occasionally it became painfully clear why so many people used alcohol as a crutch.

Walter's face contorted into a smirk. "I know who she is."

"You have my full attention." I waited as a deafening blast of thunder rolled across the sky, and at last he spoke again.

"Name's Marisol. Mexican for 'butterfly.'" I wasn't quite sure about that, but let it pass. "She don't look much like Aaron, does she?"

"Nothing at all. That's another reason I had trouble believing she was for real. There's usually some faint family resemblance. The shape of a nose, or how far someone's ears stand out, or whether the lobes are attached or detached. . . ." I shrugged, simultaneously impatient and wishing I'd never gotten into the Toronado.

"Exactly." His face squinched up even more. "Marisol is no more Aaron's sister than Hawk there is my brother. Except in the spiritual sense, of course." He threw Hawk a glance. "No offense."

"None taken," Hawk mumbled, sounding far away.

I crossed my arms as if to squeeze the answer out of the tube. "Who the hell is she, and what's her game?"

Bastey paused for yet another toke off the smoldering, near-dead roach (it really was starting to resemble a squashed bug). My lungs were beginning to burn, and I felt the first throbbings of an impending headache. He held up his hand. "We're getting to that. Now you've heard the good news. Next we need to cover the bad news." His gaze held mine. "It's my understanding that Aaron, um, sort of counted on you to cover the cost of many of his little necessities."

"Luxuries," I corrected him. "When we were getting ready to move out here—before I realized he'd be leaving by himself—I bought some of the larger items you saw him arrive with, including a trailer. Which I haven't seen yet, incidentally." I wondered whether anyone had listed the assets of the estate yet. Surely Hawk had a list. "He had the use of my Visa card, and much to my chagrin he used it much more liberally than I would've liked. But I didn't take legal action, partly because it was going to be so difficult to do. Of course I was being naïve when I kept expecting that once he got settled, I'd be coming out here, so it wouldn't matter, as everything would be shared."

"Texas is a community property state," murmured Hawk from his nest.

"Right, and I thought. . . ." I closed my eyes momentarily. "Well, never mind. When I found out that he was still occasionally resorting to the use of one of my cards, even after we'd stopped communicating, I closed that account. Closed several accounts. But not before they were run up to their limits. He went way overboard, I suppose because he was getting this new start and all. But just because you close an account doesn't mean you don't have to pay, and it has been a struggle for me."

"Why the hell didn't you prosecute again?" Hawk croaked out, more coherently than I'd have expected.

"Didn't have access to a lawyer who'd work *pro bono*, for one thing. Not like you." I couldn't resist the zinger. "I know, everybody thinks that no one sane would decline to prosecute somebody for doing that, although it isn't as simple as you'd think. For one thing, if you succeed, you'll be sending them to prison, and if you love the person, you might not want that." I checked to see whether Walter was listening, and his squinty eyes were still bright. "Years ago, my neighbor's daughter stole her sister's cards and charged them up; the police and the credit companies said she would have to either file charges against the sister or pay it off. At first she said she'd press charges, but her parents pleaded with her, said she'd be ruining her own sister's life over one youthful mistake, and that they would rather pay off the charges themselves than go pay lawyers to create a court record."

Hawk's throat rumbled, but maybe he was just clearing it.

I rolled my eyes to show that I knew how the dilemma must sound to the more hard-hearted and legalistic men. "I suppose you think I'm a fool for not starting to hate him, but I'm not a person who'll just kill anyone who gets in my way"—now, where had that come from?—"and damn the torpedoes without thinking about how my actions might affect the people I care about. Subtleties and sacrifices can be involved." I clamped my lips shut. How big was my mouth?

At least I didn't go into the song-and-dance about how if someone I love hurts me, my first reaction is not to hate them, but to wonder what I've done to deserve it. What I could've done differently to make them love me too much to hurt me again. Often I'd wondered where I went wrong with Aaron. It looked as if I'd lived in a world of delusion and denial. Even I could see it now. Too bad it had taken something this extreme to wake me from my foolishness.

"I hear you," said Walter very seriously. "Believe it or not, I get your

viewpoint." He examined the now-dead roach. Patting down his sh perhaps in search of a roach clip to extend the usefulness of the fragment, he coughed. "I'm not sure, though, that you're aware of jus overboard Aaron went."

I hadn't, in fact, examined my credit report for quite some tin knew that my credit score was lower than room temperature. Like M IQ.

"Did he ever send you any funds to cover the payments, or wha Hawk's voice oozed as from inside an egg.

"No. But he must've thought he could pay me back event because he just kept spending. And since I arrived here, I've discovered apparently he was on to something profitable. I still have no idea what it w but it had already started to make him a lot of money. From what I can t he'd expected even more income in the near future."

"Right." Walter wheezed and began to cough in earnest. He leane over and slid a metal wastebasket next to his chair. The coughing turned into gagging, and he horked up an unspeakable blob, which he spat into the can. Phlegm rattled in his chest.

"Thought you'd hurl for sure that time, buddy." Hawk chuckled. His own respiratory system didn't sound much better.

I was glad I hadn't eaten anything much, because my stomach was turning on the warning lights.

Walter recovered enough to attempt speech. "So anyway, he had you completely snowed. What you didn't know while you were being so charitable, missy, is that Marisol was the new you."

My headache had blossomed and now promised to develop into a three-star throbber. "What does that mean? She and Aaron were having"—I couldn't wrap my mind around this—"an affair?"

"I wouldn't call it that, exactly. You and Aaron hadn't been together for a while."

We'd never officially broken up, but I supposed it might seem to an outsider that we had. Or, as Zoë often pointed out, to any non-insane woman not in denial, it would be obvious that I'd been squeezed like a lime and dumped like a slime. "Point taken."

"Thus it wasn't so much cheating as it was a relationship."

"A relationship? What do you mean?" I said, knowing exactly what he meant. "I don't understand."

He shrugged. "Aaron was lonely. Marisol came to town, she set her cap for him, and nature took its course." He took a tentative hit of a new doobie. It triggered the gag reflex and he went through the wastebasket thing again. I averted my eyes as he tuned a retch into an expulsion of that tapioca pudding-like mucus he kept bringing up. The man obviously suffered from COPD or emphysema. Or both. Or was turning inside-out, slowly.

"You sure you haven't soaked that stuff in some of my barf-inducing :yote?" Hawk laughed, possibly at seeing my grossed-out expression.

One more line like that and I'd be needing that barf-bag. Already I 'asn't far from demanding a drink and some lung-ruining weed to go with it.

Walter dabbed at his mouth with a handkerchief he'd pulled out of his ›ocket, then gestured with it. "Aaron was a free agent. They hooked up like two sides of Velcro, and enjoyed the idea that the town thought they might be sinners. Both of them seemed to have an ambitious streak, hers perhaps less ethical than his. To her, Aaron represented a leg up, maybe even a way out of Marfa. The place ain't to everyone's taste, as I've explained. To Aaron—and I told him he was being naïve about this—it seemed Marisol could give him what comfort and encouragement a woman has to give, at the most basic physical level. Which is all well and good . . . except in cases like this. Men, even the smartest of them, don't always do their thinking with their brains."

Aaron generally tended to overthink things. But in this case, he definitely hadn't wasted any time in thought.

"This is crazy. I've been told that he had a fling with, um, someone else, but that made more sense."

They exchanged knowing glances.

"But this? I don't get it. That . . . woman is at least twenty years older than Aaron. And I don't mean to sound bigoted or cruel, but she must weigh close to twice what he did. Not that it makes any difference, but still, he used to ogle thinner women than me." My hands flew to my temples, where they automatically started massaging, but gave no relief. "I guess my ultimate question is, if he left me, came here, and got together with someone like her, what does that make me?"

I didn't really want an answer. Yet Walter offered one.

"In all the time I've known him, Aaron never said one negative thing about you. Take that for what it's worth, but it's the truth. There were the crazy schemes, the unworkable moneymaking ideas, the dalliance with Claudie that he soon regretted, and, yes, later Marisol. Then there was you, referred to lovingly, respectfully, much as a widower would talk about the late love of his life. Make of that what you will."

I didn't want to make anything. Except my way out of here.

But I still hadn't not heard exactly who Marisol might be or which volcano she crawled out of. "How did you find out who this butterfly—rather, this hole-eating moth—is?"

Hawk's voice rasped to life unexpectedly. "Her name doesn't mean butterfly at all, Bastey. 'Mariposa' is butterfly. 'Marisol' is 'Mary of the Sun.'"

Walter slapped his knee. "You're right, you're right. That reminds me of the old joke. Three foreigners in a bar arguing about whose language is the most beautiful. Englishman allows as to how he thinks 'butterfly' is so descriptive and lovely. The frog—Frenchman—next to him says, "Ah, but

think. So much lovelier is our word 'papillon.' Spanish-speaking gent among them says, 'In my language 'mariposa.'" Everyone nods except the German, who's been listening to all this and looking more and more consternated. Finally he barks out in his guttural voice, 'Und vot iss wronk mit 'schmetterlink?'"

The men went into hysterics. I didn't think it was that funny. And I hadn't gotten any answer to my question. "Why would Aaron's parents go along with her ruse—actually, isn't it fraud? They're defrauding the court and the insurance company by claiming she's a relative. Aren't they?"

Hawk looked thoughtful. "Near as I can tell, they think they'll get sympathy from the court by having this 'sister' who needs the money more than you do. They won't get any lawyer to take the case, especially once he or she finds out it's a fraud. And with the number of people who know or suspect, that won't take too long." He shook his head. "Don't worry about not inheriting. You've got the case won, if they keep down the road they're on. And probably even if they don't."

Oddly enough, that wasn't much of a relief or a joy to me. "Does Max Varga know about this big secret?"

Hawk calmed down with a swill of his swill. "Marisol has already been questioned by the cops." I'd surmised as much, because it had been implied at the will-reading. "I happen to have some friends on the force." Of course. "I suppose I could find out what transpired."

"We all know what 'transpired,' college boy." Walter went into another coughing spell that gave me time to think of a question for him, but I couldn't form a useful one.

It was bad enough that Aaron was involved with Marisol, but also with these two creeps—yeah, that's how I was starting to think of them—and worse that he hung out with them to drink and toke. Of course, who said they weren't lying? But I had a gut feeling they weren't. I couldn't come up with any reason for them to bother fabricating for my benefit.

I supposed that with a lack of the ballet and the symphony, Aaron had to find somewhere to hang out on cold desert nights. But he'd certainly gone wild and taken the crooked path once he'd gotten out from under my influence, it appeared.

Walter recovered. "Those two formed a ying-yangity coupling. What a pair they were as con artists. They even ran a con of sorts on themselves, in order to justify their behavior. Between them they managed to invent their own fictional version of reality, and in this story they decided that you'd done him wrong."

"Excuse me?" Walter wasn't the only one who'd reached the gagging point. "I did HIM wrong?" I could work up a pretty good head of righteous steam over this, but I needed to keep my blood pressure under control. "Here I was making those credit card payments, when all along he apparently could've been paying on them with his own cash, but instead he used that to meet his other urgent material needs. Which apparently included a top-of-the-line SUV, a luxury cabin, and dozens of fish tanks. "And he didn't even try to hide the truth from you? I'd have thought he'd be pretty low-profile about stealing from his ex."

Walter peeled the remains of the last joint apart, re-licked the paper's edge, then re-rolled it without looking up at me, "He didn't spread that part around. But when you get high with somebody on a regular basis, the way Aaron and I did, there's damn little you don't eventually hear about sooner or later. He figured you were still living the dream—rather, the fantasy—of being with him. Whatever charges he ran up, as long as he didn't go wild all at once, you paid them. Like Santa."

My pulse beat redly at the edges of my visual field. Like Rudolph's nose.

"Aaron was well aware that the credit card thing wasn't gonna last much longer. He was a brain, that Aaron. He had a knack for knowing just how far he could push something like that."

"Push someone like me, you mean." And I had a knack for being a complete and total idiot.

He inclined his head kindly. "So he and Marisol, they come up with the idea of getting you a few new credit cards. It wasn't hard. Just had to list you at the cabin's address on a couple of magazine subscriptions and on a few Web page registrations, and boom. Most every day, people get unsolicited offers through the mail. Special deals, a few months at low interest rates, all the tricks the card companies use to get you to apply. All you've got to do is respond to the pre-approved offers." He glanced up at me. His gray-blue eyes were like rounds of beach glass, opaque and unyielding. "As I say, he had a knack of sensing just how far he could go. And he obviously knew you pretty well, or thought he did; he figured as long as you still loved him, you'd forgive a lot."

"That's called being an enabler," said Hawk's voice between glugs of whatever that stuff was.

I thought I had my expression under control. I hated it when I knew I looked like someone people should pity.

Before I could form any reply, Walter made another dive for the wastebasket. Would he last long enough to start over in Kenton, Oklahoma? I wouldn't bet on it.

"Aaron knew your Social Security number, your Dallas address, your birthday, mother's maiden name, and so forth—and he could apply online or by mail, so he never had a problem with the cross-gender theft. Since he didn't care how high the interest rate was, it didn't matter that your credit was somewhat—compromised—by that time, or that they weren't offering the best deals. And he had built-in 'Plan B' safety measures, in case you and your sister, who scared the hell out of him, tracked him down and started asking embarrassing questions."

"My sister scares the hell out of me. I wish she had gotten her hot little hands around his neck." I took a deep breath so I would live to hear the entire story before I hit the floor, twitching. "I suppose Mari-poop was in on the credit cards, too."

"I suppose." His expression was amused. "The way to get around you living in Dallas with an address the card companies could check, of course, was for them to get married. At least that was the way she saw it."

I blinked. "You've lost me."

"Never made any sense to me, either." Hawk hiccuped.

"Hold your breath, Birdy," Walter said to him. To me he continued, "Marisol knew he had a line of credit with you, and she must've known why."

"What was in it for her? Just the money?"

He considered. "She's equal parts neurotic sexual desperation and naked greed, so there's no telling. I'm not sure she saw it the same way Aaron did, but they reached what I suppose you could call détente. She saw the future she wanted within reach, so she didn't let herself think about what it was doing to you. Besides, he told me that he reassured her all the time that as soon as he made his big score, he'd pay you back with interest."

"Well, that was mighty decent of her." My tone could've frozen fireballs. "I still don't see the thread of logic that leads to his avoiding problems by marrying her."

"Neither does anybody, frankly." Bastey's gagging and retching were getting to me. My stomach began to churn. Booze, marijuana, and betrayal combined would play hell with anybody's digestive tract.

Hawk stirred; he was starting to look better, less likely to slip into an alcoholic stupor. He lit a cigarette. The air grew close again.

"I got somewhere I need to be," Bastanchury said. "Business. So let's wrap this up." He seemed fairly coherent, despite the prodigious quantity of booze he'd consumed along with his nonstop marijuana intake.

I'd digested some of what they'd said, despite my stomach woes. "Let's, indeed. Why didn't Aaron just marry her and improve his own credit rating that way?"

"Good thinking. But he couldn't have." He winked. "Marisol was already enjoying connubial bliss with someone else. Theoretically."

"Theoretically married?"

"No, theoretically blissful. She was already married."

"Shit." My hands were trembling as I pushed my hair off my face. The sweat was making it cling to my forehead. "I can't get over all this taking up with married women. He used to criticize idiots who did things like that. Fidelity and loyalty used to be so important to Aaron."

"Were they, now?"

Even I could hear how outlandish I sounded, in light of the current revelations. Why had I loved that man so much, tolerated whatever he wanted to do to me? He'd often compared me to the woman in the Jimi Hendrix song "Little Wing." In the song, there's a line that says, "Take anything you want from me." Well, Aaron had taken that literally.

As Walter took a last pull on his crumpled joint, I realized the storm had run its course. The silence outside was deafening. I eyed Hawk, who seemed to be in a meditative trance. Or passed out.

I raised my hands to my eyes. "The person you're describing . . . this is not the Aaron I knew. It's a total stranger."

"It's the Aaron I knew. By this time, he had something valuable, something that could have made him a very wealthy man. He needed capital, an investor, so he could attract those buyers. That's when he first came up with the idea to get you some more easy credit. Meanwhile, Marisol managed to funnel quite a bit of money to him. I don't know how she managed it or where it came from. Maybe it was her husband's."

Hawk stirred and rallied. "She kept saying she'd gotten a quickie divorce."

"Ex, then. Although that's not what I heard. Anyhow, the guy must've been able to afford it. Never heard that she was under pressure to repay it."

"Why would she cheat on a rich man? Unless he's old and fat." Hawk looked reflective.

I snorted. "Has she looked into a mirror lately?"

Walter smiled sadly. "Well, maybe she has and maybe she hasn't. Women may be picky about their men, but men aren't as selective. There's an old saying about all cats being gray in the dark."

I was familiar with the saying.

"Be that as it may, it's true, as is my need to leave to take care of that business matter, right away." Walter stood, inhaled the last dregs of his bud, and flipped the butt into an ashtray on the coffee table. Hawk and I followed suit, minus the roach-flipping.

For a second, Walter's expression became almost fatherly. He rested his left hand on my shoulder. "I have no proof that Aaron and Marisol actually ever had sex, if that helps. I never saw them in a position that you'd. . . ."

I shook my head to dispel the image that insisted on forming in my mind. "It's all right. He was a free man, after all."

Though I'd been too stubborn to see reality when it smacked me in the face. With a wet, plucked chicken. Over and over.

He gave my shoulder a squeeze. "Why don't y'all go on out on the patio? I'm going to unhook the wolf and give him the run of the trailer while I'm gone. Best for you to be elsewhere. From here, you oughta be able to see the ghost lights pretty good." Turning his wrist, he glanced at his watch. "I imagine it's nice and clear out under the crescent moon."

"If the moon's still out. If the clouds have cleared." Hawk smiled.

"If, if, if." Walter smiled back. "Moon's gone belly-up. That means something or other, but I can't think of it just now."

Hawk headed for the door, and I followed. On the threshold, I turned back. "There's just one more thing. Who was—or is—Marisol married to?"

I knew from the sad smile on his face what he was going to tell me: "I don't know, missy. I honestly don't know."

§ § §

Outside, I took a deep breath of the new air that the storm had blown in. Walter's wrap-around deck sat at the highest point atop the Marfa plateau, and the overlook was grand, as promised.

The thunderstorm had passed over us to the other side of the mountains and river. The air was freshly washed and suffused with ozone, and it seemed I was getting a bit light-headed. But then I could be in a mild state of shock from what I'd learned, as well as having a sort of contact high from Walter's nonstop pot smoking, a headache from Hawk's cigarettes, and a queasy stomach from the pervasive odor of booze. The hint of a chill beneath the humid warmth was a reminder that summer was coming to a close.

As Walter had said, the crescent moon was lying on its back, a configuration Zoë called "holding water." Directly underneath it hung a star, as though suspended by a string.

"I used to think the stars were holes in the firmament," Hawk said in a reflective tone. "That each star was a hole in the sky through which shines the light of Heaven." He leaned over the patio railing. "Doesn't the sky look like a painting tonight? 'Desert Under the Bowl of Darkness.'"

"Or if we stand here long enough to perceive the motion of the skies, perhaps Van Gogh's 'Starry Night.'" I had no sense of direction left. "Which way is southwest?"

"Almost directly in line with where we're standing. We're very close to that government marker on Highway 90."

"Then that red broadcast tower is the place to look."

"More or less. The lights have their moods, you know. Some nights they can be playful, sometimes shy and distant."

"Are they ever aggressive?"

Hawk rubbed his chin. "Sometimes they move in close. But there's never been a story told about them hurting anyone."

I squinted, peering into the almost impenetrable blackness. Then I gasped. Something of a shade I'd call aquamarine—but that most guys would just describe as "bluish-green"—was glowing just out of reach.

"See that?" I whispered to Hawk.

"You mean that ball of fire the color of a wealthy lady's dinner ring?"

Did guys deliberately refuse to learn the names of colors, or was the old joke true, that they could only see sixteen of them anyway, like a cheap video card?

The light seemed to bloom, then began to bounce, as if playing a childhood game.

"Nobody knows what causes the lights," said Hawk. "Maybe they're the ghosts of children who wandered away and got lost. Their parents warned them not to go out into the desert night, but they didn't listen. And now they're trying to answer the calls they hear to come home, but they can't get through the Veil."

A trio of new lights appeared; from where we stood, these seemed farther away. "Blue sapphire," I said.

"Huh?"

"That color."

The lights hopped around before us like choreographed dancers.

"I wonder if they can hear us," he said, continuing his weirded-out speculations. "Come home, Lassie. Come back, Shane."

I almost laughed at his muddled, media-influenced idea of what the lights' names could be. But they must've heard and disliked his wordplay, for they were fading.

The trailer door slammed shut behind us. Walter Bastanchury stationed himself between us. "See that yella one over a little farther west? That's a big mama."

"School-bus orange," I said without thinking.

"Yeah, I guess. Them's the kind that you hear about chasin' the people who're chasing them."

"Chasing them?"

"To find out where the source is. Like finding the end of the rainbow." He paused for a beat. "Awful dark out there, though. I wouldn't do it. But like they say, there's never been anybody hurt by any light. A little shook up, for sure, but that's up to whoever is doin' the chasin'."

I looked Hawk's way: his face was impassive. What was he thinking? Better not to know, I decided.

"Well, I'm outta here," said Walter. "I'll be putting a lot of miles on my van tonight. And what with gas being up to three dollars a gallon, I'm doin' charity work in more ways than one."

As a loyal Texan, I didn't approve of running immigrants across the border illegally, but I didn't wish them any harm. "Be careful," I said.

"I try to be, missy." I had hoped he wouldn't light up another joint, but while his old fifteen-passenger bus skittered through the still-wet gravel, I caught a glimpse of his lighter flaring. As we watched the taillights disappear into the night, I sent up a silent prayer that he wouldn't hit anything or anyone.

I turned my attention back to the southwestern sky, where another trio of lights, more emerald than the earlier ones, performed their synchronized dance before separating and heading away in the general direction of Mexico. "What do you think of the skeptics who say that these are all just reflections of car headlights on that other highway?"

Hawk snorted. "That highway is twenty-four miles away, Ari. And headlights would be moving from left to right, correct?"

I thought a moment. "Yes, because that's how the traffic flows."

"But the ghost lights also move from right to left, which would mean some jackass backing up on Highway 67 at a high rate of speed on a dark night on a treacherous mountain road for long distances." He snorted. "Let me ask you: do those colored lights look like something off a car or a truck?"

They didn't. "Not like headlights, taillights, or fog lights. Not even turn signals. Besides, unless that other highway is a roller coaster that takes thousand-foot jumps, how could you explain those sudden leaps upward?"

"Exact-a-mundo." He waved his hands. "The Air Force used to try convincing people that flying saucers were nothing more than weather balloons. A lot of people bought into that fiction, too."

A single light appeared at horizon level. It seemed yellowish-brown at first, but within seconds it grew in size and brightness. I thought of the mercury vapor streetlights we'd recently had installed by the energy czars back in Renner. They took a moment to reach maximum brightness, too.

I remembered what I had in my tote. Aaron's palm-camcorder. Hadn't the Web pages I read said that some people had successfully taped the lights? And that they showed up a lot better than UFOs?

I pulled the camcorder out. Aaron had a fairly good digital model that fit into my hand. It'd been one of the gadgets I'd swept off his desk into my tote as I made my escape from those gooney birds in the cabin.

The lights were hams. They seemed to know I was recording them for posterity and possibly for CNN, and put on quite a performance. The yellowish-brown one developed pink splotches and became quite striking, putting me in mind of a dragon's egg or some dangerously enticing glass-orb gift left by a fairy. Then a blue ball appeared over the hood of the car and bounced around like one of those "follow the bouncing ball" effects on old children's shows. I could almost hear four-year-olds singing along.

Then the lights seemingly decided to flare with anger at me for taping their antics, and started to recede. All but one large orange globe, which shimmered against the dark night. It got smaller and larger and vibrated from size to size, then bounced up and down as if to beckon us. It began to recede very slowly into the distance. But it appeared to be floating right next to the main highway, moving much more slowly than even the slowest vehicle.

"Let's follow that one," Hawk said, heading down the wooden steps of the deck.

CHAPTER THIRTEEN

"What?" I stared after Hawk as he pounded towards the Toronado.

The wolf inside Walter Bastanchury's trailer howled, loud enough to startle me out of my zoned-out state. The lights had hypnotized me into a sort of half-reverie. The aftereffects of the second-hand pot hadn't helped. My stomach churned again. The chili from earlier was speaking, taking me back to the edge of nausea.

Or maybe the thought of being left alone out here was what had my guts clenching again.

"Hurry up," Hawk said. He was leaning out the Toronado's window, already behind the wheel, looking like a Native hunter on the trail of game. I tried to remember how many slugs of Scotch he'd put away during our visit. It was probably better that I didn't know.

Dust rose from the trail as he gunned the engine and nosed the car forward. I made it into the passenger seat just in time, but didn't quite get my door closed before Hawk pulled out. He slammed it into reverse, whipped the steering wheel around, and jammed the gearshift forward.

"Front-wheel drive," he said. "You'll appreciate that, riding these roads."

He was already taking the so-called road at a speed I never would've dared attempt on desert gravel. Despite the car's soundproofing, I could hear those little stones—souvenirs of floods that happened a few million years ago, if the science types had it right—bouncing off the Oldsmobile's frame.

The light, now a vivid orange, was directly ahead of us. It mocked us, hovering just overhead, then disappearing momentarily only to reappear a foot farther away. It bounced onto the hood, then danced away. But it never went out of sight, remaining a few feet off the road right in front of us, constantly backing up.

Hawk visored his left hand over his forehead. I didn't particularly want him to take either hand off the steering wheel, but the light was so bright that he probably had to shade his eyes to see the road.

I was still taping, though I knew my output was going to look shakier than the *Blair Witch* movie's outtakes. The windshield was speckled with dust and marked with rivulets where the rain had striped its way down through the grime, so I couldn't expect the tape to be broadcast quality. Plus I knew there'd be reflections off the glass. Still, I didn't feel like opening the window and hanging my head and arm out like a golden retriever smelling the air as we raced through the desert night.

Hawk pressed harder on the accelerator. We splashed through a small gully, rocking us and almost making his head smash into the roof. "Slow down," I managed through gritted teeth, checking to be sure my shoulder harness and seat belt were clicked securely into place.

The orange orb—remarkably maintaining its spheroid shape—grew larger. It kept expanding until it seemed huge enough to engulf the car. By the time Hawk caught up with it again, it looked as if it would swallow us.

"Stop chasing it. It's turning on us!" My strangled voice reflected my fear.

"That's an illusion, Ari. The lights don't hurt us."

What Hawk had told me about this car at the outset of our trip came back, and not in the most comforting of ways. This car was a 1969 model. Maybe it was a head-turner back in Marfa, carrying its colorful eccentric from office to restaurant, from the bars to whatever passed for a grocery store. But it wasn't new. How much stress could this metal take? And for how long? Who was to say that some part, something in the steering mechanism, wasn't approaching the breaking point?

He maintained his pressure on the gas pedal. The green behemoth hurtled forward mindlessly. Jouncing across the potholed gravel, we hit another rut in the road, taking another shuddering blow that had us both bouncing half out of our seats.

The ghost light, turning a shade of persimmon that I had always associated with the passage through the birth canal, was almost blinding in its intensity. Orange, flecked with blood-red. Far away, I imagined I could hear screeching.

"Painful labor," muttered Hawk. "She's not going to make it."

"What?" Now he was freaking me out. He was on a trip of his own. "Stop! I don't want to end up a stripe on this highway."

He slammed on the brakes. The retrofitted shoulder harness cut painfully into my ribcage, but I didn't hit the metal dashboard, which was all that counted. After a few moments of back-and-forth, the car rocked to a halt. Hawk opened his door, motioning for me to do the same. "Notice anything?"

Instead of cracking my door—which didn't seem like such a hot idea when there were surely night animals on the prowl—I plunged my palms against the sides of my head. "Now that you mention it, I can't hear out of my right ear. Did I hit my head against the side window?"

"How the hell would I know? I had my hands full, trying to maintain top speed on this miserable excuse for a road."

I looked down to see if my feet were still there. I might need them to walk back to Marfa. If only I had any idea where it was, out there in the windy night.

Hawk stepped out of the car. "Come on."

The light was still there, just out of reach in front of us. Something led me to open the door and slide out of the car. My feet hit the still-warm desert sand.

And then my feet, my cheap shoes, and the sand all around them, began to glow in the same orange hue as the light.

I looked skyward. There it was, complete with stripes and dots of varying hues. It was like staring at Jupiter from arm's length, uncomfortably close. I heard a faint whirring whine in my left ear. From the right, still nothing. A blockage.

"Feel the heat?" Hawk asked.

I was freezing. In answer, I just clutched my sides and shivered.

"Open up. Pay attention. It's not much, but it's coming from the light. Did you ever see anything so awesome?" Hawk's fingers bit into my upper arm. He appeared hypnotized. This was not a good sign.

I tore my gaze away from the apparition and grabbed for the car door, something solid in this world of illusions. "Get back in the car." Legends or no legends, I was getting nervous. Okay, I was afraid of the thing.

To my surprise, Hawk didn't argue. No sooner had I slammed my door and buckled in than he slid into the driver's seat and pressed the gas pedal, as if to reassure himself that the motor was still running.

A shared hallucination. The pot. There must've been something in that iced tea. Still, I didn't feel like hanging around. "Back up. Get back on the road going the other way."

He seemed spellbound again. The two of us in the car and the pulsing, bloodstone-orange light hovering above faced each other as if at a cosmic impasse. Hawk slid the shift lever forward. Into *Drive.*

"Back up," I said again. "Pay attention."

"Passionate attention," he mumbled. "Don't you see? We're so close."

"Too damn close." My heart began to race in earnest.

Gently, he punched the accelerator. The light moved with us, but it seemed to me that the space between us and the light gradually diminished. The light was holding its ground.

I glanced over at him. His forehead was beaded with sweat, and his shirt clung to his chest. "Do you feel things heating up?" he breathed out. "It's the light."

"I'm not hot. It's freezing." I was shivering, despite the car's thermometer's claim that it was still warm in the desert. I thought deserts cooled off at night.

We were going forward now, a little bit faster. The light pulsated, as though taking one step forward, two steps back.

He sounded like a narrator from some crazy SF movie. "What are they? Baby stars?"

I looked at him, then frontward again. And I screamed. It was obvious to me that the light—a star, a UFO, or whatever it was—was headed straight for us. About to smack right into us.

His voice was hypnotic. "There's no documented case of a Marfa Light hurting anyone. They've helped people. Remember the man who was hopelessly lost in the blizzard, and the light led him to a cave where he survived the night."

"This one's not leading. It's advancing."

He performed an exaggerated headshake, as if he thought it would clear his mind. All that Scotch had definitely had its effect. "Maybe you're right. Maybe we shouldn't challenge it." Suddenly he pulled the wheel to the left, turning us away from the orange light. It hovered, as though wondering what our next move would be. "Like the sheepherder said, 'Let's get the flock out of here.'" He floorboarded the accelerator. Gravel shot up, handfuls of it hitting the windshield.

The car might still be peppy and souped-up, but Hawk was having trouble keeping it from bouncing off the trail. I remembered the two fairly nasty gullies up ahead. But what concerned me was that we weren't making an escape.

The light, now with two baby lights leading the way, passed directly over the roof of the car. I squeezed my eyes shut against the bright flash I imagined was coming through the windshield. The lights pulled slightly ahead.

He coughed. "Looks like we've engaged them."

"And whose fault is that?"

"We just gotta ride it out."

One of the satellites began to dive. It seemed no more than twenty feet in front of us. It stood still for a moment. If something—I didn't know what—wasn't done, we were going to collide with it. "Please," I began, not knowing whether I was pleading with Hawk or with the unseen forces.

Suddenly we were driving through the glow. My eyes watered from the intensity of the light, the indescribable brightness. It felt as if a low-voltage electric current were running through me. Looking to my left, I saw Hawk alternately grabbing and letting go of the steering wheel, as if that would somehow break the connection.

We hit the first of the deep potholes. Maybe it was the sudden drop, but it seemed that the light was fading. The second gully dimmed it again, as if we'd punched a dimmer switch.

The sensation that the light was in the car with us abruptly stopped. Hawk sped up again, the car's frame vibrating under us as the road smoothed out a little. The orange light was still hovering overhead, but it seemed farther away, and might be receding.

I tried to shake off the feeling that we still weren't out of danger. "Remind me to turn down all future invitations to go for a drive."

"Did I invite you? I thought it was the other way around."

"You had that friend you wanted me to meet."

Hawk looked puzzled. "I wonder who that could've been."

The man was hammered beyond all reason. "Walter Bastanchury."

"What?"

"The man you took me to see."

"I wouldn't take you to see him. He's a doper. He smuggles aliens." He glanced in the rear view. "Speaking of aliens. Nobody's back there for miles. What if suddenly up ahead we see a spacecraft and a crowd of little green men waiting for us?"

If he was trying to lighten the mood, it wasn't working. "If there is, I might hitch a ride with them for safety's sake."

We hit the next gully going about eighty-five, based on the peek I managed at the speedometer. I hadn't realized that when they made speedometers that went up to one hundred and twenty, they weren't just doing it for show. "Slow down!"

His response was another burst of speed, pushing us past ninety. But at least the roadway seemed smoother.

The camcorder went dead. The screen went black, and the hard disk stopped vibrating. An orange glow suffused the car, and the very air seemed charged. It was like what I imagined an electromagnetic pulse from an atomic bomb (from the "Duck and Cover" films of my mother's childhood) would be. I caught my breath and stuffed the camera into the tote at my feet as the road went suddenly dark.

Hawk gasped. "Oh . . . oh, son of a. . . ." He stomped the brakes again, more vigorously. Above us, the huge orange orb moved on. We were, at least temporarily, in total darkness.

"What happened to the moon?" My voice came out as a choked whisper.

"Gone." He glanced into the rear view.

"Behind a cloud?" I looked over my shoulder. Nothing. Then I looked forward again. Nothing but void.

"I don't mean the moon. I mean the road." He gripped the wheel, standing on the brakes. The shoulder harnesses strained to keep us in our seats, but I rose up into mine, my butt coming up an inch off the seat the way it does on the downslope of a roller coaster. "The road's gone."

I couldn't see well enough to tell whether he was joking or not. "We're off the road?" It wasn't surprising, really. He was zonked out, and I had joined him in impossible visions. I could believe as many as three impossible things at once.

The car had slowed enough for him to be back in control. Except emotionally, he wasn't. "Oh, God." Moaning, he swung open his driver's door and leaned out.

There was the sound of retching, then splashing. The stink of Scotch whiskey out of a sour stomach reached me. "Sorry about that," he managed at a pause in the action. I clutched at my bellybutton with my hands, thinking how likely it was that I'd follow suit, until at last the noises ended. He hunched over, trembling, suspended over the road by his safety harness.

The man was a space cowboy. He could not be trusted. I didn't know why Aaron would ever have used him as a lawyer. Or Gil. Whoever it was who'd chosen this guy was . . . misguided, to say the least. And as far as my climbing into the car with him back in Marfa, I should've had myself committed instead.

The situation had gone past ridiculous to downright dangerous. I pulled Aaron's cell phone out of my purse, but couldn't get a signal. I tried to dial anyway and discovered that those "NO SIGNAL" indicators meant what they said.

"Do you want me to drive?" Of course, I had no idea where we were, but if I could just get us back on a main road, any road, leading anywhere, it was bound to eventually lead us back to civilization. Or to someone's old farmhouse where I could find a phone. Even a "Rocky Horror" scenario would be better than sitting here in the middle of a highway with him half in and half out of the car, waiting for a semi or another Marfa light to wham into us.

"No, no." He was looking up at something overhead. But I didn't see the telltale orange glow, or any sort of light, for that matter. "It's OK now. He's here."

Now he was hallucinating full-on. "Who's here?" I stiffened, preparing to wrestle him for control of the car.

He relaxed visibly. "We're going to be fine." Exhaling, he took his feet off the brake and eased the gas pedal back to a reasonable level.

"You found the road again?"

"It's the hawk. He's come for us."

I twisted my neck to look out the windshield into the empty sky. "What?"

"We need to look at the bigger picture through the eyes of the hawk."

I heard a strange, high-pitched whistle, and looked over at him, but he wasn't doing it. I couldn't tell where the sound originated from.

"Which way," Hawk muttered.

Within moments, four red-tailed hawks converged overhead, one from each of the four compass points. They began wheeling. I felt dizzy.

How were we seeing the birds in this darkness? If I had more Choctaw blood, I'd say they were avatars, guides from the spirit world or the ancestors come to rescue their namesake son. But they certainly looked real enough.

The largest raptor broke away and headed north—or was that west?

There was no built-in compass in this old gasmobile.

"We follow," said my companion. He pointed the car in that direction.

Although he'd said there was no road, as he accelerated, it was smooth sailing for our tires, as though on ironed concrete.

"Where did those birds come from?" I hadn't realized I'd said it aloud until he started to answer, in a séance-style monotone.

"The hawk, as I told you, is my totem animal. It serves as my spirit guide when I commune with Great Spirit and seek Nature's wisdom. The hawk, along with the eagle and owl, governs the East Gate, the element Air, all new beginnings, clarity, insight, and growing awareness. Since we need help, the hawk has come."

The sky was empty as he speeded up even more. I didn't see any birds in the sky now, and I knew it had to have been the power of suggestion.

Okay, I could deal with this. I was hallucinating. Who knew what that crazy nut might've slipped into the tea? I'd also breathed in that strongly scented pot. One thing was for sure, though: if I was going to be saved from the Marfa lights by Hawk's Totem Animal during a chase through the desert after which we followed the hawk back to the main road in a trance, I wasn't going to disbelieve and reject it. I'd always applauded for Tinkerbell, too.

Closing my eyes, I prayed. But when I opened them, I was still on a farm-to-market road outside Marfa. Sometimes I imagined I could see the hawk, too, flying overhead in front of us, leading us home. Not to our eternal home quite yet, I hoped.

The road got brighter and brighter. Suddenly I realized it was another Marfa light, hovering over the car. This one was bright white and difficult to look at directly. It dropped down and expanded, blocking the road. It was like driving into a searchlight.

"Watch out!" I covered my eyes as we headed straight for it. I had no breath to scream.

We drove through the giant Marfa light and we were there.

Back on the highway. In the dark, except for a sliver of moon overhead behind scudding clouds and a dim pool of pink on the pavement from a street light that seemed far away.

But the ghost lights were gone. My right ear popped open, and I could hear out of it again. And a quarter-mile down the road in the faint haze I saw the most beautiful light I'd seen all day: the lights of my hotel.

§ § §

I staggered into the lobby. It was freezing from the icy air conditioning. Or maybe because I was soaked with sweat.

Also dripping with disappointment. During our joyride, I'd been waiting for some great revelation, an amazing form of enlightenment, the key to the kingdom. The answer to why Aaron had stopped communicating with me and why he hadn't called on me to help him with whatever this great discovery could offer. I needed reassurance from the Universe that I mattered beyond being a pawn. I figured I would at least be sent a Sign, something beyond the appearance of the hawks as the lawyer's totem animal.

But mostly I felt my visit with the two in the trailer had been a waste, my mind being messed with by a couple of drunken, drugging jackasses. They'd tossed me useless "clues," and I had no idea what the true purpose of that dog-and-pony show had been, unless they'd had a one-dollar bet that they could turn me into a blibbering goon. In that case, I wondered who had won—but I no longer believed I'd been given Truth on a take-out platter.

The more I thought about it, the more credibility Hawk lost with me, and I doubted whether I'd come out breaking even on this estate deal. Not that I cared. All that mattered is that I'd gotten back here alive and in one piece. Without being sucked through into some other woo-woo superstring M-theory dimension beyond the holes in space that were the Marfa lights.

Shivering, I stood for a moment fumbling for my room key, preferring the cold brightness of the lobby lights to the solitude of my dark empty room.

I'd been far more disconcerted by the lights than I had ever expected to be. I wasn't used to or prepared for this woo-woo stuff, even if it was the result of all that exposure to second-hand smoke. That idiot must've had acid or crack in those joints, and we had experienced a delayed effect at a fraction of their hallucinogenic power.

Alternately experiencing mild nausea, vertigo, and disorientation is not my idea of a good hangover.

I just wanted to jump a plane and bail, and to hell with Aaron's estate and the memorial and whatever else I was leaving undone. I could call my sister, and she'd come rescue me. Just like she'd done when we were little.

I dialed her number, then hung up as soon as it rang. I couldn't talk to her right now. She'd ask me to put into words experiences that I didn't want to relive in order to describe. Then she'd get upset. She wouldn't understand why I was so befuddled and talking crazy.

But she'd come. And that wouldn't be fair to her. Why did I have any right to dump on her when these problems were of my own making?

It had been a while since I'd been this close to the edge, teetering on the brink of some vast emotional abyss.

Music blared from the hotel's club-slash-bar. Bright with neon, Jett was rockin' tonight, even though there were not that many patrons. In fact, right up front at a barstool was someone I recognized, obviously trolling for some defenseless girl he could pick up.

Ponyboy teetered on the stool, chewing on one of his fingernails. No, he was picking at something between his two front teeth with his right thumbnail. For some reason, my eyes were like telescopes, focusing on details in the distance. They also acted like radio beacons. I knew this because just as my gaze paused on him, he turned and locked eyes with me.

In his gaze I read a certainty—as though he'd been sitting there waiting for me, knowing I would return to find him. He couldn't possibly have set all of this up, but it certainly had worked out in his favor, if he'd wanted to see me again.

You take comfort where you find it. I needed human contact—some mundane interaction to help me shake this spooky, haunted feeling. To bring me back from the bridge I had almost crossed, insulate me from that goosebump-inducing outside world.

The sounds of life in the colorful bar offered solace. Life and hope.

Deciding, I smiled at him. Then I caught a glimpse of myself reflected in the glass doors. Looking for all the world like a print ad in a gospel magazine pointing out the Evils of Liquor—or at least the Elvis of being liquored-up—I strode into the bar as if my knees weren't still weak.

"Well, looky here who the cat dragged in." He smiled seductively and set down his Old Fashioned on a cocktail napkin emblazoned with the visage of James Dean. I knew better than to mix beer and hard liquor—and I was pretty sure I remembered him swilling down a few beers earlier. His breath reeked of pretzels.

"It was a wildcat. Batted me around the desert and clawed up several sensitive spots." I settled on the stool next to him and let him order me a drink, but corrected the guy to a diet cola. "Straight, over ice. No adulterations. I'm on meds," I lied. Couldn't trust anyone otherwise.

Ponyboy swiped the edge of his index finger along the side of his nose. "Well, you look none the worse for wear."

"I wouldn't say that." I reached for the glass as soon as the bartender set it down. It was watered down, but still gave some caffeinated relief. I couldn't guarantee that signals didn't pass between him and my erstwhile companion.

"Chili talkin' back to ya?" He punched me lightly on my upper arm, as one does to another of "the guys."

"No, not that I've really noticed." It wouldn't have been the chili's fault, that much I knew.

"Then what's bugging you?" He jingled the ice cubes in his drink, which looked like a 151-and-Coke, a favorite of one of my college boyfriends. Those things would knock me on my butt faster than an Elvis sighting.

"I got chased across the desert by the Marfa lights."

"Now, how did that happen?" He smiled again, such that I knew he was flirting. He tilted his head and fiddled with his hair. "Didja wink at one of 'em and invite it up to your room instead of me?"

"I'm serious." I gave him an abbreviated version of what had happened, omitting the part about being with the lawyer and simply saying I'd been driving alone to see if I could find the origin of the lights. "You may not believe in ghosties and ghoulies, but I can guarantee you that whether you want to call it energy fields or holes in the fabric of the material world or what, there are forces other than what science explains."

"From ghoulies and ghosties and long-leggedy beasties and things that go bump in the night, Good Lord, deliver us." He grinned and winked. "That's an old Scottish prayer."

I managed a weak smile. "Or a parody of one." Feeling too serious to delve into parody, I avoided his gaze and downed the rest of the cola. By the time I tasted the rum, it was too late.

"No, it's actually from the litany of intercessions in the old Episcopal Prayer Book and could have been taken from an original from as early as the fourth century. It's a famous example from the Scottish litany."

Suppressing a cola-burp, I stared at him. "I did not know that. And how did you?"

"Gil carries on about such things now and then." He ducked his head and tugged his earlobe. The way I read his body language, he was ready to lob a pass, but just waiting for me to indicate I was open to receive. "He's always trying to edificate me."

"Making you into a building isn't such a bad idea, I suppose. For one thing, someone else has to worry about the rent." I could see I was confusing him, and I smiled it away. "Sorry, bad wordplay. But you know, Gil never carries on like that around me. I get the feeling he never does really tell me everything. For example, I think he's hiding something. I mean, this whole deal with me coming out here stinks; he must have had an ulterior motive, because I've now been told that we didn't have to gather for the reading of the will. This estate could have been handled without my coming out here, I think. I suppose it was idiotic of me not to check on that before I hopped a plane, but I wanted to see where Aaron lived."

"Uh-huh." He was noncommittal, apparently sizing me up yet again as his gaze roved over me. I had to wonder whether he had a secret signal with every bartender west of the Trinity River.

I sighed, watching non-ghost lights dance as they reflected against a film of what looked like oil on top of my ice cubes. Maybe that was just an optical illusion from the neon. Subliminal seduction, pictures hidden in the ice cubes, the letters "S E X" etched deeply inside various cubes. I shook my head, but unlike in all those novels, the movement did nothing to clear it. Instead, I felt a little dizzy.

"What else didn't he mention? Is there something else you feel he should have told you?"

"I don't know. There's something about him that keeps me from trusting him."

"I don't trust preachers, either." He bounced his knees beneath the bar. "Or preachers' kids. PKs, as we called 'em in school. They learn at their daddy's knee how to lie and be slick." He still wasn't taking me all that seriously, it seemed. "Well, I hope you're feeling better. Anything else I can do for you?" His bright blue eyes darted around the bar (and that's hard to do—usually all a guy can manage is to bounce his gaze here and there, not throw his eyes along with it.) It seemed clear that if I didn't invite him to make a move soon, he'd be on to the next potential conquest.

I'm strong, but the evening had taken all the fight out of me. I didn't think I could live through a night alone in a hotel room.

"Something else strange happened tonight. I mean, this lights thing—it affected me physically." I described the temporary deafness, the sour taste, the fear. "I've been pretty weirded out."

He didn't laugh. "That's not unheard of. I'm an artist myself, remember. 'There are more things in heaven and earth than are dreamt of in your philosophy,' as Hamlet said." Perhaps he thought a Shakespearean quotation would be high-class enough to engage me. He patted my arm. I felt the fine white hairs rising at his touch. Static electricity, not animal magnetism. But the touch was reassuring, though I knew it was actually a grope of sorts. "Don't let it upset you."

"That's not the only thing." I took a deep breath. "I think Aaron was killed. On purpose."

He quirked one eyebrow. Raising his glass, he tried to sip, but because it was empty, he tapped it on the bar for a refill. "Why do you say that?"

"Several things don't add up." I described my visit with Detective Varga as sketchily as I thought I could get away with. "And there could be a financial reason that somebody'd want to kill him."

"Go on."

"He had an algorithm that could be very profitable. I know he was on to something big-time. Good enough that it was worth stealing. Good enough that it might have gotten him killed." A tremor ran through me.

Pony reached over to sneak his arm around my shoulders. He gave my left upper arm a couple of tentative squeezes. "You need warming up."

He was a breath away from nuzzling my temple. I should've flinched away, but I didn't want to spill my drink. Instead, I relaxed and let myself take comfort from his attraction. A living being was connecting with me in this physical plane, and in the glow of the bright neon beer signs he looked a damn sight better than a crazy pot-smoker whose companions were a metaphysically inclined Apache lawyer and a supernatural orange light.

"I don't know if you can completely trust Gil, either, frankly. He was a little weird about Aaron after, you know, all that business with Claudia. Can't get my mind around any man who was crazy enough to say he'd marry his own sister." He laughed. "I shouldn't kid. 'Course, Marisol never was Aaron's sister, or Gil's, either."

Marisol was married to . . . Gil? Ridiculous.

"She's an obvious fake. Why did everybody pretend they believed that sister act?" I asked instead of the obvious question.

He shrugged, which I felt rather than saw. The rocking felt good. Comforting. "I never did. Anyway, after their divorce, Gil didn't have any further obligation to her. But psychically he was still attached to her. Didn't appreciate her and Aaron acting like that right under his nose. Maybe he did arrange for something to happen."

"If you ask me, he targeted the wrong one." I couldn't believe I'd said that. "Of course, I know Gil didn't order a hit on anyone. And I thought you told me Gil was the ex of that other lady. Claudie." My tongue seemed too thick. "I don't know what to think."

He moved his nose next to my earlobe. "Wanna talk about it up in your room? Make you feel better." His hot breath blew into my ear canal, and my body reacted. I could take comfort from a little more human contact.

A grungy guy at the other end of the bar swung his mangy head towards us. "Get a room," he slurred.

"Already have one." I actually stuck out my tongue.

Ponyboy guffawed. The guy recoiled and turned away.

I'd been struggling for words ever since I staggered into the bar. I had to stop trying to analyze everything and just be, let whatever would happen, happen.

What the hell . . . I was a modern woman. Sometimes we need to forget, to escape ourselves.

In my defense, I never said, "Hello, sailor."

At least not aloud.

"Shall we?" Ponyboy offered his arm.

I yielded to the inevitable. "Though Hell should bar the way." I grinned, knowing he'd never place the quote from Noyes' "The Highwayman"—although perversely enough, I also thought of how my sister, queen of at least six of the seven liberal arts, would've identified it immediately—and took his arm.

Probably Heaven should've barred the way. Or at least <u>somebody.</u>

§ § §

I knew I was dreaming. They call it a lucid dream.

Still, I didn't try to wake up. Because Aaron was with me. Ponyboy was long gone, and somehow Aaron had come back. He perched on the edge of the bed and I sat next to him, tilted my head, ready to be kissed (although I knew for some reason that he wouldn't kiss me). He looked so wistful, like a little boy waiting for a kind word. I shifted my weight ever so slightly.

With a crack like a gunshot, the bed frame collapsed. The mattress halved right down the middle and dumped both of us on the floor. We rolled around on the thick carpet, laughing. The carpet turned into a field of soft marshmallows, and Aaron reached for my hand.

When I woke up, I was alone.

Except for the ghosts.
No; even they had deserted me.

CHAPTER FOURTEEN

Oh, God. What had I done?

I shouldn't have let things go this far. It was always a mistake, and I knew better. At least Ponyboy wasn't here doing the Walk of Shame this morning through the hotel lobby in wrinkled shirt and stinky jeans. If I was lucky, he had left in the still of the night and had crept past the night clerk without raising eyebrows. Or at least I could pretend he had. I couldn't look the clerk in the eye ever again.

But maybe Pony had been too drunk to remember. "This didn't happen" would be my mantra for the day.

There wasn't time to sit around and dwell on my indiscretion. I had a mission.

First, I needed to check my credit report. I'd get online and order reports from all three bureaus. I still couldn't accept that Aaron would steal even more from me, but that could explain a lot. No wonder I had been getting so many collection calls—and because I had nothing to offer to them, I hadn't been keeping track of the amounts. They never gave details such as when the debt had been incurred or who the original creditor was, and they always acted as though they knew perfectly well that you were just trying to dodge it—that you knew just what you were responsible for. Not all of those calls had been for Ricky's medical expenses, then.

I needed to close any and all credit accounts, though it would be a struggle to deny any of the charges, especially now. If I could look through Aaron's desk, I might find account numbers and bills, which could provide evidence. The thought was overwhelming. I didn't need that extra burden. However, I had to look into it right away.

But even before that, I needed to tell the police what I had learned from that crazy pot-smoking jackass and that unbalanced lawyer. Whether or not any of it was true. Some of it could be true, or all of it. Or they could have been setting me up to run to the cops with this weird info. Of course the cops might already know all of this. If they did, and they'd already discounted it, I'd look even more of a fool. Had that been the purpose of last night's little show? If so, why: who did it benefit and how?

I also wanted to go pay my respects to the family of the church lady who'd passed, Vernette. I hadn't even worn the dress that I'd borrowed from her yet. But I wanted to see what I could find out about the circumstances of her demise. I hoped it was a case of a long-time illness suddenly taking hold, but I didn't think that was going to be the case.

I showered with extra-hot water. The hotel towels were thick Egyptian cotton, and I sank into one, examining myself for bruises from the rough car ride and the even more difficult events later in the evening. I looked okay, save for two scratches on the side of my calf. I'd probably bumped into a cactus as we left the bar.

Scraping my damp hair back into a French braid, I scrutinized myself. I was presentable enough. I dabbed on some tinted moisturizer with a high SPF and a bit of blusher, pulled on my second-best jeans and a faded concert T-shirt out of my luggage that'd mysteriously materialized while I was away (courtesy of Cora, I figured—I had to do something to thank her for sending it over), and looked almost human.

I do a lot of good thinking while I'm zoned out in the shower. This time I had been thinking about that spider bite the coroner saw on Aaron. The only two spiders whose bites are lethal, in North America, at least, are the brown recluse and the black widow, if I remembered correctly. Maybe there are a few from Australia or Africa that could be smuggled over here and used to kill somebody. I needed to go online to check before I started blathering about it to that detective.

When I reached for the laptop, it was gone.

I searched the entire room. It was nowhere. I knew exactly where I'd shoved it when I pulled it out from under the pillow (so it wouldn't get knocked behind the bed or crash to the floor last night), and it wasn't in the top drawer of the nightstand. Or under the bed. Or in the bathroom, on the dresser, or in the guest chair.

Just as I was about to scream about the hotel staff, I realized they hadn't been in here today. The trash was still there, and there wasn't a mint on the pillow or a turn-down, since the bed was still a rumpled mess. Maids don't come in past a "Do Not Disturb" sign while you're in the shower. All of this was merely denial, as I already knew who must have taken it.

That son of a bitch. I knew better than to do what I did last night. But I hadn't expected he'd be a thief.

Dammit.

He must've been after something. After what I told him . . . what had I said? This is exactly why I never drink. That bartender was in cahoots with the musician. Damn those chili cookoff people for slipping me a NearBeer instead of the virgin stuff I asked for. They're dumber than Dubya, who at least knows the diff between a Duffer and a Puffer, or a Buckler's and a Burper. And to hell with pot. And hallucinations.

I didn't even have Worthless Shagging Ponybastard's cell phone number, though he had mine. Not that I expected a call.

I finally noticed my room phone's handset sitting askew next to the phone. How long had it been off the hook? That idiot must've slipped it off the base sometime during the night so we wouldn't be disturbed. The little red light was blinking. I was pretty sure that meant I had voicemail. I'd forgotten to check with the desk for messages as we came in.

I'd been pretty distracted.

I snatched up the receiver and figured out how to pick up the message. It was voicemail from my sister wondering how things were going, left yesterday evening around nine. I didn't feel like talking to her until I'd concocted a passable lie that wouldn't worry her, but if I didn't call, she'd worry.

I was trying to figure out a way to leave Zoë voicemail without risking her actually picking up the phone when somebody pounded on my door.

Damn that Gil. I was going to give him a piece of my mind, even if I couldn't really afford to lose even one brain cell. "Just a minute," I said crossly as my sister's voice came on the line.

But what she was saying didn't make sense. "Open this door right now, Airhead, or I'll kick it down, even if that triggers another episode of my gout." This speech was accompanied by pounding noises. Very realistic-sounding noises.

Zoë wasn't on the other end of the phone line. She was on the other side of the door.

I yanked the door open. "Where did you come from?"

Zoë wore her black-rimmed Buddy Holly eyeglasses and had her hair twisted up into a tight bun. That meant she wanted people to know she meant business. But she'd kind of ruined the effect with that embroidered peasant top and blue yoga pants. And, of course, the jeweled open-toe sandals peeking out underneath. But behind the glasses lenses burned a gaze of irritation that would have lasered me to bits if her batteries hadn't been low from all that traveling.

She brushed me aside and stalked in, hauling her giant Mary Poppins-style bag-on-wheels. "I told you all about where we come from when you were eight. But, as usual, you never listen."

Stopping short, she ostentatiously sniffed the room. "Oh, my God. It stinks of sex in here." She pulled a face. "No, Airhead, no. Tell me you didn't sleep with that preacher."

"Not with him." I heaved my suitcase off the folding stand at the foot of the bed so she could put hers down somewhere other than on the tainted sheets. "Why didn't you tell me you were coming?"

"When? Exactly when could I have transmitted that information? Your phones have been incommunicado." She jerked her suitcase up on the stand and threw it open, searching for something.

"Looking for a wrench to apply to the side of my head? I kind of think I might deserve a couple of whacks."

"I only wish that would help. When you didn't answer your room phone or that cell phone well after midnight, I had the desk clerk come down here and check on you. He came back and reported that he couldn't get anyone to answer the door, but gave me his personal guarantee that the noises he heard meant that the occupants were alive and well." She threw me a pained look and continued rummaging. "Very well indeed."

"Oh, God." I definitely wouldn't be meeting the clerk's gaze again.

I grabbed for my purse. Surely that worthless shagging bastard hadn't stolen Aaron's cell phone, too. No, it was there, dead as a roadside possum. I hadn't thought to bring along the charger. It had a USB connection, so if I'd still had the laptop and a cable, I could've charged it. But I didn't have the laptop. "Still, flying out here? You could've called Gil and had him come check on me." I cringed to think of the scene that would've brought on.

Her look of disgust and contempt was mixed with true worry. "What would that have accomplished? I don't trust him; he could've told me anything to pacify me. When I continued not to hear from you despite leaving increasingly panicked voice mail and messages at the desk, I got my stuff together and headed for the airport. It's amazingly cheap to fly standby in the middle of the night." She yawned. "Or early in the morning. Same difference."

"How did you find me?"

"I rented a car and drove here from El Paso, the way you should have." She cut her eyes at me as she levered open her suitcase and started rummaging through. "Why didn't you fly into El Paso, again? It's closer than the way you told me you came."

"I left it all up to Gil."

At the mention of his name, an expression of pain crossed her features. "He must be quite a piece of work. Just like Aaron, I suppose."

"Nothing at all like him."

She rolled her eyes. "Birds of a feather. Covered with the same old mites."

"No, really. I like the guy, but there's something about him. Gil is like Kudzu, surviving all efforts and crawling up your leg just when you think you're rid of it. He has that characteristic of always being on the scene, whether expected or not, welcome or not."

"You mean he's a stalker. He's been stalking you."

"No! Not that, either."

"Why has he been so nice to you? There must be something he wants. Other than the obvious." She made a face.

"Yes, I'm such a gorgeous beauty." I crossed my eyes and stuck out my tongue.

"Some women attract men even though they are plain," she said vaguely. I tried to swat her thigh with the phone cord, but she dodged out of the way. "What about this other guy? The idiot you made the little mistake with last night. Or didn't you catch his name?"

My cheeks heated up. I didn't discuss my sex life with my sister. Well, not voluntarily and not in explicit detail. "He's the musician you were so all-fired hot for me to flirt with, if you'll recall. He's a jerk. He was after the laptop all along, I suppose—Gil must have mentioned that I had it, and I confirmed that for him because I have diarrhea of the mouth." I shook my head. "To add insult to frippery, he should've known that I didn't need a one-night stand, but he took advantage. I had one little drink."

Zoë shrugged. "The way he sees it is, you're a modern woman and you ought to know how the cookies crumble." She set her lips into a line. "You should never drink."

"That's why I seldom do. In my defense, I was tricked."

"What does the guy do for a living again?"

"He's in a band."

"Oh, God. Don't tell me any more. I need a shower. And so do you; you stink of pot and beer and bad sex."

"You're imagining it. I just got out of the shower."

"Well, it didn't work." She scowled. "I ought to throw you in the tub and douse you with disinfectant soap, but I can't stand myself one more minute." She turned back to her wardrobe inspection. Finally she pulled out a couple of different outfits and frowned at them, as though finding them eminently unsuitable in the current terrain. "Just pray that I don't ever run into that creep, for the sake of his teeth."

"But I do need to see him. He stole Aaron's laptop."

Her eyes bugged out. "Let the estate worry about that. Why do you care?"

Why did I? An insight came to me all at once. "He's going to try to get the algorithm off of it. He must think I'm just too dumb to find it there on the disk. He used to be a programmer, he told me. Maybe he used to work in crypto, and he thinks he can steal Aaron's idea and sell it himself. And Gil could be helping him. After all, Bastey said Gil is on the hook for the dough from the church fund."

She just stared at me. "I know you could make that make sense. Though I'm not sure I want you to. But first let me have my shower. Everyone on this flight was a white-knuckle flyer and we kept expecting an engine to flame out any minute."

She'd really pushed her limits to come find me. I ought to be ashamed. "You are a bit whiffy. Luckily, there's one more towel. Can I use your laptop while you're in there?"

Her laptop case was strapped to that behemoth of a rollercase. She got it out and warned me not to touch any of her programs. "Only the browser. No tweaking of the settings."

"This hotel has free wi-fi."

"Glad to know it." She grabbed her shower cap and the last towel.

Underneath it were Aaron's paperbacks, the two that'd fallen out of the laptop case. Casting them aside at first, she then did a double-take. She let *Cat's Cradle* by Vonnegut fall as she clutched at *The Crying of Lot 49* by Thomas Pynchon. "Where did this come from?"

"Aaron's laptop case. I put them over there so I'd have something to read myself to sleep with."

"This was Aaron's book?" Slowly she turned.

"Yeah. So?" Aaron was a fairly wide reader.

"My God, Airhead. Don't you know what this means?"

I stared at her blankly, or as blankly as I can ever manage.

"Haven't you read it?"

I shook my head. I'd always intended to, but those particular round tuits had so far escaped me.

"Son of a—preacher man," breathed my sister. "That dumb rock of a nerd, and he's reading this book. But this explains so much." Sinking down on the bed, she looked at the book, then at me again. "Let me spell it out for you. You are living this book."

"I am not. I haven't even read it."

"If you had . . . and if Aaron did . . . maybe everything you've been told is an elaborate hoax." She waved the book in the air. "The story's about this woman who goes out to settle up the estate of an old boyfriend. He had lots of money, just like Aaron. There's a conspiracy going on that she gets all caught up in. It has to do with a secret postal system that runs under the one we all know about. Sound familiar?"

"Not exactly."

"Think, Ari. The DarkNet that Aaron was proposing to build for these people. It'd be like a secondary postal system for the Internet, a secret one. He must've left the book as a clue for you when he realized he was in danger."

I had to admit, for once I was seeing this book's appearance as a really odd coincidence. "Aaron didn't know he was about to be murdered when he left the book in his laptop case. And he couldn't know that I'd get hold of the case."

"Didn't he?" she said cryptically, examining the back cover copy. "I'll bet he figured that would be the first thing you'd go for, checking his email and such. And this would fall into your lap. He doesn't have a bookmark in, but the pages fall open to some really important passages. So anyway, in the story, she never knows whether the conspiracy is real, or is a practical joke being played on her, or is a paranoid delusion that she's sharing with her ex. She ends up in a downward spiral of self-doubt and paranoia, wondering what is reality."

"In other words, he took his revenge on her by driving her insane." I made my tone desert-dry. "It's like a Philip K. Dick novel. So? That's not even parallel to this situation."

"You aren't listening, Ariadne. It's exactly parallel. I'm saying you're being played." She tapped the book. "What if something deeper really is going on, and they're setting up their fall guy—namely, you?"

My sister has always been paranoid, but this easily beat her past efforts. "You're making my head hurt. Go take that shower."

She stood. But she paused and turned at the door of the bathroom. "If you're implying I'm all wet, you're all wrong." Her tone was ominous.

"Yeah, sure." I sighed exaggeratedly for her benefit until she slammed the door.

But she'd gotten to me. I just hadn't wanted to let her see it. Could there be some kind of scam going on?

I riffled through the book, but she was wrong: it didn't fall open to The Answer Thou Seeketh. It didn't look as though Aaron had ever cracked it.

I laid it aside and cracked her laptop instead.

No DarkNets were advertised on the 'net, or were even in existence. So far as anyone knew. But then if its existence had been revealed, it wouldn't be a DarkNet any more, would it?

And no magical algorithms surpassing RSA had turned up since that fifteen-year-old Scottish girl had done one for a science fair some years ago—an algorithm five times faster and seemingly just as secure as the dominant method—and had caused a great sensation, if I recalled correctly. Her fame lasted until a few weeks after her first paper was published, which was when a researcher pointed out the weakness of the algorithm and the reason it wouldn't be viable. Nothing comparable had come up since. If Aaron's algorithm could survive the attacks that had sunk hers, it would be invaluable.

A Web search turned up many pages about spiders whose bites could be fatal, and I verified that the most dangerous in North America were the brown recluse and the black widow. When it comes to tarantulas, the dull black American varieties are semi-harmless, as their bite is not much worse than that of a wasp. Some Sonoran varieties, more brightly colored, could apparently do the job, though; the farther south you traveled, the more formidable the tarantulas became. There were a few others flagged as being dangerous. In particular, one webpage showed a five-inch Brazilian Wandering spider, which it insisted was "one of the deadliest arachnids in the world, native to Australia." But that wasn't the one Aaron had pointed his phone-cam towards.

Was there anything dangerous that resembled the Texas tarantulas? The one that caught my eye was the male Cobalt Blue, which was actually a dull black; only the females of the variety are blue. *Haplopelma Lividum* looked similar to most Texas tarantulas, but the page said it was found only in southeast Asia. One could be ordered, said the page (I had to wonder what kind of person would mail-order deadly spiders, or who would think up a business plan to sell them), from a dealer like Hoke's Spiderworld or Swift's Invertebrates.

I compared the image to the shot on Aaron's cell phone.

It looked like a match to me.

Marfa would have both the American and the nastier Mexican kind, I figured. If someone was used to seeing them as pets, seeing a Cobalt crawling up might not be alarming (though it made my skin crawl.) Tarantulas could live comfortably in a dry five-gallon fish tank, said the website. They were reputed to be luxuriantly soft and cuddly, unless irked.

Aaron could've died from the venom of any spider breed that could prove fatal, especially in someone who had some form of heart disease. Of course Aaron's heart had been fine as far as I knew. It was mine that was broken.

Okay, I had to think. "Trying to think, but nothing happens," I muttered, reaching for a notepad and making a MindMap diagram with circles and arrows, like a spaghetti bowl.

Suppose that Aaron needed capital to get his new business off the ground, so Gil had funneled money to him from the church building fund. Gil expected to get to put that right back. Marisol talked him into it—or screwed him into it, in the vulgar sense. I ran my pen over that arrow to intensify it. What if Marisol had rooked Gil into it by dipping into the till herself and setting it up to look as if he had been the thief? Maybe he'd remarried her on the rebound when she came into town; after all, Claudia had recently divorced him, and he was vulnerable. But surely they wouldn't be able to keep it secret—and that'd be the talk of the town.

"Let's say Ponyboy knows of this situation and he's blackmailing Gil," I said aloud, adding a circle and arrows, "and that's why their friendship is so guarded now." It crossed my mind how I'd thought Ponyboy was just taunting Gil by taking me out, and I blushed; that hadn't been nearly the whole story.

If only I hadn't had that stupid near-beer and gone loose-lips at the cookoff, I wouldn't have mentioned I had the laptop. The code wasn't on it, anyway, but I suspected I knew where it was. In a far safer place.

My sister banged the bathroom door open, releasing clouds of steam. Wrapped in a towel, she stomped over to her purse and pulled out her cell phone. She made arrangements with her neighbor across the street, Zeke, to feed her cat and my fish and keep an eye on the house while she was gone ("I was called away on family business," she said, with a straight face.) She checked in with the manager at her day care business—she's part owner of the local Bitsy Bees chain of day care centers—and made sure they knew that she was out of town and that they should handle all but the worst emergencies without calling her. Then she grabbed the house phone and called for room service, only to find that the staff was tied up for another two hours catering an early wedding reception down in James Dean's den. "This isn't exactly Las Vegas, is it," she muttered.

"You noticed."

"The lack of neon was my first clue," she deadpanned. "Can we find someplace to eat around here?"

"Sure, but you're going to be awfully cold going like that."

"This is the desert, after all," she huffed, snatching her bra and panties off the bed and going to the dressing area to drop her towel. "What did you find out online?"

"Nothing much." I closed her precious computer and put it back into the case so she couldn't claim I had scratched it. "I did check out a few spiders. Wanna see?" I flipped open Aaron's cell phone again and paged to the photo. Full color, in all its hairy grossness.

She looked at her screen, then at the cell phone. "So?"

"That's the spider that bit Aaron, I'm pretty sure."

"What?" She pulled a white polyester blouse over her head. "How about we just talk about the reality we know?"

"You're going to boil alive in that."

"I don't sweat." It was true. She never perspired. "But tell me how you got to that theory about the spider."

"This is Aaron's cell phone." I ran back through all of it for her, and then went through my theory about Gil stealing the church money to fund Aaron's enterprise and the resulting mess.

My sister's face got more and more scrunched up as I talked. When I finally shut up, her hands were in the air. "You're making me hate this guy, and I've never even met him. The only reason I don't light out after him with a posse this minute—aside from my lack of a posse—is that I'm not sure this theory fits with Gil helping you get the inheritance. If that's really what he's doing." Her hands clenched into fists. "This is a fine kettle of guppies. If I'd known about all of this sooner, I'd have been out here right away."

"That's why I didn't tell you. I didn't want to worry you."

"And I'm even more not worried now?" She clasped her hands overhead to Heaven in supplication. "You've got to go to the police."

"I'm going to. It's just that, well, this does sound a bit far-out. How and what would I tell the detective about the spider bite that wouldn't sound like the ravings of some lunatic Miss Marple wannabe?"

"For one thing, there's the photo on Aaron's cell phone. They'd be interested, but would they buy the connection? And the problem I have is, if it was the spider that he caught biting him, why didn't he smash the thing instead of taking its portrait?"

"Maybe he didn't catch it because he was tenderhearted, which he was, and he didn't like to touch insects, which he didn't. He screamed if he saw a bug, the Aaron I knew did, and he'd capture them in Dixie cups and put them outside like that Buddhist monk in the old Kleenex ad whose eyes fly wide as he realizes he has killed all those viruses by blowing his nose into the treated tissue—you know, 'Thank goodness for forgiveness.'"

Zoë frowned. "If it weren't for the photo, I'd assume he had been asleep or passed out when he was bitten. First we're assuming this is even the same spider. Going forward with that, let's posit that he was awake and knocked the spider away from him. But he'd been bitten, and so he should have realized he needed to catch and keep the spider. He was a smart guy. That doesn't wash." Zoë stroked her chin, that imaginary beard she always seemed to sprout when she needed to link together disparate logical chains. "Let's say Aaron was drunk—"

"He'd stopped drinking before he left."

"If you say so. But for the purpose of speculation, let's say someone jacked up his mouth and poured in the booze, and she threw the spider on him, and he got bitten and knocked it off, lurching around, and she was mocking him for being a sissy, but he took a photo of the spider with his phone and then he passed out, yet she didn't realize he had photographed it, and she got rid of the spider and thought everything was fixed."

"And, and, and," I said. "Take a breath. I'll buy what you're selling, but. Tell that to the cops and they'll laugh as they pat you on the head."

"She could've put the spider on his foot because it was all fuzzy and she thought it would tickle him. Then it turned against her and bit him. How sad," Zoë remarked dryly. "If you don't take this news flash to the police and she did do it, won't you be complicit in hiding evidence or some such?"

She had a point. "Maybe that detective listens better with visual aids. Care to bring your laptop so we can show him the comparison between the one on the Web and the one in the phone?"

"I'm not coming with you. I have an errand."

There was no point in asking what it was. If she'd wanted me to know, she'd have volunteered the information. I couldn't stop her any more than I could stop a steamroller with a butterfly net.

"Don't worry. It's not far, and I'll be back in a bit."

"I wasn't worried."

My sister looked pretty formidable, all scrubbed and turned out in her best go-to-meeting red polyester suit. She looked me up and down critically. "And be sensible, Ariadne. Put on some lipstick. Clean up a little."

"I took a shower." But in her honor, I changed into my denim skirt and a clean short-sleeved white tee.

§ § §

Max Varga's long black eyelashes fluttered up and down as I watched him transfer the photos from Aaron's cell phone to his computer. He didn't even blink as the breast-flashing shot went past before the spider.

I had brought up the website with the documentation on the Brazilian Wandering spider on Zoë's laptop. "Don't you think these match?"

He hardly glanced at it. "We'll research it and get this picture to the coroner. She's still waiting for results from the lab, though. That'll take a while. She kept vials of blood and other fluids so things could be re-tested, but she's not expecting to need to use any of it. Especially not to run tests against mystery spider venom."

"Don't you think this is a break in the case?"

He regarded me as though I'd just said I think Dobie Gillis is keen. "In many countries, poisonous spiders are common. Redback, black widow, brown recluse, funnel web, and the like. They're all over various parts of the civilized world. Wouldn't be tough, in parts of Africa, to catch one and put it on a sleeping or passed-out victim. But here? I don't know how common these things might be or what they are. Forget about tarantulas. They aren't poisonous enough, just big and scary." He folded his fingers across his chest. "Back home in Ecuador, we have huge spiders that are mostly harmless. When I was in Australia, I saw a spider called a huntsman that is a real shocker, but harmless. It has a two-inch leg span. Try having that rappel down across your bathroom mirror in the early morning when you're not quite awake." He looked up and to the left, seemingly reliving the moment. "But you should just let them alone. They eat other insects."

"I'm a big live-and-let live type. It's just that my fian—my close personal friend Aaron wasn't let alone, and doesn't live."

His expression became more serious. "I think your scenario is plausible, except that a crime lab report on the toxin will take weeks. The local hospital only has the resources—the analysis kits—to test for toxins from common local varmints. Don't know just which insects are included, other than scorpions." He shuffled a few papers around, as though I were dismissed. "The problem I see with discussing this information with you, from a detective's perspective, is that you yourself might be either a head case or the killer. In neither case would the police investigation be helped."

Okay, I understood that. "When you interviewed Marisol—and I have it on good authority that you did"—if anyone considered Walter Bastanchury an authority on anything besides weed—"you must have found out a few things. Such as, she's not Aaron's sister as she claims, and she used to be married to Gil. She might still be; supposedly, they're divorced or they got it annulled or something, but she keeps hanging around. So why is she in cahoots with Aaron's family? Rather, why do they want to have anything at all to do with her? How do they benefit?"

He didn't blink. "I can't reveal anything that came out of an interview."

"Well, just in case you didn't find that out, now you know."

"Thank you for bringing this to our attention. I'll look at this new information and continue to work the case."

"So you won't tell me what you know about Marisol in return?"

"That's privileged information. Surely you can find someone else to ask."

"Such as who?"

"That's up to you." He raised one eyebrow. I've always marveled at people who could do that. "I just wonder how you would prove murder with spider venom. I've never heard of it, even around here where we have lots of spiders and snakes."

"That'd be a great song title." I stood and gathered my purse straps onto my shoulder. "Well, thanks for your time."

"Thanks for sharing your information. Always here to protect and serve."

Well, at least he hadn't blown me off entirely.

I hoped.

CHAPTER FIFTEEN

I hadn't mentioned Aaron's laptop to Officer Varga.

I couldn't exactly tell the cops who had stolen the laptop from me when I wasn't even officially supposed to have it. But I wasn't about to let that sorry excuse for a useless shagnasty creep get away with it. I knew exactly who I should send to knock Buck "Ponyboy" Travis off his high horse.

Gil answered the door rubbing his forehead and wincing. His right hand was swathed in an Ace bandage, with blood seeping out around the knuckles.

I gasped. "What happened to you?"

"Altercation with a parishioner. Come on in." It was the first time I'd ever seen Gil smile tentatively.

"Have you seen a doctor?"

"It's not as bad as it looks." Adjusting the bandage, he grimaced.

"Well, I'll be quick so you can go ice it down, or something." I realized my fists were clenched around my purse strap and deliberately relaxed my hands. "I need you to get in touch with Buck. Right away."

Gil's smile was sad, his voice full of regret. "Ariadne, I don't think your calling him would be a very good idea."

It struck me that Gil was examining me closely—no, looking at me funny. In fact, he acted as though I were wearing the scarlet "A" on my chest. I actually looked down to check for stains before I realized what must've happened.

"Oh, my God. You haven't talked to Buck this morning, have you?" Of course he had. His expression told the tale. "Let me rephrase that. When did he talk to you?"

"Late last night." He shrugged, looking sympathetic. No, he looked as if he pitied me.

I hate pitying glances and knowing looks. That needled me, and "pissed" overcame "humiliated." "What did that son of a bitch say?"

"Well . . . he told me what happened." Gil didn't meet my gaze. "You shouldn't have let him take advantage of you like that. I realize you've been upset, but . . . frankly, I was hoping it wasn't true." He studied his Italian loafers as if in their reflection he could see up my dress and straight into my soul. "Obviously, it is."

For a moment words wouldn't form in my mouth. I felt as if guilt were written all over me in that weird henna ink that doesn't come off, no matter how hard you scrub. "That useless shagging bastard came over here to brag about his little conquest? And you slugged him?" I sank down into the sofa, wishing it was quicksand.

"He said some pretty negative things. Took a lot of pleasure in rubbing my nose in it, too." The corners of Gil's lips turned slightly upward. "I got him right in the nose. Then when the gush of blood blinded him, I hit him again in the jaw. And that was when I realized I couldn't feel my knuckles." He cradled his bad hand in his other palm.

"Oh, God." Face in my hands, I shook my head. "You do not need to defend my honor." *If I have any left. Or ever had any.*

"It wasn't just that."

This was about Gil being into me. Liking me *that way.* Wishing I'd chosen him.

What a mess I'd made of everything. I hadn't meant to hurt him, and I hadn't meant to hurt myself.

I had no clue what to say. So I said nothing.

"I realize we all do uncharacteristic things on impulse, especially when we're upset. But still. This is not like you, Ari."

That bugged me a bit. How did Gil know what's like me and what isn't? Part of his problem was that he'd built a fantasy around me at some point, apparently before I even hit the scene in person. That was more than a little unnerving. But I had to deal with the matter at hand.

I inhaled deeply and audibly. "Anyway—I didn't come here about that. What happened, happened. But afterward, probably as soon as I fell asleep"—Gil's face crumpled, and I felt like a two-dollar whore who'd just announced a half-price special . . . to the Pope—"he stole the computer. Aaron's laptop. And I want it back."

"You had Aaron's laptop?" Gil touched the tip of his nose with his good index finger, as if considering. "Hmm, that belongs to the estate and I'll have to demand he return it immediately." He managed to look at me, but I could see hurt in his eyes.

"I'd appreciate that. I think you should turn it over to Detective Varga. He should see some of the e-mail messages that Aaron was getting. I was looking for clues."

"Clues?"

"I might as well tell you that I don't think Aaron's death was natural or an accident." Throwing caution to the wind (and it was really picking up and blowing out there; I could hear branches scratching against his tile roof), and even knowing that he might've been the cause of all this, I told him everything that I had discovered and what I thought might've happened to Aaron.

He stared at me uncomprehendingly. Or perhaps that was an expression of disbelief.

Or maybe that was just what he wanted me to think. Maybe he was the killer, and I'd just lined myself up to be the next victim.

Gil, a killer? That wussy? Looking into his guileless gaze, and seeing how soulful he always seemed to be, I couldn't take that seriously. He just didn't have it in him to kill a friend.

"And by the way, about Marisol." I became aware that my arms were crossed across my chest in a defensive posture. But I no longer cared if I looked like an angry first-grade teacher. "Tell me about you and Marisol, Gil."

He opened up that fake-sincerity smile. "I thought I'd told you. I guess with all the excitement when they got here, I didn't get a chance. She's my cousin from up north."

"And Aaron's sister. What a co-inky-dink."

His smile slipped a little. "Now, Ari. My family and Aaron's go way back."

"But she's not actually your cousin."

"Kissin' cousins. It's a term of convenience." The lie made him shift his weight from foot to foot. Maybe there was hope for this lying preacher to mend his ways, if he did feel guilty about having to do all this "white lying" (otherwise known as fibbing) to cover up his own sins.

"And not, say, a term for a temporary spouse?"

He winced. For once, I'd put him at a loss for words.

Wearying of looking through the various facets of this prismatic prevaricator ("that's a liar any way you look at 'em," as Grandpa used to say), I took a different tack. "Aaron was originally headed for Montana. How did he end up here?"

"Well." Gil perched on the edge of the sofa's arm and spread his hands as though to illustrate. "He tracked me down via the Internet—you know what a whiz he was—and called me. Said he was headed West and he'd be passing through. He wanted to stop here and rest a few days, and he'd suddenly thought about me and how he'd heard I ended up here. Of course I said, 'Hey, buddy, this Marfa place is pretty cool and still very low-priced, and you can get in on the ground floor, because it's on the upswing.' I said, 'C'mon out and I'll help you get settled—people live in Airstreams around here for practically free.' There's a snowbird couple who had let the church know they'd be willing to rent out their trailer over the summer, and so I got it for Aaron to live in while he scoped out some land."

"Aaron rented the Airstream, the one that's vacant now near the church people?"

"That's the place." Gil smiled fondly. "He started working around the community as a handyman and did a lot of fixing of people's computers and Internet connections and so forth, and ingratiated himself pretty well. Soon he had joined my church and was volunteering, was everybody's friend, and that may be one reason he forgot to write to you. Basically, he reinvented himself." He looked sheepish. I wondered whether Gil had known about my credit problems all along, including what Aaron and Marisol had been up to. "A fellow in our church had that lot the cabin's on and wanted to unload it, and was willing to do one hundred percent financing. Then several people had connections through our house-building charity so Aaron could get credit for building materials, and things just fell into place for him to build."

I'd just bet.

"Meanwhile, he had a great idea for some software that he thought would be a money-maker. He was going to make big money on that, and everyone would get a chance to get in on the ground floor of his IPO."

"Do you know what that software was?"

Gil shook his head. "He was pretty secretive about that. He'd smile and tell me I'd find out soon enough, along with the rest of the world. He hinted to me and others that he had a big break coming soon."

"But until then, he needed money to let potential venture capitalists see that he already had people believing in him, didn't he?" I pasted on an expression of naïve curiosity. "And you invested in his new concern, didn't you?"

He ducked his head. "I guess I did, sort of. About five thousand dollars of my personal savings. It was a loan. He was going to pay me back as soon as he got his first orders. I mean, it wasn't like I didn't have savings. I was glad to help him out. And I don't miss the money. I never invest unless I can afford to lose the money entirely. Play money. We got other investors, too."

"Right. By then Marisol must've been in the picture. So you and Aaron concocted the story about Marisol being his sister. Why?"

He studied his shoes. "Aaron came up with that, actually. He got a kick of telling people that after she'd moved in with him." He clapped his hand over his mouth.

"I know about that, too. This desert air does something to people. Anyway, it doesn't matter now." I went for the aorta. "Did you also know what else they were up to? That they'd come up with a scheme to charge things to me? Identity theft, credit card fraud, that sort of thing?"

Gil didn't react. "What?" he said after a few moments.

"Never mind. It's too late." No point in attacking him over his ex-wife—if Marisol was really an ex. He wasn't her keeper, any more than I was Aaron's.

"You're right about that. Whatever it was, let it go. Let the dead bury the dead." Leave it to Gil to come up with an appropriate Scriptural quotation. Out of context, naturally. That irritated me.

"I'm disappointed that he did what he did, and upset that you'd lie to me, but I'm not surprised." I stood, brushing imaginary dust off the knees of my jeans. I felt wrung out. "Can you just get the laptop back? You could go to

Mr. Hawk and explain where it is, I suppose. That might be easier than confronting Buck again."

"To tell Hawk that you had it without permission could get you into trouble with the estate."

"Doesn't matter."

"Still, let's not be rash." He rubbed his good hand across his stubble. I hadn't ever seen Gil with stubble before, come to think of it. "I'll take care of it. Last night, Buck would have gone after me but good, had I not managed to render him *hors de combat* right away. But then he came to his senses. He knows I didn't mean to incapacitate him. Not that I really did."

"Won't he be likely to press assault charges?"

"He realizes I didn't mean to hit him so hard. I told him I'd pick up any medical expenses. It'll be all right, Ari." Murmuring additional platitudes that I tuned out, Gil escorted me to the door. "Oh, by the way, Aaron's memorial service has been scheduled. His body has been released to the family."

I dodged out from under his "soothing" arm. "I suppose I should be relieved. But I'm not. I don't even want to go."

He patted my shoulder. "I know. But you'll feel better after we've all prayed and celebrated Aaron's life. It was a good life, after all. And he's gone on to that better place. We have confidence in that."

I am a believer. I knew all this stuff he was telling me, but I didn't want to hear it just now. Especially not from him.

I hated to, but I had to do the right thing by the estate, so I held out the car keys. "You should take the SUV and put it back with the estate until final disposal or whatever it's called, so there won't be any question. I've got another means of transportation available now"—assuming my sister would let me use her rental car—"so if you'll drop me off back in town, I'll be fine."

"No, that won't be necessary. Your having the car for a while is not a problem." He pushed my hand away. "Confidentially, I've already mentioned that to Hawk, and he's not concerned."

"You mean he's looking the other way because you asked him to?"

"Don't worry about it. I'm taking care of things."

I knew that I probably shouldn't go along with him, even temporarily, but I was so broke, and I still needed to do a few more urgent errands I couldn't easily do without a car before I got back together with my sister. I resolved to drop off the car keys with Hawk myself after Aaron's service. Surely he'd be in attendance.

Backing toward the door, I avoided further physical contact with Magic Man. "Listen, Gil, I do want to talk to you later, because I have something I'd like you to read aloud at the service. Right now, I need to get something to eat."

"That's just what I like to hear. Shall we head over to the Brown

Recluse for some breakfast?"

Smiling like that, one of these days, Gilgamesh was going to swallow his ears.

"No, I'm afraid I don't feel up to that." I managed to dredge up a steady, serious look that I hoped he took seriously. "I need to do some errands. Alone."

"Okay. But you'll be free this evening? Because the viewing starts at seven. Family hour is at six."

Give me strength.

He gave me directions to the place. I stood there nodding, although I'd driven past it already and you couldn't miss it.

Just to be a pain, I neglected to tell him about my sister's arrival. A little surprise never hurt anyone.

§ § §

Outside, I found that the previous night's storm had morphed into a gentle rain. I looked up at the cumulonimbus, if that was what it was, hanging overhead. But it didn't look like a thundercloud. Honestly, I had no idea whether it did or not, though Hawk or someone like him would know.

It was pleasantly cool and overcast. I hadn't brought an umbrella, but the hotel shop sold me an overpriced one bearing the image of James Dean.

"Unusual weather we're having," said the clerk. "For fall, I mean. Usually this monsoon happens in the spring."

As soon as I stepped out, I popped the brolly open. The rain was coming down harder now, but it was no toad-strangler.

I knew where I'd find my sister.

§ § §

Zoë's rental car—a late-model red Chrysler convertible, which is what she always rents—was parked in front of Hawk's building. As I'd suspected, she'd been listening carefully every time I let any information slip, and it hadn't been hard for her to locate him once she got into town.

I found them together in his office, feet up on his desk, sharing a bottle of that Rèmy stuff. My sister doesn't drink any more, so I couldn't guess how she was managing this; she must have been pouring the stuff covertly into a potted plant. I'd have to pin her down about it later. However she'd engineered it, the friendly nip had been a good idea, for the Hawk was flying. And he was circling in on "loose-tongued and loquacious."

"Sit down, little sister." Zoë patted the other leather side chair. "Woody here was just filling me in on what he's discovered about your fabulous inheritance. Namely, that it's worth about the same as a Lotto ticket that matches one number."

"What?" I sat before my knees had a chance to buckle.

"She's right," he slurred. "Unfortunately, I hate to be the bearer of ill tidings, but it seems that this estate you're wrangling over is as good as worthless. Or perhaps worse. I've done a bit of investigating and found that after all the debts are paid, there's going to be more debt left over."

I felt my face going pale. "I am so screwed," I moaned, unable to keep up the front. "That doesn't mean I owe anything, does it?"

"Probably not." He didn't sound certain.

"After everything else he took from me, this is too much. It was my credit he ruined, not his own." I hid my face in my hands.

"Your sister mentioned that. Identity theft. I can maybe help you with that, after we get this wrapped up."

"I couldn't afford you."

"I do a little *pro bono* work. As you mentioned." He thumbed his nose and sneezed. "Anyway, we'll see. She also mentioned you might like to keep that car of his."

That reminded me. I pulled the keys out of my purse. "I'm here to surrender it."

He waved them away. "Naturally it's not nearly paid for, but maybe you could take over the payments. It's with a local nonconforming lender. That means, not a bank, not a credit union." The Mafia? Chuck Norris, Texas Ranger? "Anyhow, they might be willing to let you take over the payments rather than get the car back. Let me see what I can do." He hiccuped. "You didn't tell me your sister was such an avid collector of vintage vinyl. Why, she knew a couple of names that old Bastey had recorded under that he'd never even told me about."

"We've had such a charming little chat." Before I could get a word in to thank him about the car, my sister poked me in the ribs. "Was there anything at all else you wanted to tell the Woodster?"

I rallied. "Actually, I think the estate needs to look into some money it might be able to collect." I detailed what I'd found on Aaron's e-mail. "I don't know if they owed him anything, but it's worth checking on."

"I wish you'd had the foresight to print some of those," he said sadly. "Maybe I could've pulled a few strings."

"I forwarded a few to myself at my Web-based e-mail." I gestured towards his desktop system. "May I?"

"Be my guest." He rolled away to allow me access to the keyboard.

I brought my Web mail account up on the screen and printed the messages on his laser printer. As they came out, Zoë snatched them up, scanned each, then handed the paper to Hawk.

He read through each one, then nodded. "Maybe there's something to pursue here. If they owe him any funds . . . or if they still want to buy the software, assuming you can find or reconstruct it. . . ." He waved his drink, sloshing it over on the paper. "Hell, maybe you'll come out of this with a profit after all. Let me see what I can find out."

§ § §

"You could charm the skin off a snake who wasn't ready to molt." I shot my sister a look over my shoulder as we tramped down the brick steps to Main Street.

"I get that from Daddy." She looked smug.

"And your nasty disposition from Mama," I couldn't resist adding.

She whapped me on my upper arm where my perma-bruise used to be when we were kids (she'd kept a bruise there until I was school-aged so she could easily persuade me of her superiority in many matters) But she didn't hit hard.

"Ow," I said unconvincingly.

"If you end up with anything out of this estate—say from the algorithm deal—you'd better stay away from these nutcases. This wild Indian, not to mention 'Bastey,' has a lot of schemes in mind and might want to get you entangled because you trust them. In fact, I'm wondering if Gil and Hawk aren't running some kind of con on the side. If I were Aaron, I sure would've chosen Hawk over Gil as a partner."

"I like Hawk."

"I didn't say I didn't like him. I just said he seems as likely to be part of any given con as not. Word to the wise. Or to the foolish."

Another storm was brewing in the overcast sky. The air was heavy as I sucked it in. It started misting again as we stepped out from under the building's awning.

"You didn't bring an umbrella," I said preemptively as I whipped out my new James Dean number.

"I thought this was the damn desert," was Zoë's only comment as she ducked under it.

We headed for the SUV, leaving her rental car parked on the street in front of Hawk's building. There were no parking meters. "I'm paying by the mile," was her reasoning, but I figured she just wanted to ride in Aaron's fancy car.

I decided phoning Max Varga from the car would be better than running in and out of the police station in the rain. I wanted to verify that he'd gotten the laptop. He answered his own phone, but this time he patronized me. He didn't seem interested in talking to me about anything. I asked whether the church woman's death was being investigated, and if they'd realized it was possibly related to Aaron's, and he said, "I can check on that." But he sounded distracted.

I suspected he knew a lot more than he was saying.

"Well, that takes care of everything," Zoë said as I hung up. "You've tied up the loose ends. So we can go home as soon as Aaron is in the—"

I cut her off. "OK, yes, sure. We'll leave, just as soon as that's over."

But I figured she knew I was lying.

§ § §

Zoë let me drive, as I knew where we were going. She was uncharacteristically pensive and quiet as we drove up to Aaron's cabin, an impressive approach that prompted her to yawn, elaborately covering her mouth. I parked at the bottom of the hill where Aaron's family wouldn't be able to see the SUV from the cabin.

We headed up the arroyo toward the church trailer on foot. The moment we started off, the sky opened up.

"Good grief, Airhead." My sister grabbed on to the umbrella with me. It didn't look as wide as I had thought.

Rain came down in sheets. We skedaddled, both trying to keep our bobbing heads under the small canopy as the wind whipped it around. The sky darkened as the wind picked up; trees would've been swaying, if there were more trees. Here it was mostly sand and the ragged flags that patriots had hanging limply from their flagpoles. I guessed they'd forgotten the Scout manual's advice to take the flag down in the rain. But then people forget that burning the flag is the respectful way to dispose of it. The smoke takes the essence of the item into the afterlife, into Heaven. That's the theory, anyway. What do they teach them in the schools nowadays?

Next to the Airstream were three cars parked outside that I didn't remember seeing before. A meeting: great, just the excuse for our appearance. If it was Bible study, well, I could stand a little of that. My faith and hope needed propping up just like anyone else's. Maybe more.

It was getting a little lighter, though it remained overcast. The light streaming through the clouds was strange, kind of greenish. "Is the sky a funny color, or is that just my imagination?" I asked Zoë.

"Your imagination is bleeding into my reality," she said, gathering her sodden hair between her hands and pretending to wring it out.

A sudden gust of wind almost turned the brolly inside-out. We hurried to the trailer's metal door, and I pounded.

Immediately, a tall woman in a black low-cut, long-sleeved dress suitable for any Amish prostitute let me in. "Sisters, we're glad to see you here. We always love to have people join our Bible study." She looked sad as I dripped water all over the indoor-outdoor carpeting, trying to get the umbrella closed and inside the door so we could shut it against the storm. "But today it's been canceled because of Vernette's crossing over to be with Our Lord. I'm sure you understand."

"How did she know we're sisters?" hissed Zoë into my ear.

"Shhh," I said under my breath. "Everyone's 'sister' or 'brother' here, dummy."

Behind our hostess at the round Formica dinette sat the preacher and another woman. They'd obviously been praying; a Bible lay open on the table between them under their clasped hands. They looked up as we stepped inside.

"We didn't come for the study. I'm Ari French, and this is my sister. I wanted to say how sorry I am about Vernette. I still have her black dress; she lent it to me for Aaron's funeral."

"Keep it," said the second woman shortly. "It's a gift. She'd want you to have it." She looked ready to shoo us out.

"Another thing," I said quickly. "We'd like to ask you some questions about what happened. Since both Aaron and Vernette passed so suddenly. You know."

She glanced over her shoulder as if to see whether the other two had heard. "We don't want to talk about what happened."

"Are you part of law enforcement?" Brother Ottinger's voice held a note of warning.

"No, no. It just struck me as odd that they both would, well, you know. So close together." I sensed we were at a standoff.

My sister grasped my upper arm and squeezed. This time, the perma-bruise spot hurt. "Well . . . we should be going," she said in her I-Mean-It tone. "Sympathies for your loss."

"Wait." The second woman stood, pointing at me. "You are Arrietty French, the one who inherited all of Aaron's cabin and things?"

"Yes. Theoretically." I belatedly corrected her. "Ariadne. Call me Ari."

"Ari?" She looked briefly puzzled, but went on. "God has told me that I should tell you what I know about your friend Aaron and his dealings with Gil Rousseau." Her eyes looked upward, then back to me. "I realize that might sound strange to you."

"No, it really doesn't." I flicked my gaze at Zoë, who had said something similar several times when we'd been discussing my nephew Ricky and his illness. We both believe that God speaks to us three ways: through other people (officially, by-the-book doctrine says only through Christian friends, but in practice I find just about anybody works—if you believe God is God, then this makes perfect sense), through Scripture, and through the still, small inner voice. What this lady was hearing could be the still, small voice, and what I was about to hear might be something I needed to hear.

Zoë gave me the high sign, subtly and imperceptibly. Okay, I perceived it, but no one else apparently noticed. She was good at pinching you without actually ever touching you.

"Anyway." The church lady looked down. "You were probably surprised to see Marisol Rose show up with Aaron's family. She isn't related to Aaron at all. I never believed she was, even though they told everybody that."

"They always smirked when they said it," murmured the first woman, who received for her trouble a stern glance from Brother Ottinger. She clammed up, pressing her lips together into a firm line.

"I did wonder. But now I know she isn't his sister." I stepped forward, trying not to crowd anyone despite the close quarters. This might be a way to confirm who Marisol was or wasn't married to. "Who is she, do you know?"

She glanced at the preacher. He must have given his okay with a nod, because she continued. "Marisol is Gil's first wife. She was a youthful indiscretion, like in that Rod Stewart song 'Maggie May.'" She shook her head sadly. "He was tempted into a fling with her when he tried to save her from living on the streets as a prostitute, which she was doing when he was first in the big city going to seminary." Out of breath, she stopped for air.

I wanted her to roll on. "Yes, I know, in Fort Worth at Southwestern Baptist Theological on Seminary Drive."

She blinked. "No. In Phoenix, Arizona. At a little seminary operated by our church. At the headquarters. You've probably never heard of it."

Okay, I had finally caught Gil in one of his original "little white lies," but he'd probably claim I had assumed too much.

She looked a little sheepish as she added, "Marisol is obviously way older than he is, so that's why I thought of that song."

Song? Oh, Rod Stewart's virgin vinyl, right. I nodded, speechless, as I tried to fit this piece of the puzzle into the jumbled picture that was emerging.

"Well. She got herself pregnant back then when he was in preacher school."

Odd how women "get themselves pregnant" without anyone's help in anecdotes like these. I thought it was fairly clear who else had swum past the spawning grounds to make the necessary contribution.

"She was in Vegas, where he used to go all the time on the weekends, so it was going to be a major problem, since she wanted to keep working there in some capacity." The woman looked even more sheepish as my sister glared at her, in an unconcealed attempt to elicit the exact nature of Marisol's professional goals. "He did the right thing and married her, but then she miscarried or got rid of the baby. He once told me he had always suspected she had an abortion behind his back. Although she claims it died from some congenital defect and caused the miscarriage. He said that makes him afraid that he shouldn't have kids."

"Philomena." Ottinger's tone held an admonishment.

"Well, it's true." Philomena actually defied him by looking him straight back in the eye. "This lady deserves to know. Whatever we can tell her, we should."

Wow, Gil had really opened his heart to this woman. Or did all preachers share secrets with each other, the way writers and musicians and teenagers did in their private moments?

The second woman turned out to have a voice. "Be sure your sins will find you out. Soon enough her antics were messing him up. He either flunked out of seminary or she spent up the money and he couldn't go on, so he got a diploma-mill degree. He couldn't get any position at a respectable church."

"That was years ago," put in the preacher man, under his breath.

Philomena shot her a glare and took over the story again. "He ended up working as a substitute English teacher in a suburb of Las Vegas, but he hated teaching, and they fought because he saw this as all her fault and she wanted him to 'loosen up' and find a way to make more money in some other profession, so they divorced. He married Claudia, the love of his life, who believed in him and his calling and who supported him. She'd worked as a dancer—no, really, a dancer, on the stage at the Sands or one of those hotels, not as a, you know, stripper or anything." She waited for me to nod that I acknowledged the distinction before she went on. "It was her charm that got him a new congregation and a new start out here in Marfa, because this is a very accepting and tolerant and artsy place where we accept people's eccentricities and offbeat stuff and idiosyncrasies."

Zoë piped up. Her commanding tone made it clear that she was the investigative reporter. "How did he meet Claudia?"

"He was teaching, and she was at loose ends"—I noted that this did not answer the question, which would drive Zoë bonkers—"and she saw something in him. He confided in her that he still felt the Calling. Claudie's family has some political connections, and they helped him find an offbeat independent Bible congregation forming here in Marfa where they needed a charismatic dynamic leader who knew how to preach a good sermon and could raise money." She smiled gently. "The original guy who was the focus of that congregation passed away, and there was no one to step in."

"Luck," Zoë murmured.

"Destiny," I said before anyone else could. I nodded encouragingly.

"So that worked out for them, and she and Gil settled down. Claudie and me used to talk a lot; she was at home alone and she'd come over here and we'd talk gardening and how tough it is to be a preacher's wife. She never really understood why he stayed so adamant about no children. But she coped well for a while."

"Though he never told her he had been married before," said the other lady. (I was starting to think of them as Tweedledee and Tweedledum.)

Philomena stared at her reproachfully, as if to say, "I wanted to tell that; that was my news." "I'm getting to that" is what came out.

I gave her an encouraging my-full-attention look.

She turned back to me. "Claudie soon found out that he was unhappy ministering to the flock, as he had worldly desires for material things that they couldn't afford. These are desires she really doesn't have, as she is more spiritual."

"I've met her. I like her a lot."

"Me, too. I miss talking to her." Tweedledee sighed. "At any rate, he had never told her about his past life. When Marisol showed up like the proverbial bad penny here in Marfa, about a year ago, Claudie found it was the last straw. This would've been about two years into their marriage and his preacherhood."

My sister could never stay quiet for long. "There is no legal requirement *per se*, but there is a moral one to tell your present spouse about past unions."

Tweedledum pointed at her as if she'd said the Secret Word. "Yes."

I remembered that when I went out to Claudia's shop, Claudia had said Gil lied to her and that was the final blow, though she still had feelings for him. She'd also given me a general warning. And no wonder.

Tweedledee exhaled. "So here's the situation. Claudia can't stand to stay there while this ex-wife is staying right there in the house—and Marisol insists on free room and board in the guest suite, or else she'll tattle and make trouble. Aaron offers to have her stay with him for a while. He has that extra room. It's all very friendly and chaste."

Completely different from what I'd been told about Claudia and Aaron scandalizing the town, I noted. Perhaps that was over by the time.

Tweedledum picked up the tale. "Still, Gil let his own wife move out on him. Because Claudia doesn't want him to lose his position, she doesn't tell anyone about Marisol, and they say at first that she's an old family friend. But she takes comfort in Aaron's arms, I suppose as familiarity does sometimes for a man and a woman, and, well, one thing leads to another."

I winced. This was the tough part for me. Zoë grasped my forearm, but not hard.

Both Tweedles looked sympathetic. "Sorry. I know this is painful to hear," said Dee. "But it happens. He's charming, she tells him her sadness, he consoles her. They have a little fling, and she realizes she's created a problem when it becomes a scandal. They weren't very discreet."

My sister snorted. I kicked her shin as discreetly as possible, though not very hard. After all, I didn't want her to fall down on their nasty old carpet. Not wearing her go-to-meeting best.

"Marisol wasn't good at keeping other people's secrets, and Aaron didn't give a flip. He thought up the ruse of telling people she was his sister. Sometimes they said half-sister or stepsister. They never could keep their story straight." Tweedledum grimaced. "'Oh, what a tangled web we weave.' At any rate, some believed that, some didn't. They stuck to it, though, pretty much."

"Claudia comes to the rescue," Zoë prompted.

Philomena/Tweedledee nodded. "She takes the hit and lets Marfa's grapevine and the church's gossip mill say that she wronged Gil and cheated on him for no reason, and that she's awful. I can't tell you how many times she agonized over this right here at our kitchen table, and how much we prayed over it, but she still felt it was the right way. She hurt a lot over it, but it saved face for him, in a way. So she filed for divorce from Gil and moved away to start the pottery business, which had been a dream of hers since childhood. Her family helped her, though they aren't terribly rich any more, and she's now supporting herself."

Zoë patted my arm, as though I were the one who needed consoling. "Well, at least she came out with a positive outcome."

I knew churches gossiped about members and maybe about the community, as did any group of people, but wow. However, this time I believed that instead of gossip-mongering, I was getting clues.

I met Philomena's uncertain gaze. "Thank you for telling me. This clears up so much of what I was wondering about."

"We thought you should know, as you have been getting so chummy with Brother Rousseau, and we thought maybe you weren't aware." Her gaze went to the floor.

"I definitely was not. And you were right to tell me. It was a very good deed." I smiled and reached out to pat her arm, but she flinched slightly, so I redirected it to my own hair. Turning to Brother Ottinger, I rearranged my features into a more mournful set. "Again, let me express how sorry I am for your loss."

He nodded stoically. "My wife went out having done her duty for our Lord."

Tweedledum elaborated. "The last person she helped, in fact, was that woman Orleans who used to run with every man in town. She finally heard the call and wanted to come to Christ, and she came here to pray with Vernette and learn the Plan of Salvation. Happened just a couple hours before God took her, in fact."

My pulse rushed in my ears. "What? How long did she stay?"

Brother Ottinger said, "About forty-five minutes. I feel sure she is serious, as she took home copies of study helps—here, I'll get you some." He reached into a document sorter.

I suppressed the automatic "That's OK" and instead said, "Thank you," accepting a handful of tracts. "Were you here the whole time?"

He was trying to hand my sister some tracts. I could've told him he'd have trouble with that. It was like trying to feed dollar bills back into an ATM that'd just spat them out. "No, I had to go comfort a church member." I shot Zoë a murderous look, and she finally grasped the leaflets so he could continue. "I got here just as the girl was leaving. It wasn't long after that when Vernette said she was feeling kind of funny in the head. I felt of her and she'd started to get clammy. Had a pain in her elbow, of all places." He closed his eyes briefly. A few tears squeezed out.

It was time for us to exit, stage right. "I'm so sorry." I squeezed his forearm. He was well enough socialized that he didn't even flinch.

I glanced down at the brochures in my hand. One showed a man standing silhouetted in a doorway with the caption "Which path will you take?" and another was the bulleted Plan of Salvation that our parents used to hand out themselves, fairly thick with Biblical quotations. I tucked them into my tote. One never knew when one might need reading material.

He seemed about to say something else, but he didn't get a chance, because whatever it was got drowned out by the siren.

It was the weather siren, the one they set off when somebody spies a funnel cloud or what they call a "lowering." The siren Dopplered against the metal walls of the trailer. Up, down, up, down . . . it was deafening.

CHAPTER SIXTEEN

"What is that?" I shouted over the screeching. But of course I recognized it. If it meant the same as it did in Renner, it was the severe weather alert or Civil Defense siren. Not a test.

"Unless Canada's attacking, it's a tornado," yelled Zoë into my right ear, turning my eardrum inside-out. She shoved me toward the door, but my lead-lined feet didn't seem able to budge.

"Come on!" Brother Ottinger grabbed my arm. "We can't stay in here. We have to take shelter." Tweedles Dum and Dee were rushing to grab various things and shove them into plastic backpacks which they strapped onto their backs. What would be so important they'd risk a delay just to take it along?

"Forget the records," Ottinger intoned decisively, taking hold of my sister's wrist with his other hand—which was pretty brave of him, as Zoë wore that fierce expression that she gets when she doesn't know quite what to do. "Let's get out."

He threw the door open. Rain and wind blew into our faces, and we fought to get down the three metal steps to the ground. I couldn't open my eyes against the hard rain.

Zoë and I clung to each other as we scrambled down the slippery slope behind the church members. Safer in a ditch than rolling downhill inside the Airstream, I supposed.

We struggled against the wind as it blew us back. We couldn't get our footing on the wet sand going up the hill to Cora's, or even to Aaron's, assuming those weasels would let us in or that I could find any leftover hidden keys in time. The wind was picking up even more; twigs, debris, and handfuls of sand swirled around our heads.

Philomena gasped. "Look!" She pointed. Just over the arroyo straight ahead of us, a funnel dipped down from a black cloud. "We can't make it to Cora's storm shelter. Can't be sure she'd answer, anyway."

We headed for the ditch as the wind got louder. Hail the size of English peas began pouring out of the clouds.

The Tweedles slid down the muddy slope. I followed Zoë and landed on her; she pushed me off, and the minister landed on top of the pile. Spreading his arms like wings, he covered us all as best he could with his raincoat.

The freight train ran right over us. They prayed, I prayed, we all prayed. At first I thought even Zoë was praying aloud, ending her year-long moratorium on speaking to God in any fashion (to punish Him for taking her son). But then I realized it was Philomena's voice in my ear. Just within the limit level of my perfect hearing (of the ear that Zoë hadn't deafened by yelling into) was whispered a long confessional.

"Forgive me, Father. I confess and repent of my sins. You know that I was tempted and fell prey. I confess that I got rid of the beast because I thought I should protect another sinner, because she's your child, too. But now I'm afraid I did wrong. You know my heart. Lord, please throw my sins as far away as the East is from the West, as You promised. Please forgive me for not telling what she did and for helping her get the spiders." Philomena paused. "Even though I knew not what she intended, I have sinned against you. The sins of greed and disobedience. I ask that you forget her sins and mine. I promise you that I'll make things right if You choose to preserve us here. Or if You take us, please forgive me so I can stand before you blameless in Your eternal light. Amen."

The boom-boom noises continued, terrible sounds like rending metal. I couldn't hear anything else but that and the rain. Then the rain let up and it fell strangely quiet, but my ears were roaring.

"It has passed," said a faraway voice.

Was I deaf? No, I could hear Ottinger speaking, but he sounded far away, as if he were inside a barrel. Or maybe that was me peeking out from inside the wooden staves.

We got to our knees and surveyed the quiet aftermath. The Airstream lay on its side, having tumbled off its makeshift foundation. Aaron's house was missing some shingles. Cora's looked solid, without even a roof tile missing; debris was scattered in the yards, but no trees uprooted. There were so few trees that this was a major blessing.

"I don't think it actually touched down," said Tweedledee.

"It just went right OVER us," completed Tweedledum.

The three of them started towards their tumbled trailer. I felt strange having inadvertently heard a woman's confession, and I didn't think I could keep from letting on. Plus, I definitely didn't feel that I could confront her about the spiders right now. They seemed to have forgotten us; I didn't think they even heard when I said, "We'll check on Cora and Buzz." I headed up the even more slippery slope.

My sister followed. "Dammit, trust you to take me out and ruin my best suit." Zoë kept muttering imprecations, which was her way of coping. Her hair was full of mud. I could only imagine how mine must look.

As we passed the cabin, Aaron's family poured out to examine the damage. Marisol was not with them. They weren't looking in our direction, and they wouldn't expect me to have someone with me if they did see us, anyway. We made it to Cora's back door unmolested. My first couple of pummels got an answer.

The door fell open, as did Cora's jaw.

I pushed Zoë forward. "This is my sister. We spent the tornado in the ditch."

"I don't doubt it. Look at your poor hail-damaged calves." That's what I got for wearing a skirt. Cora grabbed my hand and pulled me inside, inspecting me closely. "Child, you have a goose egg coming up on the back of your head. Or is that just your hair in a snarl?"

"Both." I touched the back of my head to find that it was mostly tangle. My head hurt, but the worst problem was the roaring in my ears.

The mirror in her front hall told all. I wouldn't have let me in, for sure.

Zoë looked grim. "It doesn't look that serious, but we'll have to watch you."

Cora had an answer. "Get into a hot shower, pronto. Down that hall, on the left."

Buzz emerged from a staircase that presumably led to a basement or root cellar and headed outside to survey the damage. "Guess I won't have to worry about that old barrel cactus any more. Storm uprooted it." He did a double-take. "Ari! And who is this striking young lady?"

He and Zoë clicked instantly and started some redneck-y conversation about the likelihood of the twister having leveled several more cacti. I saw that she was going to turn on the charm the way she always does, so I didn't feel bound to stick around and moderate.

Gratefully I closed myself up in Cora's classic 1950s-pink poodle-themed shower. I found two scratches on my chin and one on my cheek, but they weren't deep and wouldn't leave scars. Along with the "hail damage" on both my legs (those dots were going to be deep purple by the end of the day), there was a puncture wound from a thorn or something similar on the side of my ankle. Momentarily I had a crazy panicked thought about the possibility of a snake having bitten me, but there was no swelling, and it just looked like I'd banged against a cactus while we were escaping the twister. I found some antibiotic ointment in their medicine cabinet and smeared it on generously.

"Are you through?" Zoë tapped on the door. "I need to clean up." She had some hail damage on her forearms as well as her legs. That helped me feel even more guilty for bringing her out here.

My clothes weren't presentable, so I wrapped up in a chenille bathrobe worthy of a retro show. I hoped it was all right to borrow it.

While my sister showered, I went to check in with Cora in the kitchen.

Cora had wiped down my purse and washed my walking shoes in the sink to get rid of the mud, just as my mother would have when I was a child. She handed me a pair of khakis and a soft flannel shirt that'd been well loved. "Don't let him see you leaving in this shirt. I had it in the give-away box, but he didn't know that." She winked. "I think the pants'll be big on you, too, but it'll do until you can get back to your hotel. It's a crying shame you aren't staying in that house; they're a bunch of pigs. Going to ruin the place if they're not turned out before long."

She didn't elaborate, and I didn't ask. Handing me a charity tote bag, she said, "Pick out something you think will fit your sister, and take it down there to leave for her. I'm sure some of Buzz's things will fit, even though she's more statuesque."

Statuesque was the word, all right. I took her a pair of jeans and a red flannel shirt, and then returned to the kitchen. Cora was actually sitting at the table nibbling some coffee cake.

I got myself a canned cola and joined her. "Guess where I went yesterday? I saw the Marfa lights even more close-up." I told Cora about my adventure in the desert—briefly, without the gorier details—and summarized what Hawk and Walter had said about Marisol and the affairs. She egged me along by inserting "My stars," "Well, I'll be," and "Tsk-tsk" at appropriate places.

When I finished, she shook her head as though amazed. "Well, I will be dipped in chocolate." She lifted her coffee mug, but forgot to take a sip. "I swan. Did you ever?"

"No, and I'm glad I didn't." I managed a grin. And then I summarized for her what the church women had said to corroborate.

That ramped up Cora's wonder. "I swear. My stars and little fishes." She shook her head. "I felt in my bones that woman wasn't any sister to him."

"I can't imagine why they'd think that was a good ruse to pull. And why would Aaron's parents be going along with it when they must know that the estate will question that?" I pretended to be wondering, rather than fishing for input.

"That's a stumper, dear." She swirled the untouched coffee in her mug. "Gil, though, that beats all. He loved Claudie. He really did. I don't know how, but I knew there was something bad about that Marisol from day one."

"There's more. I think the cops should talk to Orleans about her hobby of keeping spiders." Without giving the game away, I explained that Aaron's body had shown evidence of a spider bite, and that I thought it could've been made by one of Orleans' pets.

Cora shuddered and squeezed her eyelids shut. "Oh, my goodness. If one of those monsters crawled up on me, I would die on the spot. I have a true phobia of spiders, especially ones up over my head. And don't even talk about one in bed with me. Anything bigger than a dime and Buzz has to come kill it or I spray it with hairspray or Raid from as far away as I can manage."

"Would she keep a spider with a fatal venom, though? Wouldn't that be dangerous? Do the people at the church even keep those?"

Cora reflected. "I just don't know. They do have snakes." Her eyelids flew wide. "Did those cages in the back of the trailer open when the storm knocked it over?"

I closed my eyes. "I hope not. I don't want to fight a plague of rattlers and adders. Or even subtracters."

"I'm even more deathly afraid of snakes than spiders," Cora said with a little shiver.

"Me, too. But I'm more worried about spiders, because they can be lurking anywhere. Most spiders don't have a lethal bite, but you can still get problems like infections or blood poisoning. The summer I turned eleven, a mystery zit showed up one morning on my outer elbow. It didn't worry me. It didn't really hurt, so I didn't pay any attention."

Zoë came walking in clad in Buzz's inadvertent castoffs, rubbing her head with a pink towel. "Are you telling about the time the spider bit you? Let me tell you, she was a little idiot at that age. Not that she's improved a lot since."

Cora smiled uncertainly.

I shot my sister a warning glance. "Not everybody knows when you're kidding, Zoë. Anyway, by afternoon my elbow felt stiff, and a red streak started up the inside of my arm. I showed it around to all the neighborhood kids, and it was a real hit."

Zoë rolled her eyes. Cora looked alarmed.

"By that evening, I had a fever. When Mother got a look at my arm, we headed for the emergency room."

"They never said for sure what it was," Zoë interrupted.

I gave her another look to shut her up. "I had to have shots, which I hated—still do—and keep the bite doctored up for weeks until it went away. Anyway, now I'm terrified of even those itsy-bitsy spiders that crawl out of abandoned stacks of paper. The doctors said that almost any spider or bug could sneak in a bite that you might not notice right away. I never even knew I was getting bitten. I don't normally check out my elbows."

Cora looked at me reprovingly. "You should, dear. We lean on our elbows and rub elbows with so many people, it's a wonder worse doesn't happen. Think of all the ways your elbows come in contact with other people's germs."

Zoë nodded. "Isn't that the truth. I carry Purewell all the time so I can squirt it on all the public handles, for instance on grocery-store carts. Did you know they've found more germs on those than on toilet seats? And on doorknobs."

I was thinking how obsessive that was when Cora said, "Oh, yes, I agree. I carry it, too." She lifted her purse and gave us a peek at her bottle of portable disinfectant gel, attached to her key chain by a rubber thread. I caught a glimpse of her heavy key chain jingling beneath, which held about twenty keys in addition to a mini can of Mace and one of those EpiPens for use in case of anaphylactic shock. Briefly I wondered whether those EpiPens could be drained of the adrenaline they came packed full of and reloaded with something else . . . such as spider venom.

"You've got to tell the police all that as soon as you can." Zoë shot me a dirty look. It occurred to me that there was no way to tell how long my sister had been standing in the hallway eavesdropping. "I would not be in the least surprised if that crazy Orleans creature had intended Aaron harm. The church ladies seemed to think she acted like a total nitwit. They thought she was faking her little 'conversion' in order to infiltrate their group. To make a scene later, I suppose."

My sister was not above "editing" the truth.

Cora smiled. "I don't doubt that for a moment." She didn't specify which she doubted—whether Orleans would make a public scene, or whether she'd harm Aaron. "And I don't blame you for not wanting to interrogate her yourself. That's police business. If I were you, I would be real careful, hon." She clucked her tongue. "I'm glad you didn't get hurt worse. Tornadoes kill people."

Idly I wondered whether I should've told Cora all that. Maybe she was the one who'd taken a spider out of Aaron's dry aquarium, the one in his cabin that was strangely empty, and while he slept . . . no, she couldn't be involved. What reason would she have?

The tornado had me shell-shocked.

Zoë pulled a Simple Country Lawyer ploy and smiled charmingly at Cora. "You're a good neighbor, for sure. I'm just glad we got out of that trailer safe."

"Those things attract wind, I think. I wouldn't stay in one overnight for anything."

We left after giving assurances that I'd see her at Aaron's viewing. Though I still wasn't sure I could make myself attend.

§ § §

Done up like a farmwife, I felt like a fashion victim from that nineties trend of wearing-your-boyfriend's-wrinkled-khakis, except that I didn't have pointy toes or stiletto heels poking out from under the rolled cuffs.

"Looking good," Zoë said in a mocking tone, as if reading my mind. "Love those Morning-After Pants."

They did resemble the attire of a fallen woman escaping from an ill-advised one-night stand. "I suppose I could find time to change again before that viewing deal."

"Don't count on me for that." She closed her eyes as we climbed into the car.

"I wasn't. Although you don't look that messed up." Her cast-iron suit had cleaned up well after a brushing with a wet rag at Cora's sink. Polyester double-knit of the twenty-first century version. The only casualty was her white blouse, which had suffered a large splotch of mud right on the jabot, and we both knew it would never come out. Texas mud has a way of staining.

"I'll manage until we can get back to the hotel." My sister was squinting out the window. "Who the hell is that? More of your Country Cousins?"

Aaron's parents were headed down the hill. "The Darlings," I growled. "They recognized the SUV, dammit."

"I told you we should take my rent car."

"You said exactly the opposite. You said you were paying per mile." I fumbled with the keys. We got rolling just as the posse arrived.

"Watch out!" My sister grabbed the crash handles over her door as I swerved towards the group. Restraining myself, I just avoided grazing Aaron's mother's big butt, and came barely six inches short of winging Marisol. Doyle pounded his fist hard on the rear fender once as we went slip-sliding past them and onto the gravel access path.

"Careful!" Zoë shouted. "Dammit, Ariadne, don't lower yourself to their level. You could have really hurt her. And what would that make you?"

I shriveled under the spotlight beam of truth. What had taken hold of me, if only for a moment? How far was I—how far were any of us—from doing something in anger or on impulse that we could never take back and that we'd always regret?

"Missed by a mile," I said in a sulky tone, because that was the way my sister and I related. I couldn't very well admit, "I'm one bad decision away from becoming just like them," could I? My only face-saving resort was to brazen it out, go on the offensive. "Now I'm even more determined to fight them for the estate. They've really pissed me off." I turned the radio on loud. "And now I'll show up for Family Hour for sure. That'd teach them."

"Or it'll kill you. But you'd be in a convenient location for it." Zoë twisted the knob right back into silence. "Acid corrodes its own vessel, Ari. You're only harming yourself."

Sobered, I drove in silence for a while.

Zoë let a reasonable interval go by, then piped up as if she'd just thought of this. "We have to find out what the software was that Aaron got his knickers in such a knot about. And got several corporations all excited, to boot."

"The code was so important to Ponyboy that he took that laptop. Of course the software itself wasn't on there. I checked." I, however, thought I knew where it was. "We need to do a little geocaching."

"Whatever." Zoë rolled her eyes as if to say that this was another of my too-frequent *non sequiturs*. "First we need to get something to eat and change clothes. I wouldn't want you to tear up Buzz's comfy duds."

"Wait until you try this Trans-Pecos cuisine." I drove through the Tex-Mex place. It would be too easy to become addicted to the vegetarian savory-stuffed sopaipillas with the stretchy Mexican cheese surrounding the soft julienned veggies and the extra-mild hot sauce. With a real glass DrPepper direct from the bottling operation in Dublin, Texas, pulled straight out of an old-fashioned ice chest, the stuff hit every spot I had.

It even impressed Zoë. "I think this salsa is the first ever that I've liked better than mine." She closed her eyes and squished it around on her tongue, obviously trying to deduce the secret ingredients. "Cilantro, of course. Roasted red peppers. Jalapeños. I don't know quite what that other whang is—cinnamon? No."

"You'll figure it out when you get home and experiment." I sipped the heavenly nectar and dipped a handful of crisp sweet-potato chips into melted cheese—not Velveeta, but real cheese that'd been melted in a cast-iron skillet, not nuked. It was like manna. "In fact, if we could get back to Aaron's, you could try out versions in his kitchen. It's really something."

She talked around a mouthful of Southwestern veggie wrap, and she hates people who talk with their mouths full, so I knew it was important. "I don't ever want to go into that cabin. It's cursed. Somebody died in there."

This was a spurious argument, of course, but I didn't challenge it. "Don't you want to see what Aaron built with his own two hands?"

She shrugged. "I don't think I care."

Back at the hotel, when we walked into the lobby, there was another surprise.

Orleans had her elbows on the registration counter and was chatting up the desk clerk. When she saw me reflected in the gilt-edged mirror over his shoulder, she sprang into action. "You bitch! Stop right there."

"Another of your friends?" my sister murmured.

Orleans whirled towards me. Zoë, ever the brave protector, stepped aside. Before I fathomed what was about to happen, Orleans slapped me across the face. Hard.

It stung.

"How dare you give them that picture of me! Where did you <u>get</u> it? When did he TAKE it?"

"What picture?" My blood paused, then slogged to a halt as I realized. "Oh, my God. The one off the cell phone." I hadn't understood what I was doing when I'd allowed Max Varga to pull all the photos off Aaron's phone.

Damn the police—they'd found a way to print out that spider photo, but they must've thought they were cool cats, because they had printed Orleans' "Girls Gone Wild" audition photo as well. That boobs-flash pic. And they must have passed it around. Sniggering, no doubt. In small towns, this stuff gets around.

She came at me again, but this time I dodged, and Zoë moved to grab her. It was slapping and hair-pulling, round two. This time she got hold of a good chunk of hair near my crown. Zoë put her in a headlock, but she twisted so that only her shoulders were in the vise. The desk clerk just stood there, watching, the jackass. I cried "Uncle." But he averted his gaze.

I writhed. "No, stop! I didn't give them that one. I mean, I did, but I didn't intend to. I gave them the cellphone for the spider picture because it might be important."

Her eyes widened like an opossum's in the dark. "The spider was on the camera?"

She ripped her shoulders loose from my sister's armlock, which meant she'd managed a huge adrenaline surge, as Zoë had at least fifty pounds on her. I do believe Orleans would have killed me (or given it all she had) if Gil hadn't walked in, leading Ponyboy by the arm.

"Hey, hey! What's happening here?" Gil ran to restrain her. He shot a look over his shoulder at the desk clerk, whose chin was on his chest with ropes of drool running down as he stared fixedly at us. Okay, I exaggerate, but why hadn't the idiot called security? If such a thing existed in this Old West faux-set. "Let's be reasonable. What has Ari ever done to you?"

"You ought to know." She spat, and he narrowly dodged it. The clerk stirred a little then, but still didn't reach for the phone.

Orleans twisted loose and faced me again. "You're going to be sorry." She stalked out.

"What picture is she talking about?" My sister didn't know that part yet. Maybe I'd left out a few little details.

"What was that all about, Ariadne?" Gil said softly.

I tried to straighten my hair. The top of my head was tender, as tender as it used to be when I was little and my mother had French-braided it too tightly for church. "I think she's upset with me."

"Well, duh." Ponyboy pointed at his head like Garfield.

"I mean, you know," I said mindlessly. "Anyhow, she's upset."

"I don't believe I've had the pleasure," said my sister, eyeing Buck. She knows just the kind of guy I tend to fall for, and when she looked at him, she saw right through him with her X-ray eyes.

"You've had it, all right, and too many times," I hissed into her ear, then said in a normal voice, "This is Ponyboy—I mean, Buck Travis. And Gil Rousseau. I'd like you both to meet my older sister, Zoë. She just got in this morning for Aaron's funeral." I emphasized the F-Word there, just to gig her a little.

"Miss French." Gil turned his high beam on my sister. She, however, is hardened against all male charm attacks. After Ricky's father skipped out and left her to make her way as best she could, barefoot, sixteen, and alone, she had figured out the ways of the world. Thrown out on the street by our "righteous" parents, she'd toughened up faster than a black walnut shell in a plastics factory.

She smiled at him and deflected his phoniness with her plus-five suit of chainmail. "Now that we've been formally introduced, you may call me Zoë. And you're the preacher who's running this Aaron show, I presume." She stuck out her hand.

He was almost afraid to take it; I could tell.

Ponyboy had no such qualms. He whipped out his hand to shake Zoë's with gusto. "Nice to meet you, ma'am. Ari has told me so much about you." He winked at her, horrifying me.

Maybe with a little lipstick and bravado I could've run into him and still held my head up. But this encounter was too soon and came out of nowhere. I tried to remember that it was all about confidence, brazening it out. He avoided meeting my gaze. On closer inspection, he looked pretty unsure of himself. He looked like a high school boy who didn't want to confront the girl he'd taken advantage of.

My sister saw our interplay (or lack of it) and looked at me. I knew that she knew. Her mouth twisted as though she'd bitten down on a SourTart. "And here he is," she said out of the corner of her mouth, "your lovely new beau, and with you fitted out like Toiletta." Toiletta Bolina was the faux mascot of our high school drama club's pep rallies; she wore a toilet seat around her neck instead of a crown, and carried a plunger in place of a drum majorette's baton.

I cleared my throat. "Pardon our appearance. We were just in a tornado."

"Are you all right?" Gil reached toward the back of my head. "You've got quite a goose egg starting there."

"She's okay," said my sister shortly. "We were just dropping by for a change of clothes, and then we'll have to head out. Nice to have met you." Her tone was dismissive. She was wearing her "this conversation is at an end" face.

"We've got some errands ourselves. But hang on a minute more." Gil looked expectantly at Buck.

Buck, I finally noticed, had a black plastic box shoved under one wing. The laptop. He held it out to me. "I was just looking for evidence or clues. After all, it ain't even yours." He was acting sheepish, but I could tell that was a put-on for Gil's benefit.

"I can't exactly report you to the police for stealing something I stole, so we have a Mexican standoff. But don't worry, because I already didn't trust you any more, anyway." I took the laptop without touching his fingers.

Gil looked at me, then at Ponyboy, then back at me. He cleared his throat. "Because you're the literary executor, Ari, I felt that the appropriate move was for you to keep looking through this to see what Aaron might've written that we should preserve."

Some bad poetry. Really bad. One of the poems was the one I'd told Gil I wanted to have read at the memorial.

And, of course, the documentation. He must've told them it was "a book," implying a novel, so they wouldn't suspect what he was up to. If only he hadn't started drinking again. He never could keep quiet after he'd had a snootful.

They seemed about to leave, so I stopped them by stepping right in front of Gil and putting my hand on his arm.

"Listen, Gil, I know you and Marisol used to be married—and maybe are again." As his jaw hit the floor, I raised my free hand. "Don't bother to protest. I've verified this with a couple of people. Are you going to tell me they're all liars?"

After a moment, he shook his head. "All right, Ari. It was a youthful mistake. She and I parted ways amicably. She fell on hard times recently, and came out here to get my help. I couldn't throw her into the street. Nor did I think everyone needed to know my entire life history."

"She's got you there." Pony—no, now he was demoted to just plain Buck—smirked. How could I ever have seen anything in him, even friendship or companionship? He just looked like the typical bummy musician, a slimeball accustomed to using up his groupies and moving on. I could've smacked myself in the forehead, but I didn't have a raw salmon handy.

I handed the laptop to my sister in case I ended up belting him one. But I turned back to Gil. "Why didn't you tell me? Don't you think I deserve some sort of explanation? I mean, other than lies."

He glanced around, catching the desk clerk's eye. The clerk looked back down studiously at his reservations computer. "I meant to talk to you about that. But now is not the time or the place." He held his hand out to my sister, but she only looked at it imperiously, like the Queen of Sheba being offered the hand of a mere peasant slave. He seemed a bit daunted. "Nice to have met you, Ms. French. I'm sure we'll run into each other again soon. Ari, I'll talk to you about everything later."

Gil seemed to be in an uncharacteristic hurry to leave. He kept looking over my shoulder, as if checking out the progress of some entity just beyond me.

Slowly, I turned.

CHAPTER SEVENTEEN

It was obvious why Gil might be feeling so motivated to leave.

Orleans Hall was back, this time accompanied by some guy in a suit. A young crewcut Marine-type wearing a straw cowboy hat and ornately carved ostrich Justin boots. "This is my lawyer," she said to me without preamble, "and he's going to make sure you don't libel me any more."

"Libel you?" Buck looked amused. "Seeing as how you're pretty well known around town, I don't know that anything she could come up with would be untrue. Therefore, no libel. Besides, libel is written. The words you two just had were oral." He smirked again at the connotations of the word, like Beavis unchained.

Her ball-bearing eyes flashed. "You'd better be careful."

"Is that a threat?" said Gil. "I hope that wasn't a threat of any kind." He shot the lawyer a you-know-better glance.

The suit next to her droned, "The last thing this community wants is a Barney Fife-style investigation instigated by any of you in order to tarnish her reputation in the community while inflicting severe emotional distress. I'm here to guarantee you that if any more slanderous remarks are made in public by any of you, we will bring charges."

"I haven't heard any remarks. But I think Ariadne has grounds for a charge of assault," said my sister the former sphinx. She ran her laser gaze up and down the two of them as if to roast them. They looked a bit nervous that it might actually work. "Must we cross swords, or let bygones be?"

Her faux-Shakespeare had a calming effect on the lawyer, at least. Buck sniggered. I wasn't entirely sure that Buck wouldn't pipe up and address Orleans as "BootyCall Woman," just to play "Let's You and Him Fight." But the Justin-booted lawyer glanced at Orleans meaningfully, and she got his message.

Orleans turned. Then she fired a parting shot. "It's her word against mine. And I am known in this town." She pointed at Buck as though to suppress any smart remarks this might elicit out of him. "I mean it. Be careful and watch your step. You never know what you might be stepping in."

After a Significant Pause, they slammed out the door.

My sister frowned. "If I were a dog, I'd bark."

§ § §

"What is it about you that attracts obsessives and smarm-o types?" Zoë shouldered her way into my room past me as soon as I had the door unlatched.

"It's not like that." I tossed my purse on the bed.

"But it is," pointed out Zoë in a reasonable tone, which made it even more irritating.

"Gil's not interested in me. He's just being nice." I hated to lie, but I couldn't tell her the whole truth.

"The musician was bad enough. But that Gil! He reminds me of Eddie Haskell talking to the grown-ups. 'What a lovely dress, Mrs. Cleaver, you old hag,'" Zoë imitated in a smarmy voice. "Sucking up constantly. Then when he gets in private with you, it's back to the old Fast Eddie. How you can stomach the man, I don't know."

"He's not all bad once you kind of get used to him." I picked at the bedspread.

"Twenty bucks says he made up that Gilgamesh nonsense because you have an unusual name. He's probably Giles . . . Gilead . . . Gilda." She snorted.

After going through the entire shower-and-change routine again (with nothing to dry off on but damp towels), we sat down with Aaron's laptop and started poking around.

Of course the e-mail directory had been wiped. The disk zap tools Zoë had on her laptop wouldn't run on Aaron's system, and we couldn't find any freeware online that would undelete it. I suspected Ponyboy had been smart enough to zero it out in some really effective way. I had to wonder what Buck might've mined first.

"Nothing left of your beloved 'SpecialProjects' folder, if there ever was anything in it." Zoë sounded a raspberry and snapped the laptop shut. "Case closed."

I groaned at the pun. "Maybe it is best to leave this to the police. They'll probably have an IT tech who can try to unerase the e-mail and so forth." This time, I wouldn't try to see the detective in person; I'd simply stop by and drop the computer and a note with the front desk clerk at the window where you pay traffic tickets and bail people out of jail. It was up to Max Varga now if he wanted to try to recover and trace Aaron's business threads.

§ § §

I left the police station and hurried through the drizzle, holding an empty manila envelope over my hair, back to the SUV, idling in a No Parking zone. "Now we're going to finally have a little fun." I tried to make my voice lively.

"Fun. We're going out in the rain on a nature trail to hell in the snake-infested desert," said my sister. "All so that you can try to find latitude so-and-so and longitude such-and-such and dig for buried treasure." She looked glum. "Prepare to shovel up pirates instead."

"Cheer up. At least it's all muddy and raining. I'm pretty sure the conditions aren't quite right for another tornado, though."

She sighed heavily and stared out the passenger side window.

The coordinates Aaron had tried to send me I had copied onto a yellow sticky note, which I now stuck to the dashboard. By doing a general-area Web search on them, I found they were somewhere behind Gil's church building.

Gil's car was in the lot in his reserved parking space, and I briefly worried that he might catch us hiking around the church yard and the woods behind it, the only wooded area anywhere around. Still, I could just say we were exploring.

We tramped through the church yard as I watched the numbers on the handheld GPS change. The digital display was so fascinating that I nearly tripped twice on loose stones and a protruding tree root.

"Watch where you're going," said Zoë. "This is wacko."

The numbers got closer and closer to a match as we headed down a steep sandy bank to a creek. The creek was running fast and splashing over its normal banks, which surprised me, but then I recalled how Gil had mentioned the rains only recently ending.

My sister flipped open the travel guidebook she'd bought at the Brown Recluse, *The Insider's Travel Guide to Marfa.* "If this thing is correct, we're looking at Cripple Creek." She began to sing the rest of the guide's information to the tune of the old Robbie Robertson song, "Up on Cripple Creek." "It's a tributary of Alamito Creek, an intermittent stream that runs towards the Rio Grande. It's dry for most of the year except during and immediately after the rainy season, when it can overflow its banks and is quite rapid. They say, 'There are no permanent streams in the county, although many dry arroyos become raging torrents after heavy rainfall.' A drunkard's dream if I ever did see one." She gave up the approximation of the tune as she gazed at the not-quite-roaring water. "It's wet enough, I suppose. I'm surprised there's even a damp rut out here in the desert. Anyhow, it claims that on the other side of this there's a waterfall where the creek comes down off a volcano-formed arroyo, and behind the waterfall is supposedly a cave that used to be an attractive nuisance to area children and teens until this property was purchased by a private party and posted as off limits." She snorted. "I suppose they fantasize that their 'No Trespassing' signs work on determined teenagers."

"Thank you, Singing Rachael Ray, for the travelogue." I rechecked the target coordinates against the display. "We're in the general area. Now what? I don't see anyplace for a cache to be."

"To be, or not to be," she quipped. "I think you'll find that anything dry would be on the other side of this creek." She glanced at the yellow note stuck to my boob, then at the screen. "No, we don't. It's even worse than that. Those numbers would be about in the middle of that stream."

I looked at the coordinates again. Stepping back and forth a few feet so I could determine by how much they changed each time I moved a foot in another direction, I did the mental calculations.

She was right.

The cache being hidden underwater made sense because of Aaron's love of Wagner's ring cycle and its imagery: the treasure under water. Especially since Marfa and environs were in a desert, so almost no one would think to look for an aquarian hiding place.

I stepped closer to the edge of the water, then held the GPS unit out as far as my arm would reach over the stream. Sure enough, the numbers changed so they were pretty close to what I wanted.

Why did she have to be right all the time?

I leaned a little farther out, then felt my smooth-soled boots slip a little. "This can't be accurate. Maybe the satellites are skewed."

"You're skewed. We have company." My sister grabbed my arm just before I would've pulled a splashdown into the muddy water.

Gil walked up behind her, grinning. Naturally, he'd waited until I was half-covered in mud. "It's a gorgeous afternoon, isn't it? That's my Ari, always out communing with nature."

Zoë glanced at me like "his Ari?" and I stared back like "he wishes." She said, "I believe I'm about communed out."

"We were taking a nature walk. Thought we might see some unusual flora and fauna." They both stared at me as though that explanation had come out of my kneecap, which it sort of had. Gil's sudden appearance had me rattled.

She extended her hand to him like some Jane Austen character. "As much as I've enjoyed being here in 'A River Splashes Over It' country, I believe I'm ready to go back to the hotel and change for dinner." Turning on the charm full wattage, she smiled at him, but I could see that she'd met her match. Now that he was rested and recharged and not facing a potential barroom brawl in a hotel lobby, they were pretty evenly yoked.

Gil broke into full Preacher Greet. "Well, we're mighty pleased to have you come out and see our wonderful area." Noticing where she was standing in the sandy muck, he held out his other hand for her to grasp as well. "Allow me to help you ladies out of there."

He hauled us out, using both hands. While I had been fooling around with the GPS on the bank, I had sunk into the quicksand-like creek bank a couple of inches, ruining my new Justins. Back to the sneaker-like Skechers for me until I could get them properly cleaned off and polished with saddle soap.

"Your back yard is really nice. But we'll take our leave now and rinse off this Texas red." Zoë actually fluttered her lashes. She had a kind of Janis Joplin charm, when she tried.

"Of course. See you two at Family Hour." He checked his watch. "I'd better get over to the cabin. I'm going to escort the family." Shooting me a look of apology, he added, "That's part of my job description."

"Sure, I know. They need you, Gil. I'll see you."

I didn't say I'd see him at that viewing thing, though.

§ § §

"That was exhausting." Zoë landed on the bed and jerked her muddy shoes off, sending clods flying. "You don't have to go, you know."

"Yes, I do. Watch the mess you're making for Housekeeping, dear. And I can't get over you. 'We must take our leave, kind sir.'" I rolled my eyes. "Straight out of Dickens."

"I got us out of there, didn't I?"

"You've got a point. I didn't want Gil to ask me to ride along with him. And I cannot bear to go alone." Then I had an inspiration. "Claudia will be going to Aaron's Family Hour."

"Sounds like a new reality show. Wouldn't that be fun—if the two of you dressed alike." Zoë smirked. I had told Zoë about our resemblance. "Put on similar hats and dresses and you can be the Toni Twins in Mourning. Straight out of a comedy of manners that Jane Austen forgot to write."

"Shut up. I really mean it. I can't go by myself, but I feel I simply have to be there for Aaron. He's expecting me." I covered my ears with my hands to drown out my sister's sarcastic raspberry at my sentimentality. "I'd better call her before she makes other plans."

When I put in Claudia's number, the cell phone started ringing and the screen displayed a Disney screen shot captioned by the name "Tinkerbell."

My mouth fell open. "Dammit! She's the last person Aaron talked to before he died."

"What?" Zoë dropped her ruined clothes on the bed.

"Claudia. She's Tinkerbell. She killed him."

"Start making sense." Zoë scowled. "She probably isn't answering the phone because she knows that's Aaron's phone number. Maybe she's creeped out, not realizing you're carrying his phone, or thinking Gil has it. She might be at home."

"I meant the night Aaron died. That's Tinkerbell." I closed the phone, cutting the connection.

My sister looked confused, and with good reason. She pawed through possible changes of clothes as I tried to explain what I was talking about. Alarm grew in her eyes as I spoke. "You're going out to confront a possible killer now because . . . why? Why not just tell that cop?"

"He won't listen. He has the list of incoming and outgoing calls—he downloaded them when he got the photos—and he apparently isn't doing anything with them. Claudia, even if she didn't do it, was there just before the crime was committed. She may know something from what he said or what they talked about that could give me a clue. I'm doing this for Aaron, to find out the truth so he can be at peace."

She rolled her eyes. "He's already fine with it. Don't pretend you believe all those horror flicks where the murder victim can't rest until the killer is brought to justice. It doesn't work that way, and you know it."

"I know it. But I think this could be important information. And no one else is going to ferret it out. I've got to try."

"Oh, God. I should've known something like this would happen." She sat up. "If you're crazy enough to insist on going out to see that woman, I'm going with you."

"No shower?"

"You didn't take another one, either."

"I'm afraid I'll melt."

§ § §

Claudia wasn't answering her door. Zoë looked approvingly around at the shop's landscaping as I tried going around back. A pickup truck sat in the driveway, but since I didn't know whether that was her primary vehicle or not, it didn't help.

I was ready to give up when a compact Sunbeam rolled into the drive. When Claudia got out, my sister gasped. With her hair in a ponytail and covered with a scarf, and what with her being dressed down almost as much as I was, the resemblance was pretty uncanny.

"Oh, hi. I wasn't expecting anybody. I've got to get ready to go to Aaron's Family Night."

"I know—that's why I came, sort of. I mean, that was the original reason I was going to contact you, so we might go together. But then I figured out that you were the last person who talked to him the night he died."

She looked alarmed. "I was? Oh, no. I hadn't realized." She fumbled with her keys. "Would you like to come in and have a cup of coffee or something while I get dressed, and then we can go?"

"No, I have to go back and dress. I tried to call you, but when you didn't answer, I came to find out what it was that Aaron called you about. It might be important. Was he worried about anything?"

She unlatched the door, letting us in behind her. "I didn't answer my cell tonight because, well, it was Aaron calling. As you know." She half-smiled. My sister landed on a kitchen barstool as I stood, arms crossed, against the back door frame. "I mean, I had this fantasy that maybe he wasn't dead after all, that maybe he was faking his death for some reason, that he'd turn up and we'd all have a good laugh. You know, the Huck Finn thing where Huck and Tom Sawyer watch their own funerals."

"Right," said Zoë. "But it was us calling."

"Well, I didn't know that." Claudia pulled a bottle of spring water out of her fridge. She raised her eyebrows, holding up bottles for both of us. Zoë accepted one, and after a moment I took the other, although I wasn't the least bit thirsty. "I'd forgotten you mentioned you had some of his stuff, including the phone. At any rate, I was also aware it could be Gil, and I didn't want any part of going to this shebang with him. Or with those nutcases in the family."

"No wonder," said Zoë.

"Can you remember what Aaron called you about?" To yank her chain, I added, "Was it a booty call? Did you rush over there and kill him?"

Her eyes bugged out as if she were a bullfrog who'd been stomped on. "No! Of course not. I had fond feelings for Aaron. And no reason to wish him ill. I do remember why he called. We had a rather long conversation, and mostly I just said, 'It'll be all right, you'll see.'" She sighed and leaned over on the granite countertop. "What happened was, there was an attack on the algorithm that he'd been working on. It was an attack that one of the buyers put forth. Do you know what I mean?"

"It's where someone points out a vulnerability or bad bug in the code."

"That's how Aaron explained it to me. Aaron had been working frantically all week to come up with a 'patch,' which was a way to fix the hole and prevent the attacks." She paused to see whether I understood, so I nodded. "But so far he hadn't come up with one, or not that he'd told me about. That was what he was working on the day before he died. He said he was desperate enough that he was thinking about asking for help and maybe even letting someone else come in on the money, if their solution worked."

"Who was this other computer whiz?"

"Gil," Zoë offered.

Claudia giggled. "Not hardly. Gil is somewhat of a power user, and he can do spreadsheets and presentations, but he couldn't debug or write programs. No, it was somebody else Aaron had become kind of close to."

My heart paused, then resumed a syncopated dance. "Tell me it wasn't Ponyboy."

"That's right. I forgot you know Buck."

My sister made a strangled noise and pretended to have choked on her water. I shot her a silencing look.

"Buck's something of a computer whiz," Claudia continued. "He used to work for a defense contractor down in Austin. Anyway, I tried to talk Aaron out of it, but the way he was hemming and hawing, I figured out that he'd already covered some territory rather vaguely with Buck, and now he wanted me to tell him that it would be okay, that Buck couldn't do a runaround and steal his idea, because he hadn't told any details, just a few sketchy bits related to the possible hole in the algorithm."

This was really bad news. "Did he think the algorithm is still viable, even if he couldn't patch it?"

Claudia looked pensive. "I think so. Of course the method, whatever it is, is still faster than those in use, but with the weakness, it wouldn't be workable as a public-key encryption system, as it gives away just a tad too much information. I have no idea what the buzzwords mean; I'm merely repeating what Aaron kept saying to me. I got the feeling it's like in a logic puzzle where you know that a digit is repeated, and you know which digits it isn't, but that doesn't really tell you which it is."

Zoë was nodding. "Like in Sudoku. It's a clue that is too easy."

I was lost, but I nodded.

"Although it would still sell as a private key encryption, that is not what his buyers want. So it's worth substantially less. Possibly worthless to the particular buyers he had who were so interested."

"That's disappointing," said Zoë.

"Well, maybe. But I could be wrong." Claudia set her half-empty bottle on the granite. "The way he talked, I kept thinking he might have written a viable patch the night he died. He talked about needing to hide the new code he had, and needing to go out first thing in the morning to back it up." She tilted her head. "Does that make any sense to you?"

"Lots of people keep offsite backups," I managed after a swig of water. "If your building burns down, it takes your backups with it. But if you have backups kept in a safe deposit box, they'll be safe."

"Of course." She straightened up, looking wistful but regal. "I hate to rush things, but I really must get ready to go."

"We've got to go so Ari can get dressed," my sister said. "She'll see you in a bit."

§ § §

I gripped my sister's upper arm hard enough to serve as a tourniquet. "Why did you tell her that? I don't really want to go. I mean, what's the point? I don't like looking at a body in a box when the occupant has moved on."

"I got us out of there, didn't I?" Zoë twisted and looked back at the empty road behind us for the tenth time since we'd left Claudia's. "I still have the feeling someone's following or tailing us."

When I looked back into the rear view, I saw nothing but the flat road ribboning out behind.

"Don't be ridiculous. How could we not see somebody behind us on this road?"

She shivered. "I just know when somebody's staring at the back of my head. And that's the feeling I have now."

§ § §

The cell phone rang. I almost didn't answer it, but during our drive Zoë had figured out how to broadcast the Bluetooth output from the phone into the car's speakers and had set up a microphone that seemed to be in the vicinity of the driver's side sun visor. What the hell: I pressed the button and took the call from Detective Max Varga.

"Good news," he said.

"You got a match between the toxin and that spider?" For some reason, I flashed on Aaron's lionfish and how he'd once told me never to reach in there, that the tank was a no-no.

He chuckled. "We have a suspect. The case is wrapping up. What I called to tell you is that Orleans Hall turned herself in this morning."

"What?" I said dumbly.

"She came in admitting that she arranged for a spider to bite Aaron, a poisonous spider, and she has been arrested. We don't know yet what the charge will be, as she described one variety of spider but kept calling it something different. The charge could be something other than murder one. We're waiting to match that toxin with any spider, and they're searching a world database. Just for clarity."

"Clarity," I echoed.

"Because we will charge her. We just want it to stick. I'm looking at precedents for damages from deliberately caused snake or spider bites. She said that the victim felt the bite but it didn't seem to hurt much at first, because he was pretty drunk. Within a couple of minutes he passed on out. She said she then watched as the site of the wound started to swell, and she then destroyed the spider and took it away and left. She's definitely guilty of something. The iffy part is whether the toxin would've killed him without that weakness in his heart."

"But he didn't have a weak heart."

He ignored me and barreled on. "We've got her for that other killing you mentioned, as well. She claimed she released a spider in the church trailer because Vernette Ottinger had told her she'd seen her leaving Aaron's house the night he passed, and asked her to repent and confess. Apparently the woman tried to minister to her, saying, 'Don't you want your soul to be safe and your conscience clean? Isn't there something you want to talk about and confess to the Lord?' Probably Vernette just meant Orleans should stop sinning with Aaron, but of course Orleans assumed she suspected her. Goes to show you how dangerous it can be to press your religion on others." He chuckled.

Once again, I was speechless.

"Another church staff member, Philomena, has confessed to procuring the spiders for Orleans"—it sounded as if they planned to farm out the insects as prostitutes—"because Orleans said she could sell them for lots of money. Philomena had some material needs that weren't being met, and she knew where to go to get arachnids, possibly connections in Mexico. A man who lives out by the winery goes down there regularly." Walter, I figured. "We're looking into all of it. But she's solid. Confession's good."

"And that's why you're telling me all this—so I'll believe the case is closed."

"Closing it right now. Rest easy that your friend's killer is in custody."

I was still thinking about how to respond when Zoë piped up into the speakerphone.

"Thank you so much for calling to inform me," my sister said in a passable imitation of me. "We appreciate all your hard work."

"No problem. Glad to close this one so quickly." The detective hung up.

"So that's that," Zoë said. "Now we can bury Aaron—you can, I mean—and get the hell out of this God-forsaken desert."

I felt contentious. "I kind of like Marfa myself. You haven't even seen the ghost lights."

"Nor do I plan to." She yawned for emphasis, inspecting her split ends.

"And that was too easy. I don't believe we've got the truth at all."

"Airhead . . . please don't tell me you aren't going to go along with the police. They know what they're doing, unlike in your silly mystery novels where law enforcement is incompetent all the way up to the Attorney General."

"The cops think they have this case sewn up with that confession. But I don't think it was Orleans acting alone. There's more to it."

"That we'll never know." Zoë tossed her hair back over her shoulder and stared at me hard. "Some things we'll just never know on this side of the Veil, Ari, and we have to accept that."

The "why?" of why God had taken Aaron—let alone Ricky—we'd never know. But there was no reason I shouldn't know the truth about who did it, about how this happened.

True, there's no reason for a lot of things that happen. As a confirmed control freak, I have a hard time with that.

§ § §

It was up to me to find Aaron's source code, if anyone was going to. I needed closure. Whether or not it had gotten him killed, that algorithm must have potential. And I wasn't above cashing in on whatever discovery he'd made. Even if all the bridges leading back seemed to be currently in flames or already turned to ashes.

After driving through Dairy Princess to get us both fruit smoothies—I wasn't very hungry, and Zoë wanted to try room service again later—I dropped my sister off at the hotel and headed to the last place I wanted to be.

I pulled up at the funeral home and opened the car door, but I couldn't make my legs move. My feet had turned to lead. I had to drag myself up the steps and through the glass doors of doom.

The whiff of flowers—not real ones, and not pleasant, but a stink mixed with preservatives and floor wax and other unspeakables—slapped me in the face along with the chilled air as I stepped inside. That awful organ music was playing softly in the background. I hadn't been able to bear Bach's "Jesu, Joy Of Man's Desiring" ever since it had played during Ricky's viewing (what a word to call such an event), and if strains of "Whispering Hope" came on, I would bolt. Our parents had allowed a neighbor of theirs, a soprano from the Catholic church, to screech that one out during Ricky's service. I closed my eyes and prayed for oblivion, but when I opened them, a solemn young woman in black was approaching me.

A very solemn-faced young woman. How could she stand to do this? What kind of person had to get a job as a . . . whatever you called what she did here? Was she from a family suffering under a curse that was working unto the seventh and eleventh generations?

"I'm the director for the Beecroft services." She led me down a dim hall towards one of those rooms. I made my feet walk, though my heart wanted to beat out of my chest and fly away, just as the hymn promised. Clutched in my hand was the reading I wanted Gil to make at the service, which I'd printed out using my sister's portable printer. (No wonder her luggage needed wheels.)

Gil met me at the door of the room where the family was gathered. All I could see were people's backs, and he walked me back down the hall a bit, letting me know without words that it wouldn't be prudent for me to be seen by any of the Beecroft clan. I was relieved not to have to actually go in there. Wordlessly I held out the printout, and he took it.

He looked over the poem, then up at me. "Don't you want to stand up tomorrow afternoon and read this yourself?"

"No." I was firm. "I'd like you to read the poem."

"I suppose that would be best, considering." He shook his head. "You'd better go. Myra became so distraught that we had to close the—that is, we had to arrange things so that there really isn't any more viewing, except by special request." He sighed. "She's really a softie, believe it or not."

"That's understandable. This is her son we're talking about." Claustrophobia or Gilphobia or death-o-phobia was kicking in. "I'll talk to you later," I lied.

I hurried out of there, avoiding the prim, serious director as she tried to catch me ("catch me if you can" being a watchword), and gulped a deep mouthful of the non-perfumed air outside. But I still couldn't breathe.

§ § §

From the look of things, I guessed that Aaron's farewell crew would be staying for a while. I could sneak back to the cabin and look for those credit card statements and other clues to Aaron's betrayals. And, if I could find it, the patch Aaron might or might not have written.

In the courtyard I found the hidden key, up on the top right-hand corner of the door frame where Aaron had always kept ours. Maybe they hadn't know about it, after all. They'd left just about every light in the house blazing, as if no one had to worry about the electric bill. It stank of collards and beans. I fanned the stink out of my face as I checked the fish tanks. Everything seemed okay.

The absence of a lionfish struck me once again. Aaron thought a lionfish in a saltwater tank was stunning. It would stand to reason that once I wasn't around to be stunned in another sense, he'd have one or more. But out here Aaron seemed not to have one, although he had all the other species he usually kept. The placid and dangerous beauty would swim contentedly in its own salt tank, separated from the others because of the high probability that it would poison and consume them. By that reasoning, they ought to keep Orleans in her own little tank.

I couldn't let myself get distracted from my mission, so I headed for the roll-top desk.

Aaron had an awful lot of office supplies and electronic junk (such as old graphics cards and all manner of ribbon cables) stuffed into its nooks and crannies. In the bottom file drawer, there they were: Pendaflex folders containing several credit card statements with my name on them. The balances were nontrivial. My heart sank to my toes as I added it all up.

The door opened behind me. I'd been too absorbed to listen for crunching gravel on the driveway. I froze; I was caught, but good. And without even my trusty official Red Ryder carbine action two-hundred shot range model air rifle with a compass in the stock for self-defense.

It wasn't the Hatfield clan, though, but Gil. "I thought you might take this opportunity," he said softly. "I don't blame you. I won't tell."

It took me a second to put my heart back in my ribcage.

I couldn't hide the handful of credit card statements I had clutched in my hand, so I brandished them at him instead. "You knew about Aaron charging these things to me, didn't you?"

To my surprise, he looked sheepish. "I had an inkling he was doing a bit of charging to you again, yes. But I didn't see any need to panic you. You'll be able to pay it all off with the proceeds from Aaron's estate, anyway." He seemed earnest; Hawk must not have told him about the situation of debt. "If this hadn't happened, I was expecting him to pay it all back within a few weeks when his big score came in. He was going to pay me back. I was into him to the tune of five thousand, remember. An investment in his future business."

"You admit that you knew?" I meant the identity theft, but he took it to mean Aaron's business.

"Not the details. I was aware he was on to something big. He had two large software companies on the hook for it. Mari thought it was a done deal."

I decided to go for the full-on direct approach—known in our family as the "Come to Jesus" talk because it laid everything on the line for repentance or denial. "Speaking of Marisol. Now that I know who she really is, I'm even more confused, Gil. About why she's hanging out with Aaron's family now. And why Aaron's parents have glommed on to her. She has no claim on Aaron's estate, does she? I mean, they were never married."

"Not so far as I know." He frowned. "I hope not, anyway."

"I can't believe you didn't just come out and tell me she's your ex. Your first wife. Not your cousin."

He looked as if I'd outed his innermost secret. "Detective Varga told you?"

"No, but everyone else did." I waved my hands in the air, nearly dropping the statements. "How could you not tell me? Especially about this identity theft."

Lowering his butt into one of Aaron's comfy leather chairs, Gil gave a sigh that sounded as if he were deflating. "It's complicated, Ari. I didn't know how I was going to tell you. But I would have, as soon as we'd gotten this will probated and the estate settled. I thought I'd have time. That you'd be staying here forever, and then I could figure out the best way to explain."

"Maybe you could give it a try right now."

He studied some imaginary stain on his sleeve. "Marisol hung around until she was sure I wasn't going to be available to her, and saw that she could latch on to Aaron. I was happy enough to unload her. Aaron and she were enough alike that they got along, and I couldn't see any problem with it if it made them happy. They were both schemers, but none of their big plans seemed very likely to bear fruit. You know the drill with those types—people who talk a good game, but never actually carry anything out. It seemed harmless." He shrugged.

"So they came up with a scheme to get more money to live on and have luxuries until his ship came in." I crossed my arms, suddenly cold. "She egged him on to apply for the credit cards, and he did it."

Gil looked miserable. "At first, I had no idea. I didn't know you, and I believed you were sending him money and that you had some sort of an arrangement."

I rolled my eyes.

"Yeah, I know. It all sounds so transparent now. But con artists are convincing. They can be quite persuasive. As you already know. Aaron was one of the best con men I've ever run across." His lips curled upward. "The only con artist I've met who could beat him is my ex-wife."

"How did she have her hooks into you?" Waiting for some cosmic signal that'd clear all this up, I tilted my head, but the signal was still static-filled. "She must have had something on you, or you'd have told her to leave you alone way before this." Then it dawned on me. "You said you invested in Aaron's company. You used up your savings."

"That's right." His arms were crossed now. We were like two forts facing each other across the barren desert.

"But that wasn't enough. Aaron wanted more. She got you to 'borrow' from the church, didn't she? Petty cash or the collection plate?"

The panic in his eyes told me I was on track.

I held down my freak-out and pretended all of this had only just come to mind. "The church has a building fund, doesn't it? All churches do nowadays, because they all plan to build a behemoth of a stadium and tear down the little brick building they started in, because they feel their mission is to become a megachurch that attracts crowds and has a television broadcast, rather than being content to serve the community and tend a small flock. I've seen it happening everywhere."

Gil's Adam's apple bobbed as he swallowed—hard.

I knew I'd uncovered the root of Gil's last temptation.

CHAPTER EIGHTEEN

"She tricked me," Gil said miserably. "I never intended to let them use that money. Once she pulled her stunt, Aaron said he'd pay me back immediately as soon as he got a commercial investor. He needed cash to get this company going."

"Tell me you didn't really fall for that."

"You're one to talk. Look what you fell for." He almost managed a smile. "Marisol stole a check out of the drawer and forged my name on the first one. After that, she had me. When she threatened to expose everything, I gave them another small amount as a loan, fully expecting to put it back. Aaron promised me up one side and down the other that he was about to score big. Then we'd put back all he'd 'borrowed' and more. No one would ever know."

How did people get sucked into this stuff? But they did.

Suddenly Gil's confession of several days ago came back to me. *"If you hadn't been here, Aaron's estate would have gone to the church building fund."*

He kept talking, as if I were his mommy and I could fix it if only I'd understand and see it his way. "Certainly I knew I was in trouble. My ex is thoroughly immoral, and she attaches herself to opportunity like a magnet. She listens, she analyzes, and she strikes. There's something repellent about her, but it attracts some people."

"Like maybe you?"

"Low blow, Ari." He sighed again, but there was little air left to escape. "By this time I was well and truly screwed by the whole mess. You see, my family and Aaron's family go back a long way—to World War II, through our grandfathers. Of course they knew Marisol slightly, and she had gone to Aaron's parents when this all started and sold them this sob story about how abusive I was and so forth."

"Were you?"

His basset-hound eyes reproached me. "Of course not. But she knows how to play the part when she needs a lie to be convincing. Anyway, she told them she was his fiancée. That she had to play at being his sister because of the repressed morality of this small town—you know, a guy marrying his best friend's wife and so on. They might've even actually believed her tale of being secretly married to Aaron. She knows places you can go to get forged documents, from birth certificates to marriage licenses. Probably wouldn't hold up to the scrutiny of the court, but the Bees might buy into it."

"They're not bringing the potato salad to the Mensa picnic, for sure. But you didn't warn them?"

"I kept quiet because I was happy to be rid of her. So the Marisol deception started out as a scratch-my-back thing. Any public figure has to keep up appearances, and it was important to me back then that I seem above reproach. Of course, I was in denial, as everyone in town was talking already."

I had to remember that underneath the façade, Gil was just another vulnerable human being. Beneath being a minister and a pillar of the community, he was just plain Gil. He wasn't some sort of superman, but only human, with human weaknesses. When this guy was in his twenties, he had ministered to Marisol, who was then a whore in her thirties coming for a handout to the church where all the seminary students went on Sundays, and he thought he could rescue her. She'd trapped him because he was weak. He wasn't God, but just another mortal man who could fall into sin and regret it.

It hadn't escaped me that if Gil were the killer, this moment would be a great opportunity for him to create an "accident" to eliminate me.

"I've got to go before they get back." I circled around the long end of the couch towards the back door.

"They've gone to dinner. We have some time."

"I'm afraid time is running out." Sometimes we let loose with Freudian slips of a major magnitude. "I mean, it's about that time."

"Ari, don't leave. Not without telling me that you understand. That you don't judge me, that you don't think I'm a terrible person. 'Judge not, lest ye be judged by the same standard.'"

This was not the time to point out that if judged by the same standard, I would probably pass the test he had failed, because I'd never defrauded or stolen from my friends or a church or, well, anybody. Assuming you didn't count the time I broke into Zoë's piggy bank when I was eleven and took her change so I could go get the latest CD by some teen idol or other I'd completely forgotten about by now.

He stood, blocking my exit route. "I'm serious. I need you to tell me that you know how these things are. You can understand the position I was in, can't you? That I really had very little control over what started happening, once the snowball began rolling down the hill and gathering momentum?"

"Of course." I sidestepped a chair, putting it between us. "These things happen. Look at history; it's filled with examples of good men who make bad mistakes. It'll be all right, Gil."

"Ariadne, I want to make it all up to you." His sweeping gesture took in the cabin and contents. "Let me. You'll inherit all of this, and we'll pay back everything that got . . . borrowed." His voice was unnaturally low and quiet, yet it carried as if he were a Shakespearean actor playing to the balconies. "It isn't that much, considering this estate and what it must be worth." He absolutely must not know what Hawk had told me about the estate's true value. "We'll take care of everything, and I'll never make such a mess of things again. And then we'll have a life together. It could be so good."

"My life is back in Dallas."

"But I love you."

"I know you think you do. But it's too soon. You don't even know me." Why was I parroting all the lines that the women in slasher flicks always said just before the psycho lost it and strangled them? I took another step back and stumbled against the leg of a side chair. "We'll talk about this later, I promise. I've got to get out of here before they get back."

"They're at the diner. They're the type to have dessert." He advanced on me.

I heard a car door slam. The rednecks were to be my salvation—in a manner of speaking. In my panic, I couldn't fully appreciate the irony.

Gil twisted around, grabbed at the curtain, and stared out the front window. "That's them. Hurry! Go."

Even Gil in crazy mode wasn't up to a confrontation with them.

As I hit the back door, I glanced over my shoulder. Aaron's desk was pulled apart, papers everywhere, just as I'd left it. I wondered what sort of explanation he'd offer them. Probably that he was looking for some important financial data. Or he might throw me under the bus to save himself.

In a way, he already had.

CHAPTER NINETEEN

The Clochandichter, in Scotland, is the last rock you can stack on the cairn pile before the whole heap comes tumbling down around your feet. Not the one that makes it collapse, but the one juuuust before. I needed to find that one so I could make a quick study of the whole scam structure before it came tumbling down around the murderer.

Early the next morning, while everybody else was busy getting primped or otherwise mentally prepared and ready for Aaron's memorial at two (and while my sister sat stubbornly on the bed watching an old movie and eating a huge room service breakfast), I set out with the GPS unit to find what Aaron had hidden at the coordinates he'd tried to send me.

The numbers led me back to the creek lot behind the churchyard. Gil's car was parked in his usual spot, so I circled behind and slogged through the sand where I imagined snakes and spiders lurked. Snakes or Gil: it almost seemed a toss-up by now.

Back at the stream's edge, I balanced on a rather steep incline covered with a combination of loose rocks and sandy soil. It seemed a lot more precipitous than it had when Zoë had been with me. There could be snakes, and cactus dotted the area despite the shade from the ridge at this time of day. How to find a cache? Especially sub-aqua? I had no clue.

Most of the accounts I'd read on the 'net talked about digging among tree roots or climbing to find caches secreted under a loose rock. Sunlight dappled the water, and I wondered just how fast the current flowed. I scanned the surface of the creek and despaired.

Out of the corner of my eye, I caught a glimpse of something shiny.

Near the base of a downed tree, a key glistened on the surface of the water. How could that be? Metal doesn't float. I scrambled down the slope across the pebbles and damp sand, ruining my Skechers and getting the hems of my jeans all sandy. I should've rolled them up.

I saw that the key was knotted on a length of clear monofilament fishing line attached to the tree. The key floated on the water to show you where to pull up the line.

Wading into the creek, I got hold of the line and started coiling it around my arm. On the end of the line was an old 35mm film container wrapped in duct tape that had a Velcro-tabbed opening. I cut the fishing line with the nail clippers I always carry in my purse and pulled it the rest of the way up.

When I ripped the Velcro open, the film container slid out. It rattled promisingly.

The top of the container had a Valkyrie icon taped on top.

I knew I'd found Aaron's software.

Inside was a USB stick—a flash drive, a thumb drive. I slipped the stick into my bra and started crawling back up the slope.

"Ari!" came Gil's voice. It wasn't so mellifluous now; it sounded almost plangent with urgency on the otherwise silent desert air.

He lumbered towards me. Why did he seem so clumsy, almost as if he were limping? Probably the way he was hurrying across the difficult terrain. He'd figured out that I was on to his game. He thought Aaron's software would give him the means he needed to get back his money and become a player in the world of software, to boot. I could kind of see why he'd fallen into the temptation.

"Wait for me. You're in danger!"

From him, of course. I wasn't exactly playing in my home stadium, and this was practically his church's back yard. He knew this territory better than I did, and getting out was likely to prove harder than getting in. As if to bring the point home, my rubber soles skidded on a patch of loose gravel.

"Ariadne!" Gil called again.

Under the waterfall that Zoë's guidebook had shown us, I recalled, there was supposed to be a cave. Instinctively I headed for it, Gil limping behind me, shouting something else I couldn't quite make out. Did it matter? Was I interested in the details of why he needed to bump me off? How important it was to him that I hand over the data stick and join him in his plan for us to "live happily ever after"? In the life hereafter was more like it, I suspected.

The slippery stones leading across the deep part of the stream were like something out of *Deliverance*. Uneven, unsteady, treacherous. And the fast-running water of the bloated creek created a recipe for disaster, serving twelve. I hopped across the rocks on my toes and prayed, giving special thanks for the gummy bottoms of my Skechers and also that I'd had occasion to change back into them.

Praying all the way, I managed to wade through the shallow currents churning beneath the waterfall. The quiet desert air had become thunderingly moist and humid. I brought my right foot down, hard, on what looked like a darkish patch of sand at the mouth of the cave.

A gigantic black tarantula—it looked like the biggest spider in the world—leaped from its hidey-hole in the sand to the middle of my bare breastbone. Five feet, easily. A fraction of a second ahead of my scream, it panicked and began scrabbling for purchase, its hideous hairy legs flailing as it tried to establish a foothold on my throat. I shrieked full-voice and started an automatic windshield-wiper attack with both hands, but I couldn't seem to brush the monster off me. It dodged and sent out another thread, coming for my face.

"Don't worry about that spider," Gil called out. "It's only a black tarantula. Harmless."

Between the Devil and the deep blue sea, Scylla and Charybdis, the proverbial rock and a hard potential roll down the muddy bluff into the water. Perhaps it hadn't been the wisest idea to run for a cave where I could be trapped, after all, but there was no time for second thoughts. I couldn't divide my attention further, as I already had the two threats of Gil and the spider. I couldn't trust his assurance that it wasn't a killer.

The spider was a tenacious devil, and even in my panic I had to admire its resolve. Every push down prompted a scramble back up. I'm super-ticklish in certain areas. Of all the sensations you can imagine, nothing's quite like the feel of a tarantula's legs as it crawls up your neck. Sort of like a lover's caress, soft and tender, but one step away from sinking a pair of good-sized fangs into your flesh.

My heart beat out a jungle tattoo, my pulse surely pushing a hundred. Our Aunt Glad had died of what Mother had insisted was a fright-induced stroke when a rattlesnake wound around her leg on a nature hike because she'd stepped on its neck right below the head, and the tail reacted automatically. I gulped deep breaths, hoping they'd help slow my pulse before I hyperventilated.

Gil was in full view now, though I perceived him only as a dark blur out of the corner of my left eye. The tarantula seemed to be raising its fangs and studying my flesh, angling itself for the perfect bite.

Black tarantulas aren't lethal. Their sting is much like a wasp's. I recalled those Wikipedia lines from my Web surfing, but they provided cold comfort in the face of the imminent fangfest, seeing as how Wikipedia entries could be edited by anyone who felt like giving it a shot. I managed a kind of bird-flap sweep across the side of my neck, remembering how much like a burn from a cigar a wasp sting felt before the numbness set in.

All at once it was gone from my chest. I felt a tickle on my cheek. I couldn't suppress a full-out scream.

Before my conscious mind registered it, my hands had slapped the spider off my face. The monster lost its footing and fell to the floor of the cave. Before it could send out another spidey-line or pull another five-foot jump, I brought my foot down on it as hard as I could. Talk about squicky.

Perhaps unfair to end a life like that. But I was in survival mode.

Gil was negotiating the tricky waters at the bottom of the falls. He was catching up to me, but at least he hadn't made it inside the cave. He was soaking wet and I saw no sign of a weapon: no gun, no knife, nothing he might be able to use against me. But he was a lot bigger than me, and fists are useful—even if the idea seemed completely out of character for him. Or did it? He hadn't hesitated to put them to work on Buck. At this point could he afford to be gentlemanly and not strike a lady, no matter what?

"Ari?" He called my name, a little uncertainly this time. Out of the corner of my eye I saw the spider's legs start to move. Was that part of its death agonies, or was it regrouping for another attack? I put all my force into an unladylike stomp, then ground the sole of my shoe viciously back and forth.

That had been completely out of character for me. Similarly, I couldn't assume that simply because Gil had always seemed mild-mannered, he'd remain peaceable toward me if I didn't agree to whatever plan he had for "us" to take the software and run—and be Together Forever. If he got upset, no telling what he might pull.

I looked deeper into the cave. Nothing but darkness. No guarantee of a rear exit, either. Bats swooped in my chest, wings beating against my ribcage.

"There you are. Get out of sight," Gil shouted. "I'll try to misdirect him so he can't get to you. He's gone insane!"

What?

Gil appeared in the mouth of the cave, eyes bugging, but before he could get a word out, there was a soft pop and he fell forward.

In the movies, people leap immediately to see how they can help the fallen. I froze, unable to process what Gil had been saying.

Ponyboy stepped over Gil.

I could breathe again. "Where did you cross the creek? You must've taken a shortcut when you saw him chasing me."

Then I saw he was pointing a shiny silver stick. A gun.

A gun?

CHAPTER TWENTY

I put my hands up playfully. "Hey! Is that real? Don't wave that thing around." Then my slowed-down mind acknowledged that he hadn't just pushed Gil down.

"Silencer," he said, indicating the gun's extra-long barrel. Apparently he'd taken my blank stare for a lack of understanding as to why I hadn't heard a loud bang like in the old Westerns on TV, whereas it was really because I was trying to revise my former belief that he was rescuing me from Gil.

One look into his suddenly hard, flinty eyes took care of that little fantasy. Affection, or whatever he and I had shared for a brief moment, had nothing to do with why he stood here. He lusted after something else, something not even distantly related to the desires of the flesh.

I shrieked. My hands flew to cover my mouth as if they anticipated that his next words would be, "Quiet down." But he merely chuckled. We were behind a thundering waterfall, so no one would be nearby, let alone hear me.

Glancing briefly down, I saw red seeping into the sandy dirt on the cave's floor. It came from under Gil's shoulder, but I couldn't tell whether he had a sucking chest wound or had only been grazed on the arm and was playing possum. I thought of the spider after my first stomp; Gil didn't seem gone, only out for the moment. I sent up a quick prayer that it was the latter as I returned my attention to the guy with the gun.

"That thing's real," I said stupidly, mostly because he wasn't talking.

Ponyboy squeezed off a shot into the cave roof. Clods of dirt rained down on Gil's back, and I dodged a large rock.

Backing up by reflex, I nearly stumbled on a root. Tangled roots near the water first, and now a scrubby tree in here. What were the odds? More to the point, what were mine?

He backed me farther into the cave. It was unbelievably dark past where the sunlight dribbled in. My eyes blinked, trying to adjust. I shivered, and my arms reflexively crossed under my breasts. And then I felt the fishing line wrapped around my left arm, between my elbow and my hand.

The line I'd salvaged from finding Aaron's thumb drive. It was still coiled around my shoulder. Still transparent.

Ponyboy was oppressively close, seeming to enjoy dragging this thing out. A power trip, no doubt. But I had to keep from glancing down at the line or touching it in any obvious way, or I'd draw his attention to it and lose what was probably my last chance for survival. Buying time worked on TV.

I pointed at his wrist, where he wore something that wasn't a wristwatch. "What's that?"

"This?" His head moved a fraction as if he were about to fall for it and glance down, but he caught himself. "Ain't it cool? Custom. Homes in on the radio beacon that's attached to Aaron's GPS. He added the electronics so he could track the unit if it got lost; it's the $400 model, after all. When it's queried or pinged, the tracker sends out its coordinates on a given radio frequency, and they show up here, on the display of what used to be a cheap digital watch. That's how I knew you had gone out to see Claudia, and that you probably were close to finding the code. Though I knew she wasn't interested, her being above the world and all"—his eyes flashed—"but I figured if she knew anything to tell anybody, she'd spill to you."

Because we looked a little alike? Because we had loved the same man? This wasn't the time to question his logic.

"You kept track of all my movements while I hauled that thing around in my tote like a little fool."

"You said it—I didn't." That Terry-Thomas midline diastema was really ugly, come to think of it.

"My sister will be looking for me by now. She'll call the police, and she already doesn't like you."

"I noticed. She fought like a jaguar. You can be proud of her."

My head spun. "What have you done? Where's Zoë? You'd better not have bothered her. She had nothing to do with this. She knows nothing about it."

"I verified that. Don't worry; she won't suffer."

"You bastard! She's already traumatized. She's very fragile." His gun morphed into a mere nuisance, something I would get past unharmed because I had to. I had to get out and rescue Zoë. "At the funeral, they'll all wonder where I am. They'll come looking."

"Not anytime soon. Trust me, you won't be missed by the Bees during the service. They'll buzz around when Gil doesn't show, but someone else will surely fill in and officiate. It isn't my problem. I'll be miles away by then. Got a buddy in Vegas who's hooked me up with a gig there."

For him to tell me all this meant he knew I wouldn't tattle, as he intended me to fly across the Veil between worlds right behind Gil. I had to buy more time, get away, rescue Zoë. "There's a possibility that the algorithm isn't perfect, that it needs to be patched and tested some more. Are you sure you can maintain it all by yourself? I'm a good debugger. That's how Aaron and I met, when we were both in secure communications programming. I worked test and quality." I fluttered my lashes. "We can work together."

"I work alone."

"But you have to deal with those companies. You and Aaron look nothing alike."

"Neither do you and he." He laughed. "I'll be transacting business online first, and only later in person as Aaron. The companies haven't met Aaron, so there'll be no problem." The gun jiggled up and down slightly, and I couldn't help watching its business end. "I've got all the e-mail, and I understand what was going on well enough to pull this off."

I figured he could. "But you don't have the code."

"I will." He held out his hand. "I saw where you put it. Hand it over now, or I can get it the hard way."

"There's an easy way?" Slowly I reached in and retrieved the stick. "There could be, you know. A very pleasant way for both of us to profit from this."

He wasn't buying. Nothing lay behind those eyes but a steely resolve. I had been notch nine hundred on his, um, bedpost, but nothing more. "So you're going to kill me no matter what. First at least tell me. What really happened to Aaron?"

"Can't you ask him when you get to Heaven?" His smile was concentrated evil.

"Yes, but I'd like to hear it from you now, as well. Let's say I want to compare your stories." I crossed my arms tighter as if I were in control, because I had nothing left to lose anyway; I might as well act tough. Also, that posture stilled my quaking a bit. "Tell me how you did it. What did Orleans have to do with this?"

"Very little. She thinks she did it all, of course. I switched that spider that the church woman managed to get—which wasn't the killer it was advertised to be—with a less harmful spider, so Orleans wouldn't kill herself with it by accident. I went to her place and made sure I 'accidentally' saw it, and carried on about how dangerous it was. I had her convinced it was a killer. Looks fairly similar to one that comes from the Australian outback." He snorted. "She managed to get the thing to bite him after he was crocked. I watched from the shadows in the courtyard. After she left, I milked the toxin out of Aaron's lionfish, wearing rubber gloves, and shot it into the area of the bite while Aaron was passed out on the sofa."

I'd always known it would lead to trouble for Aaron to be so enamored with those poisonous pisces.

"And the bit about Aaron having a heart defect. You're the one who fabricated that and spread it around town, to make his collapse and death seem more likely." I was gripping the stick so hard I was afraid I might crack the plastic. "Did you also do the church lady?"

He shook his head. "That was Orleans. She was convinced that the preacher's wife had seen her going in and out of Aaron's house. Something about the woman urging her to confess and repent. She wasn't sure that Vernette wouldn't go to the police and do the confessing for her, so she took care of that with one of her own pet spiders. At least she thought it was one of hers. Actually, I slipped a substitute into one of her cages anonymously when she told me what she planned to do, because I knew mine was the real thing, not just one of those that makes you sick. I'd managed to get hold of a real doozie by mail. I figured she was just blowin'—that it was the booze talking. I could hardly believe my luck when she went ahead and worked up the gumption to do it. Now no matter which one of us that church lady saw leaving the scene, it won't matter: I'm covered."

"Orleans confessed to you that she killed Aaron? And that she was going to do the same to Vernette?"

"Not in so many words, but she knew I'd figure it out, and she didn't care. People talk. She and I had an understanding for a while."

"She might well mention you and implicate you. She's confessed to the police, you know. Or didn't you?" I cocked my head brazenly.

"I don't think that'll be a problem. Orleans wasn't making a lot of sense in her confession, way I heard it. Overwhelmed by guilt, supposedly, and hysterical. Anything she says about me, they'll take with a saltlick. Remember, I know people around here. They trust me. I'm one of the good old boys."

I kept buying myself time in such tiny increments, and I didn't know for what. Something would come to me. I hoped. "What I don't understand is, how could you do this to Aaron? He was a good person. All this killing over a mere piece of code?"

"Not just any piece of code, as you well know. An algorithm for public key encryption that's four to five times as fast as the one commonly in use? Whoever implements and licenses it will write his own ticket. Aaron knew it. If he'd been able to keep his stupid trap shut when he was drinking or toking, he'd still be around. But he was weak. Trusting."

"He shouldn't have trusted you. Neither should I."

His head swung slowly back and forth like the MGM lion's. "Depends on your point of view. Worked for me." His lips curved upward. "Problem was, when I searched his computers, I never did find any code or any executables. That had me stymied for a bit. But I knew he'd have backups. Just a question of where he kept them." He paused. "It seemed as if you were well on your way to figuring out where the source code was. You told me at the chili cookoff how you intended to keep looking."

"You must've gotten frustrated waiting for me to pick up the GPS and come get this. That was you the other day who followed us over here. You were patient, knowing I would eventually find or figure out the part you didn't have—the real coordinates."

His smile widened, turning him into a jack-o'-lantern. But not one of the happy ones. "As the song says, you ain't quite as dumb as you seem. Unfortunately, you smartened up too late. Still, the way this played out is a shame. Until your sister showed up, I'd hoped we could find the code together and cooperate. I really was fond of you, you know."

"Glad to hear I wasn't just the latest scalp on your virtual belt."

Ponyboy smirked like a smug politician. "The latest? Come on, Ari. The groupies have paid a few visits since I 'visited' you. Why do you think I like the music business so much?" He tilted his head. "You know, you forced me into this. If you'd just handed over the code, this wouldn't have been necessary."

Horseshit. He'd have had nothing to lose by killing me anyway.

I could not believe that a hoary old cliché out of every "B" movie would come out of my very own mouth, but it did. "You'll never get away with this."

His eyes gleamed as the sun sent a momentary beam between us. "Of course I will. Orleans has already confessed. They have their killer. And you? You just fell into the creek and drowned looking for that silly software that I told you not to bother with. All the spiders and snakes around here, a city gal like you could panic pretty easy. Not the wisest little Nancy Drew ever, you squashed a spider and the gunk is all over your foot. Won't necessarily wash off easily, either. They'll buy it because they'll be looking for stuff like that. Poor old Gil jumped in after you, and who knows whether he'll survive? People will understand why he tried to save you. He really had it bad for you, you know." He touched his nose bandage gently and chuckled.

"Gil has a bullet hole."

"Don't worry. I have a plan." He gestured with the gun.

I could throw the USB stick into the water and let it float away, and he might go with it, like Gollum. That might be my best hope.

On the other hand, this algorithm was Aaron's life's work, his legacy. I couldn't force my arm to make the pitch. Besides, it was as likely that Buck would shoot before he leaped. He'd have plenty of opportunity to recover the stick from the mud, by claiming he needed to find my body in the creek where I'd "fallen in." He might well get the entire town to dredge it, for all I knew, as he had friends in high places. As well as the lowest.

I pinched the stick tighter. In my fantasy, I'd envisioned that an invisible filament of fishing line stretched across the mouth of the cave would be an option for slicing the head off whoever was coming after me, and I could finish him like Wonder Nerd. But that wasn't to be my path. I'd have to run the line between my hands instead and try for an *ad hoc* snatch. I felt the line cutting into my palms already. If I were to have any chance, I'd have to entice him to come closer, so that ruled out throwing the drive. And first I had to get my hands into position.

He stepped toward me.

I kept his gaze locked with mine in a pleading fashion, mostly to keep him from refocusing and seeing the line glistening in the partial sun. "Who's that?"

The old movie-serials ploy had been worth trying. He stopped advancing on me momentarily, glancing around behind him as if to make sure there'd be no witnesses. I got my line into position as he turned, eyes flashing. It was embarrassing to be caught looking, wasn't it?

"Made you look," I said to egg him forward. "You've thought about how you need to drown me without having to shoot me, too, as bullet holes would bring up questions when I was found floating downstream. Gil's bullet hole and mine, the same caliber. A possible hitch in your plan."

"I won't hesitate to shoot, even if it means changing my plan."

I didn't doubt him.

The thought of drowning, suffocation, gulping water when I no longer had any gills, was giving me an anxiety attack. But with that came a surge of adrenaline, and along with it, strength. My back stiffened, along with my resolve.

He gestured with the gun again. "This is getting boring. Hand it over."

I held out the stick just past the line I'd imagined in the dirt. When he lurched angrily forward, I stepped back. That enraged him, and he surged toward me just as I jerked a length of my impromptu rope off the coil at my shoulder and caught it to settle between my wrists, just like when I was a child and I'd served as a yarn-holder for my grandmother's knitting. He grabbed the stick, but I lunged so that the line hit him in the Adam's apple.

My judgment of his height had been accurate. Not a giant after all, but another mortal man. About Zoë's height.

He glugged and reared back, making choking sounds as he lost his footing on the loose rocks. I took the advantage of distraction to unloose the kind of kick ladies aren't supposed to indulge themselves in unless their virtue is in imminent danger of compromise. As ironic as it was appropriate.

I knew I'd get only one chance, and my guardian angel surely approved, for my kick hit home. Ponyboy's eyes clenched shut, and he curled forward like a shrimp. The wail-screech he made reminded me of something you'd expect from a spoiled brat who'd fallen off a swing. But a lot louder.

He was still more or less upright; I knew what I had to do, and my next kick caught his forward-angled chest. He tried to correct his posture, but the pain was too much. The stick was clenched in one fist, except both fists were now cupped around his zero zone. He staggered back a few steps.

I already knew that the brain could process time differently in a crisis. I've never believed that time exists as we experience it anyway, but merely as a mental construct. After all, doesn't God exist outside of time, and step into time when He needs to intervene? We can perceive time as running faster or slower in crises, such as when we are near the interface between this world and the next. The apparent slowdown of events now illustrated my theory.

Buck's expression of surprise just before he tumbled backward into the ravine of rushing water made me sick to my stomach. I truly hated to see that happen to anyone, but if poetic justice had ever been served on a silver bed-tray, this had to be one of the times. He must've hit his head on a protruding rock on the way down, because just before he hit the surface, he went limp. Almost immediately, he sank under the water.

As soon as I got my arms untangled from the line—which had cut into my palms and the sides of my hands slightly, like a deepish paper cut—I managed to dig out Aaron's cell phone. Of course I still couldn't get a bar of signal. The worst part was that the only reason I could think of for rescuing Buck Travis and bringing him to justice was to make him tell me where Zoë was.

I contemplated crawling down to get him, maybe reaching for the toe of the boot that still stuck out of the water, but I knew I couldn't get to him without falling in myself. The water moved surprisingly quickly up close. And I didn't know how deep it was. A black stick floated by. No, it was a cottonmouth. Another poisonous snake.

I retreated from the bluff's edge. Just as Buck's face slipped under, I accepted the truth: there went Aaron's code. Clenched in his stiffening fist.

But I didn't care. It had caused enough trouble. I supposed I could tell Gil, and the church people could dig around for it as well as Buck's body, and if they found it, fine, let them have the money to replace what Gil had—

Gil!

I crawled double-time back to Gil. He was clammy, but not cold. I put my ear to his chest and thought I heard a ragged breath. Perhaps there was hope.

Gil's cell phone had one bar; he used a different service provider, working off a different cell tower from Aaron's. As 911 rang, I wondered what the sticky mess all over my cheek could be.

Watching the creek below, I felt I was riding the tide as it came in over and over. Wave after wave, rocking eternally, a boat against the current, borne back ceaselessly into the past.

§ § §

The EMT response must've been amazingly quick, though it seemed to me like forever. They pulled a paramedic engine and an ambulance into the church parking lot, very up-to-date, nothing like the ragtag volunteer fire department that I'd envisioned, without even a Dalmatian or a little boy ringing the bell hanging off the back. It took me a minute to convince them that I wasn't a casualty after they saw Gil's blood caked down the side of my face. After a Sani-Wipe cleaned me up suitably, everyone turned to the problem of taking Gil across the water on an inflatable raft. They didn't think they could keep their footing on the sandy rocks of the creekbed.

I rode across on a second trip with an EMT.

Gil was still on the gurney behind the engine, getting hooked up and worked on, when one of the paramedics and I simultaneously heard the trunk of Gil's car raising a fuss.

The EMT reached the car first, circling around to the trunk. "Do you have the keys to this vehicle, ma'am?"

That prompted my sister to beat on the trunk lid even more furiously, shouting hoarsely for help.

At first I imagined Gil must've been tricked into helping take her. You see people jumping on other people to throttle them, like Homer Simpson does to Bart, in cartoons. I never thought someone would actually do it, but I couldn't help myself: I fell on him, shrieking. This alarmed the rescuers, who pulled me off. Before killing him, I decided to let him get to his keys with his good hand so we could get her out.

Zoë was pretty wracked. She's claustrophobic, so car trunks are not her favorite venue. When we popped the lid, she dropped the tire iron she'd been banging against every available surface and practically shot into the fireman's arms. She was all shouted out, her clothes clinging to her with sweat, and she stunk like a mule who'd been pulled through tall cotton . . . but she was OK.

"I thought he had you for sure, you airhead," was the only understandable thing she got out before she fell on my shoulder, sobbing. We said more, but we were both sobbing too hard to understand each other.

"Ma'am? Would you two come right over here so we can check you out?" The EMT led us over to the paramedic engine. As we passed Gil, I moved towards him again, but Zoë stopped me.

"It wasn't Gil," Zoë managed before they made her lie back on a second gurney and take the oxygen mask. "It was Guitar-zan, that long-haired asshole you slept with. Just him alone. Pretty strong, for a musician."

Of course she had to tell the world that I'd slept with him. I couldn't look my attending EMT in the face. I'm pretty sure he didn't even chuckle, though I know he heard her.

Pony'd had keys to Gil's car, as a trusted "friend." Of course. He had that stupid truck with no trunk to lock her in.

"You were so lucky that Gil's car was parked here at the church already. Buck might've done something really awful," I said.

"As if he didn't." She was still fragile, but she wasn't cowed.

Gil cleared his throat and weakly raised the good hand, the one with the IV needle in it. We both turned his way. He had rallied so much that I wondered if he'd been playing possum.

"I'm afraid this is at least partly my fault for not doing something earlier. I saw him stalking you two the other day over here. Then I knew he was after something. I was reluctant to confront him for various reasons . . . things I'd rather not talk about with the police, and that I was certain he'd find reason to bring up with them if I irritated him." He took a ragged breath. "A couple of hours ago, he was sitting in his truck out front; he must've had you by then." He gestured at Zoë, then winced. A paramedic restrained that hand and rescued the IV needle before it pulled loose. "I didn't see you, though. And I'm so sorry about that, but I didn't know. I just thought he was working up the courage to come in and confront me about—about some of the stuff we were arguing over earlier." He shot me a glance. Like maybe Buck's broken nose, for instance. "And then I saw Ari park. I went down to the creek after her, and he must've thrown you in the trunk about then. He cut across and stopped me halfway down. We argued, and he socked me a good one. Anyway, I went down. I guess I hit my head on a rock." Or maybe Ponyboy kicked him with a boot? "When I could get up again, I saw the muddy footprints of boots in the wet sand and I knew he was going after you. I could hear him . . . I just couldn't go very fast. At least I thought I couldn't. I prayed for strength, and God sent me an angel. Buck wasn't familiar with where the cave is and how to get up there, but I realized where you must be headed. The angel helped me get to my feet and I started running after you, but you didn't hear me. I guess I didn't have the wind to shout loudly enough."

I had, as usual, played the fool.

"The angel stayed with me after Buck shot me. We floated above my body, watching everything. You were magnificent. Then I knew it was time to come back to my body, and I don't remember after that until I was floating across the creek with these gentlemen."

The EMT gave me a dirty look. "Sir, please don't try to talk any more. You've lost a lot of blood."

I felt another pang in my chest. "Is he going to be all right?" I asked the paramedic.

"It's a high shoulder wound. He'll probably need orthopedic surgery. But what I'm concerned with is the amount of blood he's been losing. Bullet must've nicked an artery." The EMT scowled and bent closer to the bandages. Guilt drowned me the same way I'd been afraid the creek would.

Zoë pulled off her oxygen mask. "This stuff's making me light-headed. Shouldn't someone call the police?"

I turned to see that lovely Cheap Detective's sedan pulling into the parking lot.

CHAPTER TWENTY-ONE

For once, Max Varga seemed confused; he looked like a fish—one of the particularly unintelligent species—complete with staring eyes and gaping mouth gulping at empty air instead of life-giving water. "What's going on here?" he asked me, probably because I was one of the few civilians not hooked up to something.

"The Hundred-Year Flood," Zoë answered from her sidesaddle perch on the other gurney. Her worried tech hadn't been able to convince her to put the mask back up to her face yet.

"In the desert?" The detective blinked.

"As Grandma always used to say, 'The first hundred years are the worst.'" Zoë actually smiled. This alarmed her EMT sufficiently that he made her lean back and tied the mask back on.

The detective didn't get it at all. Neither did I, but then I started laughing. I guffawed and hooted, and then I went into hysterics the way my best friend in third grade and I used to be able to do, laughing until tears squeezed out of my eyes and I choked.

The detective grabbed my wrists as I bent over, trying to catch my breath. "Are you OK?"

"Not really." I waved him away and grabbed for the hot coffee that one of the techs was suddenly offering me, poured out of an old-fashioned plaid thermos. It was both bitter and sour, but it did burn an airway through the mucus. I coughed that out, and in a moment I could talk. "I just got ticked—I mean, tickled—there for a minute." Another snippet of subconscious commentary.

"Okay." He backed away a bit, which was also good. "When you're ready, then, maybe you can tell me what the hell happened."

§ § §

Once my sister had caught her breath, she waved away any further concern. "I'm fine." I noticed a few places on her thighs and upper arms that would become bruises later—she bruises slowly, and it takes days to clear—but she didn't have cuts or scrapes, so after they pulled away carrying Gil to the hospital in Alpine, we turned back towards each other.

"Let's get this over with," Zoë said.

I nodded. Thinking she meant we should go back to the hotel and get packed to leave, I headed for the car.

But she surprised me. "Where are you going?"

"Back to—where did you mean?"

She was walking towards Gil's church. "I know we're way late, but whatever."

The parking lot on the west side was full of cars. The service had obviously started before the ambulance and all the fuss arrived. Zoë wanted to go inside, to . . . Aaron's funeral?

"What?" I said dumbly. "Looking like this?"

She glanced over her shoulder. "It doesn't matter. God understands. We'll sit in the back."

Just as we stepped inside the church, the chapel's front doors opened and people streamed out.

Zoë stopped short. Then she looked at me. "See what you made us do, Airhead? You made us miss the whole thing."

"Sorry," I said. "Let's get out of sight before Myra and Doyle see us. I don't want to upset them further."

"You mean you don't want another fistfight. Come on." In the car, she half-smiled. "Should we follow to the cemetery?"

That would put me way too close to the combatants, and it would be asking for another unpleasant scene. I didn't want to ruin things. "I'd rather remember him as he was. Besides, we look so bad they might try to toss us in after him." I sighed. "A year ago in this situation, I probably wouldn't have minded."

"Shut up, Airhead." But she made her seat recline and leaned back, apparently satisfied that we'd made an effort. "Take me to the hotel. But first let's drive through that Tex-Mex joint. I think I need a double Sopaipilla Ecstasy Plate."

§ § §

For once, Zoë didn't get her way. I wanted to check on Gil.

"What's going to happen to Orleans?" I took a bite of the brownie that Cora offered me, although as soon as I tried to chew it I realized I couldn't possibly swallow, that I wasn't the least bit hungry. But because Cora hadn't passed around any napkins yet, I had to swallow it. "She didn't really kill anyone. Unless she killed the church lady, as Buck claimed. I have my doubts on his word alone. Anyone know yet what happened there?"

"They're investigating. Yes, there's a spider bite on Vernette. No, they don't know whether it killed her." Gil fiddled with the controls on his hospital bed, raising the head, then the foot, probably trying to get comfortable. He'd only been out of surgery a few hours, but he seemed fairly chipper and not in as much pain as I'd imagined. "Fellow I talked to tells me that there's forensic evidence from crimes committed last year that still hasn't been analyzed, because they have so many cases backed up. It's tough, even in larger cities."

Cora was peeking down the hall, head hanging out the door of Gil's hospital room. "Nurses nowhere to be seen. You'll have to lie there all crunched up until one of them comes back who knows how to work that thing." Obviously, she didn't consider a scrunched-up mattress a call button offense. She came over to me carrying a gift sack. "I brought you something from the gift shop. A little remembrance of your time in Marfa."

"You shouldn't have," I said out of obligation, but dug into the rainbowed tissue happily. Inside was a ball. A clear round plastic orb. I must've looked confused, because she said, "Cup it in your hands."

I did. After a moment, the ball lit up from inside and began a gentle vibration.

"It's a Marfa light." She laughed, and everyone else followed suit. Zoë rolled her eyes.

"It'll be perfect for my mantelpiece." I grinned.

"That's not all." Buzz winked. "She never gives just ONE present."

Underneath the rest of the paper was a silver frame. It contained a picture of Aaron and me from about three years ago. It was his favorite photo of us; I wondered where she'd found it, but thought better of asking. We stared into our bright secure future, his arm encircling my waist, his eyes—the eyes of a dreamer—unfocused and probably seeing something ahead that was going to turn into the magic talisman that would make everything all right and then some. Right for him, right for Doyle and Myra, maybe even right for loyal, trusting, naïve Ari.

I hugged the photograph to me. "I don't know what to say."

"Now when you miss West Texas, you can look at your keepsakes and remember us," said Buzz. I thought I saw my sister tear up a little. I suspected Buzz reminded her of one of our crazier uncles, way back from when we were little.

I really would miss West Texas . . . about like you miss the sound of city traffic when you drive out here into the country. But her people were gems.

Some of them, at least.

§ § §

"Do we have everything?" Zoë looked around the hotel room. We were headed to Gil's, where we'd been invited to stay until we could figure out how we were getting home. For some reason, Zoë had been willing.

"Let me check." I reached into my tote. My fingers touched something metallic and solid. I'd forgotten about the camcorder. And the tape of the Marfa lights. "Wait a second." I plugged it into the hotel television. "Take a look at this. This is footage from when we were being chased through the desert."

Zoë scoffed. "That's too blurry to see anything clearly. Just a big orange smear in the darkness. Overwhelming your camera and overexposing."

I stared at her.

"Give me a break, Airhead. It looks like you went on some carnival ride, an indoor roller coaster or a fun house. They had one of those traveling carnivals in town, didn't they, the kind that they put up in a supermarket parking lot on Friday and pack up to leave on Monday morning, and in the meantime they had these cheesy neon-outlined rides." She snorted. "You just got drunk and went into the Ghost Train with those crazy idiots on either side of you, and they convinced you that you were seeing something supernatural." She shook her head. "You know better than to drink. You know you can't handle the stuff."

I knew what had really happened. But I snapped the recording off. "Think whatever you want." I closed the camcorder's ports, jerked the cables free, threw it all back into my tote, and stalked out to the car, abandoning my sister to her under-the-breath mutterings about me and my irresponsible attitude and crazy ideas. I was glad I hadn't told her every idea I'd ever had.

§ § §

Gil had been released from the hospital after one night, which amazed me. But the day we left, his arm was still in a shoulder sling, and I could tell he was in a lot of pain. Physical therapy loomed ahead of him. He'd arranged, as promised, with Mr. Hawk to allow me to take over the payments on the car. The family was getting their lawyers together to try to repeal the will or whatever, but for now they'd vacated the premises and were regrouping somewhere on the road. An aquarium hobbyist Hawk knew in Alpine had arranged to lease the cabin and all its furnishings and take care of the tanks and their occupants for the time being. It would be months before we'd know the final disposition of the other assets of the estate—if there turned out to be any that weren't in hock. At the moment, everything was still iffy.

We swung by Cora's to say our goodbyes. Cora had made chocolate chip pumpkin muffins. Zoë immediately slathered melted butter on one and praised it to high heaven, and Cora recited the recipe for her as she scribbled it down in the back of her Marfa travel guide. "Wouldn't want you to go hungry, in case you run out of Stuckey's," Gil said, looking amused.

Gil had something for me. Buzz was carrying the gift sack because Gil still couldn't carry anything heavy and he wasn't supposed to use his bad arm. With a wink, Buzz said, "Here you go." Inside the sack were a couple of photo albums.

"Pictures we all took during the housebuilding, and stuff that Aaron did around town. I had a bunch of them on my disk drive, and I printed them out for him. Apparently he made these albums. I found them before, and, y'know, I was going to hang on to them, but. . . ." Gil smiled. "I know you'll appreciate them more."

I opened the top album and there was Aaron hanging on to a ladder with one hand; I flipped to the last page, and saw him with a bunch of guys with their arms around each others' shoulders in front of the finished cabin.

"The other one is mostly his old pictures, from what I could tell. Myra and Doyle didn't want them, so." He cleared his throat. "I looked for those photos of you that Aaron always had tacked up on his corkboard, but I could only find a couple. Best I can tell, Orleans took them down at some point. But I did find a few around the house." I wondered whether he had carried them for a while himself. "I put them all in there for you. To remember the good times."

I choked up to where I couldn't even thank him. As I hugged the books against my breast, Zoë (ever at the ready to speak for me, as usual) said, "That's so thoughtful of you. She doesn't know what to say."

Gil traced the bottom edge of his lower lip with his "good" index finger. "Don't say anything."

§ § §

Marfa was receding in the rear view mirror when Zoë piped up. "It's been real. No, actually it's been unreal. I still wonder. . . ."

"What?" I got on the interstate and flicked the satellite radio into life. One thing I could say for the Navigator was that it stayed pretty comfy on long hauls. It had swallowed even my sister's oversized luggage—and an appalling amount of gasoline as we filled up to head home—and its tail hadn't even sagged. We needed to take our time getting back and see a few sights. If there were any.

"You didn't go inside on family night for Aaron," she pointed out. "Neither did I. And we missed the service. We never saw Aaron dead. I just wonder."

Gil had told me at the viewing that they'd closed the casket early and it would remain that way. . . .

Zoë whistled low. "Do you think Claudia could be right? That he faked his own death . . . and that whole song-and-dance about a closed casket for the family's sake was to help cover that up . . . and that crazy peyote-chewing lawyer is keeping quiet about it, or maybe even he doesn't know?" She paused for breath and raised her hands in the air pre-emptively. "I'm not saying that I really believe he could pull it off. But hell, Airhead, with what all has gone down out here, who could say for sure?"

As we left Marfa for good, I started to slip the chain with Aaron's ring off over my head to stash it away, then thought better of it. It felt right as I dropped the ring back between my breasts. I'd keep it on until I could put it safely into my jewelry box at home. No sense letting it burrow into one of the car's leather seats, what with its history of getting lost. It was a keepsake. No, it was the ring that Aaron had never given me. I didn't feel the least bit guilty about having it.

And it felt right to be going home. I popped the top on a diet ginger ale and handed one to my sister. She held the cold can to her jugular and leaned back, enjoying the frigid air conditioning. "I can't wait to get home," she said.

"Yeah." I heard a tinge of sadness in my own voice.

Marfa receded in the rear view mirror until I saw nothing but a dusty red haze and the peaks of the Chinati mountains beyond.

—THE END—

ABOUT THE AUTHOR

Denise Weeks has been writing since she could hold a crayon. She has been writing novels since she had chicken pox at age six and her father sat by her bedside and told her that books didn't drop from the sky fully formed, but were written by mortals. She graduated from Southern Methodist University with bachelor's degrees in computer science and in mathematics (with a minor in English); she worked as a software engineer for several years. All the while she was scribbling, scribbling.

Like many homegrown Texas humorists, she isn't funny. Novelist, pianist, belly dancer, baton twirler (but no fire batons ever again, by order of the Renner Volunteer Fire Brigade), and amateur radio operator, she has published many short pieces in anthologies, magazines, and journals, along with faithfully maintaining her blogs (which are not "diaries": diaries pretend to some version of the truth, and writers don't hold with strict veracity. We prefer stories, because they make more sense.)

She has worked as a software weenie, soft-serve cone maker at Dairy Queen (she perfected that little twirl on the top of the dipped cone), and secondary school math tutor. Her favorite foods are curried yak, chocolate, and French fries. She knows (but is not telling) a plethora of alchemical and occult secrets. Homeland Security has identified her as a person of interest. (Okay, just kidding. She doesn't really eat curried yak.) She is currently at work on yet another novel.

She and her husband live happily in a northern suburb of Dallas, Texas, with their two beloved pets: a yappy Pomeranian and Denise's elderly mother. Write when you get work.

Visit my blogs at http://deniseweeks.blogspot.com
http://jackiesjotting.blogspot.com
http://shalanna.livejournal.com
Author's Website: http://tinyurl.com/bvffdml

Made in the USA
Coppell, TX
26 October 2022

85288359R20144